ASSASSIN *of* TRUTHS

a Library Jumpers novel

ASSASSIN *of* TRUTHS

a Library Jumpers novel

·BRENDA DRAKE·

entangled teen

an imprint of Entangled Publishing LLC

Entangled Publishing, LLC
2614 South Timberline Road
Suite 105, PMB 159
Fort Collins, CO 80525

Entangled Teen is an imprint of Entangled Publishing, LLC.

Visit our website at www.entangledpublishing.com.

Edited by Liz Pelletier and Stacy Abrams
Cover design by Cover Couture
Interior design by Toni Kerr

ISBN: 978-1-63375-738-7
Ebook ISBN: 978-1-63375-739-4

Manufactured in the United States of America

First Edition February 2018

10 9 8 7 6 5 4 3 2 1

For those not afraid to jump into the battle.
And to Jacob, my son, who is a warrior.

CHAPTER ONE

There were moments when I wanted to scream. When I just wanted the world to fall away and leave me behind in the quiet rolling hills of my new home.

Home? Right. It was nothing like Boston.

If a person had to hide out somewhere, I couldn't think of a better place than Ireland. I adjusted on the rock wall that'd become my escape from everyone in the large farmhouse just down the hill. Vines crawled over the two-story building and many of the retaining walls cutting through the green hills that surrounded it. The wall I sat on had a smooth top and a rock that stuck out just at the right height for a footrest.

Even though it was barely autumn, I couldn't seem to get warm. The ground was always wet and muddy, and the scent of manure hung in the chilly air. The view was beautiful, though. The Irish hills were dressed in shades of green mixed with shocks of purple flowers. *Afton would love to paint a landscape like this.* My heart sank at the thought of my best friend. Leaving her, plus Pop, Nana, and Uncle Philip, had been like tearing away a piece of me. It was as if I'd left half my heart behind.

I wasn't me anymore, just some ghost walking among the living, trying to remember who I used to be. Gia Kearns—even the name sounded foreign to me. Somewhere along the way, I'd become Gianna Bianchi McCabe, Sentinel—a magical knight protecting the libraries and the human race from dangerous creatures. Bianchi was my mom's last name, and McCabe belonged to my birth father, Carrig.

Separated from Pop, I was more afraid of being alone than wielding a sword. Though he was my stepfather, he was the only parent I'd ever known. And he was a damn good one, at that.

We'd been in hiding for nearly two months already, and I was getting anxious. My days were filled doing battle drills and chores with the other Sentinels. During my downtime, I'd think about my best friend and cousin, Nick. It was the first time he hadn't celebrated my birthday with me. Seventeen years. We'd known each other since birth. Things felt off without him around.

Then the dark thoughts would come. Was Conemar torturing Nick? What evil plan did Nick's biological father—the most dangerous wizard of the Mystik world—have for him?

Momo raced in and out of cracks in the wall, her furry body squeezing into the tiniest of places. I never thought I'd love a ferret so much. She'd been my alarm while trapped in the wastelands of the Somnium, alerting me when one of the frightening beasts was around. I couldn't leave her behind in that magical void.

Normally, her playfulness would be a distraction for me, but my mind kept replaying Nick's kidnapping. Conemar's Sentinels shoving him into the back seat of Miss Bagley's Subaru. The look of despair on Nick's face as the vehicle disappeared around a corner.

I'm sorry, he had mouthed.

He was sorry, when I was the one who had failed him. I shouldn't have hesitated. There was so much going on in the battle around me that I'd lost focus. Pop would've been killed if Faith hadn't rushed in front of him and taken the dagger meant for him. But I had hesitated, not knowing what to do. Everyone I loved had been in that fight.

I swore never to falter again, but it was too late for Faith and Nick.

And for Kale and Gian. Both had died that day with Faith. I'd let all my friends down.

Faith. I touched her gothic-style pendant with thorny, silver-stemmed roses encircling a bloodred crystal. She'd become a good friend and protector, and missing her hurt so badly that sometimes thinking of her made it hard to breathe.

Flipping through Gian's leather-bound journal, I inhaled the scent of aged pages. My great-grandfather wrote this for me to find. He was a powerful wizard, and Gian had given up his life to save mine. I knew there was something important in the pages but couldn't figure out what. He'd also left a poem containing clues to finding the Chiavi—seven keys hidden as objects within the libraries. Each one held a special power. In their original forms, the keys would unlock a prison containing an apocalyptic beast called the Tetrad. Whoever released the creature could control it and bring both the Mystik and human worlds to their knees.

I tapped against my lips the laminated prayer card he'd used as a bookmark in the journal and reread the poem titled *Libero il Tesoro*, which meant "Free the Treasure." It was a spell to release a Chiave from its hiding place. The poem was a list and held clues to artifacts in the libraries where Gian had hidden the keys.

A religious man's charm hangs from his vest. The first line. It was a necklace with a cross pendant Gian had found in the Vatican Library.

A school of putti, one of which sees farther than the rest. A telescope Nick and I had recovered in the Abbey Library of Saint Gall.

Strong women flank the ceiling; the one in Sentinel dress holds an enchanted point, small in size—which I found totally by accident after a battle in the Senate Library in Paris.

Behind Leopold he stands, one hand resting on a crown and the other holding a rolled prize. Nick and I discovered it in the National Library of Austria.

With numbers in her mind and knowledge in her hands, on her brow a crown does rest. We stumbled on it in the Monastic Library in Ulm, Germany, while looking for another Chiave.

I read the final part of the poem, hoping for something to stand out.

In front of the world, he wears his honor on his chest.

Beneath destruction and rapine, he scribes the word, while time falls.

All these things are within the library walls.

After circling the last two clues to the missing Chiavi, I folded the paper and slipped it into my pocket.

Gian's journal was just a log of slips into the Somnium, which were pockets of wastelands created when the wizards shielded the Mystik realm from the human world. They were like glitches in a computer program, the trapdoors blinking in and out of the libraries.

His notes went into detail about the areas surrounding the traps. But nothing really stood out…except for one. I turned the page. In black marker, he'd written "can figs" at the top.

"Why would he want a can of figs, Momo?" Her pink nose sniffed the air. "Did he start a grocery list? Do figs even come in a can? No, it has to be another clue. An acronym, maybe?"

Deidre's squeal rolled up the hill to me. My Changeling had morphed into her own person. From bleached hair to the clothes she wore, she was nothing like me. And who could blame her? The Fey had grown her in the Garden of Life to be me. To take over my life after I was born, when my parent faery would have come to switch us and take me away so I could become a

Sentinel. That is, if I hadn't disappeared with my mom.

Royston chased Deidre around with a bucket, water sloshing over the rim. I used to have fun like her, but the survival of both worlds wasn't on *her* shoulders. And I guess it was on Royston's, too. He was the chosen one. The one who could bring down the Tetrad.

Though Royston looked nineteen or twenty, he'd been alive for hundreds of years. Stuck in the Somnium, where time was frozen, he had remained the age he was when he'd fallen into the trap. With his long, light brown hair and thick shoulders, he was like a feral god.

Cadby's bat-like wings twitched on his back as his eyes followed Royston and Deirdre. He'd been Royston's guard since he was a boy. Mailes never expressed any emotions—it wasn't in their DNA. Cadby had said his people were fiercely loyal. The way he watched over Royston proved that statement.

Cadby ran a hand across his bald head, his pale skin nearly matching the yellow paint on the house. The straight line of his mouth and those alert eyes, the color and shape of black pebbles, definitely masked his emotions. If there were any to mask.

Sinead and Carrig prepared breakfast in the kitchen, the sheer curtains fluttering with the breeze entering through the open window. Carrig lifted a spoon to Sinead's lips for her to taste something he'd cooked. My biological father and his wife were cute together. I'd be lucky to have such a loving relationship as theirs one day.

The other Sentinels on my team kept busy. Demos and Lei sharpened their swords. Though we hadn't used them in months, Carrig insisted we clean and hone them weekly. He said it was a Sentinel's duty to have presentable weapons at all times. Jaran carried a basket of vegetables from the garden to the house and glanced in my direction before entering. He was checking on me again, worried I'd have a breakdown. What he didn't know was that I was too numb to have one.

Unlike Jaran, Arik—our leader and my ex—avoided eye contact with me as he fed a bottle to an orphaned baby goat. Since our breakup and his claim that he still loved me, we'd barely spoken about where we stood with each other, or about my feelings for Bastien. I supposed there wasn't anything else to say. Relationships were the last thing I needed to worry about with Nick gone and the recent deaths crushing my heart.

Cadby climbed the hill, heading in my direction. I returned my attention to the journal, hoping he'd get the hint and leave me alone.

He didn't.

"Breakfast is almost ready," he said, stopping in front of me.

"Hopefully it isn't figs."

"I'm not certain what the meal is. I don't believe it's figs. I enjoyed figs. They were a treat when I was a boy."

I pointed at the page. "This acronym spells out CAN FIGS."

"What are you reading?"

"Gian's journal," I said, not bothering to look up. "It has a list of libraries and the trapdoors he found in them. Then this random notation."

"The initials stand for something?"

"I think it's an acronym." I frowned.

A look of concern crossed his face. "What's the matter?"

"I thought he might have some clues in here. Something that said what I needed to do. I have no idea what it means to be Royston's protector or guardian or whatever I am."

His wings hugged his back as he rubbed his bald head. "You are a warrior. Follow your instincts. In time, you will know what to do."

"I'm glad you have faith in me." The sarcastic tone of my voice suggested I didn't. I needed to get out of my own brain, stop the insistent fear from freaking me out. I placed the prayer card into the journal and closed it.

"May I see that?"

I gave him a quizzical look before removing the card. "You mean this?"

"Yes," he said.

"It's just a prayer card." I offered it to him. "There's some writing on it. I can't figure out what it means."

Cadby flipped it over as he studied it. "The church on this directs to the clue you seek?"

"I think so."

"In older times," he said, "people would hide love letters and notes of treason in or around prayer candles. They'd write the whereabouts of such secrets on handkerchiefs and other items to pass the clue to the intended receiver. This"—he pointed out the handwriting on the backside of the card, and I followed along as he read it—"prayer candle, seventh row, three in. It's directions to the candle in this chapel." He handed it back to me.

"That's clever," I said, taking the card.

If it's still there.

My eyes went to his. "Listen, don't tell anyone about this, okay? I'm not sure who's trustworthy anymore, and I have to keep Royston safe. With my luck, you're probably on the wrong side."

"I assure you, I am on your side, Gianna. We must think of Royston's safety before all else." Cadby glanced over his shoulder at the others down the hill. "But your safety matters, as well. Without you, he hasn't a chance against the Tetrad. You have inherited a great responsibility. It's best you stop acting on your emotions and use your head. Let others help you."

Even though he was right, I started to protest. "I don't act—"

His hand went up to stop me. "I don't mean that as an insult. We all let our emotions direct us. Remove the heart so the head can think." He turned and plodded back down the hill, not waiting for a response from me. His injured wing lay flat against his back while his good one twitched and moved as he walked. He'd broken it while saving me right before I'd crashed Nick's motorcycle. The wing had almost healed, and he was able to do short-distance flights now.

The Tetrad. Hearing him say the name scraped at my thoughts. A high wizard back in medieval times had created the beasts by sewing animal parts to four slain warriors and connecting them with one soul. The beings were frightening and haunted my dreams. One creature resembled a lion with a cleft lip and claw-like hands. Another had a boar's head with sharp tusks sticking out of its jaw. The third had two large ram horns coming out of its forehead, which pulled and distorted its face. And the final one was part lizard, with razor-sharp teeth and scales. Each could command one of the elements, but they could never separate from one another or they'd die. The creatures were a myth to me, yet I was key to their destruction.

All I had to do was find the seven Chiavi, which, when combined, would unlock the beast from its prison, buried in some elusive mountain somewhere in a world full of mystical creatures. Simple. I rolled my eyes before returning my attention to Gian's journal.

CAN FIGS?

It must be a puzzle.

There were seven letters in the clue. There were seven Chiavi.

I sat up straighter.

Which meant there were seven libraries.

We had retrieved five of the keys. I wrote down the names of the libraries where we'd found them, but none of the initials matched the letters in the acronym.

It's not the names of the libraries. What am I missing? I stared at the page. *Maybe it's the* location *of the libraries.* I printed them next to the libraries. No matches.

Countries?

I scribbled on the page—*Austria, France, Italy, Germany, Switzerland.*

That has to be it. I just need two more letters. One starts with a "C" and the other an "N."

I removed the list of libraries with artwork that could be a Chiave. Nick and I had assembled it with Uncle Philip's help. I compared the clues for the final two Chiavi with our notes and circled the Czech Republic. Uncle Philip had suggested a painting in that library for *In front of the world; he wears his honor on his chest.* It was a portrait of some royal guy from the eighteenth century. He wore a uniform with a badge on his chest. It was the only library that could represent the *C* in the acronym.

We'd already figured out the final clue—*Beneath destruction and rapine, he scribes the word, while time falls*—or actually, Nick had. The thought of him made my heart tighten again.

Conemar won't hurt him. Nick's his son. I tried to reassure myself.

Nick believed the final clue described a mural named *The Medieval Scribe* in the McGraw Rotunda of the New York Public Library's main branch. He'd gone there with his family a few years back. The image stayed with him only because he'd pretended to like it for nearly twenty minutes to impress some girl.

A smile tightened my lips as I imagined how silly he probably acted around the girl. Nick was a goofball at times. It was what I liked most about him.

But the other letters represented countries. I scanned the list of possible libraries.

A light went on in my head, illuminating the answer. He couldn't put America down. There were too many states. He'd narrow it down to one of them. That's what I'd do. I couldn't explain it, but I knew that's what he'd do, too.

So "C" for Czech Republic and "N" for New York. I had solved can figs. And I had the locations of the final Chiavi.

Arik passed Cadby on his way up to me.

I slipped the list back into my pocket and put my notebook on top of Gian's journal, opened it to a page, and pretended to read. When he stopped in front of me, I kept my head down, acting too engrossed in what I was reading to notice him.

But I had noticed him. I noticed everything about Arik. The way he fought in practice with hardly any effort. The way he cared for the animals on the farm. And the way he would look at me with his hopeful, dark eyes. There always seemed to be an unanswered question between us. One I didn't want to answer and he didn't want to ask.

"What are you doing up here by yourself?" he asked, his English accent lacing his words, and he flashed that smile he used only around me. It was sort of forced and held a hint of uncertainty.

Glancing around, he waited for my response. He seemed nervous around me. It probably hadn't helped that I'd kept to myself when I wasn't doing chores or practicing Sentinel skills with the group.

"I know where the other two Chiavi are hidden," I finally said.

"That's fabulous," he said, sitting down beside me. "Where are they?"

"I want to go alone," I said, purposely not answering his question.

He raised a brow at me, his eyes full of disappointment. "Have we come to a place where you don't trust me?"

I bit my lip and considered his question. Out of everyone in hiding with us, I knew where Arik's heart and loyalties lay. "It's not that. It's *because* I trust you that I want you to stay. You must protect Royston while I'm gone. I can't go if you're not here with him."

"I'll send someone with you," he offered.

"No," I said. "It's too dangerous. Conemar's men have been attacking anyone traveling through the gateways. Uncle Philip said he believes they have one of the missing Monitors. Whoever jumps with me will register."

I waited for his response as he thought over my words. There were only four Monitors left. The parrots had a gift of sensing the gateways and registering those who jumped through the books. The other Monitors had died when I'd thrown my battle globe at a trapdoor to save Bastien and Gian. The action had caused a magic blowback that unlocked the traps and killed many of the birds.

Arik picked at some grass growing in the crack of the wall and said, "All right, then, but Lei and Jaran will keep an eye on the gateway page for any dangers. They can wait in the Dublin Library."

I would feel safer with two Sentinels watching my jump. "I'm good with that."

Arik tossed the grass to the ground and watched Deidre shake her wet shirt as Royston stared at her. I knew that look on Arik's face. He was worried about me.

"Don't worry." My fingertips went to the crescent scar on my chest. The bumpy flesh was a reminder of the shield charm Nana Kearns had branded on me. "I'm a ghost in the gateways. I can handle myself. Two quick jumps and I'll be right back."

The corners of his mouth lifted slightly, dimples hinting in his cheeks. "You've come quite a ways, Gia Kearns."

There was that name again. The one that no longer felt like my own.

"I'm proud of you," he added. "There's no one I'd rather have fighting beside me in a battle. Stay alert. Don't let your guard down, all right?"

"Promise."

Arik stood and brushed his hands across his pants. "We received a message from Bastien. Carrig will meet him in Asile and bring him to our hideout. Though the Wizard Council believes Carrig had nothing to do with your disappearance, they're still monitoring his jumps. So it will take a few days to get here, since they can't go through the gateway. They have to travel through the human world, but you should see him soon."

"That's great." Excitement swelled in my chest, but I kept my cool and smiled up at Arik.

Though my response held an even tone, there was a hint of disappointment in Arik's eyes. What did he expect? I'd moved on when I thought he'd broken up with me to date Emily. The witch. Literally. She'd placed a love spell on him, freeing me up to get close to Bastien while trapped in the Somnium.

Nothing brings a couple together like surviving a frozen wasteland filled with beasts hell-bent on consuming them for dinner.

Arik nodded and turned to leave, but stopped. "The remaining Chiavi. Where do you believe them to be?"

I glanced down at my notes. "I can't say. Uncle Philip gave me orders to tell no one." My uncle had become the new High Wizard of Asile after the previous one was murdered. As Sentinels, we had to follow his orders. And Arik, being a strict rule follower, would never allow me to go against them.

He nodded again and again turned to leave. "You should go tonight, then. Alert Philip of your jump schedule," he said over his shoulder as he started to trot down the hill. "Are you coming? The meal is ready."

I closed my notebook, hugged both it and the journal to my chest, and trailed him.

Arik's pace picked up as mine slowed, the distance growing between us. Unlike his normal confident posture, his muscled shoulders were slumped.

Bastien's face flashed across my mind. Without him, I wouldn't have survived the Somnium. The memory of his kisses and gentle touches tingled across my skin. I missed him.

I shook my thoughts away and plodded across the lumpy grass. My love life would have to wait. There were life-threatening things to consider.

CHAPTER TWO

Decked in their Sentinel gear, Lei, wearing her samurai-like helmet, and Jaran in his horned one, looked ready for a battle as they stood guard for me. I spoke the spell to retrieve the gateway book and waited.

The Long Room in Dublin's Trinity Library was dark and quiet. The two-story bookcases soared to the arched ceiling. I created a light globe on my palm and strolled down the center of the room, my messenger bag bouncing against my hip. I'd stuffed my cat-shaped helmet in it. My boots clacked against the polished floor as I passed the red ropes lining the bookcases on both sides of the room.

"I'm curious." I glanced at Jaran. "How do you get into Tearmann from here?"

The Irish haven intrigued me. Carrig's roots were there, which meant mine were, too. I hoped to visit it one day.

"You step on the spiral staircase in this library," he said. "Then say the charm that opens all the entries into the havens."

"Good to know." I rubbed a tickle from my nose.

"It's unwise that we don't know where you're going," Jaran added. "What if you don't return? How can we come to your rescue?"

Jaran had been a rock I'd clung to when my world seemed to slip away after Arik broke things off with me. He'd kept me company. Watched horror movies with me. Listened when I'd talked excessively about Arik and Emily's new relationship. Had held me while I'd cried over the loss.

"If something happens," I answered, "you call Uncle Philip. He'll tell you where I went."

Perspiration dampened my T-shirt and caused my leather pants to stick to my legs. Inside the library, wearing both my Sentinel gear and a trench coat, it was like being in a sauna. I tugged at my breastplate. Faith's pendant and the glass locket Uncle Philip had given me with Pip's white feather inside clanked against the metal. I removed the elastic band from my wrist and tied my hair up with it.

Where is that book? It never took that long for it to float over to me. I spun the watch that Carrig had given me on my wrist. It was ancient and clunky, and way too big for me, causing the leather to rub against my skin. When we left Asile in the dark of night to go into hiding, we had to leave our cell phones behind out of fear of someone tracking us. It was as if we were in the Stone Age using watches and landlines.

I decided to search for the gateway book and headed down the center of the room.

Plaster busts of famous men sat on built-in pedestals between the alcoves lined with bookcases. As the faces came in and out of my light, I read the names—Aristotle, Cicero, Homerus, Plato—

Jaran kept to my side. "Why isn't the book coming?"

I stopped, glanced in both directions, and shrugged. "I don't know. That's strange. *Sei zero sette periodo zero due DOR.*" I repeated the numbered charm to locate the gateway book. A scraping sound came from some ways down from us. I went to the area and said the charm again. On a shelf labeled "*ll*," the book shook but didn't come to me, something preventing it from moving.

"It's stuck." It was too high for me to reach, so I climbed the ladder. Jaran grabbed the sides to keep it steady.

I reached for the book and paused. "Someone tied a rope around it." My fingers followed the braided hemp. "The ends are nailed to the wood behind it."

"That's curious," Jaran said.

Lei sighed, startling Jaran and causing him to bump into the ladder.

The ladder wobbled, and I clung to it. "*Jaran*," I hissed.

"Sorry," he said, then looked over his shoulder at Lei. "Perhaps you shouldn't sneak up on someone in a dark library."

"I'd apologize, but we both know it wouldn't be sincere." Lei inspected her nails. "The Wizard Council sent out an order to all the havens. The gateway books are on lockdown ever since some rogue Mystiks attacked Mantello. Most likely, they were part of Conemar's band of evil misfits."

The wizard havens were realms cloaked by magic and connected to the human world through secret entries within the libraries. There was too much unrest in the havens, and we weren't sure who could be trusted. By binding the gateway books, it looked like the council was also in doubt.

"Wait." I glanced down at her. "What would happen if I jumped and there's another secured book on the other side? Would I get through?"

"Of course you would." She looked disinterested in my questions but answered them anyway. "It's a charm that opens the book when someone jumps through it, then locks it afterward."

I opened my mouth, but she stopped me.

"And before you ask, humans can't see the bindings or the book. Isn't magic a wonderful thing." The deadpan way she said it sounded like she thought it was anything but.

"Right. Good to know." I glanced down at her. "Do you

know the charm to release it?"

"*Liberato*," she said.

"*Set Free." That makes sense.*

"Didn't Philip give you the charm?" Jaran asked.

"No. It must've slipped his mind."

"Nothing ever slips his mind." Lei returned to inspecting her nails. "This is going to be a long evening."

She was right. Could his new role as high wizard be wearing on him?

I spoke the charm and freed the book. It was difficult to climb down the ladder with the heavy reference volume. Lei grasped my elbow and supported me as I stepped off the last wrung.

"Thanks," I said, smiling at her, though there was a dullness to her eyes. I missed my playful friend. She hadn't called anyone *ducky* since Kale died. The spell tattooed on Lei's hand—a radiant lotus between her thumb and pointer finger—had subdued her emotions; losing the love of her life had to be torture. I understood her need to not feel anything, but she'd become unrecognizable.

She gave me an impassive look. "Put your helmet on— you'll want to protect your vital parts. There have been reports that the spell disabling human weapons in many of the libraries is broken. Probably happened when your globe hit that trap."

I wrenched my helmet out of my messenger bag and secured it on my head. The silver casing covered half my face and was shaped like a cat's head and decorated with sapphires.

Jaran rested his hand on my shoulder and leaned over to my ear. "Listen, do you still call Nana before leaving the libraries?"

It had become routine for me to phone her just before jumping out of a library. I'd find a landline or swipe someone's cell phone and make a two-second call. "I'm okay," I would tell her.

"Yes," I said. "Why?"

He handed me a slip of paper. "It's Cole's number. Can you ring him for me? Tell him I'm alive and well? I can't use the phone or computer here. Carrig said they aren't safe."

Cole was the student council president at the school we'd attended while hiding in Branford, Connecticut, and Jaran's boyfriend.

The separation from his boyfriend had to be difficult for him. I got it. Being away from Bastien sucked.

Bastien's face flashed across my mind, and it was as if a dart hit my chest, piercing through flesh and bone, piercing my heart. Missing him was like my soul bleeding out. Memories of us together kept me up at night, and every minute away from him was like an eternity.

"Gia?" Jaran's voice pulled me from my thoughts.

I stuffed the note into the front pocket of my pants. "Of course."

"You're the absolute best." He winked and stepped away to guard the other side of the room from Lei.

I riffled through the pages of the gateway book until landing on the one with the National Library of the Czech Republic in Prague. The photograph was in motion. There wasn't anyone inside the reading room. It was definitely closed.

"See you on the flipside," I said.

"What was that?" Lei glanced over, her mouth a straight line, her eyes unfocused.

"It's just an old saying." When that didn't seem to register with her, I sighed. "Never mind. I'll be back soon." I spoke the key, *"Aprire la porta,"* jumped into the book, and tapped the page with my hand to turn it before fully entering the gateway.

It was a dangerous move, but they didn't need to know where I was going. If I was attacked in the library, I'd be spared because I could find the Chiavi. Lei and Jaran would be killed.

The coolness of the gateway welcomed me. I plunged into

the darkness, not bothering to ignite a light globe. With my feet under me, it was like surfing in the nothingness. The wind howled in my ears, and my mind was as blank as the void in front of me.

I flew out of the book, and my boots smacked against the marble floor, the sound echoing off the frescoes on the arched ceiling. The book rose from the ground and returned to its place on the shelf. Leather straps instantly wrapped around its spine, securing it.

Good thing Lei was right. Missing the exit and being stuck in the gateway was certain death. By luck or an act of God, Afton, Nick, and I had made it through that first time when we accidentally jumped into the book.

Since the library was empty, I removed my trench coat and draped it over my arm.

Twisted wooden columns between the bookcases supported the gilded, wrought iron railing around the upper gallery. I hated galleries. If I was going to attack someone, that's where I'd hide.

I passed a row of various sized globes displayed on wooden stands. Something buzzed behind me. I'd heard the noise before. I spun around. Aetnae, a book faery, hovered in front of my face like a humming bird.

"Hello, Gianna," I could barely hear her say.

"How are you?" I asked. Every time I'd see Aetnae, her praying mantis form and green skin always threw me off for a second.

"I am well."

Another faery flew up to Aetnae's side. It was a boy about her age. Maybe. How could a person tell with such a small, insect-like person? He had cropped brown hair and olive colored skin and was a little larger than Aetnae, with a wider wingspan.

"So what are we doing here?" he asked.

"*We?*" Aetnae snapped at him. "Why are you always following me? Don't you have something better to do?"

A worried expression crossed his tiny face. "I thought we could, you know, go together."

"Go away," she said, the exertion of hovering in one place causing her to sound breathless. "I'm working."

"All right," he said. "I'll see you at dinner. I'll save you a seat." He flew off.

"Goodbye, um…" I didn't know his name.

"Sen," he said from somewhere in the library.

Aetnae landed on my shoulder, grabbing my ponytail, draped over my collarbone, to keep from falling off. "I hope you don't mind, but I'm losing the energy to keep going."

She was practically weightless, and I could barely feel the pull on my hair.

"No problem," I said. "I think that boy likes you."

She groaned. "He's such a bug. Always at my side. And he prefers the modern libraries and all those graphic novels. Doesn't appreciate the architecture of the older ones. Or the classics."

"Well, he's definitely smitten."

She glanced in the direction he'd disappeared, a tiny smile tugging at her lips. "You think so?"

"Anyway, you needed to talk to me?" I wanted to hurry her along. If I let her, she'd talk endlessly, and I had a mission to do.

"I must get a message to Sinead. A travesty has happened in the realm of the Fey." Her words were so soft I had to strain to hear them. "Not a single Changeling hatched in the Garden of Life, so the Fey couldn't retrieve the newest batch of Sentinels. They're lost somewhere out there in the human world. Unless…"

She didn't need to finish her sentence. I knew what she would have said. The new Sentinels could be dead or might have never been born.

My neck was starting to ache from craning it to look at her. "Do they know what caused it?"

She let go of my hair, her fists landing on her hips. "The elders believe it's because of what you did."

What I did?

"I've never been to the Garden," I said. "How could it be because of me?"

Losing her balance, she grasped my hair again. "It's because of your battle globe. When you threw it at that trapdoor, it destroyed the charms securing the Somniums and messed with the enchantments surrounding the Fey realm. Everything is connected in the Mystik world, you know. The elders think it did something to the magic in the Garden. The Changeling pods withered away. I've never seen such a thing, not in all my hundreds of years."

Great. Now I was responsible for the destruction of an entire generation of Sentinels.

Way to live up to the Doomsday Child rep, Gia.

"Message received. You can go now." I continued down the row of stands holding the variety of globes. Aetnae took flight and flitted along with me, and she actually pointed her toes when she flew. She was like a graceful bug.

She harrumphed. "Your face isn't as pretty when you scowl like that."

"I'm not scowling. Just busy."

Seriously. It was as if an annoying gnat were following me.

Her wings worked double time to keep up as she tossed a bunch of questions at me. "Are you seeking a Chiave? How many do you possess? Is there one in this library? Want me to help? I'm good at finding things. Found a spool once for Laila."

Aetnae had helped me several times with searching for the Chiavi and finding the Shelter when I needed it. We'd become good friends. I could count on her.

"I am. We've found five." A lump formed in my throat.

We found. Nick and me. Thinking of him was like an ice pick to the heart. "There's one somewhere in this library," I said, shaking off the thought of him.

"And what are we searching for exactly?" she asked.

I stopped. "That."

By the subject's white wig and the uniform he wore, the portrait had to be from around the eighteenth century. One of his hands rested on a parchment unrolled across on a tabletop, and the other was placed on his hip. Pinned to his military jacket was a gold badge of honor with a cross on top of a starburst, and a large ruby in the center.

I grasped my locket with Pip's feather inside and chanted the spell to release the Chiavi. "*Libero il Tesoro.*" Release the treasure.

A gust of wind swirled around me, blowing Aetnae away.

Gasping, I turned away from the painting. "Aetnae?"

She was gone.

"Why have you called me only to ignore my entrance?" A man's voice came from behind me.

I faced him. "I'm sorry. It's just that my friend—"

He held up his hand to stop me. "I am the spirit of the Chiave you seek. Go on now. Remove my badge, but carefully, you understand. You aren't to ruin the material." He pushed out his chest and lifted his chin.

Oh gosh, someone thinks he's special. I dropped my trench coat and worked to free the clasp with nervous fingers.

"Hurry. I haven't all day, simple girl."

Simple? Better than being a royal jerk like you. Of course, I would never say that to him. The dude was full-on scary.

The clasp finally opened, and I removed the badge.

He snapped around and pulled himself back into the portrait.

"Wait," I said.

His eyes went to me as he placed his hand back on the table.

When I didn't continue right away, he snapped, "Out with it."

"Aren't you supposed to tell me what the Chiave does? The other spirits had an entire spiel about what theirs did. You know, other than actually being one of the keys."

"Must you annoy me?" A frown deepened the lines around his mouth as he settled back into his pose. "But since you asked, I'm obliged to tell you. It's a shield, but don't dally with it. The spell won't last but a few minutes."

I glanced down at the metal in my hand. It was a heavy badge. The arms of the cross were thin and widened at the ends, and the ruby was dull with age. "A shield? Will people be able to see me?" I glanced up. He had already frozen in the portrait. "You must've been a rude man when you were alive."

A squeak came from behind me. If the library hadn't been so quiet, I wouldn't have heard it.

"Aetnae?" Rushing around the globes, I shoved the badge into the main pocket of my messenger bag. "Where are you?" I called.

Another squeak.

I stopped. My boot was just inches from Aetnae's tiny body sprawled on the marble floor. Gingerly, I picked her up. She was unmoving in the palms of my hands. I sucked in a breath and tensed as if any movement would make her crumble.

Oh my God, she's dead.

I gently poked her shoulder. "Aetnae?"

She groaned and pushed herself up into a sitting position. My muscles relaxed, and I expelled a breath. "Are you hurt?"

She brushed her tangled red hair from her face and stood. "No, but that was quite a ride."

"Listen, I have to go to New York," I said, placing her on top of one of the globes. "Will you be okay here?"

"Of course." She inspected her wings. "Who do you suppose took care of me for the few hundred years I've been alive? I'll give you a hint—me. But I should go with you. I'm tiny and make a good watch out."

"A lookout?" I checked the time. "No. It's a little after ten here. That means it's around four in the afternoon in New York. The library's still open. Someone will see you."

"As if you won't look suspicious with all that on." She waved her hand at me.

"You're right." I searched for my trench coat.

Aetnae followed me, bouncing a little unsteadily on the air. The coat had been blown up against one of the globe stands. I snatched it, and a square piece of paper dropped from the pocket and floated to the floor.

"I've got it." Obviously recovered, Aetnae zipped down and grabbed it. She flew it over to me. "Directions to St. Patrick's Cathedral. Is that where you're going?"

"Yes," I said, putting on my coat and tying the belt in a knot. I removed my helmet and shoved it in my bag.

"That bulky bag looks awfully suspicious," Aetnae said.

She was right. The helmet bulged out as if I were hiding a volleyball inside. I removed it and placed it on the globe. I'd have to retrieve it later.

"Dettor?" I asked.

"Guess so. I don't know why I can't go with you. At least to the library." The pout on her face made me smile. The kids I used to babysit would make the same one after I'd announced it was bedtime.

"Next time, okay?" I said, giving her a reassuring smile.

S ince the New York Public Library was still open, I couldn't collect the Chiave, not with a crowd around. So I decided to investigate Gian's prayer card. But first, I had to do that thing for Jaran. Strolling down the middle aisle flanked by rows of desks, I looked for an unattended cell phone. Preferably belonging to someone immersed in a book or work. And one without a passcode.

The teens in the room never let go of their phones. They didn't even glance up from them as I passed. Then I saw it. My target. A flip phone sat on the table beside a man with a beard, outdated clothes, and Birkenstocks. Perfect. The phone was ancient, and most of them didn't require a password or a fingerprint. And definitely not face recognition.

I'd gotten good at phone snatching, but still my stomach shifted uneasily. What would I do if caught? I picked up an abandoned stack of books from one of the tables and headed for the man, pretending to stumble when I reached him. The books shot from my arms and tumbled onto the table and floor.

The man jumped in his seat.

"I'm so sorry." I feigned embarrassment.

"You should watch where you're going." He didn't say that very nicely before bending over to pick up the books on the floor.

I gathered the ones spilled over the table, along with the phone.

He stood and put the books in his hands on top of the stack in my arms.

"Thank you," I said.

He grunted.

How rude. It's not as if he knew I meant to toss all those books at him. Of course, I'd just borrowed his phone without asking, but he didn't know that. And hopefully never would.

I abandoned the books on a table at the end of the row then searched for somewhere to use the phone. The bathroom was my best option, so I found one and went in.

An Italian-looking woman wearing gray plaid pants, a white shirt, and a red scarf came in after me. I ducked into a stall and didn't come out until she left.

After pulling out the slip of paper Jaran had given me, I dialed the number on it.

Cole answered his cell on the first ring. "Hello," he said, sounding anxious.

"Hi, Cole, this is Gia. Do you remember me?" The door to the restroom banged open. I paused and peered through the crack between the stalls. A woman with red hair, wearing all black except for the floral scarf around her neck, went into the last cubicle.

"I know who you are," Cole said. "You're Jaran's friend. Do you know where he is? The home for the foreign exchange students is empty. They're all gone." His disappointment tugged at my heartstrings and tied them into knots. He missed Jaran.

"Their funding fell through," I said. "Listen, I don't have much time. Jaran is visiting relatives in Africa. He wanted me to let you know. Said he'd contact you soon."

"Did he say anything else?" There was hope in his voice this time.

"Oh, yeah, I almost forgot." Jaran would shish kabob me with his sword for what I was about to say. "He said he loved you."

"Really?" Now he sounded excited. "If you talk to him again, can you tell him I feel the same, and that I'll wait for him? Tell him to email or text me when he can."

He loves him. Aww…

"I sure will."

"Great," he said. "And thank you for calling."

"No problem. Bye." I pushed the end button then dialed Nana's cell phone number. It went straight to her voicemail, so I called her home. No answer. I'd have to try reaching her another time.

I flipped the phone shut and decided I'd better return it.

The table the man had occupied was now abandoned. I placed the phone on the chair he'd sat on. When he realized it was missing, he'd come back and find it there.

I found the exit and dashed outside. Buildings lined the streets and soared into the sky. Everything was crowded—the streets, the sidewalks, and even the clouds overhead. The church was about ten blocks away. People on Fifth Avenue rushed from one place to another. I weaved around them and headed in the direction of St. Patrick's Cathedral.

Thin beams of sunlight broke through the clouds and spotlighted parts of the city. Fall leaves danced over the sidewalks, pushed along by the breeze. My trench coat fit the cold day.

The cathedral was a gothic-style building spanning an entire block, made of white marble, with spires reaching into the sky. My brain felt overwhelmed by the many details—from its lattice accents to its tall stained-glass windows, all of it was awe-inspiring.

I stood in front of the massive bronze doors with statues of the Holy Family, Saint Patrick, and other saints inserted in square niches within the metal. If only I had my cell phone, I could text Afton pics to put in one of her architecture scrapbooks.

"You can't enter through there," said a woman with a messy bun at the top of her head and a little boy pulling on her arm. "Admittance is through the side doors."

"Thanks," I said and went around the column to where she'd pointed.

A man with a buzz cut in a dark suit inspected my bag at the security check and held up the Chiave badge.

"Part of a costume I'm designing for a show." I answered his question before he could ask it, keeping my arm close to my side so he wouldn't notice my sword under my trench coat.

Please don't ask me to remove my jacket. I concentrated on breathing normally as he stared at me for a long moment.

He finally handed me my bag and nodded me through. I

could hardly believe he hadn't checked to see if I had anything under my coat. How safe was that? It had to be a mistake. I wanted to run to the prayer candles before he noticed, grab whatever Gian had hidden there, and hurry back to the library.

Rows of polished wooden pews ran the length of the gothic-style cathedral. I measured my steps and headed down the right aisle on the far side of the pews, imagining Gian there in the 1930s. The place probably looked the same back then as it did now. The tall stained-glass windows were even more beautiful viewed from the inside. There were so many artifacts and statues my eyes couldn't take them all in.

Prayer candle stands were everywhere. I wasn't sure which altar held Gian's secret, so I retrieved the laminated prayer card from my bag and studied it. *Prayer candle, seventh row, three in.* It was the only clue written on the card. I turned it over and there were no marks on the back. I'd have to check every stand for the correct candle. This was going to take some time, and there were way too many people around.

In the alcoves on each side of the pews were altars and votive stands. The fourth one on the right caught my eye. There were three statues of women, probably saints, in the center and an angel on each side of them. On the backside of Gian's prayer card was a small picture of it. I hadn't thought the other stuff on the card would be clues. The photo's label read, Altar of Saint Rose of Lima.

This has to be it.

A man and woman in their fifties or something were at the stone railing in front of the prayer candles. The woman stood on the kneeler aiming a fancy looking camera at the center statue of a saint cradling a cross with a wreath of flowers on her head. I decided to sit in the nearest pew and wait for them to finish.

The crowd seemed to be thinning. A group posed together in front of the main altar, a girl angled her phone with a selfie stick to capture herself in front of another statue, and others shuffled around, heads thrown back, trying to take in all the treasures adorning the cathedral.

Once the couple left, I waited until three women passed before stepping over the barrier. The candle stand looked too modern to be from Gian's time. Starting from the right side of the stand, I counted seven rows down, three in, and searched the circumference of the votive hoping to find something, but came up empty. I did the same with the candles on the left. Nothing there, either.

Disappointment slumped my shoulders. I was at a dead end. The candle stand Gian had put his message in must have been replaced ages ago.

At the sound of someone approaching, I hid behind the wall of the arch. A priest rushed up the aisle, and I held my breath, only releasing it when he'd disappeared around the corner. I glanced at the flickering wicks on the few prayer candles still lit on the stand.

Maybe I missed something. It wouldn't hurt to try again, I reasoned.

Tightening my hands into fists and then stretching out my fingers as wide as a Ping-Pong paddle, I tried to control the nerves bubbling inside my stomach.

What would happen if I was caught?

Fist. Paddle.

They'd just kick me out. That's all.

Fist. Paddle.

No need to freak out, Gia.

I relaxed my hands and peered around the wall. A few tourists were across the way from me, their backs turned. Carrig had drilled during our practices that sudden movements would attract attention. Slow, fluid ones and you'd blend into the environment, he'd said. I eased out of my hiding place and crossed over to the stand. He was right—no one noticed me.

Though the chapel was cool, sweat beaded on my neck. My fingers shook a little as I ran them over the copper stand, hoping to find whatever it was Gian had hidden. But there was nothing. Or if he had left a clue there, it was gone, lost to time.

Frustration settled in my gut. I might never know what he'd left for me. He wouldn't have gone to all the trouble of hiding it if it weren't something important. Whatever it was, its loss could be bad. But I had no idea what level of bad it would be.

The cool chapel suddenly felt hot. Stifling. I had to get outside.

Get some fresh air.

At the same moment I turned to leave, a man's cough startled me. My heart jerked in my chest, and I bumped into the copper stand, the flames on the candles flickering. My foot kicked some sort of metal rod sticking out of the floor under the holder, and it moved forward slightly.

Another cough came from one of the pews, and I darted a look over my shoulder, listening. The man's back was turned. He hadn't seen me. I dropped to a squat and inspected the rod sticking out of the tiles.

It had to be a latch or something. I tugged it forward the rest of the way.

Stone scraped against stone.

One of the bricks beside the angel on the right slid out from the wall.

I found it! Adrenaline sparked through my veins, and I struggled to push my excitement away. I had to stay focused.

Stay calm.

I did another quick check over my shoulder to make sure no one had noticed before reaching inside the drawer and grabbing the leather cylinder case inside. I moved the rod back into place with my foot, and the brick drawer shuddered as it closed, the noise causing me to pause.

Still no one noticed. The sound must've mixed in with the murmur of voices and the shuffling of feet in the cathedral. I climbed over the barrier and knelt on the step right before the priest who'd passed earlier returned. He nodded at me, and I lowered my head and pretended to pray until he was a safe distance away. Then I slowly tucked the leather case into the pocket of my trench coat.

The flames on the candles flickered as a shadow moved across the altar in front of me. Deciding to let whoever it was have privacy, I made the sign of the cross and was about to stand, but froze at the sound of her voice.

"I wasn't aware you were religious," Veronique said sweetly, as if we weren't sworn enemies.

CHAPTER THREE

I pushed myself up from the prie-deau and faced her. "There's a lot you don't know about me."

"I highly doubt it." Veronique pressed her perfect rosebud lips together and slipped her hand under the flap of her coat. The candlelight flickered across the hilt of her sword.

"We're not doing this here," I said, eyeing the blade. "Isn't there a rule about holy ground or something?"

The Cheshire Cat grin on her face boiled my blood. It was the same one she'd flashed me during the battle on my front lawn last spring. It was only after I'd failed to stop Conemar from taking Nick that I'd learned Veronique had killed Kale. I held back the tears threatening to escape at the thought of him.

"Rules," she said without her strong French accent. Her blond hair was longer and twisted in a braid. The smug look on her face deepened the corners of her mouth. "Once you learn to break them, Gianna, you'll be the warrior Agnost believed you would be."

Agnost. I hadn't heard his name in a long time. Not since I first learned about the Mystik world. Nearly two hundred years ago, he had predicted that a child born of two Sentinels would be the coming of the end. And because my parents couldn't resist each other, I was the lucky winner of that gene pool.

I had to stall her. Figure out an escape. "Where's your accent?" Dumb question for a time like this, but it did put her off guard a little.

"A charm." Her eyes followed me as I eased right, hoping to find a way around her. "It helps me blend in—not get noticed."

I highly doubted she'd ever go unnoticed.

"What happened to you?" I backed up, the heels of my boots stopping against the kneeling step. "Why did you decide to join Conemar?"

She took a step toward me, her hand still resting on the hilt of her sword. "You've risked all to save the ones you love. Do you think I am different from you?"

She meant Bastien and Gian. To save them, I had thrown my globe at the trap door into the Somnium where we'd been stuck, releasing all the evil creatures imprisoned there. My stupid actions started what could be the destruction of both worlds. I *had* risked everything for them, without knowing the consequences.

"Why did you join Conemar? You're a Sentinel. Trained to stop men like him."

"Because I'm his daughter," she said.

I swore my jaw hit the floor.

"You're his *daughter*?"

"You heard me."

I just stared at her, waiting for my mind to catch up.

Why did no one know this? Or if they did, why hadn't they told me? I had to keep her talking. Distract her so I could figure out an escape.

"How could Conemar hide that you're his daughter from the council?"

She answered, "My father replaced a Sentinel with me when we were infants. Poor thing is at the bottom of a lake, weighed down with rocks. At six, when my magic hadn't come in, he had my parent faery convince the council that all I needed was private training."

Bastien had mentioned she'd trained with a private coach in the French countryside.

"Wait. Then how do you have a battle globe?"

She glanced down at her hand, and I took the opportunity to do a quick scan around her. I could go to her left. There was more room on that side.

"I'm a daughter of a wizard. I have little magic, but I can make fire look like a globe." Her fingertips sparked. She stretched her fingers out, studying her hand. "Damn it. There's a charm over the chapel. I suppose the sword will have to do."

"So that means you're Nick's sister." The thought made my stomach feel like I'd eaten a bag full of sour grapes. "Have you seen him?"

Her head popped up. Hatred flared in her eyes, and her grin vanished from her lips. "I know what you're trying to do. Distract me. There's no escape. The cathedral is surrounded by Sentinels more skilled than you are. Hand over all the Chiavi, and perhaps your death will be quick and somewhat painless."

All the Chiavi? She thinks I have more than one. "I don't have them all."

"Oh, I'm sorry. I should have been clearer." Her voice carried a sinister tone. "I only need the final two. We have the rest. And that ancient book, too."

My heart sank. "How—?" I couldn't speak. The other Chiavi were in Asile, locked in a safe. In the high wizard's chambers. Uncle Philip's chambers.

"How do you think?" She leaned forward. "We took them. Not but an hour ago. Asile is less a few guards and a Sentinel," she said. "I'll let your mind process that information. Wonder who could have perished in the attack. Was it someone you know?"

Oh no—Carrig? He was to meet Bastien in Asile, bring him to the hideout in Ireland. I wanted to crumple to the floor. *Please don't be Carrig.* My throat swelled, and I swallowed hard. Crying was not an option. I couldn't let her see she'd punched my weak spot.

Focus, Gia!

A fire burned in my stomach, consuming and angry. I wanted to crush her. But just over her shoulder, I could see tourists in the middle of the chapel, sitting in pews, clicking pictures on their phones, and I took a deep breath and released it slowly. There were innocent people around. I couldn't risk them getting hurt.

"It's my lucky day," Veronique continued, her hand going to the hilt of her sword. I recognized the intricate woven metal on the hilt—the Chiave. "I was on my way to deliver our spoils from the attack to daddy dearest when my spy found me with information about your whereabouts."

Someone told her where I'd be. Who?

"There's security here." I grasped the hilt of my sword. "They have guns."

A sinister snarl twisted her lips. "Not to worry. They'll be taken care of."

She started to pull her sword out of its scabbard just as a large group of men and women wearing choir robes cut between us.

I needed to take her by surprise. My boots scraped against the tiles as I got into my kickboxing stance—left foot forward, feet shoulder distance apart, fists up to my cheekbones, elbows in by my sides.

The last two women passed.

I charged at Veronique. A jab to her face. Cross punch to her cheek.

The tourists who witnessed my attack gasped and backed away from us, but I didn't let the commotion distract me.

An uppercut to her ribs.

Veronique stumbled.

A side kick to her chest.

She flew back and collided with the pews.

Boots hitting the tile floor sounded to my left. A man and a woman Sentinel headed our way.

In the pew, Veronique struggled to get up. I readied my stance again.

Someone grasped my arm and pulled me back through an opening in the wall. The bricks slid into place again, sealing me in a darkened room with a stranger.

What was going on? Veronique had the other Chiavi. I had to get them from her.

Slamming my palms against the stone, I shouted, "Wait! Let me out." I faced whoever had dragged me in there and ignited a light globe on my palm. The priest who had passed me twice in front of the altar stood there with a sympathetic look on his face.

"The others with her were coming for you," he said. "They would have killed you."

"But she has something I need. Something dangerous." I pushed on the wall. "I have to stop her."

"This way." He nodded for me to follow him.

I hesitated, glancing at the wall.

As though he had read my thoughts, the priest lightly touched my arm. "There will be another opportunity to acquire what you've lost."

He was right. I had to move forward. "All right," I said. "Lead the way."

He bowed his head and started down a tunnel.

"You know of the Mystik world?" I asked.

"The church has always known of it. The Vatican remained as a bridge between the human and Mystik worlds when the latter went into hiding."

Our footfalls echoed through the tight passageway. "How did you know I was here?"

He rushed along at a brisk pace. "Antonio alerted me. Said he owed you."

Alarm bells went off in my head. If both Veronique and Antonio knew my location, I wasn't as stealthy as I thought I was. "Then how did Antonio know?"

"Because of the recent attacks on humans, the Vatican has guards posted at many of the libraries during hours of operation. They wear street clothes to blend in, so you wouldn't have noticed him or her."

"I see." *Guess it's not a good idea to jump during the day.* "Well, next time you speak to Antonio, thank him for me."

"I will."

I really hadn't done much to save the Vatican's Sentinel during an attack in a library several months ago, only thrown my pink globe to protect him from a fireball that Nick had unleashed, which had been about to hit Antonio.

I followed the priest through the maze of tunnels until we came to a stairwell with stone steps.

"Do you know what happened in Asile?" I hoped that maybe he'd heard something.

He kept glancing over his shoulder as he spoke. "Yes, Antonio told me. He keeps me up-to-date on Mystik news. He said a small group had attacked the castle. Killed several guards and a Sentinel. They broke into the high wizard's chambers and took something valuable."

"Did Antonio give you a name of the Sentinel who died?"

"It was an older man," he said. "Just out of retirement."

Carrig had never retired. He remained as an instructor after his term of duty. It couldn't be him. *Thank God, he's okay.* The intense feeling of relief caused tears to gather in my eyes, and I turned my head so the priest wouldn't see, wiping them away with my fingertips.

We ended up at another tunnel, and the priest climbed into a golf cart. I got in on the other side. He turned the key, pushed on the gas, and the cart bumped down the tunnel.

"What's your name?" I asked.

"You may call me Father Peter," he said.

The headlights illuminated the rock walls, and dank air hit my face. We traveled for about ten minutes before the cart coasted to a stop. He scrambled out, and I followed him up a narrow staircase until it came to a dead end.

He placed his hands on the wall and leaned forward to look through a peephole. "This is the public library. You have a head start. The cathedral's security will detain Veronique and her gang for as long as possible."

When I didn't answer, he looked back at me, and I nodded that I understood.

He returned his eye to the peephole. "Ah, here she is. Time for you to go."

"I don't know how to thank you," I said.

"No need." His smile was full of warmth. "It is I who should be thanking you. Without you, we are all lost."

"I'm scared I'll fail everyone," I said, so quietly I wasn't sure a mouse could hear me, let alone Father Peter.

"I have faith in you, Gianna." Wow, he had good hearing. "You are more than a prediction. If ever you or yours need a place to hide, come here. There is a tiny silver starburst at the bottom on both sides of the wall: push it, and this door will open." He bent over and pressed it. The wall slid aside, making an entry into the library.

The Italian woman from the bathroom earlier, wearing gray plaid pants with a red scarf tied around her neck, was on the other side of the wall.

"Good day, Father," she said before nodding at me. "Gianna."

"Thank you for meeting us," Father Peter said. "Gianna,

this is Agata. She will help you from here."

She turned, looking left, then right. "The library is still open. We should be on our way before someone sees this door."

He gave me a warm smile, the wrinkles at the edges of his eyes deepening. My bet was that he must smile often to have such deep lines. "Now go," he said.

"Thank you." I ducked through the opening.

His words were an echo in my head. *You are more than a prediction.* I may have started the apocalypse, may even be the Doomsday Child, but I could turn it around. I could stop it all. I simply had to release the Tetrad and have Royston destroy it.

But how? The answers must be inside the leather case Gian left for me. For his heir.

Though I knew I should go straight to the Rose Reading Room and jump through the gateway book to safety, I couldn't leave the Chiave behind. Veronique may have stolen five of them, but I wasn't about to let her have the remaining two.

Agata headed down the hall expecting me to follow her. When I didn't, she whirled around. "This way."

"I have to get something first," I said.

She shook her head in protest. "We must hurry before Veronique and the others get here."

"Both worlds depend on me getting it."

She studied my eyes before giving in. "All right. I'll keep a watch on the entrance. But quickly, you hear?"

"I will." I took off down Aster Hall—a large space with soaring ceilings. Charging up the two flights of stairs to the McGraw Rotunda, my breaths grew heavy.

Dominating the wall at the right of the entrance to the Catalog Room was *The Medieval Scribe*. The mural reached almost from the floor to the high ceiling. The artwork was of a monk sitting at a drawing desk and copying a manuscript while another man watched. The sea, a castle, and a burning barn with two men attempting to calm a bucking horse made up the background of the painting. Just below the mural was a stone bench and a sign with the library hours on it.

A girl sat on that bench reading. The rotunda was crowded. People shuffled from mural to mural taking in the artwork. As I studied the monk, I thought of Gian's clue, *beneath destruction and rapine; he scribes the word, while time falls.*

While time falls. "What does that even mean?" I asked under my breath as if someone would answer me. There were open books, a rolled parchment, and a discarded quill at his feet. On his desk were a bunch of quills secured together with a red ribbon, an inkwell, an hourglass, and an open book. Any of those could be the Chiave.

Tourists flowed in and out of the rotunda. My hands shook at my sides; I couldn't wait for it to empty. Veronique and her Sentinels could show up at any time. The girl sitting on the bench in front of the mural stood, gathered her things, and walked away.

Witnesses or not, I decided this was my chance.

I recited the charm to release the Chiave.

"*Libero il tesoro.*"

Cold air circled me, the chill raising the fine hair on my arms. Voices sounded around me. Quick intakes of breaths.

"What's happening?"

"Did you see that?"

"It's moving."

"Not to worry, everyone," Agata said. With my eyes on the mural, I hadn't seen her enter. "It's a new interactive show we're trying."

Good one.

The monk in the mural set his quill down on the table while the man above him shifted his gaze to me. The horse, men, and burning barn in the background were all in motion.

Clearing his throat, the monk stood and lifted an hourglass off the desk. His gray hair was like a wreath around his bald head. His white robes were clean and crisp. But it was his eyes that startled me—soft blue and full of sadness.

"You are just a child, daughter of the Seventh. I am Frances, the keeper of the Chiave you seek. This hourglass will allow the holder to slow time for as long as the sand lasts." He leaned out of the mural and extended the artifact to me. I stepped over and took it from him.

"Thank you," I said.

He bowed his head slightly, returned to his chair, and lifted his quill off the desk. The man above him, the thrashing flames on the barn, and the horse with the men chasing it all froze into their places. The magic always seemed to surprise me, even though I'd seen it several times before. The breeze halted, and the rustling pages of the book on the desk settled back into position.

"Now, off with you," Agata said from behind me. "They have arrived."

I twisted around to find her retreating back. She was racing toward Veronique and the other Sentinels. I soared across the rotunda.

My boots sounded against the high-arched hallway. The library was active, people were everywhere, but I suddenly felt alone.

A shiver quaked my spine.

Quit being a baby. I stopped and adjusted my messenger bag across my body while trying to catch my breath. The Rose Reading Room was gigantic. Sunlight came in through the large arched windows and shone on the metal reading lamps stretching across the rows and rows of long tables. Brown stuccowork with intricate gilt on the ceiling surrounded murals of cloudy skies. Several chandeliers, covered in shadows, lined each side of the room.

The hourglass in my hand was ancient. Made of wood and glass, it seemed fragile, so I gently tucked it into my messenger bag next to the badge and called for the gateway book, not caring who heard or who saw the book fly over to me.

Balconied bookcases surrounded the room. Arik had told me once that he felt the libraries were his secret garden. There was a time when I would have agreed with him, but not anymore. Libraries were beautiful creatures, but they hid unknown dangers behind their bookcases and among their artworks.

Where is it? Come on. I darted looks over my shoulder, my hands sweaty, breath quick, certain Veronique would find me.

There're too many people. There're too many.

Stop!

Focus.

I couldn't put anyone in danger. How was I going to keep them all from getting hurt?

A fire alarm blared through the library.

Agata. She's causing a diversion.

The people sitting at tables around the room picked up their things and rushed to the door. I shoved my trench coat into my messenger bag. Not too long after, I noticed a faint flapping sound coming from one of the balconies. Another trapped book.

I maneuvered between the tables to a door. Inside were stairs that led to the balcony. I bounded up them and found the book strapped to a bookcase.

"Seriously. This is getting annoying."

Agata ran into the reading room.

"I'm up here," I called. She skirted around the row of tables.

I tucked some loose hair behind my ear and spoke the charm to release the book, "*Liberato.*"

The straps fell away, and the book shot out of the case. I caught it and flipped the pages with shaky fingers.

Something made a crashing sound below, and a fireball flew over my head, hitting the bookcase above me. I spun around.

Another Sentinel had joined Veronique and the original two. He stood in an aisle between the rows of tables, a fire globe blazing in his hand.

Where's Agata? I dropped to a crouch and peered through the railings. She lay motionless on the floor, a few chairs toppled around her. Ice crackled across her skin; her stare was frozen on the ceiling. Veronica stood over her, a satisfied snarl on her lips.

No, no, no, no. She's dead. Air rushed into my lungs, and I choked back my sobs. I had to get out of there. I crawled to the books strewn across the floor, searching for the gateway book.

A ball of fire hit the bookcase. Charred books fell from the shelf and burned pages floated around me. I formed my battle globe and tossed it over the railing. The sphere looked like a crystal bubble; I'd never seen that before and wasn't sure what it would do. It grew as it soared through the air and shattered on a table below, glass spraying up in the air. A large shard stabbed through the man's throat. A surprised look crossed his face—blood squirting out of the wound—before he crumpled to the ground.

A fiery glow left him and hit me, heating my body. I patted down my clothes expecting to be on fire, but there was nothing.

I killed him! I. KILLED. HIM. Bile rose in my throat.

"Get it together, Gia," I ordered myself. There wasn't time for a freak-out. I moved my messenger bag to my back and continued searching through the shelves.

Flames consumed many of the books. Dark smoke drifted to the ceiling, causing the sprinklers to turn on. A purple sphere exploded by my hand. Call it fear or instinct, but I instantly formed a glass globe and sent it over the railing with great force.

An agonizing howl came from below. I didn't dare stop searching, afraid to look. Afraid to see what I'd done, to see another death.

A purple light rushed me, hitting me in the chest. *Crap. He stunned me.* But I could breathe. I could move my hands. It didn't work. My hand touched the familiar fine leather of the gateway book. I wiped the water from my eyes and tossed open the cover.

Something hit the bookcase to my right. Ice spread across the spines of books on the shelves and snuffed out the burning books on the floor. The water spraying out of the sprinklers froze and dropped, pelting me, stinging my exposed skin. I found the page to the Dublin library and stood, hunched over to make myself less of a target.

Veronique threw a fire globe. It hit my shoulder and part of my chest, catching my vest on fire.

"*Shit*," I yelled and tugged it off. Pain seared my shoulder. Thankfully, my breastplate had taken the brunt of the assault. During my distraction, the girl Sentinel had climbed onto the balcony. She charged at me, tossing another ice globe. I dodged it, and an explosion of ice and snow fell around me.

I didn't want to kill the girl, so I hesitated to throw another globe at her. Squaring my shoulders, I got ready for her attack. When the girl got close enough, I threw a kick to her gut and slammed my fist against her jaw. She stumbled back against the frozen railing. It broke free, and she fell over the side, landing on a table below. Her body was half on and half off the table, her neck bent at an odd angle and the bones underneath pushed against her skin.

Is she dead?

A shimmery light left the girl's body and flew to me, smacking my chest. I took a step back, expecting to turn into a human Popsicle, but nothing happened, only a chill that rushed across my skin and quickly ended.

"You killed her," Veronique yelled as she stepped up on a chair and onto a table. She charged the length of it, heading for me.

I dropped to my knees and flipped through the pages of the gateway book. My heart galloped like a thousand racehorses on steroids. I needed to escape.

Where do I go? I can't lead her to the others. I stopped on the photograph of the Boston Athenæum. *Home? To Nana. Afton. No.* Veronique knew where Nana Kearns lived. I couldn't risk going there. I tossed over more pages.

Just then, Veronique pulled herself up onto the balcony and let loose another fire globe. The flames licked the air and smoke trailed it like a comet. The fire grazed my cheek, pulling a sharp gasp from my chest.

Her breaths were loud—panting. The sound of a siren drew nearer. We'd have company soon.

A feral look on her face, Veronique plucked a dagger from her shoulder sheath. A velvet bag, weighed down by something heavy inside, was tied around her waist.

The other Chiavi? I had to get them. I grasped the strap of my messenger bag.

"You can't win, Gia. You're weak. Unskilled. A sniveling child."

"I beat your ass, and I took care of your friends." Meaning the three Sentinels lying dead on the floor below us. I forced my eyes to stay on hers, acting brave, though their deaths were like an overweight barbell on my conscience.

Her step forward caused me to step back. "That was dumb luck," she said. "This will take skill."

She ran for me. I drew my sword and swung at her. She ducked, the blade barely missing her. Before I could get another swing in, she tackled me, our bodies smacking into the bookcase, my sword knocked from my hand.

A satisfied look crossed Veronique's face right before she stabbed my upper arm with her dagger. Her blade cut across my cheek. A horrified scream rattled my throat. My knees buckled and thudded against the floor.

"*Shit!*" The pain shocked me. I wanted to roll into a ball on the floor, to have this end.

She's going to kill me. I'm going to die.

Fear gripped me.

Then anger.

Fight, Gia! The voice in my head was strong and forceful. It pushed me. Pushed me to my feet.

Pushed me to take action.

Your globe. Stop her before she takes you down.

I ignited one and busted it against her thigh, the glass pieces cutting into her leg.

She shrieked and teetered backward.

Dropping to a squat, I spun around and sweep-kicked her calves, knocking her to the floor. Her head slammed against the ground.

She laid there, unmoving.

"Unskilled," I spit out like a distasteful word. "Who's unskilled now?"

She started to move.

With pain shocking my shoulder, cheek, and chest, I opened the gateway book and collapsed on top of it. I couldn't move anymore. My arms and legs shook. Blood trickled down my cheek and into my mouth, and I tasted copper on my tongue.

"*Aprire la porta,*" I said and hugged my bag to my chest, then remembered the Chiavi tied to Veronique. I felt a tug across my entire body. "No. Stop." A swirling wind engulfed me and dragged me into the page.

Veronique jumped in after me and wrapped her arm around my neck, clinging to my back as we fell through the pitch-black void.

CHAPTER FOUR

The air rushing across me cooled my burning cheek. Blood from the wound in my shoulder soaked my sleeve. Fear rocked my bones, and I wanted to give up, just let the dark take me somewhere else, not there, not in the gateway of hell with Veronique. Her fist connected hard against my side and knocked me to my senses.

She can't win.

I threw my elbow back and clipped her chin.

Veronique lost hold of me and spun away.

Unable to see where she was, I formed a light globe and tossed it in front of me. The sphere flew with us, illuminating the gateway.

Veronique struggled to unsheathe the Chiave sword. I threw my battle globe to stop her. It barely missed her, so I threw another, and it shattered against her side.

Her shriek sounded over the wailing wind, and she lost hold of her sword. The blade careened past me and nicked my thigh.

I broke through the gateway and landed hard on a marble floor. Books from a nearby case scattered around me, and my light globe popped at my side.

The handle of the Chiave tapped the tiles at the same time Veronique landed on top of it, the blade impaling her chest.

Glass rained down on us, several pieces embedding into my skin, and I winced.

With some effort, I crawled to her. My stomach rose and fell like an angry sea at the sight of the blood pulsing out from where the sword had pushed through her breastbone. The blade shook with each of Veronique's shocked breaths.

No words came to me. My mind was numb, but my body was alive with pain.

A gurgling sound came from her mouth.

Veronique coughed, her bright blue eyes focused on me. "Don't be weak, Gia. You're a Sentinel for the Wizard Council. I would have killed you." Her breathing went shallow, and her next words came out quiet and pained. "We are all between good and evil. Make sure yours is the right side—" A cough cut off her words. "They lie to you. Seek The Red. He knows—" Her final breath cut off her words.

She's dead. Her stare had frozen, her body was bloodied and stiff, and she was still beautiful. I'd never know why she wanted me to find The Red. I didn't know where the beety Laniar lived. My eyes slid back to her.

The sadness surprised me. She'd killed Kale, after all, and tried to kill me. She deserved to die. But as I stared at her face, I could see a six-year-old girl training to be a killer like her father wanted. Trying to please him while he used her. Most likely, she'd never received love. Not like the Pop kind of love that I grew up with.

Forget her. Wipe it away.

A Monitor had to have picked up her jump. I had to get out of there before someone came to investigate. But I had to get the Chiavi, and one was sticking out of Veronique's chest. I untied the velvet bag and removed it from her waist. I opened it, and the other Chiavi and ancient spell book were inside.

My eyes slid to the sword. The blade had gone all the way through her chest. Her back was lifted a little, propped up by the handle sticking out the other side.

"Okay. I can do this. There're two worlds full of people at stake."

I heaved her onto her side and grasped the handle of the sword. With my eyes closed, I took a deep breath and yanked and yanked and yanked until the sword was free. A slurping, then a gushing sound came from her. Blood pooled around her, and I recoiled from it, my back crashing into a bookcase.

Blood ran down the sword. There was nothing to wipe it clean except a corner of Veronique's trench coat. I ran the blade across the material, slid it into my empty scabbard, and tied the velvet bag to my belt.

I went over to the gateway book, my fingers trembling. Blood dripped from my sleeve and hit the pages. I flipped all the pages, leaving bloody prints on each so no one could tell that I'd jumped to the Boston Athenæum.

The library was quiet when I landed. Its familiarity was welcoming—like coming home. I struggled down the stairs, my injuries causing me to wince with each labored step. There was a phone at the reception desk, and I used it to dial Nana Kearns's number. It rang five times, and I was about to hang up when someone answered.

"Hello?" a girl's voice came through the receiver.

"Katy—Katy Kearns." My voice sounded scratchy. I swallowed. "Is she there?"

"No. Who is this?"

I recognized that voice.

"Emily?"

Hearing her brought back memories of Arik breaking up with me to go out with her. She'd used a charm, becoming his puppet master, pulling the strings to make him do things he never would've if not for her evil, devious plans.

"Gia, is that you?"

Nana wasn't there. I needed help. She'd have to do.

"I'm hurt. Can you come and get me?" I wanted to lie down, close my eyes, and pretend this night hadn't happened.

"You're hurt?" Emily said, panic in her voice. "Oh my gosh, how bad is it?"

"I'll be fine. Just come now."

"Where are you?"

"The Athenæum. Meet me at the graveyard."

"Be right there." She hung up, and I dropped the phone.

At least the charmed keycard Arik had given me unlocked the library's door on the first try. The rest of the night had gone horribly wrong, and this little thing working gave me hope. I slipped outside and hobbled to the street, then up Beacon to Tremont. It wasn't a very long walk to the Granary Burying Grounds, but with all my wounds, it was laborious. The velvet bag holding the Chiavi grew heavy as I grew weaker. The rope tied around my wrist dug into my skin. I waited for an older couple walking a Pomeranian to pass before unlocking the gate and entering the graveyard.

Weak and tired, I hid behind one of the stone columns of the arched entrance. The grave markers were silent concrete bodies lined up in the ground and cloaked in darkness, some of them seeming to lean in sadness against the others.

With my back resting on the wall, I slid down and sat on the ground. I closed my eyes, just wanting to sleep. Maybe when I woke up, this nightmare would've been a dream, and the pain would be gone.

Don't sleep.

I pushed myself back to my feet. If I was standing, I couldn't fall asleep.

Nearly forty minutes later, a small white car pulled up to the curb and stopped. The passenger window whirred and screeched open.

"Gia," Emily called, somewhat louder than a whisper.

I dragged my beaten body out from behind the gate and hobbled to the car. Every bit of me ached as I settled into the passenger seat.

"You look bad." She switched the car into drive and sped off. "What happened?"

The world spun, and my stomach reeled. "Veronique. She attacked me."

"Oh no," she said. "I will kill her one day, I swear."

"Too late. She's dead…" I trailed off as the darkness squeezed around me.

Something cool and wet dragged across my forehead, and I opened my eyes to see Emily staring down at me. I tried to sit up, but she gently pushed me back down. I recognized the antique dresser and squeaky double bed. They were from Nana Kearns's guest room, but I wasn't in the room in Mission Hills. The windows were different and on the wrong side of the room.

Emily's dark hair was pulled back, and the frown she was giving me wrinkled her forehead and moved her widow's peak. "Don't get up," she said. "I have Nana's gunk holding your wounds closed."

"Where is she?" My voice sounded like I had swallowed a handful of gravel. I pushed myself up the pillows to sit.

Emily grabbed a glass of water off the nightstand. "In Seattle. She's trying to get a flight home. I'm supposed to keep you down and cool. You're a mess, and you have a high fever."

"This isn't her house. Did she move?"

"Yes," Emily said, handing me the glass. "They sent us into hiding for our safety. We're in Jamaica Plains. It's a pretty cool place."

"Nana has the same phone number. Someone can track you here."

"She didn't want to change numbers in case you called. She placed a ward on the line. No one can trace it back to this house."

"You said *they* sent you into hiding. Who are they?"

Her eyebrow rose slightly as she gave me a concerned look. "Asile's guards, of course. Why do you ask?"

Did they know Pop's and Afton's locations, too? I'd been hiding from everyone for months, except Uncle Philip. Veronique had said she'd learned my whereabouts from a spy. Having Asile know where my family and friends were sat uneasily in my mind.

"Nothing," I said. "I'm just groggy. How long have I been sleeping?"

"About three days."

I took several sips of water from the glass and handed it back to her.

She placed her palm on my forehead. "Man, you're boiling."

"I feel fine," I said.

"That's because I poured a great deal of Nana's elixir down your throat. You should be floating." She placed the glass on the nightstand and picked up one of Nana's jars of ointment.

I was definitely floating. My arm felt heavy as I touched the gauze taped to my cheek.

"See, all your moving around opened that shoulder wound." She must've noticed the worry on my face because she paused. "Give it time to heal. The scar should be faint. A little makeup will hide it."

A little? I doubted it. It was a pretty deep gash. But I appreciated her attempt at easing my fears. "Nana's been training you well, huh?" I said.

Her fingers plunged into the gunk, and she dabbed a blob of it onto the wound in my shoulder. "Listen, I know you don't like me. I'm so sorry about Arik. I would never have placed that spell on him. It wasn't me, you know? It was that Bane Witch's spirit Conemar used to possess me."

We'd gone over this before. "I know. It's fine. Stop stressing about it."

"I just want to make it up to you," she said.

"You are right now," I said. "I have to get back to the hideout."

"You're safe here. Only Carrig knows where you are. Nana said you are to *stay put*. Her words, not mine."

Someone came in the room, but I couldn't see who it was with Emily blocking my view. "Oh, I forgot you have a visitor. He's been waiting for you to wake up."

Arik? Great. He was going to be pissed at me. I should have just jumped into the library and grabbed the Chiave. Going after Gian's canister without help was careless.

Emily stood and crossed the room, passing him as she went out the door. He walked over and sat on the chair Emily had just vacated.

Bastien's smile stopped my breath. It was as if I'd been in the dark so long and the sun finally came out. His blue eyes held so much concern. Tears formed on my lashes, the sight of him overwhelming me. I wasn't sure he was real. With great effort, I reached a hand out to him, and he grasped it, his touch speeding up my heart.

"You're here... I thought... Carrig..." My words were as broken as my thoughts. As broken as my body.

"We had left shortly before the attack." His head lowered, and he stared at the folded paper bag in his other hand. "If I'd known you were... Well, I'm here now."

"There was a woman with me, Agata." My chest tightened at the thought of her lying motionless on the library's floor.

The expression on his face was as solemn as his voice sounded. "She's recovering in Mantello. The curers believe she'll make a full recovery."

"She's okay?" A shaky laugh escaped me, relief loosening my chest.

"She is."

"How did you get here? You could've—"

"Nothing could keep me away." Bastien let go of my hand and placed his open palm on my uninjured cheek. "I was so worried."

"My face is going to be scarred."

"No scar could ever hide your beauty." His smile returned, and though he'd only smiled a minute ago, it was as though it was my first time seeing it, and my heart lifted in my chest. He pressed his lips against mine. It was a gentle, careful kiss. "You're so hot."

"You probably say that to all the injured girls you know." I laughed, then winced at the pain stabbing my ribs, reminding me that Veronique had punched me there.

A worried look crossed his face. "Your fever comes and goes. I'll have Emily give you something for it."

"No. Please stay." The tears I'd been holding back rushed from my eyes and down my temples. "I'm scared."

I wiped my eyes with the tissue he'd tugged out of the box on the nightstand. He slipped off his shoes, and I moved over for him. The bed squeaked as he sat on the mattress and leaned against the pillows.

He removed a book with a green linen cover from the paper bag.

"I thought I'd read a familiar book to you," he said. "Perhaps it'll free you from your thoughts."

I noticed the book before I read the gold lettering: *The Secret Garden*. By the cover, I could tell it was a first edition. His thoughtfulness made the corners of my mouth lift.

He grinned, and there was a tilt to his lips. "Come here."

I scooted closer and rested my head on his chest. He

wrapped an arm around me, his nearness so comforting. I'd missed him. I'd missed his eyes that watched me as if he were memorizing every one of my expressions. Most of all, I missed the tiny moments with Bastien where he'd really listen to me, no matter what silly or bizarre thing I said.

"You'll have to help turn the pages," Bastien said.

I flipped them over and stopped on the first chapter.

He began, "When Mary Lennox was..."

Each word he read was like a soothing lullaby. His fingers continually combed my hair, calming me. I could listen to him read for an eternity. The world fell away, and there was only us getting lost in a story we both loved.

I'd look up at him now and then, admiring how the lamp by the bed lit up his beautiful face. A piece of his dark hair fell across his forehead, and a crinkle formed between his eyebrows as he read. It was cute how he changed his voice to represent different characters.

By the end of chapter three, my head kept bobbing as I struggled to stay awake. He closed the book and placed it on the nightstand. "I think it's time you slept," he said.

"I don't want you to go."

He adjusted onto his side, facing me, and took my hand in his. "I'm not going anywhere."

Our heads rested against each other.

"Better?" he whispered.

"Much." I squeezed his hand with what little energy I had. "I killed them. Veronique. Those Sentinels. They're all dead." Tears pooled in my eyes, and my lip shook. He wiped my tears away with his thumb.

"You were defending yourself," he reasoned, parroting the words I'd repeated to myself. But no amount of reasoning could make me forget their deaths. The attack replayed in my head like a slasher movie.

"My globe," I said. "It's fragile now. Like glass. When I

throw it, the sphere grows and shatters against whatever or whoever it hits. It cuts people."

"That's curious." His breath brushed my cheek. "It must have happened when you tossed one at the trap door to save Gian and me. When you are well, we could have one of our professors of magical sciences examine your globe."

"That doesn't sound very appealing," I said. "I don't want to be someone's specimen."

"We can talk about this later." He kissed my forehead. "You should rest."

His body so close to mine reminded me of the many cold nights we had spent trapped in the Somnium together. He felt safe. The rhythm of his breathing and the hint of his cologne eased me gently into a deep sleep. Nothing played in my mind, no nightmarish images, no replay of Veronique's death. Nothing.

Light tickled my eyelashes, and the smell of autumn came in from the window. *They lie to you. Seek The Red. He knows...* I opened my eyes. Veronique's voice sounded as if it came from inside the room. I sat up against the pillows.

It had been five days since the fight in the New York Public Library. Five days since I'd killed Veronique. And two days since Bastien left in the middle of the night while I slept. I almost thought he was an illusion, but Emily had assured me it wasn't a dream.

Bastien had risked his safety to visit me, and I wished he could've stayed, but his haven, the wizard realm of Couve, needed him. He would've accessed the haven through an entry within the Senate Library of France in Paris. There'd been several attacks in that library lately, and I worried about his safety.

The door opened, and Emily came in. "Good morning. I came for your breakfast order. What do you feel like having today?"

"I'll come down and eat." I flung my legs over the side. My scabs and bruises were healing fast due to Nana's magical gunk, and the puncture wound in my shoulder only ached when I raised my arm.

Emily picked up my robe and handed it to me. "Oh, I almost forgot." She dug into the front pocket of her jeans and handed me Carrig's watch. "I managed to get all the blood off it."

"Thank you," I said, putting it on, relieved to have it back.

"You talk in your sleep, you know that?"

I shot her a startled look. "What did you hear?"

"Everything. How Veronique died. What she said. That you have to find The Red." Her almost black hair was longer than I'd remembered it. With her pronounced widow's peak, her pasty white face still looked like a heart. One of her dark eyebrows shot up. "You don't remember any of this, do you?"

Do I? No. I shook my head.

She sat on the bed beside me. "I think we have to go find that Red person."

"The Red? *We?* Oh, hell no, you're not going with me." What was I saying? I wasn't going, either. Maybe if I hid out at Nana's house, the apocalypse would blow over without me. Besides, I had all the Chiavi.

The Chiavi. I sprang to my feet and plopped right back down, my ribs screaming at me. "Where's my bag?"

"Right there," she said, pointing at my messenger bag on the high-back chair in the corner.

"Not that. The velvet one."

She grinned and crossed the area rug to the closet. "You don't think I'd leave the Chiavi just lying around the room, do you? I hid it." She reached inside, pushed against the wooden panel lining the back wall, and a section popped open. She dragged the velvet bag out and brought it over to me.

I undid the tie and placed the Chiavi and the ancient spell book onto the comforter, then lined them up. My fingers brushed over the crown and continued over the sword, telescope, cross, and scroll.

Emily sat on the foot of the bed, facing me. "They're beautiful. Nana said they have individual powers."

"Yeah, they do. I just have to figure out how to use them." I slipped out of the bed.

"Where are you going?" Emily bounced to her feet. "Nana said you have to rest."

"I'm fine. I just need my bag." I shuffled over to the chair, grabbed it, and rejoined her on the bed. My trench coat was balled up on top and I took it out. I retrieved the hourglass, badge, Gian's journal, and the leather canister and placed them on the mattress beside the other Chiavi. Before I touched the ancient spell book, I stopped, as though touching it would give me a curse.

Emily flipped through the ancient spell book. "This is in Latin. And look how old these pages are. I'm surprised they're not crumbling in my hand."

A strange scent, like licorice, escaped the leather case as I tugged the cap off. I tipped the cylinder over and two vials landed on the comforter. One was empty, and the other had a thick black liquid in it.

"That's a strange smell," Emily said.

"Yeah, I think it's from the stuff inside that one." I carefully removed the slip of parchment stuck inside the cylinder and unrolled it. The handwriting was familiar—the script matched the one in Gian's journal. The paper crinkled as I flattened it on the comforter.

Emily turned another page in the spell book and studied it. "I can't read any of this." She waved her hand above the book and chanted, "*Ad mutare anglicus.*" She then ran her finger across the sentences as she skimmed the page. "That's better."

"What did you do?" I asked.

"I'm using a spell to transcribe the words to English," she said. "So, what does the note say?"

I read it aloud.

To my heir,

On a page a bit past the halfway mark within a book bearing my name, within the house of books in the city of my birth, you shall find the entry into a mountainous, frozen land. The Four sleeps under the tallest peak, but be careful, for traps will deter your journey to finding the creature you seek.

The Chiavi, I have transformed into items, magical ones. Use them to get through the traps blocking your way. Find the etched clues to know which to use. Once through, change the Chiavi to their original forms by commanding, *modificare.* You will be left with seven rods. There are seven matching holes in the door holding the beast. Before inserting each rod into the door, recite, *accendere,* and the rods will glow. Once all rods are in the prison door, use the charm, *rilascio,* to open the door. Whoever opens the door will then control the beast.

The moment the door opens, the chosen one must drink the spell. Mix the blood from the heirs of the seven original wizards with the potion I have included in the canister. The mixture was concocted by Mykyl to create the beast. If mixed correctly with the blood of the heirs, the liquid will turn golden. The donors must be the closest living heir. Consuming the spell will change the chosen one to match the Four. For only the purest heir can consume them all and defeat the Tetrad. Make haste for the spell will end quickly, and *the Seventh Heir will be lost.*

Heir to heir, blood to blood, lies the cure.

Trust your wit. Trust the inner voice. For it was all determined before your birth.

May Saint Agnes guide you on your journey.

Gian

Mykyl. He was Athela's father and the High Wizard of Esteril. The creator of the Tetrad. Conemar had used his recipe and Mystik creatures to create a new species, the Writhes. They were now deformed and scary creatures with sharp teeth, able to contort their bodies. I shuddered at the thought of them. Conemar had them attack me in the Mafra library, and I barely survived it.

Emily's eyes shifted from the page in the ancient book she was staring at to the parchment. "Chosen one? Purest heir? Who's that?"

Her questions made me wonder if I should have read that out loud. Nana's elixir was fogging my judgment.

I glanced at her, not completely sure if telling her about Royston was a good idea. After all, Conemar once controlled Emily. But Nana trusted her, and Emily had come to my rescue after Veronique tried to kill me.

"It's the one who will destroy the Tetrad."

"The what?"

"It's a monster created centuries ago as a weapon. It can control all the elements and destroy both worlds." I decided she didn't need to know that Royston was the chosen one. My fingers felt foreign as I carefully rolled up the parchment.

"That's creepy." Her attention returned to the ancient spell book. "This is so cool. There are so many spells I haven't seen in Nana's books." She looked over at me. "A page was ripped out."

"Yeah, it had a shielding spell on it." I lowered the collar of my pajama top, revealing the crescent scar on my chest. "Nana used it to brand the spell into my skin. It prevents the Monitors from seeing me jump through the gateway books."

Something banged against the window, startling us and causing Emily to drop the book to the floor.

Neither Emily nor I moved from our places on the bed. Another bang came from the window.

Emily started. "What is that?"

"I don't know." After grasping the Chiave sword, I pushed myself up from the bed. "Put everything in the bag and get in the closet."

CHAPTER FIVE

Emily scrambled around retrieving all the Chiavi and books, and she'd barely finished when I reached the other side of the room. I waited for her to close the closet door behind her before peering through the opening between the curtains.

"Afton?" I pushed open the curtains at the same time she was about to bang on the glass again.

She jumped back, tripping over a garden stone and landing on some purple aster flowers. Her big eyes found mine, and she pointed to the front door.

"Why didn't you ring the doorbell?" I asked, as if she could hear me through the thick glass.

Emily pushed open the closet. "Because it's broken."

I dropped the Chiave on the bed and headed for the hallway.

"Oh no," Emily said. "You're supposed to be resting."

"I feel fine."

"Nope," she bit back. "I'm not getting in trouble for letting you walk around. I don't want to cross Nana. She can be scary."

"Her? She's easy."

Emily frowned. "I doubt that. Now get back in bed." She

nodded toward the bed before leaving me.

Not too long after, the front door opened and shut. Afton's excited words were muffled against the walls, but I knew that tone. Something was wrong. Like, *way* wrong. I slipped out of bed and struggled to change into my gear.

The bedroom door flew open, and Afton rushed in with Emily on her heels.

"We have to leave now—" Afton stopped when she noticed I was slipping on my cargos. "Oh good, you're getting dressed."

"What's going on?" I pulled my T-shirt over my head, wincing at the pain in my shoulder.

Afton paced the carpet. "I don't know. Nana said to head here and get you out. I think the whereabouts of this hideout has been compromised."

I struggled to get my foot into my boot. Emily knelt down and pushed the left one on, then the right.

"Where are we going?" I asked, fumbling with the straps. Every movement caused pain to shoot through my wounds. My muscles felt petrified from being in bed so long.

Afton's eyes darted from me to the door. "We're to meet someone at the Boston Athenæum. I'm not sure who because I lost service, and Nana didn't answer when I called back." She crossed over to the window and peeked through the opening of the curtains.

"Is Nana okay?"

"She's fine," Afton said, keeping her post at the window, rocking from foot to foot and wringing her hands.

The strap to my boot kept slipping out of the buckle. I heaved a long sigh before asking, "What's Nana up to? She's not in Seattle. Do you know where she went?"

"Okay, I lied," Emily said. "She told me not to tell you. The Wizard Council has been enforcing more and more restrictions on the covens. Nana went to the Mystik League meeting in Eelsteed."

Restrictions? The covens were home to the many different creatures in the Mystik world. I'd thought Nana and I were beyond lies now. She'd promised never to keep secrets from me again.

"Why would the council do that?" I lost hold of the strap again.

"She didn't say." Emily brushed my hand aside and secured each buckle for me.

"Thanks," I said.

Emily straightened and wiped her hands on her jeans. "No problem. Now let's get out of here before any uninvited guests show up." She gathered the ancient spell book, and Gian's journal and canister, and shoved them into my messenger bag. The sword wouldn't fit in there with the other Chiavi, and she frowned at it.

"I'll wear it." I fastened my empty scabbard around my waist and slid the Chiave in.

There was a sound like hoofs hitting the cobblestone sidewalk outside.

I put on my trench coat and tightened the belt, tying it in a knot

"Too late." Afton turned from the window, panic shocking her words. "Duck!"

I dropped down to the floor beside Emily at the same time Afton dove onto the carpet. The window exploded, sending shards of glass shooting through the room and raining down on us. The pain from my wounds almost stopped me, but I clenched my teeth and hobbled up. With a flick of my wrist, I created my battle globe and threw it.

A flaming ball soared from my hand and grew in size before hitting a creature, half bull and half man, climbing through the window.

I glanced down at my hand. *What the hell?*

My globe had changed again.

A Laniar, a creature that looked more greyhound than human, leaped into the room, baring her teeth and readying to pounce. Her dark eyes burned like coals against her pallid skin. The look on her face was fierce and determined. I created another globe, and it was cold in my palm. The sight of it caused me to pause. It wasn't mine. This one was white as snow.

The Laniar charged, and I hurled the globe at her. It exploded against her body and ice crackled across her skin until she was completely frozen.

Emily pulled on my arm, my messenger bag slung over her shoulder. "Come on!" she shouted. "This way."

Afton followed us into the hall. "How did you create those globes?"

"I-I don't know." My voice didn't sound like my own. *How did I do that? What's happening to me?*

Emily opened the basement door. "We can't hide down there," I said. "We'll be sitting ducks. Let's go out the back."

"No. This is the way." Emily pounded down the stairs with me on her heels and Afton on mine. She wove through the moving boxes stacked around the room and over to an old-looking furnace, the kind used as a gateway to hell in scary movies. It dominated most of the back wall and looked as if it hadn't been used for centuries. She pushed on one of the bricks in the wall beside it. The furnace swung out, revealing an opening into a dark tunnel.

I created a light globe. "Where does it lead?"

Emily entered the tunnel. "I don't know. Nana said to use it in an emergency. We're to follow it to the end."

I stepped inside, trying not to think about what kind of insects or tiny critters would live in the cool, moldy-smelling cave. Afton came in behind me. Her measured breathing told me she was just as nervous and scared as I was. Emily lifted a handle by the opening, and the furnace closed.

"I don't like this," Afton said.

From the other side, we could hear voices, and boots clapping down the stairs.

Emily lifted a finger to her lips to quiet us. She motioned with her head for me to start down the tunnel.

I rushed down the tight passageway, leading the way. The light from my globe bounced against the brick walls. Tree roots had broken through the packed dirt, and we had to climb over several of them. Water leaked down on us from the many cracks above.

"What is this place?" I asked.

Emily adjusted my overstuffed messenger bag on her shoulder, the Chiavi inside clanking against each other. She'd added the velvet bag, and the flap to the bag barely closed. "Nana said it was used during the Revolutionary War," she said. "The patriots transported guns to the center of the city. That house we were in was a makeshift armory—"

A thunderous *boom* shook the tunnel's walls.

Another bang resounded quickly after.

"Guess they figured out where we went." I hurried my steps and glanced over my shoulder at Emily and Afton, both with frightened looks on their faces. "Keep up. We have to get out of here."

We rushed as fast as we could over the roots and fallen piles of bricks where there must have been a mudslide. One pile was so massive we had to crawl through a tiny opening at the top. It was difficult to keep my light globe going while climbing, and I dropped it several times. The darkness that enveloped us terrified me until I could get another one lit. Whoever was following us didn't bother being quiet, which succeeded in freaking us out even more.

It sounded like the group was gaining on us. I slipped down a brick pile and waited for Emily and Afton to get on the other side before creating a battle globe in my free hand. A purple ball of light pulsed on my palm. "What is this?"

"How are you doing that?" Afton asked.

"I have no idea." But that globe wasn't going to help me in this situation. Or would it? I gently placed it on the ground, trying not to pop it or snuff it out. It worked. The globe sat in wait just under the opening.

"What's that for?" Afton asked.

"To stall them, I hope—" A sharp pain hit my shoulder, and I stumbled.

Emily caught me before I fell to the ground. "You're bleeding through your bandages."

"It feels like it's on fire." I inspected my shoulder. A stain had bled through my trench coat.

"This isn't good," Afton said. "You have to rest."

"Can't." I straightened and tried to focus. "It just hurts. I'll be fine in a sec."

"Why didn't you say so?" Emily reached into her front pants pocket and tugged out a small glass bottle. "Nana's elixir. It should ease the pain."

I took the bottle she offered and popped off the cork.

"Only half," she warned. "Or you won't be able to move. And we can't carry you."

The sweet taste drenched my tongue as I gulped it down. "Okay, let's get some distance between us and them," I said, returning the cork and slipping the bottle into my vest pocket.

It was then I noticed I'd forgotten to put on my breastplate. Veronique hadn't worn hers, and she'd ended up dead. I suddenly felt vulnerable. If I wanted to survive, I had to stop making careless mistakes. A warrior doesn't take risks. They calculate. I glanced from Afton to Emily. It was up to me to get them to safety.

The elixir was kicking in, so I hurried my steps. Behind us, there was a soft punch of air, and a purple light flashed through the tunnel. Someone had stepped on my trap.

We stopped at a thick wooden door with wide, rusty

hinges and an ancient looking handle. It took all of us to get the heavy door open. It creaked and squeaked so noisy, I worried whoever might be on the other side would hear. The footsteps and voices behind us grew louder. Whoever or whatever followed us was getting closer. We threw our bodies against the door, and when we pushed hard, it moved an inch.

"Harder," Afton yelped from her spot nearest the opening. "They're here."

We threw our bodies repeatedly against the door. Inch by inch it opened until we could squeeze through one at a time.

"We have to close it," I said and pushed the door as hard as I could, blood from my shoulder staining the wood. Emily and Afton joined me.

"Again," Afton called, and we shoved it again.

A long hand with claw-like nails reached out at the same time as we threw our bodies at the door with one last heave, closing it with so much force it snapped off the creature's hand. It thumped to the ground, blood spraying across the stone floor.

Afton screamed.

I pulled her away from it. "Don't look. Keep moving."

"That was seriously gross," she said. "Will this nightmare ever end?"

"No." I shook my head, surveying the room we were in. "Once you know about Wonderland, you're never the same, Alice."

Afton crossed her arms. "That's not funny. It's cold in here."

We were in a room with brick walls.

"There are stairs," Emily said, adjusting my messenger bag before climbing the steps to the top. "Get up here. I think this is the way out. We should exit together—no telling what will happen."

"That's comforting." Afton uncrossed her arms and climbed. I followed, darting quick looks over my shoulder in case someone got the other door open.

A rusty brass knob stuck out of the rocky ceiling. Emily pulled on it, and nothing happened. She pushed, and that didn't work, so she twisted it, and dirt dumped in her face. The top slid aside, opening up to the outside world. Fresh air rushed in, and I breathed deep, filling my lungs with its sweetness.

Once we were out, I glanced around. We were in the Granary Burying Grounds. We'd exited through the tall obelisk that marked the grave of Benjamin Franklin's parents in the middle of the cemetery.

"Did you see that? They came out of the memorial." A woman's voice caught me off guard, and I realized we had an audience. Families with small children, a group of women in their sixties, and some teens stared at us blankly. It was daytime, and there were tourists in the graveyard. Behind me, the memorial moved and slid back into place, covering the tunnel we'd just exited. My eyes found Emily and Afton. Both were stunned to their spots, not knowing what to do.

The obelisk shook. Someone was trying to figure out how the knob worked.

"We must get these people out of here," I said. "Afton take the right and Emily left. I'll take the center. Tell them all to go."

I ran to the group of six women. "You have to go. There's bad crea—" I stop myself from saying creatures. They'd think I was pranking them or something. "Men. There's bad men coming."

The women smiled, and one asked, "What is that, dear?" Her eyes went wide, and I spun around.

The obelisk shook and slid to the side. First, a Laniar came out, followed by a horned man and a creature that resembled a six-foot troll.

Panic made my heart flip in my chest. *I can't beat them. I'm outnumbered and hurt.* I had to get out of my head, push back the fear, and fight. There were too many people around. Someone could get hurt, or worse, killed.

I couldn't tell if it was two women or all of them who screamed. But they did, their screams matching the ones blaring in my head.

"Get out of here," I ordered them. The women, some still screaming, dashed for the gate. I summoned my globe, and fire swirled on my palm. Taking a few running steps, I chucked it at the creatures. It hit the horned man, setting his clothes on fire.

I launched globe after globe at them—stun, fire, glass.

Ice.

Missed my target, but it spread across the steps of the memorial. The creatures slipped around trying to get their footing.

I shot a purple globe, and it stunned the troll-like beast. It collapsed to the concrete with a reverberating *thud*. The stun would stop his breathing. He would die if someone didn't release him from it.

The Laniar stooped to all fours and soared off the steps. The ice globe I propelled smacked him in his wide chest, freezing him in midair. He crashed to the ground, his body breaking into several pieces.

Noises came from the tunnel under the obelisk. There were others and they'd be out soon.

"Running would be good now," I yelled to Afton and Emily, sprinting down the pathway to the street. I followed the last of the people scrambling to get out of the cemetery. With all the adrenaline rushing through me, I had renewed strength. Afton and Emily panted behind me. I darted up the street and headed for the Boston Athenæum.

"Emily, get my membership card," I said over my shoulder. "It's in the front pocket of my bag."

She unzipped the pocket and took it out. "Got it."

I slowed down as we approached the library. "Keep close to my sides so the desk person won't notice a sword hiding under this trench coat and the blood on my shoulder."

Afton bit her bottom lip as she stared at the red-leather salon doors of the Boston Athenæum. "That's not going to work. You'll have to remove your coat. And they now have lockers in the lobby for bags."

"I have one of those entry cards," I said. "We'll have to find an emergency exit."

"Entry card?" The confused look on Afton's face said she didn't remember the magic Arik had used to open the library doors before.

I retrieved the card from the breast pocket of my vest. "It's magic."

"Right, that," Afton said, tugging her cell out of her back pants pocket. "I'll search Google for a floorplan of the library."

Several minutes later, she looked up from the screen. "Got it. This way." She led us down the sidewalk.

A black cloud of dread hovered over my head, and I searched the road. Maybe the creatures inside the tunnel hadn't seen which way we went.

I slid the card across the lock on the emergency exit and opened the door.

The street filled with screams and crunching metal. I tensed and fought the fear turning my stomach. Afton and Emily needed me. I couldn't give up.

"Get inside," I said, opening the door wider. "Beacon Hill just met some scary Mystiks."

"We have to hurry," Emily said, shutting the door behind us.

"You and Afton go ahead of me," I said. "Make sure the coast is clear. I don't want anyone freaking out about this blood. I'll be right behind you."

Afton gave me a slight nod, and I responded with one. It was our secret signal, our way of saying we had each other's backs. She hurried after Emily.

Each step forward sent pain surging through my body and fear to twist in my stomach. The elixir was losing its edge. I took the bottle from my pocket and downed the rest of the liquid inside.

We passed the Children's Library and got to the elevator leading to the fifth floor without running into anyone. Excited voices came from the foyer just around the corner. They all must be gathering by the entrance to see what the commotion was on the street. We dashed inside the elevator.

The voices turned to screams, and feet scrambled across the marble floors. Inhuman growls and grunts rushed over the library. A Mystik, tall and lanky, with long arms and grayish skin, came around the corner. I'd seen one of his kind before, after the council hearing with Bastien. I'd found out later he was a Grigiolian. Panic pinged my stomach like moths hitting a porch light.

At spotting him, Emily and Afton sucked in a collective breath.

The Chiave's blade *shiiinged* as I drew it out of my scabbard. I willed my hands to stop shaking.

Don't show fear.

Keep calm.

But my body ignored me.

Emily's finger kept stabbing the fifth-floor button. The noise alerted the Grigiolian to where we were, and he charged after us. The door started to close, but it was too late. His long-fingered hand stopped the door. Our backs slammed against the walls of the elevator as he lunged inside.

Afton and Emily shrieked at once.

I held up the Chiave. The blade picked up the light from the overhead lamps.

"Gianna, you needn't fear me," he said in a growling tone before I could take a swing at him. "I was sent by Katy. She said to say she loves you and something about a bug. Not quite sure about that one."

I love you, Bug, I could almost hear Nana say. It was her

term of endearment for me.

Emily's and Afton's backs were still pressed against the wall.

"It's okay." I inserted the Chiave into my scabbard. "Nana did send him."

"Anyway," he said. "I'm Doylis of Grigiol. I have met you once. You were with the honorable Bastien." He practically pushed me into the corner as he stepped in and let the elevator door close.

The space was already too small for my comfort. Adding him made it stuffed. *You will not freak out,* I tried to convince myself.

"The Mystiks following you were not too far behind me," Doylis said. "Go straight to the gateway book. Don't stop. Don't look back."

Afton slipped her hand into mine. "You're okay," she whispered. She knew me well, knew my fears and quirks. I had to get myself together.

The elevator doors slid open. A great commotion resounded up the staircase. Our pursuers must have reached the library.

The fifth-floor reading room was empty.

"*Sei zero sette periodo zero due DOR.*" I recited the numbered charm for calling the gateway book. I wanted to get as far away from there as possible. But we needed to lead those bad Mystiks away from the Athenæum before they hurt anyone.

Amid the shouts and screams, a loud bang came from somewhere below us, as if a heavy wall-to-wall bookcase had tipped over. The shattering of glass made me flinch, and I glanced at the elevator.

I have to go back. They need help.

Doylis must have noticed my concern. "Don't worry. My men are there. They'll protect the humans. We must get you and yours to safety."

The rustling of pages sounded through the room, and I scurried toward the noise. The others raced behind me. The book was tied to a bookcase. I recited the charm to release it, and fetched it from the shelf. "Where are we going?" I asked.

"Scotland," he said. "The Central Library in Edinburgh, to meet Aetnae. She'll lead you to Katy."

Aetnae. I hadn't seen the faery in a while, not since the day Veronique attacked me in New York.

Emily twisted her hands. "Are we really going to jump through that book? Nana told me about it, but I never thought I'd go through one."

I paused flipping the pages of the gateway book and glanced over at her. "Don't worry. It's not too bad."

"Not too bad?" Afton gave me a look that told Emily I wasn't being that truthful. "It's like freefalling through a black hole."

Emily swallowed before clearing her throat. "I'm not afraid. You all have done it. I'm sure I can."

"That's the spirit," Afton said with a dash of sarcasm.

Duylis's head snapped in the direction of the entrance. "Someone's on the stairs."

I stopped at the photograph of the library in Edinburgh. "Got it. How are we doing this?"

"You're going without me," he said. "I must stay here and see that no one goes after you. And I must aid my men in protecting this library."

"Are you with the havens' guards?"

He shook his head. "No. I'm with the Mystik League. Now go."

I placed the book on the floor, grasped Afton's hand then Emily's, as I slid a look at her. "Whatever you do, don't let go. I'll lose you if you do."

"That's encouraging." Emily gripped my hand tighter, and

my fingers grew numb.

I turned my head toward Doylis. "Thank you, and be careful."

He nodded without a word before returning his focus to the entrance.

Afton adjusted on her feet. "Let's just do this already."

"Okay. Here we go," I said and then spoke the spell to launch us. "*Aprire la porta*."

Open the door.

A blast of wind hit my face and sped around us like a lasso, squeezing Emily and Afton against me.

"Jump up with me," I called.

A yelp escaped Emily's lips as we jumped together and the book sucked us into the page. Without my hands free, I couldn't form a light globe, and the darkness engulfed us. Emily and Afton were gray silhouettes beside me. Afton had gotten good at transporting, not making a sound, and keeping her legs down.

Emily's legs flew out from underneath her. "I don't like this," she shouted over the wind's howling. Her free arm and legs flailing, she almost broke my hold on her hand.

"Stop pulling from me!" I shouted. "Try to get your legs down."

"I don't like this, I don't like this, I don't like this!" Emily screamed, the arm of the hand I held jerking up and down.

"Calm down!" My panicked command tumbled into the void.

Emily's hand was yanked from my grasp.

CHAPTER SIX

Emily's ear-piercing scream shattered the darkness. I caught a sleeve, clutching the material in my shaking hand.

The familiar light at the end came into view, and we shot out of the gateway book. Emily landed on her side, tumbled across the mauve carpet, and crashed into a chair at one of the nearby tables.

"Oh crap." Afton hurried over to Emily and helped her to feet. "Are you okay?"

"I'm fine, I think. Just some carpet burns." She inspected her shaking palms "I never want to do that again."

My eyes swept our surroundings. The soaring walls of the room were a warm yellow and accented with white-painted trim. Tall arches led to wide nooks. Narrow, wrought-iron galleries ran the length of the dark wood bookcases.

Aetnae zipped into the room. A boy with cropped dark hair and big brown eyes, and another boy, looking very much like Bastien might have looked when he was young, trailed her. Behind them, a little girl with auburn curls walked with confidence, her chin up and her shoulders back. Their clothes looked like uniforms.

"Who are the kids?" I asked.

"They're the last of the eight-year-old Sentinels," she said, landing on the table. "I found them hiding here."

Afton stepped closer. "The last?"

"As I told Gia before"—Aetnae sounded annoyed—"the new batch of Changelings hadn't hatched. Well, it's worse. Something is killing off the eight-year-olds. A disease. It's been spreading through the Mystik covens."

I didn't know what else to say. It sickened and saddened me to think of children dying.

When I didn't respond, she added, "Katy is working with the curers. Maybe she can help them."

The little girl stuck out her chin. "Excuse me. We were told to go to Asile." Though she wasn't very big, her attitude sure was—strong-willed and a bit on the pushy side.

A warning bell dinged in my head. "Who told you?"

"Our trainer. We were at a training camp in Greyhill." She lowered her head. "He got sick and died. So did the others. The ones like us."

Afton's hands covered her mouth. "How horrible."

I got down on one knee in front of the girl and grasped her hand. "What's your name?"

Her head popped up, her eyes a multicolor mix of brown, yellow, and green. "I'm Peyton. That's Knox"—she pointed with her free hand at the boy with brown eyes, then aimed her finger at the one that resembled Bastien—"and Dag."

The dark circles under Dag's eyes concerned me. He looked barely able to hold up his head.

"Well, I'm Gia. It's nice to meet you."

"Are we going to die?" The girl bit her bottom lip and stared intensely into my eyes, so seriously I wanted to turn away from her to hide my doubt.

Instead, I answered, "No. Of course not. But we can't go to Asile. We have to see my nana. She's a Pure Witch skilled at healing people."

Aetnae lifted off the table. "Are you ready?"

"We're ready." I put on a brave face to hide my worry, even though my insides were swirling in a sea of dread. Dag might've caught the illness that had killed most of their generation of Sentinels.

"Follow me," Aetnae said. "The entry is in the children's library downstairs." She zipped off to the door.

Afton held a hand of each of the boys. Emily moved my messenger bag to her side and offered Peyton her hand, but the little girl ignored it. We plodded down the stairs to the children's library. Aetnae landed on my shoulder and directed us to a reading area.

"It's in one of those pop-up books." She pointed at a bookshelf.

I crossed over to the case. There were many picture and pop-up books lining the shelves. "Which one?"

"*The Secret Garden*," she answered.

My mouth gaped.

Her eyes widened, and she glanced around. "What's wrong?"

The Secret Garden? I couldn't believe it.

"It's her favorite book," Afton said.

I'd found it in my mom's collection of books and had a strong connection to it the first time I'd read it. It was probably why Arik's parent faery read it to him when he was a boy.

"It's one of my favorites as well," Aetnae said. "Our queen's grandmother chose this book when it was time to change the realm's door. The entry into our realm moves every hundred years. I'll be sad when it changes from this one. Wait until you see. It's quite lovely." She raised her hand and spoke something in a language I couldn't understand.

A thick picture book slid out from the bottom shelf of the bookcase in front of us.

Aetnae tugged on my hair. "Stand back. Don't want anyone getting hurt."

I moved away as the book opened and grew. Emily scooted back. Afton dragged the three children with her to the other side of the room.

The pages flipped as the book grew. Pictures popped out and folded in, rustling and crinkling with each turn, until it stopped on a page with a three-dimensional image of a gate nestled in a vine-covered wall. The book quit growing when it reached the ceiling.

The detailed artwork on the heavy gauge paper was awe-inspiring—the weathered gate, its wood splintered with age, the vibrant green leaves on the vines yellowing at the ends, and the bricks with cracks and pockmarks. It all seemed so lifelike.

Emily took a step forward. "You don't see that every day."

"There are many things I've seen lately that you don't see every day," Afton said. "But this is so much better and a lot less scary."

The gate slowly crept open, revealing a lush garden with pointy flowers of various colors dotting the greenery. Cutting through the middle was a glittering sandstone pathway. The birdsongs and low-toned chirping of insects created a soothing melody. A peaceful feeling loosened muscles I didn't know had tensed.

I'd never seen such beauty. It was what I imagined the Garden of Eden would look like, but magnified.

"Can we go inside?" Peyton asked, standing by my side, her eyes wide.

"Yes. Follow me." Aetnae flitted into the garden.

Peyton grasped my hand, and I gave her a no-need-to-worry smile as we plodded to the book. There was something special about her. Strong and determined. I bet she bossed the other two eight-year-olds. But the way she kept glancing back at them, I also bet she took care of them.

Passing through the gate was like walking into a dream. The temperature was perfect, and the air smelled of sweet honey. A balloon of excitement and fear inflated inside me—I was thrilled for a new discovery, frightened of the unknown.

Emily came in after us, then Afton with the boys holding tight to her hands. Once we were through, the gate behind us shrank and disappeared into the vines.

Emily rotated, taking in our surroundings. "Is this for real?"

"It's amazing," Afton said.

Aetnae hovered in front of us. "Welcome to *Tír na nÓg*."

"Tir...what?" Dag asked, then hid behind Afton.

"It's the name of the faery realm," Aetnae said and zipped up the pathway. "This way."

Knox rubbed his nose. "Will they have food?"

"Of course. They have to eat, too," Peyton said, and then whispered, "I just hope it's not bugs."

I pressed my lips together to stop a laugh from escaping. There was a crack forming in the walls around Peyton.

We followed the pathway winding through cottages of varying sizes—large ones with curved doors, small ones like birdhouses hanging in the trees, and others built into their wide trunks. Beings of different sizes, some with wings, some without, looked out windows or stepped onto their porches. The tiniest we saw zipped in and out of the shrubbery. Their moth-like wings, hair made of twigs, and bodies resembling sticks helped them to blend into the woods.

"What are they?" Peyton asked, keeping up with me.

Aetnae buzzed around us. "They're sprites. There are many different species of faeries in the Fey realm. Some can be tricky and others not so nice, but mostly all are friendly. So keep on your toes until we reach the castle."

The pathway curved and trails branched off to unknown places until we came to the end. A magnificent city, crowded with extremely high buildings made of glass and copper, spread out across the land under a sky bluer than any blue I'd ever seen.

An expansive bridge constructed of twisted wood and vines arched over a large body of water that cut off one side of the city from the other. Riders in one-person aircrafts that looked like metal birds mingled with the many different faeries flying overhead.

In the distance, an enormous castle sat on the tallest hill. The sun dancing across the walls made them sparkle like crystals.

Aetnae landed on my shoulder and grasped my collar.

"I'm dreaming," Afton said.

"If you are, then I am, too," I said, stepping onto the bridge, my boot clacking over the tightly placed stone pavers.

Emily came up to my side. "Too bad I forgot my cell. I could've snapped some pics of this."

Aetnae gave her a disapproving look, which, since she was so small, no one noticed but me. "Cell phones don't work here. Our magic blocks human technology. It's damaging to the environment. And we don't have many humans visit the Fey realm. You all being here is a rarity."

By the curious looks we were getting from the citizens of *Tír na nÓg,* I'd bet many of them had never visited our world, either. The majority of the faeries on the bridge reminded me of Sinead. They had pointy ears and no wings like her. I wondered how she and the others were doing at our hideout in Ireland. I missed them. They'd become my family. My strength.

Such thoughts always led to Pop. How was he doing? Did he miss me as much as I did him? Even though I knew staying away ensured his safety, I wanted to run to him, to have him protect me as he had before all this otherworld shit hit the fan.

"Afton?"

"Yeah." She glanced over at me.

"I didn't have time to ask you. Have you seen Pop?" I held my breath, hoping he was okay, but knowing she'd have told me if he wasn't.

"He's good," she said, guiding one of the boys over to the side to let a group of faeries pass. "Been hanging out with my parents at a Cape Cod rental, under my mom's maiden name. No one can find them."

I released my held breath and all my worries with it. Pop loved fishing at the Cape.

"Your parents are back together?"

"Yeah. They're working on it." Her voice sounded doubtful.

I sidestepped to avoid colliding with an older woman hunched over by age, her ears long and pointy. Her cloak and dress were as green as the leaves. Her sleeves were flared, the hem of her skirt dragged across the ground, and thin gold cords made a swirling design sewn to the material. Another woman, much younger, passed wearing a similar outfit except in midnight blue. Most likely, that was the style in the faery realm.

As we approached the emerald glass doors of the castle, they slowly opened. Somber men and women with pointy ears met us. The castle and the way the faeries were dressed reminded me of a modern-day court in Versailles, less the corsets and bustles.

A young woman with a long neck and platinum hair gathered in a loose braid broke from a large group of faeries. Her ears were like bat wings sticking out of her hair. She couldn't have been much older than I was. "Good day," she said. "I am Queen Titania. Welcome to *Tír na nÓg.*"

Are you kidding me? She was actually the queen of the Fey realm. And her name was the same as in Shakespeare's *A Midsummer Night's Dream.* I glanced at Afton. The shocked look on her face matched mine. Maybe we were dreaming.

Emily slid a look at me and then down at the bag hanging

across her stomach. She was thinking the same thing as me. If they knew what was in it, would they take the Chiavi away?

"Gianna Bianchi," Titania continued. "It is my great pleasure to meet the presage. Agnost was my half brother. He had dreamt of you since he was a boy. It is sad he cannot be here for this momentous time."

What does a girl say to something like that? It was odd and uncomfortable for people to put all their hope in me. My biggest fear was that I'd fail at whatever I was destined to do. Besides, I was just a seventeen-year-old girl, and barely, at that.

"You haven't faith in yourself." Her eyes, the color of coal, studied me. "That is good. If you have too much faith, you will not try as hard. Don't lose your fighting spirit, Gianna. We all need you."

Titania's stare found the eight-year-olds. "Aetnae, who are these children?"

Aetnae lifted off my shoulder, flew over to the queen, and bobbed on the air in front of her. I couldn't hear what Aetnae said. It must've been about the children, since Titania's eyes kept darting to them as she listened.

After Aetnae had finished, Titania waved a man over. He was your typical tall, dark, and handsome type, except for the large ears with sharp points. She said something to him, and he strode over to Afton and the boys.

"The children are to come with me," he said, clipped and direct.

Peyton looked up at me, her face a mask hiding her fear, but I could see it in her eyes.

"What will you do with them?" I asked, hoping to get answers for the little girl.

"They will be well cared for and protected." Titania went to Peyton and knelt to look into her eyes. "I won't let anyone harm you, dear one. Your friends need a curer."

I squeezed Peyton's shoulder. "It'll be okay."

"All right." Her lips pressed together, and she extended her chin, that brave look returning to her face.

Peyton gripped the boys' hands and the man escorted them down a long hallway.

"Our guards will take you to Katy Kearns," Titania said as she turned to leave. The group of faeries followed her down a different hallway.

Three faeries, two men and a woman, wearing some sort of uniforms with capes lined in gold, led us down a long stairwell and escorted us into a laboratory. The lab was like others I'd seen—white and sterile.

My heart soared to the ceiling. Nana bent over a tall table, staring into a contraption with a copper arm holding a large oval glass. Her short, silver-gray hair fell in waves around her jawline. She had her favorite pair of dark jeans on, and a white button-down shirt. On either side of her were two older women, one tall and lanky with a thin face and long nose. I recognized the shorter one grasping a cane with a slight hunch to her back. Morta. She had taken care of me after I'd returned from the Somnium.

"Nana?" My voice sounded shaky, and tears spilled over my lashes. All the warmth from my childhood came rushing in, and though we were in unfamiliar surroundings, I felt like I'd just come home. Nana always said a place or town wasn't a home until it was filled with people you loved.

She spun from the table and charged over to us. "Oh, my dear Gia. I've been so worried."

I met her halfway and threw my arms around her. The familiar scent of her lavender soap and floral perfume filled my nose. "It's really you."

"Now, now." She patted my back. "It's okay. You're safe."

"Why are you here?" I drew back to look into those soft gray eyes of hers. The eyes that had always shown so much love and care for me. But they were stormy, her lids heavy from fatigue. Something was wrong.

"I was summoned." She let me go. "Emily, you did a great job. She's a little battered, but looks well."

"I had a good teacher," Emily said. "She wouldn't stay still. Kept opening the wound in her shoulder."

"Let me see." Nana eased the right side of my trench coat off my shoulder and inspected the wounds. "Ena, we'll have to stitch this."

"Stitches? Do I really need them?"

"You do. Now, sit over there." Nana pointed at one of the stools.

I collapsed onto the seat, teeth clenching in anticipation.

The glances Nana and the other women were giving each other concerned me. They were keeping something from us.

Ena clopped over to a table, grabbed some supplies, and joined us. She lined up the items on a table. Nana tied a rubber tourniquet around my arm and inspected it. "There's a nice vein."

Ena passed her a silver syringe with a long needle attached.

My eyes narrowed on the sharp needle as Nana aimed it at my arm. "I don't think— Ow! *Nana*, you didn't even give me a count-to-three warning."

"It's better to get it over with than to think on it too long, dear." Nana pushed the plunger, delivering the clear liquid into my arm. Her lips were pursed tight as though she wanted to say something but held it back. It didn't take long for the pain in my shoulder to subside, and she began stitching up the cut.

Nana turned to Afton. "Thank you for getting them out of that house in time. I couldn't risk calling. Not after I learned Conemar discovered the location of our hideout."

"I'd do anything to keep Gia safe," Afton said.

"I know you would." Nana rested her hand on Afton's cheek. "We need your help here."

"Certainly. What can I do?"

"There are so many sick and not enough hands to aid them." Nana tied the final stitch in my skin and lowered her hand. "The curers could use your skills. Ena, please get Afton clean clothes and show her to the infirmary. She'll need instructions, but she's helped the curers before."

After Ena and Afton were gone, I followed Nana to the contraption she was using when we arrived. Nana definitely wasn't herself. It was as if a dark cloud hung over her.

Emily dropped onto one of the stools surrounding the work area.

"Why did you need me here?" I leaned my back against the counter, watching her. "I have to get back to the hideout in Ireland. Have you heard from Arik?"

"She has." His voice, with that English accent of his, sounded foreign in contrast to the sterile room. His dark hair was messy, and his Sentinel uniform looked like he'd been in a war.

"Arik?"

Emily straightened her back and brushed her dark hair from her face. When we were hiding out in Branford, Conemar had put an evil witch spirit into Emily that had forced her to place a charm on Arik that made him like her. He'd broken up with me because of it. She was supposed to get information about Nick and me from Arik and feed it back to Conemar, but she had resisted and helped us during the battle on my front lawn. By her actions, it seemed she definitely liked him in a more-than-friends way.

Arik crossed the room. "You look quite a bit better, Gia."

I look better? "How do you know how I looked?"

"I came to the house in Jamaica Plains to see you." His eyes went to the bandage on my face. "You were completely out. Peaceful. Disturbing you would have been cruel. I would have stayed, but I was called away." A sadness hung on his face, and he had dark circles under his eyes.

"Why are you here? What aren't you telling me?" I pushed myself away from the counter and walked over to him. "You're keeping something from me."

He lowered his head. "While I was gone, our hideout was attacked."

It felt like everything collapsed around me. "What? Where is everyone?"

Arik's hesitation scared me.

"Was anyone hurt?" Tears burned the back of my eyes as I searched his eyes for answers.

He bit his bottom lip and lowered his head.

Oh no.

"Are they dead?"

CHAPTER SEVEN

The suspense was killing me. "Arik, please, what happened?" Nana startled me when she came up to my side and wrapped her arm around my back. She was preparing me for what Arik said next.

"The night Veronique attacked you," he said, "Lei and Jaran went missing. I searched, but there wasn't any sign of them It was as if they'd vanished. There was nothing for me to do, so I returned to the hideout." He grabbed the back of his neck, his pause warning that he was about to hit me with more bad news.

"Deidre and Demos were unharmed," he continued. "Cadby had escaped with Royston. They're all in Asile." He dropped his hand, his eyes finding Nana's as if to ask permission to continue.

"And Carrig? Sinead?" I pressed.

"Those who attacked us took Carrig," he finally said. "I'm not sure who they were. They wore cloaks, and it was night. Sinead must've gotten hurt during the fight. She's in the infirmary here."

After catching Emily's gaze, I shifted my eyes to my

messenger bag, indicating that she should watch over it.

She nodded slightly.

"Take me to Sinead." I spotted a nearby door and marched over to it.

He followed me. "Gia, you need to let her rest."

"I have to see her." I opened the first door I came to. It was a supply closet. "Arik, please."

"All right," he said. "Follow me."

I shut the closet door. If she died, or if they killed Carrig, I wasn't sure I could survive the blow of losing them.

Arik opened a door in the back and held it for me to pass. I had expected a small room, but instead it was an enormous area with three galleries surrounding the main floor. There were about twenty rows of beds filled with patients on the first floor and several more on the balconies above. There had to be more than a hundred Fey and other Mystiks in them.

"What's wrong with them?" I slowed my steps, glancing from one bed to the next, searching for Sinead.

Arik put on a surgical mask and handed me one. "Here. Don't touch anything. It's a disease that's spreading through the Mystik world."

I took it from him and secured it over my mouth and nose. "Where is Sinead?"

"Third floor. Isolated from those with the illness."

I slid a glance at him. His worried face scared me. The fear in his beautiful brown eyes mirrored my own.

"She's that bad?"

"She's in a faery sleep," he said, darting looks at me. "She'll be all right. I'm worried about Carrig. And, of course, not knowing Lei's or Jaran's whereabouts is maddening. There is all manner of evil out there. The human news channels are full of reports. Attacks on humans. Creatures roaming their streets. We must end it."

His words strangled the hope out of me. I couldn't bear it

if something horrible had happened to Carrig, to Lei, to Jaran.

"Are you all right?" Arik's voice seemed like it was miles away.

"I'm fine. Where's Sinead?"

He nodded in the direction of the main row. "That way."

I kept pace with Arik down the aisle, my eyes roaming over the row of beds.

The faces of the sick struck me as I passed each one. A faery with sores around her mouth, blanket pulled up to her chin, stared at the towering ceiling. A bird person, breathing heavily, missing feathers to the point that he was balding, mumbled what sounded like a prayer to himself. A curer pulled a sheet over the face of a Laniar. I only caught a glimpse of him, but blood from his sores had streaked his chin, and his dark eyes were glazed over, lifeless.

Each face took a bite out of my soul. The linen mask sucked in and out with my stuttering breath. I staggered alongside Arik, walking on numb legs.

Someone had to do something to save them all.

Down the row, Afton sat on a stool beside one of the beds. She blocked the face of the child under the covers. I detoured down the row toward her.

The sound of Arik's boots hitting the floor followed me. "Where are you going?"

"Afton?" I approached her.

She twisted on the stool to look at me. A linen mask covered her nose and mouth, surgical gloves were on her hands, and her hair was pulled back in rows of braids. Just over her shoulder, I could see the boy's face.

Dag.

I stumbled back, and my hand flew to my mouth.

Afton shot up to her feet, blocking the boy's view of me. "Don't frighten him," she whispered.

"Will he be okay?" I whispered back.

She didn't answer—the tears welling in her eyes told me it all. He might not make it.

I sucked in my emotions and forced a smile behind my mask before going over to the bed. A sore had formed at the corner of his mouth. His almost-black hair stuck to his sweaty forehead. I reached out to brush it away, but Afton caught my hand with her gloved one.

"Don't touch him," she said. "You could catch it."

I dropped my hands and leaned over him. "Hello, Dag," I said.

His eyes fluttered open.

"Why can't I be with Peyton and Knox?" His voice was scratchy and quiet, his words ripping my heart into pieces like an unwanted note.

I hesitated, not sure how to answer him, not wanting to lie.

"Once you're better, you can see them," Afton answered for me.

"I have to go," I said. "But I'll be back later, okay? Is there anything you want?"

"Do they have ice cream here?"

"I'll see." I gave him one last smile before returning to Arik.

It was as if the world collapsed on me, the weight of it unbearable, suffocating. "Take me to Sinead," I said, trying to compose myself.

Arik led me down the aisle, up two flights of stairs, and stopped at a glass partition. A willowy girl with doe eyes and hair so shiny it was like an iridescent oil slick opened the door. The gemstone piercings lining her pointy ears glinted in the light.

"We're here to see the patient," Arik said.

The girl nodded before opening the door then closing it behind us. We stopped at another partition and waited for her to let us through. Six beds lined the walls in this part of the infirmary, but only one was in use. A cocoon-shaped apparatus made of glass covered Sinead. She looked peaceful in her sleep. My emotions were still so raw from seeing all the sick people, from seeing poor little Dag, that I almost didn't notice the new set of tears burning my eyes.

I placed a shaky hand on the barrier, wanting desperately to hold hers. "Has she spoken to anyone?"

Arik crossed his arms in front of him and shook his head. "No. She was unconscious when we found her in the barn. She's in a faery sleep. The curers have done all they can for her. It is now up to her to do the rest."

I turned away and wiped the tears now falling from my eyelashes. "How do we get her out of it?"

"We can't." He lowered his head as if he feared I would see something in his eyes.

"What are you hiding from me?"

"It's nothing."

"I know you better than most. We're battle partners. Tell me." I swiped away tears still lingering on my lids. "Tell me, Arik."

His face lifted, his eyes capturing mine. "When Sinead married Carrig, their lives became tethered together. She can't live without him, but he can live without her. Since she isn't dead and is in this state, we believe Carrig is still alive."

There was a silver thread in the midst of all the sadness. "So there's hope," I said, my gaze going to Sinead.

"By the state Sinead is in, Carrig is barely holding on to life."

And the world collapsed again. I rested my forehead against the glass and closed my eyes.

Carrig is strong. He'll be okay. He has to be okay.

I couldn't fall apart. Carrig and the others needed me. I took several deep breaths, releasing them slowly, then turned to face him. "What are we going to do now?"

"Return to Asile," he said. "Not straightaway. You need some rest."

I nodded, too tired to speak.

"We need a break from all this despair," he said. "Shall we get some air?" The sincerity in his voice softened his accent. It was soothing and held strength, even though I was sure he was hurting inside just as much as I was.

Arik had always been strong; I'd rarely seen him weak. It seemed so long ago we'd bumped into each other at the Boston Athenæum. So long ago that we were more than just sparring partners. So long since we'd shared intimate words, and he'd been the only star in my dark universe. I held on to hope that we could be true friends, not just cordial.

I walked beside Arik in silence down a long hallway. The glass walls and metal fixtures were cold and unwelcoming. When we exited a door and ended up in the lush outdoors of the Fey realm, it was a completely different feeling. It was warm and colorful, with floral smells and the musical humming of life around us—a paradise wasted on two people at odds with each other.

The path cutting through the thick shrubbery ended at a cliff with a decorative wrought iron barrier blocking it.

Wrapping my hands around the top of the fence, I arched my back to stretch it. My entire body was tense. "Wait. This isn't iron," I said, trying to ignore the weakness in my muscles. "Is it copper? It seems like everything here is made with it."

"Yes, it is. You won't find any iron in *Tír na nÓg*," he said, watching me intently. "It burns faeries."

"Like their Kryptonite?"

"Sort of," he said, pulling his stare from me and turning it to the valley below.

"It's so beautiful here. It's too bad we can't stay forever." My thoughts played back what I'd just gone through. Time was running out. For the sick. For our missing. Staying in the Fey realm wasn't an option.

"We have to find Carrig and Nick…Lei and Jaran. We can't

waste time here." I released my grip on the barrier and stepped away from him. If I kept moving, maybe the image of Dag in that infirmary bed wouldn't catch me.

But it did chase me. His image blinked in and out of my mind. Dag with shadows under his eyes and a sore at the edge of his lips.

Arik followed me. "We sent tracers to search for them all, but our efforts were futile."

"I can't just sit around and do nothing."

Dag's hopeful eyes.

I strolled into a meadow full of bluebells just off the side of the pathway, disturbing several sprites sleeping under the foliage. They zoomed around and darted off across the grass.

Ice cream. Dag wanted ice cream. Such a simple request.

The grass sighed under Arik's boots. "You're as stubborn as guilt, if I'm honest. Will you please just do this one thing that I ask?" he said. "Once there is word, we will go. For now, just take a moment and breathe."

Breathe? I was suffocating. "I'm worried."

"I share that feeling," he whispered, his face hidden in the shadows. "Seeing you bloodied and hurt in that bed nearly killed me."

Maybe he was beginning to forgive me. Possibly, we could be friends and partners again.

Dag alone, wanting Peyton and Knox.

We came into a bloom of light from a crystal lamppost.

My stomach grumbled.

His lips twisted at the corners, and his dimples deepened. "You're hungry. We should find something for you to eat."

I wasn't sure I could hold anything down. I'd rather curl up in a ball somewhere quiet and sleep.

Fall into nothingness and forget.

...

After having a quick meal of roasted chicken and vegetables, Arik and I returned to the lab. Nana and the curers were studying data on a large computer screen. Emily sat on a nearby stool reading the ancient spell book. When Nana heard us enter, she quickly turned off the screen. Emily's face brightened at the sight of Arik.

"Hi, Arik," Emily said, closing the book and hopping off the stool. "It's good to see you again."

"Hullo," he said without looking at her.

His rudeness was like a slap across Emily's face. The smile slipped from her lips, and she stood there like she didn't know what to do next.

As I brushed by Arik on my way to Nana, I whispered, "You don't have to be rude to Emily."

"I wasn't—" He stopped when I'd moved too far away for him to protest without Emily hearing.

"What have you been up to, dear?" Nana said when I reached her.

"We visited the infirmary."

Her eyes flashed in my direction. "It's a horrible sight. But you aren't to worry. I will find a cure."

"Are you continuing your research?" Arik's stare followed Nana as she removed a bottle from within a cabinet and brought it over to me.

"Now, take a few sips of this before bedtime, and it'll help you sleep," Nana said, obviously ignoring Arik's question. But he was determined to get an answer.

"The Wizard Council sent an order for you to cease your research," he continued.

Nana folded her hands on the counter. "The Fey have insisted I continue my work to find a cure. The council doesn't rule here. Now, if you don't mind, I have work to do."

"Are you excusing me from your laboratory?" The firm tone of Arik's voice startled me.

"I am," Nana said. "I'll let you know when I have what you need ready."

"All right, I see how it is." He turned to Emily. "My apologies. I didn't mean to be rude." His eyes found mine again, and he hesitated. "I'll check on you later."

"Okay, I'll see you then," I said.

Something was going on between Nana and the Wizard Council. And I could tell by Nana's actions that she wasn't going to tell me with Arik around. She waited until we heard the lab door shut behind him before she clicked on her computer screen.

"Come here," she said. "I want to show you something."

I shuffled across the floor and leaned over her shoulder to view the screen. She had two windows up. One image looked like a twisted ladder and another resembled a dandelion. "Is that a DNA strand? What's the other one?"

"It's DNA from a Sentinel." She pushed a few buttons, and three-dimensional versions of the images came out of the screen and floated in front of us. "See this sequence here?" She pointed out a part of the strand. "It's the Sentinel gene. It's very rare. Without wizard DNA, it's useless." She pulled up another image. "This is your DNA. You have the same wizard gene as others, but your Sentinel one is longer, most likely because both your parents are Sentinels."

"Where did you get my DNA?"

"Morta went to the hideout in Boston," Nana said. "I had her gather a blood sample from you and bring it here."

I glared at her through the 3-D image. "Without my permission?"

"You were out cold, dear. I couldn't ask you for it." Nana gave me one of her how-could-you-not-take-in-that-cute-kitty looks. She used that stare a lot to soften Pop. That was how she got us to give Cleo, my cat, a home.

"Lives were at stake," she was saying. "The cure we created from another Sentinel's blood only lasts a few days, then our subjects go back to being sick. We tried other donors, and had the same results. But what we do have, though temporary, is keeping many patients in that infirmary alive a little longer until we can save them."

I studied my DNA. "Exactly when did you become a scientist?"

Nana clicked off the screen. "I did have a normal human job in a medical lab before retiring. Being a Pure Witch isn't my only skill."

That makes sense. "But I don't remember you working."

"When your mother passed away, I decided to stay home to help your pop out with you." She gave me a warm smile. "Best decision I ever made."

"I'm glad you did." I returned her smile. "Okay, what do you need from me?"

"She needs more of your blood," Emily said.

Nana looked smaller sitting in the chair in front of the computer. She was worn out. Worried.

I placed my hand on her shoulder. "What is it?"

"After we make more of the cure, we must test it. Then I need you to sneak out of *Tír na nÓg* and deliver it to the Greyhill coven. Bastien will meet you. He'll make sure the sick receive the cure. The entry is in the Abbey Library of Saint Gall."

The thought of seeing Bastien quickened my pulse. But going against the Wizard Council's orders made it thud to a stop for a beat. What would they do if they discovered our plan? I didn't even know what the punishment was for such an action.

"I don't understand," I said. "Why doesn't the Wizard

Council want to share the cure? And why can't I tell Arik?"

Nana rubbed her chin. By the bags under her eyes and the slump in her shoulders, I could tell she'd been pulling late nights working on the cure. "Arik will never go against the Wizard Council's orders. How many people knew you were going to New York that day Veronique found you?"

I shot her a puzzled look. "Only Uncle Philip. Why?"

"Veronique didn't just happen to be in the neighborhood."

"I know. She said her spy told her I was there. That whoever it was had spotted me."

"This spy just so happened to spot you? I don't believe it." Nana covered my hand with hers. "Someone told her you'd be there."

"Uncle Philip?" I didn't want to believe it. "But he could've had me killed many times. Besides, I tested him with my truth globe, and it showed that he was trustworthy."

"I'm not saying it was Philip." She cut me off. "He must've shared your jump schedule with the council. There is unrest within the havens. It started with the high wizard murders during Toad's trial. There are many new high wizards. We're not sure if we can trust them all. Tell no one about the mission I'm sending you on. Many lives depend on your success."

If the council was corrupt, I had to convince Arik to see the truth. He'd listen to me. See that we had to get the cure to the Mystik covens. Just then, I remembered something from when the council had questioned Bastien about Conemar's disappearance. It was during the dispositions regarding our part in Toad's escape from the gallows under the Vatican.

"The disease is spreading to the havens, too," I said. "Akua of the Veilig haven in Africa mentioned it at a hearing I attended."

The vials clanked against the counter as Nana set them down. "That explains why Arik has instructions from the council to bring a substantial amount of the cure to Asile. He was told it was for testing, but they wouldn't need as much as they requested for that. They'd save the havens and not the covens. Merl would never have stood for such cruelty."

Merl had been the high wizard before Uncle Philip. He'd died during an attack on Asile. He and Nana had a little romance thing going before his death. By the sadness in Nana's voice, I wondered if she missed him.

"Why would the havens not want to help the covens?"

Nana picked up a vial and inspected it. "When the Mystik world was first created, it was to hide the magical and unusual beings from human persecution. The high wizards in that time believed the havens and covens could live in harmony. But there were some xenophobic wizards who didn't much like that idea. People in the havens were divided. Most wanted to remain connected to the covens, while a few wanted separation."

"The attacks by those rogue Mystiks didn't help," I said.

"No, they didn't." Nana examined another vial. "Conemar was one of the wizards who wanted the separation. I wouldn't be surprised if he was behind the attacks as a way to scare the havens into closing off the covens. The Wizard Council shut down Conemar's movement in 1938 just after Gian's death… or rather, disappearance."

Conemar had tried to kill Gian, but my great-grandfather had escaped through a trap into one of the Somniums, only to die during the battle on my front lawn.

"Okay," I said, wanting to move past the memory of Gian. "So when do I go?"

She retrieved supplies off the shelf: gloves, syringes, tourniquet, vials, alcohol pads, and gauze. "We'll test the cure on a volunteer first. Make sure it works. If it doesn't, there's no reason for you to go. When it's time to leave, I'll come for you."

Nana slipped on the gloves. "Have a seat."

"What about Afton?" I sat on one of the lab chairs at the counter.

"I told her we were heading out soon," Emily said. "She wanted to stay and aid Nana. Doesn't want to leave the eight-year-olds. Been mothering them ever since we got here."

That didn't surprise me. Afton loved kids. Whenever I needed someone to take over a babysitting gig for me, she'd step in. Actually, sometimes she would join me to help and not even want half the pay. But I couldn't leave her. It was another realm, after all. What if she got stuck and couldn't return to the human world?

Nana's face softened with an understanding smile as she tied the tourniquet tightly around my arm. "I'll watch over Afton. She'll be safe with me."

The needle gleamed against the light coming from the ceiling. A surge of anxiety hit me, and I shuddered.

Emily grasped my hand. "Here. Squeeze my hand if you want. It's just a prick. Won't even hurt that bad."

I smiled at her. When I'd first met Emily, I thought she was an evil bitch. It wasn't her fault. She had been controlled to do the horrible things she did to me. Her kindness toward me, and the whole taking care of me while I was hurt thing, showed she was trying to make amends. She was growing on me.

As for leaving Afton here—though I've never seen her do it, and I definitely never wanted to witness it, Nana was skilled in the magic of Incantora, which gave her the power to make a person erupt in flames and burn from the inside out. She never let me down all my seventeen years, and I was confident she'd give her life for Afton. Knowing that didn't settle the worry bubbling inside me.

Morta came into the lab. Behind her, two men guided a rolling bed with an older man lying on the mattress. There were sores around the faery's mouth, and his face was flushed with a fever.

The needle pierced my skin, and I flinched, clenching my teeth. Nana filled a vial with blood. After the third tube, my stomach got queasy. Morta must have noticed and, using her cane for support, brought me a glass with a vibrant red liquid inside.

I took the glass from her. "What is this?"

"Fruit juice from berries that grow here in the Fey realm." She hobbled to a nearby chair and eased herself down on it.

Nana carried the vials holding my blood over to a worktable with flasks and other glass containers, along with an apparatus I didn't recognize, a microscope, and miscellaneous lab equipment. She snapped on some rubber gloves and picked up one of the vials with my blood. Morta brought her a beaker from another glass refrigerator.

"What's that big metal tank over there for?" Emily asked, spinning around on the stool.

Morta glanced at it. "That's to do a bigger batch of the cure. We'll use it to make a vaccine later."

Nana picked up one of the vials of my blood and poured some into the beaker. My blood swirled in the clear liquid as she mixed it with a glass stirrer. She put some of the cocktail into a small bottle and screwed on a rubber top. Morta handed her a syringe. Nana took it, punctured the rubber with the needle, and pulled back the plunger, filling the barrel with the mixture.

"Shall we see if this works? We don't want to keep our volunteer waiting." She held the syringe, needle up, and carried it over to the sick man on the table. I looked away as she shot him up with the stuff.

Emily hopped off the stool. "Now what?"

Nana removed the rubber gloves and tossed them onto the worktable. "We wait and see if the patient gets better."

"How long will that take?" I asked.

"A night, possibly," Morta said. "That is, if it works as the other cure had." Morta's cane hit the floor as she shuffled across the floor. *Thud-scrape, thud-scrape, thud-scrape.* She was out of breath by the time she reached the patient. "You may return him to the infirmary," she said to the two men attending him.

"Can we try the cure on Dag?" I asked, remembering his hopeful eyes. "He's bad, and I'm worried he'll ..." *Die.* I couldn't say that word for fear of making it come true.

Nana pushed a strand of her silver hair away from her face. "Once we see how our volunteer does, we'll give it to him right away."

When the men had left, Nana leaned against the counter in front of me. "I believe we have something else concerning to discuss. Afton mentioned your magic changed. You were able to create a fire, ice, and stun globe."

The nightmare of the incident in New York ripped through me like a jagged knife. "After I'd killed the Sentinels with Veronique that day in New York, I think I absorbed their globes."

"That is curious." Nana went over to several books lined on one of the shelves against the wall. The spines were old and tattered and in a foreign language. She pulled one out and flipped through the pages.

Emily and I exchanged confused looks.

"Nana, what are you looking for?"

She stopped on a page and ran her finger down the length as she read. "This is one of the Fey's medical books. There's a section on Sentinels. I know there was something about power transfer in here. Now, where was it?"

Power transfer? That must have been what happened.

Nana cleared her throat. "It says here that in cases where there is a longer Sentinel gene strand, the subject may attract power when he or she kills another Sentinel. When the power leaves the body of the dead, the dominant Sentinel absorbs it."

"Has this happened before?" I asked.

"Yes. It was a regular occurrence in the beginning when the

Fey created the Sentinels, before they had found the correct mix of wizard blood in the formula."

"What else does that book say about us?"

"It mentions that the Fey chose to create Sentinels from a mixture of human and wizard DNA," Nana said. "They wanted their magical knights to have an affinity for both worlds. They send the magical mixture out into both worlds every eight years. It seeks fetuses with a rare genetic mutation from both worlds and infuses the unborn with the magic. Once the babies are delivered, its match grows in the Garden of Life."

Emily hoisted herself onto the counter. "That's creepy. What kind of mutation?"

Nana crossed her arms over her chest. "Some mutations cause diseases in people. This one isn't harmful. It just enables the fetus to absorb magic."

My arm was sore from where Nana had drawn blood, and I rested it on the counter. "Why don't the Fey just grow their own knights in that garden?"

Nana closed the book. "They tried but failed. Faeries were resistant to the magic."

A young faery girl came in and stood by the door as if waiting to speak to Nana. Her back was straight, her brown hair pushed behind pointy ears, and her hands stiff by her sides.

"We're done here," Nana said. "Go and rest. It may take a few days to produce an ample amount of the cure. This is Nysa. She's your host while you're in the Fey realm and will show you and Emily to your rooms."

"Follow me," Nysa said and exited the lab.

"Sounds good to me. I could sleep for days." I stood and headed for the door Emily held open.

"And Gia," Nana said before I left. "Remember, not a word about our plan to Arik."

"Yeah, got it." I closed the door behind me.

I'd always been able to trust Arik. He was the leader of

our Sentinel band. We might be at odds with each other, but we had been battle partners. When he discovered I'd gone against his orders—and he *would* find out—all my attempts at regaining a friendship with him would crumble.

But I would risk it all to save the sick Mystiks and faeries in that infirmary. To save the covens. To save Dag.

CHAPTER EIGHT

The ceiling leaked in the dark room. My nose and ears felt like ice; I pulled the rough covers tighter around me. It was strange that the temperature had changed so drastically. Since arriving in the Fey realm, it had been a perfect seventy-two degrees. I sat up when a door creaked open.

I wasn't in the same room I'd gone to sleep in.

"Your Highness," a deep man's voice said behind the flame of a candlestick in his hand. "You asked to be awakened with any news from Asile."

"That I did," Athela said, swinging her legs over the side of the bed. I was in the head of Royston's mother, my ancestor who'd lived hundreds of years ago. She was an enchantress, hijacking my dreams ever since I'd entered the Mystik realm, showing me things from her past. Things she felt I needed to know to help her son destroy the Tetrad.

The man turned his back as Athela crossed the cold floor, a flimsy nightgown flowing around her legs and her blond hair swaying against her waist. She grabbed a thick, red robe from a chair and slipped it on.

"What have you heard?" she asked, her voice shivering a

little in the cold.

"Taurin's sons have been murdered. The whereabouts of the Chiavi are unknown. Mykyl—" The man cleared his throat. "Your father's body rots while the people of Esteril celebrate his crucifixion. Shall I send an army to retrieve it for burial?"

"No." Athela tied a gold rope around her waist and stared into a distorted mirror. She was older than the last time I was in her body, most likely in her forties. "All is how it should be. My father betrayed our people. Betrayed me. Let them have their revenge."

The anger Athela had for her father mixed with my sadness for her. She never felt the love from her father that I had from Pop. It must have been hard growing up with a father as cruel as Mykyl.

Why am I here? I thought. *What does she want me to know?*

The man kept looking back at the door. "As you wish, Your Highness. We must leave. You are no longer safe here. The uprising sends an assassin to your door as we speak."

"Very well," she said, turning from the mirror. "Alert Cadby. We leave tonight."

His eyes went back to the door. "The council has sent Cadby to a Somnium for your son's murder."

She covered her mouth with a shaky hand. "He was wrongly accused. My son is not dead."

"There is no reasoning with the Wizard Council," the man said. "They fear the uprising. Those who want to overtake the human world won't stop until you are dead. Taurin's vision of two separate worlds won't last. It is only a matter of time before those who want to rule all will rise."

"My death will shock them all. It will cause the people to vote for a just high wizard to lead the council." Athela grabbed bottles filled with what looked like insects and herbs. She opened a leather-bound book that I recognized. It was the ancient spell book that Nana had found and Emily now used.

It was her book.

"Taurin's sons and daughters will keep the peace for many generations." She read one of the pages of the book. "But it cannot last. His or her time will end, and another ruler will take over. The council will want to use the Tetrad to bring the Mystik world out of hiding. To enslave humans." She dumped the contents of the bottles into a mortar bowl and worked at grinding them with a pestle.

A loud thump sounded somewhere in the castle, and the table shook.

The man adjusted his stance, his eyes darting to the door. "The assassins are ramming the door."

She lit a match and set the crushed items in the bowl on fire. "They may kill me, but my spirit will not leave. I will send my own assassin. An assassin of their false truths."

Her eyes closed and darkness overtook me. She chanted something, and a brightness lit the back of her eyelids. A loud boom resounded through the room, and her eyes flew open. The man lay unmoving under rubble from the ceiling, blood staining his beard and the candle by his hand snuffed out.

"Daughter of the Seventh, you are my chosen one."

Is she talking to me? A chill ran through my thoughts.

"I've waited hundreds of years for you," she continued. "I've cried thousands of tears for peace. It is up to you to guide my son in achieving what he is meant to do. You are the Assassin of Truths. Expose the evil choking the Mystik world. Destroy the weapon they mean to use."

The roof collapsed, crushing Athela. A tugging sensation overcame me as her soul departed her body. It was as if someone had pulled a plug and everything suddenly turned dark. I was left there alone and cold within her mind.

Sadness hit me, so painful it cut through my soul. She was dead. And without doubt, I knew she would never enter my dreams again. She had shown me all I needed to know.

It was her way of connecting with me, touching my heart so that I would understand her cause. So that I would do what she wanted. To expose the truth. To destroy the Tetrad. To finish what Taurin believed was the only way for the Mystik and human worlds to exist. One without the other. Separate. Because those with magic could control those without.

"Gia, wake up." A whisper tickled my ear.

I opened my eyes. Emily leaned over me. Her pasty, heart-shaped face glowed in the spotlight of the moon coming in through a nearby window. It was warm again. Colorful crystals hung from the ceiling, and white sandstone walls surrounded me. The cushions on the chairs and bedcovers were various shades of blue. I was back in the bedchamber in the Fey realm.

I hadn't seen much of her the last two days. She had been locked up in her room studying the ancient spell book.

"You're crying."

"Bad dream," I said and noticed my messenger bag on the bed. "Thanks for keeping my bag safe."

"No problem." She smiled. "Anyway, I found something cool in here." She flipped open the ancient spell book to a page she'd dog-eared. "This is going to sound awful and somewhat barbaric, but hear me out. I found a charm that can hide things on a person's body. Wizards used it to keep thieves from stealing precious gems and other stuff. It's going to get tough carrying around the Chiavi everywhere without someone noticing. And considering both worlds depend on them *not* falling into the wrong hands, I think we should try it."

I sat up. "Go back to the part where you mention it's somewhat barbaric."

She exaggerated a breath. "I have to brand them into your skin."

"What?"

"That's just a response, right? You did hear what I said."

"Yeah, I heard you." My fingers went to the crescent moon

scar on my chest. Nana Kearns had branded the charm on me when I was a baby. It shielded me from the Monitors. I could jump through any gateway book unnoticed. "My nana branded me once. She used a numbing spell on the area before doing it. Do you know how to do one?"

The apologetic look on Emily's face told me she didn't know. "I'm not even sure I can do the branding spell. We can try one in a place not visible. See how it goes."

"How about some of Nana's elixir?"

She shook her head. "The lab was locked, and Nana didn't answer when I knocked on her bedroom door."

Nana used earplugs while she slept. Even the smallest noise would keep her up.

I stared at my hands.

Come on, Gia. Toughen up. It would be hard to travel with a bag full of Chiavi clinking on my side. And it was better if they were hidden.

"Okay, let's do it."

She nodded and placed the book on the bed. "Where do you want me to put them?"

Where do I want them? Not the arms. Someone would notice. Stomach? No. Someplace it was easy to hide. "My side. How do I get them off when needed?"

"I'll teach you the charm for removing them. We'll practice."

I turned my side toward her and removed my shirt. Thankfully, I still had my sports bra on. "Okay. Let's get this over with."

She passed me a thick piece of leather.

I took it. "What's this for?"

"You know, to put between your teeth and bite down on so you don't scream or bite off your tongue or something."

"You've seen too many movies." I turned the tan piece over in my hands, inspecting it. "Where did you get this? Is it clean?" There was no telling where that thing had been or what germs were on it.

"I washed it. I cut it out of a chair in my room." She looked over her shoulder at the door. "Let's get this done before someone comes."

"Okay. Torture me."

"Funny," she said, adjusting her position in front of me.

The leather was stiff between my teeth and tasted like my sweaty kickboxing gloves. Emily opened my messenger bag to retrieve one of the Chiavi. She pulled out the cross and placed it on the bedding in front of her. It was the size of her palm, made out of silver, decorated with gemstones, and attached to a chain. After reading over the spell in the book, she held one of her palms over the cross, placed one hand on my side and said, *"Abscondere."*

"Nothing's happening," I said around the leather piece in my mouth.

"Hush. Let me concentrate." She lowered her head and mumbled to herself.

Still nothing.

"Abscondere," she said in a forceful voice. It didn't even sound like her. There was a darkness to it.

A burning pain hit my rib cage, and I bit down hard on the leather, groaning. It was more like a guttural screech. I slumped forward, leaning over my lap and holding back my screams. Tears stung my eyes. My skin was on fire. I took several deep breaths, releasing each slowly.

"Are you okay?" The worried look on Emily's face scared me.

"What does it look like?" I strained to view the brand on my side. A cross the size of a thumbprint was burned into my skin. As I stared at it, the angry red mark faded until it was a white scar. "It's really small."

"And it healed fast." Emily flipped the page in the spell book. "Do you want to try and remove it?"

"I don't know if I can do this six more times," I said.

"Maybe it won't hurt as much the next time. You know, as they say, the body gets used to pain."

I doubted it. "Okay, how do I get it off me?"

"Place your middle and index finger on the brand. It has to be your dominant hand. Think of the cross and only it. Then say, '*Reditum.*'"

The scar felt raised under my fingers. I concentrated on my first memory of the cross. I was playing around with my mom's red umbrella, waving it in the air like a weapon, when the handle detached and the top of the umbrella went flying across the room, almost hitting Afton. The cross was inside the handle.

"*Reditum*," I said.

It was like ripping off a very sticky Band-Aid when the Chiave tore away from my skin and slowly grew to its normal size. The cross hovered in the air, the silver chain swinging underneath it. I grasped it.

Emily's mouth gaped. "Now, that, you don't see every day."

"How do I put it back?"

"Like I did. You say *abscondere,* and it will brand into your skin."

"Great." It was anything but great. Each time I used them, it would be painful.

"What do you think?" Emily adjusted on the bed, crossing her legs. "Do you want to put them all on you?"

It took me several beats to get up the courage to answer her. Having the Chiavi hidden on me was the best way to keep them safe. Only Emily and I would know how to release them. But the pain of having them branded into my skin made me hesitate.

Stop being a baby. Just do it.

I nodded several times, swallowing back my fear. "Okay, I'll try."

• • •

After branding all the Chiavi into my skin, Emily went back to her room. I'd let her keep the ancient spell book. She was coming into her own as a witch, and it felt like the book belonged to her. My heart sank as I kissed Gian's journal. I no longer needed the information in it, but it tore me apart to leave his words behind.

You have to travel light. I placed the journal on the crystal nightstand. My wounds still ached, but the pain was now dull as I pulled on my pants then a long-sleeved T-shirt. My fingers went to Faith's pendant and then the glass locket with Pip's white feather inside. I should leave them behind, but I tucked them inside my shirt instead. They were like lucky charms, and I was afraid to part with them.

The black trench coat Emily had found to replace my bloodied one fit snuggly around my body. One of the pockets had a hole in it, so I buried Gian's leather canister holding the two vials and instructions in the other one. Since I didn't have my sword, I left my sheath on the bed and made sure my dagger was secured inside my boot.

Before I met Nana, there was something I had to do. The hallway was vacant. The sound of my boots hitting the polished rock floor bounced off the bare walls. I eased the infirmary's door open and slipped inside.

The lights were dim, but a lamp attached to Dag's bed spotlighted Afton. She sat on a stool, her soft voice drifting over the other beds. She was reading to Dag.

Afton heard me approaching and stood. "Hey, what's up?"

"They have books here?"

Her eyes went to the chapter book in her hands, then passed it to Dag. "They borrow them from the libraries. You're not here to talk about a book, though, right?"

She knew me well. "I'm leaving tonight. Just wanted to check on Dag and say goodbye to you."

"He's improving by the hour. The cure is working." She spun on her heel, glancing around the infirmary. "It's healing them all. Dag gets to stay with Peyton and Knox tomorrow."

"That's wonderful." I bent over and brushed the hair away from Dag's face, the face that reminded me of Bastien and made my heart ache for him. "You do look much better. Did you get ice cream?"

The corners of his mouth turned down. "They don't have it here. But I did get some treats."

"Well, maybe you can have some when you return to Asile." I ruffled his hair and straightened. "I have to go, but I hope to see you again."

"Me, too," he said and continued studying the illustrations in the book.

There were tears in Afton's eyes when I turned around. "What is it?"

"I miss Nick," she said. "If you find him, tell him...tell him—" A sob cut off her words, and she covered her mouth with a shaky hand.

I gave her arm a gentle squeeze. "I'll tell him. I'm sure he loves you, too. We'll get him back. Whatever it takes, I'll do it."

A tear dropped from her eyelashes and skittered down her cheek. "I know you will. You should get going. I'll be fine."

My eyes traveled up to the third-floor gallery.

"Sinead's the same," Afton said. "Don't worry. I'll take care of her."

We hugged, neither of us able to let go first. I gave in and released her. "I'll come back as soon as I can."

I turned quickly and bounded down the aisle, not wanting her to see the tears in my eyes. Fear settled in my stomach like a seed growing and branching out, its roots threatening to take over my body. I wasn't sure I'd ever see her again.

So I wouldn't get lost, I hurried back to the corridor my room was in and passed the door.

Two lefts. Then a right. Then up a long stairwell. I replayed Nana's directions to where we were to meet.

A painting on the wall stopped me. It was of a man lying on his back with a woman cradling his head. They both wore Sentinel gear. A battle was happening around them. There was a cut on the woman's hand, and she held it over the man's mouth. I read the Italian writing on a scroll by the woman's knee.

Erede di erede. Sangue per sangue. Si trova la cura.

I translated it under my breath. "Heir to heir. Blood to Blood. It is the cure." Gian had written that on the parchment I found in his leather canister. He must have seen this painting before, walked these halls.

"Gia?" Arik's voice startled me, and I spun around.

"Um... Hi," I said, totally sounding like I was up to something and just got caught.

He measured his steps to me. "What are you doing awake?"

I could ask you the same thing. But I didn't, fearing it would sound too defensive.

"I couldn't sleep, so I took a walk." I glanced up and down the hall. "Guess I'm lost. I can't find my room." The lie made my lip twitch, and I sucked the flesh between my teeth to stop it.

His eyebrow went up as he watched me.

Did he notice? He knew the twitch in my lip was a telltale sign I was either nervous or lying or both.

He couldn't know where I was going. Nana had warned me about telling Arik what we were doing. He would never let me go against the Wizard Council's orders, and I wasn't about to let innocent Mystiks die. Not if I could save them.

Arik nodded the way he'd just come. "It's back that way. This castle can be confusing. There aren't many distinctive markers or artworks, and every hallway looks exactly alike.

I'll escort you."

My heart practically thudded to a stop. I would be late to meet Nana, but if I refused, he'd know something was going on. I forced a smile. "That would be great."

We walked side by side in an awkward silence through the corridors.

"Are you angry with me?" He broke the silence.

"No. Are you mad at me?"

"Do I have a reason to be?"

He's suspicious.

"Of course not. I'm just nervous about Sinead." Which I was, so it was only half a lie, but it still tasted bitter on my tongue.

"Here we are," he said. "Perhaps you could join me for breakfast tomorrow morning?"

"Okay. That sounds good." Another lie.

"You understand why I mustn't let the cure go to the Mystik covens, don't you?" he asked.

His words broke my heart. How could he not want to do the right thing?

"I don't understand," I finally said. "The cure was tested. It's working. The sick here are getting better by the hour." Frustration and anger bubbled up in my chest like a geyser waiting to erupt, but I held it back. "Listen, I admire how loyal you are, Arik, but sometimes it can be a mistake to trust without question. I hope you will reconsider your decision. So many lives depend on it."

"I gave my oath as a boy to do whatever the Wizard Council commands of me. I don't know how to be any other way." His eyelids weighed on his deep brown eyes. He was tired and worried. "If this cure indeed works, the council will have the same results as Katy's tests and will distribute it to the sick."

We didn't have time to wait for the council to do their tests. But I didn't say that to him. The effort would be wasted.

Instead, I smiled and said, "Thank you for showing me to my room."

"Sleep well."

I opened the door. "Good night, Arik." I closed it and leaned against it, holding my breath and listening to his boots clack against the floor and fade down the corridor.

Once I was certain he was far enough away, I breathed again. The minutes seemed like hours as I waited to make sure the coast was clear. Not wanting my boots to make noise, I took them off before leaving the room.

Two lefts. Then a right. Then up a long stairwell. I found a door there, and I stepped out onto a balcony that resembled a helicopter launch pad. Parked in the middle were two single-driver aircrafts. The moonlight danced across the black bodies of the bird-like machines. About half a dozen faeries secured leather boxes with straps to the back of the crafts while Nana supervised.

Bastien was beside one of them, and all my frustration toward Arik dissipated. He wore a black leather Sentinel outfit. A copper helmet that resembled an acorn was on his head, and another one just like it in his hand.

He spotted me, and a spectacular smile stretched his lips. It was a smile that said he'd missed me as much as I did him.

I dropped my boots and ran to him, crashing into his arms and almost knocking him to the ground.

He laughed. "Easy there."

"You're here?"

"I believe so." His breath teased my cheek.

Leaning back, I stared into his striking blue eyes. "I thought we were meeting in the library."

"I had nothing better to do." He grinned, the one where his lips had a little bit of a smirk to them.

"Oh really?"

He brought his lips to my ear, and his whisper sent shivers

across my skin. "I'd kiss you, but your grandmother is watching us."

My eyes went wide, and I pulled away from him. I'd totally forgotten where we were. Nana was doing a horrible job at pretending to be busy discussing something with a red-haired girl.

I stared up at him. "You have an acorn on your head."

That smirk was back. "And I look good in it."

He was right, but I wasn't about to tell him so.

Nana walked around the craft to us. "Gia, what took you so long?"

"Arik caught me in the corridor. I had to ditch him."

She glanced down at my socked feet. "Why aren't you wearing your boots?"

"The heels were making too much noise in the hall." I went over to where I'd dropped them and slipped them on.

Bastien offered me the helmet he'd been holding when I was done. "Here. Wear this."

"Now, you must be careful not to break any of the vials," Nana said. "Especially when jumping through the gateway. We don't want any of the cure wasted. Emily will meet you in a few days after I have the vaccine ready."

"We'll keep them safe," Bastien said.

Nana looked at me. "Do you remember Sinead's tracers?"

"Yes," I said.

Nana waved to the girl with the red hair. The girl rushed over carrying a shimmery butterfly on her fingers.

"Raise your hand, palm up," the girl said.

I did as she said.

She spoke to the butterfly in a language that sounded ancient. It fluttered over to me and landed on my wrist, its body and graceful wings flattening onto my skin. It was so light, like a faded tattoo.

The girl grasped my wrist and inspected the butterfly.

"She's on good and tight. When you need to summon someone, just blow on it. The tracer is already programmed and will know what to do when you give it an order."

"But the Monitors will pick up Bastien's jump," I said while twisting my wrist, studying how the wings slightly glinted under the lights.

"My travel plans were sent to the Monitors," Bastien answered. "It's believed I'm here to discuss the cure with the Fey. They'll ignore my jumps."

It was a smart plan, except for one problem. "But you're not going home from here."

"I included several libraries in my plan." He placed his palm on my cheek. "Don't worry. I'm traveling all the time. They won't suspect a thing."

Nana cleared her throat, and Bastien's hand dropped away from my cheek.

"Once you deliver the cure to Greyhill," she said, "you mustn't use the gateway books. You are to use the Three Barley Flower Passage. It's an address in Greyhill. It's in the basement. Push on the brick farthest from the stairs and follow the Talpar's tunnel to the end. You have to hide from the Wizard Council."

A Talpar tunnel? I didn't like the idea of going underground. The Talpars were a Mystik race that looked like a cross between a mole and a human. The Red had used one of their tunnels to escape after the attack on Asile when we'd lost Merl. There were many tunnels, but most of them were secret and only the Talpars knew their locations.

"It will lead you to a library," Nana continued. "Use the tracer to call Aetnae. She'll take you to a place where you'll be safe. Oxillia will show you how to operate the aircrafts."

The young faery with the red hair had bright amber eyes and was just a little shorter than I was. She wore a fancy tool belt around her waist. "Have either of you ever ridden one of those human motorcycles?"

"I have," I answered, leaving out the fact that I'd also crashed one before. But really, it wasn't my fault. I was dodging battle globes while chasing after the Subaru speeding off with Nick.

"I've never been on one," Bastien said.

Eyeing the craft, a sinking feeling soured my stomach. "I don't think we should drive them. What if we crash?" I put on the helmet.

"Try not to." Oxillia cocked her head in the direction of the two crafts. "Get on. I will give you a quick lesson. It's not as complicated as the human vehicles."

Placing my foot on the running board, I hoisted myself up and straddled the seat. Bastien easily threw his leg over and adjusted on the cushion of his craft. After we went through her instructions a few times, Oxillia pushed a button in the middle of my handlebars, and a three-dimensional GPS blinked to life.

"I've programmed your crafts to take you to the entry leading to the portal back to the library." Oxillia pushed another button. The metal bird roared to life. "All you have to do is keep it upright and lean into the turns. Simple." She went over to Bastien and turned his on. "The tough part is landing," she yelled over the noise. "Don't press too hard on the brake."

"What happens if we do that?" Bastien asked.

"You'll crash," Oxillia said matter-of-factly. "When you're ready, just lean forward and you'll take off. It's a quick ride to your destination. Try not to throw up. It'll blow back in your face."

Just then, the door leading into the castle flew open, and Arik came storming out onto the launch pad.

CHAPTER NINE

"Gia! Stop, or you'll be charged with treason." Arik ran to one of the other parked aircrafts.

I gave Bastien a quick look. "Go!" I shouted and leaned forward. The aircraft took off, weaving between buildings and trees. My stomach lurched and dipped with each turn. Bastien's machine kept up with mine.

We blew past several slower flying faeries, and I closed my eyes, fearing the craft would hit them. But it avoided them, maneuvering around the group with precision. Several times, it got close to a building or a tree, and I was sure it would crash.

I risked a glance over my shoulder to see if Arik was following us, but couldn't see very far with all the buildings and trees blocking my view. I had to act as if he was. There was too much at stake for him to stop us.

We crossed low over the bridge, causing the faeries on it to gasp and duck.

"That was close," Bastien yelled over the buzz of our engines.

The force of our crafts careening past the trees rocked the tiny birdhouse-like homes. I worried about the inhabitants.

inside—it had to feel like there was an earthquake shaking them. A launch pad, much like the one on top of the castle, came into view. It was in a clearing between the crowded trees. Panic fluttered my stomach.

"Straighten to stop," I reminded myself. The craft was so fast that I sat up too quickly and too late. The vehicle dropped and landed hard in the clearing. It tipped over on its side and slid across the pad until it bumped up against a tree.

Bastien landed his craft and it hopped a few times over the ground before stopping.

A green-skinned man with bat-like ears hurried over to me. "You hurt?" His voice was deep and scratchy.

I rolled off the seat and lay unmoving on the ground for a second, dazed. My shoulder throbbed, but nothing seemed broken. "Surprisingly, I'm fine," I finally answered.

Removing his helmet, Bastien ran over to me.

The man offered his hand, and I grasped it, letting him help me to my feet.

"We need to hurry. Arik is not too far behind us." Bastien unstrapped the two boxes from my aircraft, opened the lid, and inspected the contents. "Only three broke."

Only three? That meant we couldn't save three Mystiks. Three souls might die because of my accident. Three souls would suffer as Dag had. I wanted to kick myself.

"You follow me, please," the man said, pulling me out of my funk.

I had to forget about the broken vials. I couldn't fail the others. There were so many more I could still save.

Bastien handed me the boxes, and I slipped the straps of both over my head, carrying them as I would my messenger bag. He retrieved his, and we followed the man into the woods.

I leaned close to Bastien and whispered, "What is he?"

"A goblin."

The goblin stopped at a tiny sandstone building the size

of a coat closet. "This is it."

"Wait," I said. "This isn't the same way we entered the realm."

"This is a secret portal." He pulled a handle beside the door, and it slid open, dust puffing into our faces. "The Sentinel following you will exit the other one. This way is quicker."

"Is the other Sentinel close?" I glanced behind us.

"The woods sent me a message. He isn't far behind." One long, green finger pointed at the entrance. "Now, you go."

"Thank you for your assistance," Bastien said, following me inside.

It was dark in the building, so I ignited a light globe. A *whoosh* sounded behind us as the door closed. In front of me was a wall with folded corners.

As I stepped closer, the wall moved, the corners pushing up and out. "We're in the pop-up book."

The paper rustled and popped until we faced the back of a gate that slowly opened. I held the straps to the two boxes crossing my body and stepped through first, then Bastien. The page folded back and the book shrank to its normal size.

I turned and walked backward, watching *The Secret Garden* float over to a nearby shelf and slide into a gap between two books. "That's so wild."

"We're not in Edinburgh." Bastien pivoted on his heel, taking in our surroundings, the boxes he carried bumping against his body, the vials inside clanking against each other.

"Careful," I warned. "We don't want to break any more."

He grasped my hand, and we crossed the carpet to the middle of the room. My palm in his felt as natural as breathing. That was, if breathing came along with tingles and a heightened awareness of his skin against mine.

We were in a library I recognized. Fake trees reached to the ceiling, one of them with fall leaves, its roots hugging plaster replicas of books. A large sculpture of a book canopied the entrance. Little creatures, one of which was an owl, peeked out of holes in the trunks of the wooden pillars that held up the structure.

My gaze touched all the fantastical murals, trees, woodland animals, and the many book sculptures dominating the walls.

"I know this library. I've been here before. We're in the Brentwood Library in Tennessee." Nana had brought me to the city for one of her conventions when I was twelve. Going to the library was my reward for surviving the boredom of sitting in a room with old women talking about herbal cures. Now that I think about it, it was probably a witches' convention.

Jumping through the gateways, I'd never ended up in a modern library before. The Fey were always changing the entrances into their realm, so it made sense they'd branch out to newer places. The library was a children's fantasy. I wanted to sit down on one of the large, stone books like I had five years ago and enjoy all the magical artwork around me.

"This must be a secret exit," he said.

"I hope there's a gateway book in this library." I adjusted the straps to the leather boxes crisscrossing my body. "*Sei zero sette periodo zero due DOR.*" I spoke the charm for calling the gateway book and listened for any sound that would lead me to it.

A fluttering noise came from just outside the children's library.

"Is that a bird?" Bastien let go of my hand and marched toward it. "It's the book."

"Oh good. It's not tied down."

Bastien followed the book as it passed him and flew to me. I caught it and thumbed through the pages until I came to the Abbey Library of Saint Gall's photograph. I gripped the book tight at the memory of Bastien and me being sucked into a trap there and dumped into a barren Somnium. We could have died, but luckily, we had escaped when I'd thrown my globe at the trap. But I'd also released Conemar from his prison, along with tons of Mystik convicts.

Bastien placed his hand on my back. "Are you okay? Your knuckles are turning white."

I loosened my hold on the book. "Yeah."

"Don't be frightened." His voice was soft and soothing. "It won't happen again."

He was right. It wouldn't happen again. I'd broken all the traps and released the Somnium's creatures into the libraries. It took weeks and a few human lives before every one of them was captured.

I placed the opened gateway book on the floor.

"I'll go first in case there're guards in the library," Bastien said. "They won't suspect me. Give it ten minutes before you leave."

He clutched the straps to the boxes and jumped into the book.

I paced as I waited. It had to be the longest ten minutes ever before I plunged into the gateway. There was a slight tug on the leather boxes as I went, but then they slacked and sped along with my body. The black coolness of the gateway engulfed me. I stretched my arms out. Fresh, cold air rushed over me and filled my lungs.

The strap on my right suddenly loosened. I pushed against the wind trying to reach the strap. The box tore away before I could grab it.

No, no, no.

Panic caused me to lose my balance, and I tilted forward. I quickly righted myself.

Think, Gia. You have to catch it. But how?

I created a light globe to search for the box. It was behind me and too far away to reach. *Air resistance.* The flat bottom and sides of the box were slowing it down. I'd reach the exit to the library before it would… All those cures. All those people.

I couldn't let it crash into the library. I had to stop myself.

An idea came to me. The globes.

I reached down and tore my dagger away from my boot. In my free hand, I ignited a globe. Fire? That wouldn't work. I tossed it and formed another. Glass.

No.

A light dotted the blackness in front of me. The exit.

"Come on. I need ice," I yelled above the wind's howl, anger taking over me.

A shimmery white sphere sprouted on my palm.

"Yes!" I tossed it at the blooming light, hoping it would spread as it had across the bookcases when that Sentinel had thrown it at me.

I was getting closer, and adrenaline shot through my veins at a speed faster than I was going.

The globe hit the side of the exit and ice rushed around the opening, crackling and fanning out, growing until it covered it. I landed hard on the ice, the vials in the box I still had clinking against each other. The heel of my boot went through the frozen membrane. I stabbed my dagger into the ice and used it to hold on.

The box got closer. It was too far left. I would miss it. I tried to stretch more, but it wasn't enough. I kicked my other boot against the ice to make a foothold. Facing the ice, my boots holding me up, I removed the dagger and stabbed the ice as far as I could reach in the direction the box was heading.

I rolled to my back to face the gateway and punctured my heel into the ice to keep from slipping. The box landed on my stomach and punched the air out of me. I clung to it with my free hand, not moving, trying to catch my breath.

"Great. Now how am I going to get through the exit?"

I had to break the ice. With as much force as I could, I kicked my heel against the ice. It cracked but didn't budge.

I kicked again.

Crack.

And again.

Crack.

The crack spread across the surface.

On the next strike of my boot, I broke through, shooting out of the gateway. I turned and fell backward, keeping the boxes in front of me. My body dropped hard onto a marble floor. One box landed on my chest and the other on my stomach.

I laid there, stunned, my back stinging. "That hurt."

The bookcase I'd flown out of was dripping, the ice thawing and slipping down the spines of books.

"Gia." Bastien fell to his knees beside me. "Are you injured?"

"I'm not sure." I pushed myself up to a sitting position and, surprisingly, I hadn't broken my back. Bastien lifted the box with the broken strap off my chest. I placed the other box on the floor, opened it, and examined the vials. Two were broken, liquid puddled at the bottom. Each damaged one represented a life I couldn't save.

"What happened?" he asked.

"The strap broke. It must've torn when I crashed the aircraft."

Bastien unsnapped the other box and lifted the lid. "No others are damaged in this one. Just the three broken vials from before."

"So now what?"

"We need to summon Doylis and my guards," he said. "They're waiting for us. Can you use the tracer?"

My fingers touched the silver tracer on my wrist. I'd forgotten about it. I blew on the butterfly form. It pulled from my skin and hung in the air in front of me.

"Find Doylis." The tracer jetted off, bouncing along the display cases filled with antique books until disappearing around a corner. A dim light shone across the dark wood and gold leaf accents on the pillars and bookcases surrounding the large room.

"We should get to a place less in the open." Bastien lifted two of the leather boxes and carried them into a nearby alcove surrounded by polished bookcases. I followed him with mine and placed the carriers on the floor, sat beside them, and hugged my legs, resting my head on my knees. Bastien put his down next to mine and took a seat beside me.

"I messed up." The weight of my mistake crushed me. "I damaged vials."

Bastien slid an arm around my back. "It was an accident. You never flew an aircraft before."

I tilted my head to look at him. "People will die because of me."

He lifted my chin with his fingers. "There are forty vials in each box. You will save one hundred and fifty-five beings."

A deep voice called Bastien's name from the reading room.

"It's Doylis." He released my chin, stood, and offered me his hand.

I gripped it, and he towed me to my feet. He kept hold of my hand all the way to the reading room.

With Doylis were five older Sentinels—two women and three men in their late twenties or early thirties. Bastien let go of my hand and crossed the room to them. "I'm so glad to see you, dear friend."

Doylis towered over Bastien and the others. "Glad to see you made it, as well."

The tracer flew over and bounced in front of me. I lifted my wrist and it sank into my skin.

The gateway book flew out of the bookcase, water spraying out as it opened. Arik jumped out of the thawing page, followed by Demos.

I sucked in a ragged breath and quickly backed away from them.

I hadn't seen Demos since our hideout in Ireland. His

Sentinel gear was a little banged up. A few of the red plumes on his Roman-style helmet were bent, the visor dented.

Arik straightened, water dripping from his clothes and hair. His brown eyes peered through the eyeholes in his helmet and surveyed Bastien and the others before landing on me. "What is this? Gia, you need to come with me." He held out his hand, his fingers motioning me over.

Three of the Sentinels moved between us.

"If you go with them," Arik said, hurt sounding in his voice. "You will be deemed a traitor."

My hands curled into fists. "You would let thousands die? How could you? Arik, please, don't do this." The look on his face told me no matter how hard I pleaded with him, he wouldn't listen.

Demos's face screwed up in confusion. "What is she saying?"

My gaze went from Arik to Demos. "There's a cure for the disease spreading through the Mystik covens. The council has forbidden its release."

"Why don't they want to distribute it?" Demos asked.

With my eyes back on Arik, I said, "Ask him."

Arik pulled his fingers through his wet hair. "It hasn't been tested. Get your battle globe ready."

"They'll die without it." My fists tightened, nails biting into my skin. He had to understand. Had I really misjudged him this much? I believed he'd fight to save people. "It's been tested. It works. I'm doing this with or without you. Try to stop me."

"We have our orders." Arik formed a fire globe on his palm. "Gia, if you go against them, you are an enemy of the Wizard havens, and I must take you in. Don't turn this into a fight."

Demos stepped in front of me, faced Arik, and sprouted a green globe. A faint howl came from the swirling wind in his hand. "We may have pledged our allegiance to the council, but she's the presage. We are sworn to protect her."

By the look on Arik's face, Demos's betrayal had gutted him. His jaw stiffened, and he squared his shoulders. "Back down," he warned. "The council comes first."

A rope of blue light shot across the room and wrapped around Arik's arms. He fell, his knees thumping hard onto the floor, and struggled against the electric bindings.

Bastien manipulated the stream with his fingers, keeping Arik down.

Demos turned his globe toward Bastien. "Release him."

"Not when he wants to arrest Gia," Bastien said.

"All right. We'll tie him up." Demos lowered his hand, and the green sphere popped. "Does anyone have something I can use?"

Bastien and Doylis glanced around as if trying to find something. As I searched myself, my fingers grazed over the belt securing my trench coat. "Will this work?" I removed it and handed it to Demos.

Demos inspected it. "It should do," he said, then turned to Arik. "I'm truly sorry."

Arik scowled at him. "You'll regret this."

"I'm sure I will." Demos tried to move one of Arik's arms behind his back, but Arik fought him, breaking free from his grip, and then wincing when the electric rope shocked him again.

"Let me help," Doylis said, holding Arik's arms together so that Demos could secure the belt around Arik's wrists.

Demos avoided touching the electric rope while he tied a final knot in my belt. Doylis released Arik's wrists.

"Now, remove the lasso," Demos directed Bastien.

Bastien lowered his hand, and the electricity snapped from his fingers, the rope disappearing in a series of sparks. Arik sat back on his heels, his hands tied behind him, and he took a deep breath.

"The longer we stay, the more likely we'll be caught." Doylis kept a hold on Arik. "Where is the cure?"

"I'll get the boxes," I said and headed for the alcove. My lip trembled, and the tears pooling in my eyes blurred my vision. At the same time that Bastien's love was filling my heart, Arik's resolve was breaking it. Betraying Arik, going against him, felt wrong. Since entering the Mystik world, he'd been my rock, protecting me and guiding me through this scary adventure. I missed him, and letting go was tearing me apart.

Bastien came into the alcove. I lifted one of the boxes and slipped the strap over my head. His hand on my shoulder stopped me before I could grab another one. I turned, and he cupped my face in his hands.

His eyes were like dark pools in the low lights of the library. "You know what I admire most about you, Gianna? It's your ability to empathize with others."

"It hurts too much."

"You care for Arik, and that's okay. It's similar to how you feel about Nick. And you feel guilty...as if you're betraying Arik. The lives we can save matter more than his battered ego. He'll come around and see our side of things, eventually. I just hope it's sooner than later."

How did he always know exactly what to say or how I was feeling?

"Stop being so perfect," I whispered.

"It can't be helped." Amusement lit his face, and he pressed his lips against my forehead. It was a brief and tender kiss, but it held so much emotion, causing a warmth to rush over me. He released me. "Now, we better get out of here. We have those lives to save."

He picked up two boxes, and I took the last one. Doylis held Arik's arm and followed Bastien and me to the other room. Demos took up the rear, darting looks over his shoulder in case anyone jumped into the library. We stopped at the third bookcase on the east wall.

"Ammettere il pura," Bastien spoke the charm.

The bookcase shuddered as it moved across the floor.

Admit the pure. The charm was a way to keep out those with evil intentions. But did it really work? Veronique had entered Asile when I'd first come to the Mystik world, and she was rotten to the core.

What she said before she died hit me. *We are all between good and evil. Make sure yours is the right side—*

It was as if chilly fingers ran up the back of my neck. I had been on the wrong side without knowing it. I believed in the Wizard Council because Arik and Uncle Philip put all their faith in it.

I stepped over the proverbial good versus evil line and followed Bastien down the steps into the dark tunnel.

CHAPTER TEN

I stood on a balcony of the tall, lean building that housed the leaders of a movement that was against the Wizard Council. Many wizards and Sentinels from all the havens had band together to save the Mystiks. Emily had joined us in Greyhill, bringing the recipe for the vaccine and cure. Nineteen hundred and seventy-two cures had been administered to those with advanced symptoms of the disease. Their bleeding sores had stopped, and their extremely high fevers subsided. The ones we couldn't save, their organs had failed and their deaths were painful.

The crowded buildings prevented me from seeing any countryside. I wasn't even sure if there was one or not. Small walkways cut through the beautiful brick structures, and rope bridges stretched from building to building. The sky was more purple than blue. Smoke puffed from chimneys, and the noises from the roads below rose in murmurs to our fifteenth-story flat.

I tightened my grip on the shawl one of the curers had given me, absentmindedly rubbing the raised scar on my cheek. I had to find out what had happened to Jaran and Lei—and

Carrig. Arik had said *they* took him.

Who were they?

A group of birds flew in a circle just outside the window. They were beautiful with their winter-blue feathers and bright red beaks.

Nick. We had searched for him for months. Every lead we'd received led us nowhere. His loss was like a wound that never healed—gaping and painful.

He has to be okay.

My dreams about him the last few nights felt real. He was in the dark. Cold. Scared. When it got too much for him, he'd scream out my name, and I'd wake up.

I was getting restless. With my wounds healed and the curers having enough of my blood to make more of the antidote, I was ready to go. Ready to find my friends. My father.

I hated leaving Bastien without saying goodbye, but I didn't want him stopping me or getting caught. I turned and walked back into our dorm-like bedroom.

Bastien lay on his bed, his bare chest rising up and down. The silky pajama bottoms provided by our host kept slipping down his waist, like they were right then, exposing the V-shape line just below his abdomen. He looked so peaceful when he slept, which wasn't often lately. He'd spent late nights delivering provisions and cures throughout the covens. I carefully lifted his keys off the pile of his clothes on a chair beside him, placed a note I'd written him on top of his jeans, and tiptoed to the dresser.

Emily's bed beside mine was a mess. She never made it. Demos's was perfectly made—I could probably bounce a quarter off it. They'd left an hour ago for breakfast. I was meeting them there after I got Arik out of his cell. I'd convinced them that I had to go alone. If caught, I'd be the only one arrested, not all three of us.

If I was going, it had better happen fast, before Bastien

woke. I had to stop hesitating. But the sight of him sleeping there, so peaceful and gorgeous, made it tough to leave.

Just go already.

I slipped on my leather cargos and long-sleeved tee. Darting glances at Bastien, I grabbed my boots and trench coat and crept out of the room, easing the door shut behind me with a faint *click*. Quickly and quietly, I finished dressing and hurried down the hallway.

The glass elevators ran on the outside of the buildings, and not wanting anyone to see me disappear to the basement, I decided to take the stairs. The lower level of the building was where they housed prisoners, which was only Arik at the moment.

I hoped Emily would be able to follow through with our plan.

Two guards looked up as I came out from the stairwell into the basement, a little breathless and very determined. One of them was a Laniar with a pronounced underbite. The other looked human, with thick eyebrows and hardly any hair. Both didn't look scary enough to stop an attack if there was one.

It took a few seconds to catch my breath before talking. "I need to speak with Arik."

Another guard came off the elevator. She had thicker arms than my thighs and her black hair was pulled back in a tight bun.

"Do you have permission?" the guard with thick eyebrows asked.

I handed him the note from Bastien that I'd spent hours forging.

He studied it while the woman guard watched me curiously. *Does she suspect something?* If I avoided eye contact, she'd get suspicious. So I kept my eyes on hers until she conceded to our stare war and crossed over to a chair. "You need a break?" She directed the question to the Laniar.

"Yeah, I could use one." He went over to the elevator and pushed the button.

Eyebrows finished scrutinizing the note. "All right. This way." He led me down a narrow hall to a barred door. Arik lay on a cot, one arm resting above his head and the other on his stomach. "Don't be long."

Whatever they used to clean the hall and rooms made the place smell like basil or some other type of herb.

"Can't I go inside?" I asked.

Arik sat up at hearing my voice.

"Sorry, no one is allowed in with the prisoners. I'll give you your privacy. You have ten minutes." His boots clanked back down in the direction we'd come.

"What are you doing here?" Arik pushed off the cot and came to the door. He looked tired. His hair was a mess, and his face and arms smudged with dirt.

"We don't have much time," I said. "So please listen and try to see things differently."

"Differently than what, precisely?" His tone sounded harsh, but his accent made the words seem soft.

I sighed and grabbed the bars. "You know. How you see things. Stop putting all your faith in the council. You don't always have to follow their orders. Not when they're wrong." I glanced down the hallway to make sure it was still vacant. "Listen, only Uncle Philip knew where I was going that day I went to New York. Veronique said her spy told her I was there."

His eyebrows pushed together. "Are you saying High Wizard Philip arranged to have you murdered?"

"I'm not saying that. I hope it wasn't him… I just don't know. Maybe he told someone on the council, and that someone sent Veronique after me."

He rubbed the back of his neck.

"Okay," I said. "I know I'm not going to convince you here, but I am breaking you out. You can go back to Asile. Protect

Royston and the others."

"Gia." He grabbed my hands, squeezing them tight around the cold bars. "Come with me. You don't belong in the middle of this."

"I was born to be in the middle of this," I said. "Please, promise you won't let anything happen to Royston, and you won't try to escape. You're the only one I can trust to protect him. We're the same, you and me. I know if you promise to do something, you'll do it."

He released my hands. "We're the same, all right. Both stubborn in our beliefs. I can't convince you the right thing is to go with me, and you can't convince me what you're doing is right."

"You're wrong, Arik." I unclutched my hands from the bars. "I wish you could see that. There's too much at stake. Too many lives at risk."

He stared at me for several seconds. His brown eyes were cold. "I won't try to escape, and I will protect Royston at all costs. That's all I can promise you. Now, perhaps you should execute your plan before the guard comes back."

I removed Bastien's keys from my bag.

"Perhaps she should," Bastien said from behind me.

I dropped the keys and spun to face him. He was leaning against the wall, kicked back as if there wasn't anything wrong with this situation. And he probably had been listening to everything I'd said to Arik.

"I...um..." I didn't know how to respond. He'd caught me red-handed. So I settled for, "Don't sneak up like that."

The collar of Bastien's distressed leather jacket was tucked inside, and his shirt was wrinkled. He must've dressed quickly to chase after me. He combed his fingers through his dark brown tufts several times to tame his serious bed-tossed hair.

Bastien pushed from the wall and strolled over to me. "You're not as quiet as you believe yourself to be."

I picked up the keys. "You're not stopping me."

"I don't plan to," he said and took the keys from me. "Did you think I would? Is that why you didn't include me? I thought we trusted each other."

"I do trust you." We locked eyes, and I hoped he could see the sincerity in mine. "I didn't want to risk you getting caught. You could lose your position in Couve."

"I believe my position is already compromised. Arik knows my role in distributing the cure." His steely blue eyes lingered on my face. "I'm in this with you. With Demos and Emily. With the covens and those in the havens who are on our side. I won't let you face the storm without me. If you fall, I fall."

His words caused a fluttering in my chest. I knew he would take a fall with me. He proved it when he couldn't pull me out of that trap into the Somnium and, not wanting me to face the barren wasteland alone, jumped in with me.

"All right," I said.

Bastien found the key he was looking for, inserted it into the lock, and opened the door. "So what are we doing? What's your *plan*?" He glanced at me before his eyes landed on Arik.

A look passed between Arik and Bastien—one of disdain or distrust.

"We have to get to the outbuilding," I said, pulling their attention from each other. It was a lie. We weren't going to the exit. I couldn't tell him the real plan with Arik there. "Emily and Demos are waiting for us at the bakery."

"Right, then, lead the way." Bastien stepped aside to let me pass, then Arik.

We walked single file through the narrow passageways between the brick buildings, with me at the front, Arik in the middle, and Bastien behind us. The stones were ancient, and the bottom of the structures had mud stains, which made no sense, since there wasn't any dirt to make it. We ended up on a cobbled road not much wider than the passageway.

"See how the doors of the buildings are all higher than the walkways?" Bastien answered the question he knew was playing in my head. "When the river overflows, it rushes through the streets. That's why there are rope bridges overhead."

"Does it flood a lot here?" I glanced back at Bastien. He wore a deep frown on his face.

"Yes, and we should hurry." He pointed up at the sky. "See those dark clouds? It doesn't take long for the rivers to flood with the heavy downpours here."

Arik glanced up. "Surely we have plenty of time. It hasn't even started to rain."

"This coven is unique," Bastien added. "It happens in a flash. You don't see any villagers about, do you? They know."

"Well, we're here." I pounded up the five steps to the entrance of the bakery where Emily had instructed me to meet her and Demos. The rusty bell on the door jingled, announcing our arrival.

Demos and Emily were sipping steaming liquid from chipped mugs. The remains of their breakfasts stained the thick, white plates on the table. Emily paused mid-sip and glanced our way.

"What took you so—" Her gaze landed on Bastien. "What's he doing here?"

"He's helping. We definitely could use a wizard on this quest." I rested my hand on the back of Emily's chair. "Demos, you and Arik better get going before the rain starts."

Arik shook his head. "He can't go with me. I'll arrest him the moment he sets foot in the library."

Demos let out an exasperated breath. "Oh, come on. Really?"

I was about to give Arik a swift kick in the butt.

Bastien must've noticed my frustration. He came up to my side and lightly brushed my hand with his. There was a spark between our fingers, and I wasn't sure if it was from the worn-out carpet I'd just crossed or the strong connection I felt between us. He was going with me on my search for The Red. He didn't know where, but he was going without hesitation, just as he'd done when the trap had pulled me into the barren Somnium. He'd held on, regardless of the outcome for him. And he wouldn't let me do this alone.

"You'd really do that?" The surprise in Demos's voice matched how I felt when Arik had said I'd be an enemy to the Wizard Council for delivering the cure to the Mystiks.

Arik's eyes slid over Bastien's and my hands before darting to Demos. "You went against a direct order *and* you tied me up. That's imprisonment. Because I'm your leader, it's most certainly mutiny as well. I have agreed to protect Royston, but I go to Asile alone."

"Blimey, you certainly can hold a grudge, can't you?" Demos picked up the linen napkin in front of him and wiped his mouth with it. "Why let insignificant things like my disobeying and binding you ruin our friendship?"

Arik pressed his lips together as if he were trying not to smile at that. "This is quite serious. Don't test me. I won't hesitate—"

"Enough," I said, cutting him off. "Emily will go with Arik. Demos, you come with Bastien and me."

Emily perked up at that.

I continued. "Unless you'd lock her up, too."

He stared at Emily for a long moment. The tightness in his jaw loosened as he watched her. "I suppose I wouldn't. She isn't of our world and only aided you. Most likely, she didn't know of the Wizard Council's orders."

"I didn't tell her about anything." I hoped Emily would go along with that story.

"That's right," Emily said. "I just took care of her at the house in Jamaica Plains. When we were attacked, I ended up with her in the Fey realm."

"I don't need a babysitter," Arik argued. "She isn't even able to jump on her own."

Bastien stuffed his hands in his pockets, his eyes going from me to Arik. "I wasn't let in on *the plan*. But possibly, there's another reason Gia is adamant someone goes with you."

"There is," I said. "To make sure he returns to Asile."

Demos removed some silver cuffs from the pocket of his trench.

Arik eyed them. "Cuff locks? You mean to use them on me?"

I gave him an unsure smile, worried he'd lose it on me. "It's only until you're in Asile."

"You know I can come right back here." He glared at me. "With guards."

"We'll be gone before you return," I said. "And what are you going to do? Arrest all of Greyhill for getting the cure?"

"I see," he said. "And I'm to jump with Emily, hands bound?"

"*Pfft.*" Demos fidgeted with the cuffs. "You could master the gateway blindfolded and with your feet tied."

Arik raised his chin. "All right. I just want out of here."

"And you'll protect Royston?" I added.

"I promised I would." Arik offered his wrists to Demos. "What are we waiting for? Put them on so I can leave already."

Demos clamped the cuffs on Arik's wrists and waved a hand over them. The cuffs glowed blue, securing Arik's wrists in front of him.

I grasped Emily's elbow, led her over to the pastry display case, and whispered, "Give this note to Cadby. Whatever you do, don't let Arik see it. I know you still like him, but please don't cave. Our lives depend on it. Both worlds depend on it."

Emily frowned, took the note, and leaned closer to me. "I may like the guy, but he's completely wrong on this. And I'd never let Nana down. She told me to help you, and I will."

"Thank you," I said. "Stay with Cadby. He'll keep you safe. Okay?"

Arik was staring at us, so she just nodded. Demos placed his trench coat over Arik's shoulders to conceal the fact that he had the magical cuffs on his wrists.

Demos held out a steel ring to Emily. "Put this on your pointer finger. If he tries to run or leave you behind, you only have to pull your finger in to stop him. To move him, point in the direction you want him to go. He won't be able to resist the magic."

She slipped it on her finger and grinned. "I'm going to like this."

"I bet you will," Demos said and laughed.

"Can we go already?" Arik growled.

Bastien opened the door. "By all means. I'll be happy to see you go."

Arik pushed by Bastien. He didn't look back, just stomped out.

After Emily and Arik had exited the café, I felt a sudden rush of regret. *He'll never forgive me.* How did we get to this place? A place where we were fighting on opposite sides of a battle. A place that broke my heart. And a place from which there was likely no return.

Just then, Bastien glanced at me, a crooked smile on his face that made my heart stutter. "Now, what about that plan?"

Right. Back to business.

"Do you have a window rod?" I asked.

Bastien nodded.

"Great. Have your guards leave Greyhill and meet us in the library."

A round, stout woman with graying hair pulled away from her face stood behind the counter. Flour caked her floral apron, the grin on her face welcoming.

"Have you forgotten the rain?" Bastien removed his window rod from his jacket pocket and pulled the two pieces apart. A screen ignited between them. "I can do this walking. I'd feel much better if we get out of here before a flood hits."

"Yeah. Let's—" I looked over at Bastien and caught a glimpse of someone passing outside. Though the window was made of thick glass and a little distorted, I knew that hair and that walk.

I pushed past Bastien on my way out. The old door stuck a little when I yanked it open, the bell attached jingling angrily. My boots slipped on the last step down, and I righted myself.

He was a ways down the passageway, looking from side to side as if he were searching for someone. It was only his back, but I knew him almost as well as I knew myself. We'd spent nearly fifty thousand hours together since he was born. A perfect image of him was burned in my memory.

Nick?

CHAPTER ELEVEN

Three Greyhillians, fine feathers covering their faces and thin plumes falling around their shoulders like hair, blocked the passageway. The slight curve of their bodies told me they were girls. Except for all the feathers and beak-shaped noses, they looked and acted like teens from the human world.

"Did you see how he was staring at you?" one of the girls with blue and yellow feathers said.

"He wasn't looking at me. Stop teasing," the girl with yellow feathers and black plumes answered.

"Excuse me," I said to a girl with red-tipped white feathers.

Her black, marble eyes studied me as she stepped aside to let me pass. "You should get to higher ground," she called after me. "The rains are coming."

My boots pounded against the bricks as I flew down the passageway. Nick was getting farther away from me. He disappeared into the blackness of a tunnel cutting through one of the tall buildings surrounding us.

"Nick!" I slowed down before stopping outside the tunnel, my eyes stuck on the entrance. "Nick!"

I could barely make out his white shirt in the darkness.

He turned and sprinted for me.

My lips tugged into a smile.

He's okay. We found him.

He was getting closer.

Nick was free.

I wanted to cry. Why was I just standing there? I started to take off, but someone caught my wrist, stopping me.

"Wait," Bastien said. "Look at his eyes." He moved in front of me and ignited an electric ball between his hands.

My gaze went to Nick's fierce glare. His black pupils were so large I could hardly see any white in his eyes.

No, no, no, no, no. He's compelled.

A loud crack sounded over our heads, and rain dumped down so hard that it stung my skin. My hair and clothes were instantly drenched.

Nick was almost to us. Like a charging bull, there was no stopping him. He was coming fast. Bastien pointed his hands in Nick's direction.

I grabbed his arm. "Don't. You could kill him."

"He could kill us," he shouted over the clapping of rain. A bright flash and another rumble of thunder shook the buildings.

"I won't hurt him." Bastien shrugged my hand away and let go of the charge. It exploded by Nick's foot. He stumbled to a stop. Another charge left Bastien's hand and hit Nick's shoulder. He slipped and landed on one knee. His glare rattled me. I'd never seen such evil.

"Hey," Demos yelled from the bakery's steps.

I glanced back at him.

He pounded down the steps. "Do you see it?" He pointed up the passageway. Water trickled down the cobblestones. "Get inside. The flood's coming."

Just as he said his last word, a river rushed him and came fast at Bastien and me, knocking us off our feet. Demos collided into me and grasped my waist.

"Hold on," Demos cried.

The debris-filled water stung my eyes, went up my nose, and scratched my throat. We were going to drown. I caught a glimpse of Nick climbing a wire trellis on the side of a building.

Bastien.

Where was he?

Think, Gia. What did Pop always say? *Keep your feet pointed downstream in a flood.* I struggled against the water until my boots were aiming in the direction it was going. Demos, still clinging to me, did the same. We rushed by Bastien; he'd made it to some steps and was climbing up them.

Demos's hand slipped from mine. My head went under, and I choked on the rush of water. I pushed up, my head breaking out of the waves. Heavy coughs tore from my chest.

"Gia," Demos yelled. "See that wrought iron on the side of the tunnel?"

I nodded, then realized he couldn't see me and shouted, "I see it!"

"When we get closer, I'll grab it."

"Okay." The muscles in my arms burned as I pushed them through the raging water and wrapped them around Demos's neck. He reached out his arm, readying to grab what looked like an open gate pushed up against the brick wall.

Angry water slapped my face, blurring my vision. I could barely make out the tunnel as we came up to it. Demos grabbed the gate at the same time a wooden chair crashed into me. I lost hold of his neck, the flood taking me into the tunnel. The darkness was terrifying. I reached out, hoping to find something to grab on to, but there was nothing.

I couldn't form a globe. It took both arms and all my strength to keep from going under the water. And what good would it do, anyway? I had no control.

All I could do was keep my feet pointed downstream.

Keep my head up.

Try not to drown.

I gulped in some more rancid water and gagged, trying to catch my breath. My body twisted in a swirl of water while exiting the tunnel. A *swoosh* sounded above me, and then another one.

Another gate.

I crashed into the metal and clung to it.

Hands covered in white feathers with red tips grasped me under my arms and lifted me out of the water. We went high, the ancient city with its tall buildings and rope bridges falling away. She headed back the way I'd come, my stomach roiling.

The girl descended and placed me on one of the rope bridges. She lowered herself and stood on the planks in front of me, her marble black eyes narrowing. "I told you to get to higher ground."

Water dripped from my hair and soaked clothes, wetting the planks of the bridge. I shivered, my lips shaking and my teeth clattering against each other. "Th-thank you. I don't know how to—"

Her hand raised, stopping me. "I know who you are. My parents talk about the presage all the time. You don't look like much. I'm not sure how you're going to save the worlds; you can't even save yourself from a flood."

She was definitely like some of the girls at my school—a lot of attitude and no filter. "And thanks for your vote of confidence," I said. "What's your name?"

"Shyna. Not like you'll remember it." She stretched out her wings.

"Did you have those earlier?"

"They retract into my back. I must go. I'm late." She flapped her wings and took off into the sky. No *goodbye* or *see you later*. She just left.

Nick.

He was somewhere around here. I glanced over the ropes.

The street was nearly three stories below. I searched the buildings up a ways from me where he'd climbed out of the flood. There wasn't any sign of him.

The rope bridge stretched across the passageway from one tunnel to another leading into the buildings. I wasn't sure which way to go. The one in front of me led in the direction Nick had gone. The one behind me would take me to Bastien and Demos, hopefully.

I turned and headed for the second tunnel. The bridge shook, and I grasped the rope, catching a glimpse at how far it was down to the bottom. My stomach lurched. But I straightened, carefully putting one foot in front of the other.

You're not going to fall. Just don't look down.

"Gia." Nick's voice stopped me.

I held up my palm and ignited a battle globe. A purple ball appeared. *Stun.*

Shaking from the cold, or from the fact that my best friend was behind me and most likely possessed, I faced him.

His eyes were soft brown again, and his face pained. "I'm sorry."

I dropped the globe and teetered to him, my arms flying around his shoulders. I hugged him tight. "Oh, Nick." I buried my face in his shirt and cried. "I'm so sorry. I tried to stop him from taking you."

"I know," he whispered against my ear. "I saw you."

"What has he done to you?" I sobbed into his shirt. "You mean so much to me. I love you, Nick. I won't let anything happen to you again. We've never been without each other. I'd die if something happened to you."

"I love you, too. And it wasn't your fault. Don't blame yourself, okay?" He pulled my arms from him, held my wrists between us, and stared into my eyes. "I don't have much time. The flood must have broken the connection between my compeller and me. You have to get far away from here. I won't be able to stop him. He'll make me kill you."

"I can't leave you." Panic swelled in my chest. "Don't ask me to."

"I mean it, Gia. I'm not Nick."

"Yes, you are." I reached for him, and he shrugged me off. Tears slid down my cheeks. "You're scaring me. Please, come with us. Uncle Philip can help you. We can break the compulsion."

He took my face in his hands. "You mean the world to me. Promise you'll fight me and not give in if it comes to that."

I shook my head against his hands. "I can't."

His eyes pleaded with me. There was so much pain behind them. I lowered my head, and he lifted it back up. "Promise me, Gia."

My heart was crushing, but the look in his eyes told me he needed this.

"I promise."

He smiled, one full of longing and hope. "I wish we were in the North End right now. You drinking a latte and me my Vitaminwater."

I smiled back at him, mine weak and full of defeat. "Me, too."

He kissed my temple, released my face, and bounced over the rope bridge back the way he'd come.

"Wait." My voice sounded as broken as I felt.

He stopped and turned.

"Where are you going?"

"As far as I can get from you before—" He couldn't say it this time. And I didn't want to hear it, either.

But I couldn't help but think it. *Before he's no longer in control. Before he can kill me.*

He continued across the bridge and ran toward whatever horror awaited him. Back to Conemar.

And I just let him.

Without a fight, just rocking on the rope bridge, staring at his retreating back.

Alone.

He's alone. I crumpled, my knees smacking against the planks. I covered my face with shaky hands and sobbed.

Demos and Bastien rushed out of the tunnel, the bridge swaying under the force of their boots. Bastien dropped down in front of me and pulled me into his arms. I buried my face in his chest.

"Are you hurt?" Bastien asked.

I shook my head. "It's Nick… He was… He was here. You were right. He was compelled. He's supposed to kill me."

"I'm here. You're okay." Bastien's arms were warm around me.

"I just let him go." I swallowed down a sob. "I should have done something."

Bastien brushed my wet hair from my face. "There's nothing you could have done."

"It's Nick. I should be with him." I wanted to stop shaking. Why couldn't I stop? "All my life he's been there. It's always been just us."

"I'm here. I'll never leave you." Bastien took his jacket off and put it over my shoulders. "We'll get him back."

"That boy's messed up," Shyna's voice came from above us, and I looked up. She was on the roof. The clouds had parted, and the sun shone over her. Her hand shaded her eyes as she watched something in the distance. "You should get out of here before he comes back. He did tell you to run."

Demos grabbed the ropes with both hands, staring off in the direction she was looking. "We should do as she says."

Bastien touched my cheek. "Can you get up?"

I nodded, and he helped me to my feet.

"Where are we going?" Demos asked.

My legs felt wobbly, and I leaned into Bastien's hold. "There's a Talpar's tunnel," I said, my teeth still clattering.

"It's in the basement of a building around here. The address is Three Barley Flower Passage."

"A Talpar." Shyna exaggerated a shudder, her wings flapping around her. "They're Undergrounders. Their long noses with those feelers attached to them, wiggling all over the place like that, creep me out."

"Why do you sound so much like a teenager from my world?"

"Human television. I'm obsessed." She flew off the roof and landed on the bridge, shaking it. Her wings retracted into her back. The feathers ruffled into place, covering the holes in her shoulder blades. "Follow me. I'll take you there."

Demos leaned in toward me. "You okay?"

"I'm fine."

"It's kind of odd," he said, "but I find Bird Girl a little attractive."

A small laugh escaped me, and then a pain twisted my heart. Demos's humor was like Nick's, and it reminded me of how my friend must be suffering.

I won't let you down, Nick. I'll get you back.

Shyna led us through tunnels and over rope bridges until she stopped at a door. "Here it is. Take the stairs down. It'll lead you to the tunnel."

"You've been a great help," Bastien said and opened the door.

"Anything to help the presage." Her eyes went to mine.

"Thank you." I squeezed her hand. The feathers covering it were soft under my touch.

The corners of her mouth went up slightly. "I'm sorry about saying you weren't much. I think you're everything. All the Mystiks have hope you'll be like Gian and fight for us."

"I'll never give up." I smiled at her and ducked inside after Demos. Bastien followed me and closed the door behind him.

∙ ∙ ∙

The tunnel led us into the Abbey Library of Saint Gall in Switzerland.

After I was through, I turned. The door to the tunnel was still open. "How does it close?"

Bastien searched the walls. "I don't see anything."

Demos fiddled with a golden filigree attached to the bookcase. It moved a little, and he turned it. The wall closed, and the bookcase settled into place. "You two would be horrible in an escape room."

"Wait," I said. "When did you go to an escape room?"

"Back in Branford. I used to go all the time with Ka—"

He stopped, unable to mention Kale's name or unsure if he should. Not mentioning Kale felt as if we were forgetting him. He'd lived. He was here. And he was taken away from us too soon.

"Kale always loved puzzles, didn't he?" I smiled at the memory of him trying to solve a crossword in Pop's Sunday paper.

Demos smiled, one that said he appreciated my comment. "That he did. I had to cheat to beat him...on occasion."

A smirk formed on Bastien's lips. "Only on occasion?"

"Okay, it might have been more than that." Amusement sounded in Demos's voice.

Bastien paced the floor in front of a display case. "Where are Doylis and my guards? They should have beaten us here. I better contact them. Excuse me." He pulled out his window rod and spoke Doylis's name.

I rested my back against the wall, wondering how much longer my legs could hold me up. With all the adrenaline rushing through my body earlier, I hadn't noticed the pain from where I'd bumped around in the flood.

Demos leaned against the wall beside me. "Good thing the wall doesn't need us to hold it up."

I chuckled, turning my head to face him. "Good thing. So how are you doing?"

"Better than you, I'm certain." He winked. "It really rots about Nick. It's hard to lose a friend."

"Yeah, it does, and it is." I flicked my gaze in Bastien's direction. "He doesn't look happy."

Bastien snapped the window rod closed.

I pushed off the wall. "What's wrong?"

"They've been detained," he said. "We better go on without them."

"Well, I guess we should call our escort then," I said and raised my arm and blew on the silver butterfly embedded in my wrist. It pulled from my skin and flew across the room. I hadn't really looked at the library until then. It was a beautiful room covered in polished, dark wood with gold-leaf accents and a domed ceiling made up of murals and decorated with elaborate filigree and white frames. The two-story, balconied-bookcases would make a great place to hide for an ambush.

"I'm going to find the loo," Demos said, crossing the room with confident, measured steps. "Don't leave without me."

When he was gone, Bastien came to my side and took my hand in his. "How are you faring?"

"I've been better."

He squeezed my hand. "This will pass."

"How are *you* doing?"

"Better now that you're not being tossed in a raging flood. Danger seems to find you at every turn."

I tilted my head to look at him. "Please never leave me."

A worried smile spread across his lips. "You couldn't chase me away."

My heart loosened as if it had been bound tight with hurt and fear.

He wrapped his arms around me and kept me in his embrace for a long while. His chest rising and falling against my cheek with each of his breaths was like a lullaby—soothing and relaxing. If I weren't standing, I'd probably fall asleep. I inhaled, his scent filling my nose. He had always smelled like fresh laundry and a hint of his cologne, but not now. There was no cologne, and he smelled of the herby soap that we all had to use in Greyhill.

"Now, isn't this sweet. All this love stuff makes me miss my new girlfriend." Demos leaned against one of the many display cases that held antique books as he studied his hands. "I wonder if she misses me."

"Do you mean Shyna?" I asked.

A grin pushed up his cheeks. "Yes. *Shyna*. Such a pretty name for a pretty bird."

Bastien exaggerated an eye roll at me; he wasn't hiding it from Demos.

Demos ignored the gesture. "So who does the tracer summon?"

"Me." Aetnae's tiny voice startled us.

"A book faery?" Demos pushed himself off the display case.

She landed on my shoulder and grabbed my wet hair. "Eww, what happened to you?" She wiped her hands on her skirt. "You smell rancid."

"Nice to see you, too." I frowned down at my wet, muddy clothes. "I could use a bath."

"Or a fire hose." Demos laughed.

Aetnae gave Demos a disapproving look before taking off from my shoulder. "We need to use the gateway book."

Demos turned to us and shrugged. "I thought it was funny."

Bastien shook his head at him. "I'm not certain this is the proper time for fooling around."

"I think it's the perfect time. It lightens the mood." I smiled at Demos.

Bastien called for the gateway book. When it didn't show up, he went off looking for it, and Aetnae zipped along with him.

I spun around, scanning all the beautiful woodwork and the many colored spines of books.

"What are you doing?" Demos's eyes followed me.

"There never seems to be enough time to explore the libraries."

Demos's eyebrow rose. "Did you hit your head?"

"I'm serious." I sighed. "We have this gift to transport ourselves to any library anywhere in the world. It's amazing, but we never get to enjoy it, to just sit in one and read books written ages ago."

"There was a time we could do that," he said. "Perhaps we'll be able to do it again."

When Bastien and Aetnae returned, we jumped to Chetham's Library in Manchester, England. Like a dark blanket around me, the gateway was chilly, and I shivered. My boots slid across the floor when I landed.

"This way." Aetnae zigzagged in the air as she led us down a small aisle.

On one side, books on the shelves were behind small, chained fences. The other side had dark bookcases that stood single file behind gates resembling saloon doors. Large wooden beams crisscrossed the white vaulted ceiling. It was like walking in history. The floorboards were old, the books fading with age. I wanted more time to be there. More time to explore and marvel at all the details that were hidden to first glances.

"You're taking us to Barmhilde," Bastien said, pulling my attention from the book stacks.

"I am," she answered and hovered in front of a dark wood paneled wall. "This library is nearly four hundred years old, and was one of the first to hide Mystiks from human persecution. Not many from the wizard havens come here. They're afraid of the creatures living in the coven. Call them heathens. Uncivilized without belief in a god. So I've heard. But in reality, they're just like us, but some have scary exteriors."

"That's sad," I said.

"It is," Bastien said. "Many of my friends are here. Some of the nicest beings you'll meet." His eyes slid to Demos. "There's no going back for you. The moment you sided with Gia, you became a fugitive like me, like her, and like everyone behind this panel."

"I'm aware of the cost." Demos nodded in my direction. "Without her, there is no hope. Arik will come around. He'll join us."

I doubted that.

Aetnae whistled and flew to my shoulder.

"What was that for?" I craned my neck to see her. Before she could answer me, the silver tracer flitted to me, landed on my wrist, and seeped back into my skin.

"If you need me, you know what to do." She dove off my shoulder and flew into the darkness of the library.

Bastien placed his palm on the door and spoke a charm different from the one we used to enter the wizard havens. The panel slid open, and we walked onto thick grasses that buried our boots. The panel shut, and we crossed the field to dense woods. We followed a tight trail to a small village. The many tiny homes were low and crumbling.

As we walked down the muddy road, the villagers' faces turned to watch. There were Mystik races I'd seen before and others that were new to me. We approached a man with a boar's face and tusks sticking out at the corners of his mouth. His large biceps flexed as he slammed an ax into a thick log.

The man spotted us and charged in our direction, ax in his hand.

I ignited a globe, not knowing which one would appear. A

white, frosty sphere balanced on my palm.

Okay. Don't freak out. Big scary men fall harder, I thought, trying to convince myself.

I waited for him to get closer, planting my feet shoulder width apart and drawing my arm back, ready to launch the globe.

CHAPTER TWELVE

Bastien placed his hand on my arm and lowered the globe. "He's not a threat."

The man dropped the ax and almost tackled Bastien in a hug.

"Ah, Renard, my dear friend." The man clapped Bastien's back. His eyes went to me, panting so hard the skin around his tusks waggled. "Who did you bring with you? Outsiders aren't welcome."

"You forget, I'm an outsider," Bastien said, his tone light.

The man laughed. It was more of a roar, really. "That is not entirely true. More like a savior. We owe our lives to you."

Bastien's smile was bright. "I'm not owed a thing. Gianna, this is Enoon." He rested his hand on my back. "And this is Gianna Bianchi McCabe and her guard, Demos."

Enoon smiled, placed his hand on his chest, and bowed.

I leaned against Bastien. "What's he doing?" I whispered.

"The Mystiks considered Gian their king. To them, you are like royalty."

My great-grandfather. He had fought for the Mystiks' rights.

"Not in all my days did I believe you would come," Enoon

said, straightening. "My father told me of this day, but I never thought it would be while I was alive. My life is yours. I am your servant."

"Um." My gaze went to Bastien then to Enoon. "No one needs to serve me. If there's a fight, we stand together."

He may have looked menacing, but his eyes were kind. "Such a young girl, but a brave heart."

If he knew how terrified I was, he'd be disappointed. I didn't know how to respond to him.

Bastien helped me out. "We need to find The Red," he said.

"He's here." Enoon inclined his head over his shoulder, gesturing toward the town. "Made a camp just outside the village. Follow me. I'll take you to him."

We traveled down a narrow dirt road full of potholes and jagged rocks embedded in the ground. It snaked around mud-caked buildings with thatched roofs. They looked poorly made, or they'd been put up in haste. A bell rang somewhere, followed by a woman's voice yelling out names. Somewhere from a road or two away came the clanking of metal against metal.

"How long has this village been here?" I asked, just as my foot landed in one of the potholes.

"Be careful, you'll turn an ankle," Enoon said. "Our village was destroyed by a horrible fire. We sent out distress calls, but no aid came. We lost everything. Many lives. This place is temporary until we can rebuild."

Bastien's foot slid across some pebbles, and he righted himself. "It was a beautiful village. The loss was devastating."

Enoon patted Bastien on the back. "Bastien here saved us. Without supplies from Couve, our people would have starved."

I gave Bastien a bright smile. "He's definitely a saint."

"A little too sure of himself for his own good," Enoon teased. "But with a heart bigger than Throgward Canyon."

Bastien gave me a side-glance. "She has no idea what Throgward is."

Enoon nodded at a woman working in her garden. "Then I will assure her it is quite vast."

The villagers stopped whatever they were doing to stare at us as we passed. But there weren't many of them outside. Two children resembling Enoon followed beside us. The girl looked to be about ten and the boy maybe six, but they didn't have tusks.

"She's too thin to be a Sentinel," the boy said.

The girl smiled up at Demos, a dreamy look on her face. "Do you have a girlfriend?"

"You don't stand a chance," I told her. "He's smitten with a bird girl."

"I didn't ask you," she said and sniffed the air. "You smell."

I must reek. I'd kill for a bath but doubted there was indoor plumbing here.

Enoon waved his hands at the kids. "Shoo. Off with you. Check on your mother. Make sure she doesn't need anything."

"Pa, do we have to?" the boy whined.

The girl gave him a stern look. "Of course we do. Get moving." The two ran off, heading back the way they'd come.

"Is something wrong with your wife?" I asked.

Enoon's face scrunched up in confusion. "What is this wife?"

"She means partner," Bastien answered.

"Aye. She has the sickness." Enoon kept his eyes in front of him. "Most of the village came down with the disease."

"I'm sorry," I said, wishing I could tell him I had the recipe for the cure. Nana had warned me that the curers in the covens might not have all the items needed to make it. And I didn't want to give him false hope.

In a field just outside of the village was a large camp with rows of pod-like tents. The murmur of voices hung over pitched canopies. Smoke rose from somewhere in the center of them. As we neared, one of the guards, a buff Laniar with silver hair, turned and darted down a row of tents. I recognized the other guards from when they'd attacked Nick and me in one of the libraries. One was rust colored with horns, and the other was stocky with a partially bald head and bushy sideburns.

Enoon stopped at a line of small rocks stretching across the road. "We wait here until The Red invites us in."

Bastien and I came up to stand on Enoon's right side, and Demos on the left. "Why must we wait?"

"It's the agreement we made. No entry without permission. He protects the village and we leave him and his band alone."

I saw his hair, the color of fire, just over the tents before he came into view. The Red. His long, scraggly hair had been cut short, and he no longer had a beard, which made his large snout less noticeable. He actually looked younger and kind of good-looking in a feral way. His broad shoulders and thick neck and arms seemed even larger than the last time I saw him during the big battle in front of my home in Branford.

He had helped us fight Conemar and his band of evil Mystiks. The Red had come for his sister, Faith, and we lost her that day. I felt a connection to him after that. We both loved Faith, and her loss was painful. I touched her pendant hanging from a chain around my neck, and it clanked against the locket with Pip's feather inside. It didn't belong to me. I'd have to give it to him soon, and I knew when I did, I would feel the loss again.

"Gia," The Red said, approaching. "You've made it."

His gang trailed him.

The smile on his face was strange to me. I was used to it having a menacing scowl. Possibly finding Faith and losing her had changed him. They had been separated for so long only to reunite briefly during the battle. I'd think he would be angry at the world.

"It's good to see you," I said, uncertainty coating my words.

He laughed. "No need to be afraid. This is your army."

What is he talking about? An army? Me? No. Not happening.

"My army? I don't think so."

"I see. You'll need time to get used to the idea."

"We appreciate you giving us refuge in your camp," Bastien interjected before I could completely freak out.

"It is our pleasure." The Red's eyes traveled over Demos. "You're a Sentinel. From Asile?"

"I am." Demos rested his hand on the hilt of his sword and eyed the men behind The Red.

"You needn't fear them," The Red said. "The others will be pleased to see you."

"What others?" Demos asked.

"Gia!" The sound of Jaran's voice almost made my knees buckle. My eyes went to where it originated. Jaran dashed across the field with Lei just behind him.

I covered my mouth with my hand, stopping a sob. They were alive. And they were here. All noises silenced. The voices around me sounded muffled. It was as if Jaran was moving in slow motion. I wanted to run to him, but my feet wouldn't take off.

Jaran finally reached us and caught me in a hug. I squeezed him back. "You're here. And alive." My heart swelled almost to bursting.

"I'm sorry if we scared you, but we couldn't send word." He released me. "You look horrible. What happened?"

"It's a long story," I said.

"Okay, tell me later." He winked.

Lei stopped in front of me. "Hullo, ducky."

Ducky? I hadn't heard her use that in a while. Not since she had her emotions subdued with a spell.

She wouldn't be the first to hug someone, so I dragged her into my arms. "I'm so happy to see you."

"I missed you, as well." Lei pulled away, her nose wrinkling. "What is that smell?"

"Wait—you seem normal."

She screwed up her nose again. "Define normal."

"Less drugged up," I said.

She raised her hand. The spell tattoo of a radiant lotus between her thumb and pointer finger was gone. "I decided it was better to feel something, no matter how painful, than nothing. And you are in dire need of a bath."

Demos put his arm around Lei's shoulder. "It's been maddening without you. I missed passing insults with someone."

She wrapped an arm around his back. "I think that's about the nicest thing anyone has ever said to me."

"Arik mentioned you two went missing from the library," Bastien said. "What happened?"

Jaran's smile slipped, and his face went serious. "We were on our way out of the library when a band of guards and Sentinels pulled up in vans. They had Carrig. He'd been beaten and bound."

My stomach twisted at the thought of Carrig being hurt.

"We decided to fight them," Lei said. "It didn't look good for us. We were outnumbered. My lightning globe took several of them down. That was before one of their Sentinels figured out he could stop the flash by stunning it."

Jaran slid a look at The Red. "If it weren't for The Red and his gang, we'd be dead now."

The Red adjusted his stance. "Actually, it was a book faery who alerted me."

Aetnae? Or maybe it was another one, but my bet was on her. She did more than protect books from humans and natural forces, the nosy little faery. And I was thankful for that.

Lei turned to The Red and said, "We would have lost Carrig if you hadn't been there."

"And our heads," Jaran added.

My spirits jumped. "Carrig's here? Where?"

The grim look that passed between Jaran and Lei deflated all the excitement inside me.

"What is it?" My voice sounded as shaky as my hands.

"He's not dead, is he?"

"No," Jaran said quickly. "He's injured but stable."

"I want to see him."

Lei shrugged Demos's arm off her shoulder. "Follow me. But first, you need a bath and some fresh clothes. Then I'll take you to him."

After I'd bathed, which was in an actual metal tub that several boys and girls filled with hot water, I followed Lei to Carrig's tent. The clothes Lei gave me to wear were epic warrior style. I decided to go with the long beige tunic top over leather pants, and boots. The rest of the gear I left on the mat in the tent assigned to me.

Carrig lay on a cot, blankets wrapped tightly around him.

I sat on the stool beside his cot and picked up his hand. It was warm and limp. His eyes closed, face slack, he looked peaceful. "Has he woken up since the attack?"

"No," Lei said. "He was out cold when we rescued him and has been this way ever since."

"Sinead is in a coma, too," I said. "They found her in the barn."

"That makes sense," she said.

I kissed his hand and placed it by his side. "Why do you say that?"

"When a Fey marries a human, their lives are connected. So when their human spouse dies, they do as well."

I could lose them both.

She lifted the flap to the tent. "I'll leave so you can have some privacy."

I nodded. "And Lei..."

She paused and looked at me.

"Can you get the others together? I have some stuff to tell you guys."

"Will do," she said and ducked out of the tent.

I rested my cheek on Carrig's chest. His breathing rocked my head. He was warm. Alive. "You have to get better," I whispered, absentmindedly twisting his watch repeatedly around my wrist. "Sinead needs you."

I swallowed the lump forming in the back of my throat.

"I need you."

I'd gotten close to my birth father and his wife while in hiding. Deidre probably didn't even know her parents were still alive. She was safe in Asile with Royston and Cadby. But now that the Wizard Council considered me a traitor, going to them wasn't an option. I just hoped Emily could get my note to Cadby—he had to get Royston to me. We needed to free the Tetrad and stop Conemar and whoever else he was connected to before they got control of the monster.

The Red ducked into the tent. He practically filled the entire space at the foot of the cot.

"Your Sentinels are gathered and waiting for you," he said. "What will you have my men and me do?"

I pushed myself off the stool. "Can you join us? I think you should know it all."

He nodded and lifted the flap, holding it for me to exit. "As you wish. I am anxious to hear what you have to say."

Several werehounds gathered around the tent, heads pointed in our direction. On all fours, their bodies came up to my waist. The largest one, and one of the medium sized hounds, had brown, matted fur. Two had black fur, and the smallest, gray. As I passed, each one sniffed my legs.

"They must've heard of your arrival." The Red petted a gray one that was smaller than the others. "We call them Gian's pack. They loved him so. Wherever he went, there were a few around protecting him. I suspect while you're here, they'll show you the same respect."

I held my hand out to a large, brown one, and he nuzzled it. Or at least I thought he was a he. It was hard to tell. "Do they ever change to human form?"

"Most choose not to. It's very painful and temporary."

"So they have a choice?" I reached out to another one, and she pushed her head against my palm.

"They do."

"Thank you," I said, my gaze touching each one before I continued following The Red.

A recent rain had dampened the ground. The mud slurped at my boots as I sloshed after The Red to a large tent. The group sat on pillows around a fire pit. Smoke snaked up from the logs and exited through a hole in the top of the tent.

Muddied shoes lined one side near the opening. I tugged off my boots, then found a seat on a pillow between Bastien and Jaran. The Red took the one between Lei and Demos.

I inhaled a deep breath and released it slowly. "Thanks for coming," I said and crisscrossed my legs. "I'm just going to jump in. Um…okay, so that day the hideout was attacked, Veronique and three Sentinels found me in New York. They tried to kill me but died before they could."

"Wait a second," Lei said. "Did you kill them all?"

"Yes, but by accident."

"They were attacking her," Bastien clarified, resting his elbows on his knees. "She defended herself."

A grin spread across Lei's face. "I didn't say it was a bad thing. I'm just impressed."

"Let her continue," Jaran said and gave me a nod. He had a way of sensing when I needed him. When Arik broke up with me, Jaran was the one who'd gotten me through the tough times.

"Only Uncle Philip knew where I was going." I swallowed. It was painful to say, not wanting to believe he had anything to do with Veronique's attack. "I'm not sure if he sent her or if he told the council and one of them did. But the recent murders of high wizards on the council are pretty suspicious, wouldn't you say?"

"What's more suspicious?" Bastien said. "The wizards who've replaced them have always been strong voices in favor of breaking from the Mystik League and segregating the covens and havens. All but Philip Attwood."

"He's neutral," The Red said. "He hasn't taken a side, which to me is more damning than showing your hand."

Bastien leaned back. "Then we must test his loyalties."

I shot him a startled look.

He rested his hand on my lower back. "It's the only way to be certain."

I knew it was the right thing to do, but I hated the idea of it.

"There's something else." I uncrossed my legs and stretched them out in front of me. "The Fey have a cure for the disease spreading through the covens. But the council sent an order halting its distribution. I disobeyed that order when I delivered it to Greyhill, and now the council wants to arrest me." My gaze went to The Red. "Are there any curers in the village? Nana sent me with the cure's recipe."

"The oldest and wisest curers are from Darmbilde. I'll take you to them after we're through here."

Demos cleared his throat. "You failed to mention that I am also on the wanted list. And you left out the part where Arik is enforcing the council's wishes and won't listen to reason."

It probably wasn't nice of me to flash him a glare, but I couldn't help it. "I was getting to that, but it's more complicated. I think I know Arik better than most."

Shit. Way to insert foot in mouth, Gia. I wanted to take that last bit back the instant it left my lips, worrying it would hurt Bastien.

But obviously it didn't because he said, "She does. And I put my faith in her judgment."

When I smiled at him, he gave me one back. "Arik will process what I told him, observe the council, and come to his own conclusion. And he'll realize what we all do now. The Wizard Council is trying to get rid of the Mystiks."

"What is your plan?" The Red's wide chest expanded with each of his breaths. Laniars resembled greyhounds, but he looked like one on steroids.

"I sent Emily with Arik. She'll deliver a note from me to Cadby. I told him there will be someone coming for Royston, Emily, and him next Friday." My intense stare on the fire made my eyes water, but I couldn't look up. I didn't want anyone to see the fear in them. "That gives me three days to gather what I need to release the Tetrad."

"All right, then, what are we doing?" Impatient Lei had also returned after the spelled tattoo was removed.

"Bastien will go with me. Demos will stay with Carrig. Jaran and Lei will return to Asile with an elaborate story of being kidnapped and escaping or something. Once there, take up a normal routine. Make sure Cadby, Royston, and Emily are ready. On Friday at two in the morning, The Red and his gang will library hop through the gateway books at the same time, to different places. All the activity will throw the Monitors into a frenzy."

Jaran sat up and nodded. "I get it. That's when Lei and I will jump with Cadby and the others. The Red's Mystiks will mask our departure. Brilliant plan."

"One problem." Lei looked doubtful it was brilliant at all. "What about Arik?"

I hadn't forgotten about him. The thought of what I would ask them to do turned my stomach. Could I do it if asked? No. How could I expect them to?

"Avoid him. But if he tries to stop you—" My emotions halted me, and I cleared my throat, not wanting to continue.

Oh, Arik. How did it come to this?

CHAPTER THIRTEEN

Lei's and Jaran's glares unnerved me, and I lowered my head.

The words sticking on my tongue tasted like poison. I wanted to spit them out, but I couldn't. Arik was one of us. Or, more important, he was like them—I was the outsider. He was their leader, and I was asking them to disobey him. I had loved him, I still cared deeply for him. And now every memory of us twisted my heart and made it difficult to breathe. His Sentinels' betrayal would destroy him.

Lei's stare bored into me. "I see. You want us to kill him?"

"*No.* I didn't say—"

"I won't harm him," Jaran cut me off. "We'll find a way to remove him from the situation. If it comes down to Arik or this mission, I will pick Arik."

It was Bastien's stare boring into Jaran this time. "You would sacrifice two worlds filled with innocents for one Sentinel?"

He didn't use Arik's name. It was his way of removing the intimacy from his question.

"If you can't get him away"—my voice sounded shaky—"try

to convince him to come to our side. If not, you have to stop him. But do whatever you can to not harm him."

The Red laughed and slapped his knees. "You all are missing the perfect way to get a boy distracted."

"You have a better idea?" Bastien asked. "Then tell us."

"Gia," The Red said. "He loves her. I saw the longing and concern in his eyes for her during that battle in Branford. Tell him she's in danger, and he will search for her. Send him on a wild goose chase. It's that simple."

Demos rubbed his chin. "That would work. Arik has it bad for Gia." He glanced at Bastien and said, "No offense."

"None taken. Then we're all set." Bastien stood and brushed his hands over his pants. "It's late, and I'm tired. We've been through a rough time getting here." His eyes went to The Red. "Thank you for your hospitality. The tents are quite comfortable." Bastien pushed the flap aside and walked out into the darkness.

What's up with that? I was pretty sure he was mad about what The Red and Demos had said about Arik and his feelings for me. Which just pissed me off.

The Red, then Lei and Demos, exited the tent.

Jaran reached his hand out to me. "Come on. My tent's next to yours. Want to walk together?"

"That would be great." I grabbed his hand, and he yanked me up to my feet.

"Splendid." He winked. "We have a lot of catching up to do."

After I'd put on the comfortable cotton nightdress someone had left on my bed, we sat on the thick mat in my tent, and I told him about Veronique's attack. The way she and the Sentinels with her had died. About how their battle globes became mine and that I had no control over which one I summoned. I finished with my time in the Fey realm. The part about Arik accusing me of treason and Uncle Philip possibly betraying me formed tears in my eyes. I wanted to tell Jaran everything. Unload it all so that it wouldn't weigh me down any longer.

And he listened.

He listened as only a true friend does, with sympathetic nods, his hands holding mine tight.

And when I'd finished, he pulled me into a tight hug, and I rested my cheek on his shoulder, tears falling from my lashes.

"I wish you hadn't had to face that alone," he said. "I believe you're right, though. We can't go to a professor of magic to help with your globes, not when we aren't certain whom to trust. Lei is a master, though. She could help you learn to control them."

There were wet spots where my tears had fallen on his shirt. I rubbed them as if it would make them dry. "Look at what I did. I'm sorry."

He inspected his shirt. "Don't worry about that. It's nothing."

I sniffled. "Thanks. You're so good to me."

"That's what one does for a friend." He released me. "You contacted Cole on my behalf when asked. We have, as you've said, 'each other's backs.'"

"Oh, right." I covered my mouth with my fingers. "He was worried about you. Said he'd wait for you and that he loves you."

Jaran adjusted on the mat, a wide smile spreading across his lips. "He just told you that? Not knowing who you were?"

I dropped my hand. "He knows me from school. Anyway, what does it matter how he told me? He said it."

The nervous tick in my lip shuddered.

"*Gia...*" He said it like Pop would whenever he suspected I'd done something wrong. "What are you hiding from me?"

It was time to come clean. Besides, I should have never told Cole how Jaran felt. "Okay. I may have said you loved him first, but you had to hear him. He was so sad and...and...and he did say he loved you, too."

Jaran grinned, his eyes dancing with excitement, until suddenly sobering. "I would have preferred for him to say it first." He picked at a loose thread on his shirt.

"What if he was waiting for you tell him? Someone has to say it first, or no one would say it."

He glanced up at me, tossing the thread to the floor. "Yeah, but what if he just said that because you told him I did?"

"Are you serious?" I yawned and rubbed my eyes. "He loves you. You should be ecstatic."

"I am, and you're tired." He placed his hand over mine. "Thank you for contacting him. It is nice to know how he feels and that he'd wait for me."

"He knows a good thing when he sees it," I said.

He watched his hand on mine. "I dream of running away with him. Fleeing the Mystik world and never returning. He spoke of us going to college together. Living in a studio apartment." There was sadness in his eyes when he glanced up again. "I want that dream."

"Why don't you? Just leave."

"Unlike you, I'm not shielded from the Monitors." His hand slipped off mine. "They'd find me and send me to the gallows under the Vatican. Besides, I won't leave you. I'll fight beside you until the end, Gia."

His words were a sledgehammer to the chest. I hated thinking of him in danger because of me. It would crush me if anything happened to him. But I didn't tell him that—he'd just argue with me—so instead I said, "I'm frightened."

"I know." He stared at something across the tent. "I am, too."

"I kind of miss high school and all its drama right about now." I yawned again.

"I should let you sleep." He started to get up, but I caught his arm, stopping him.

"Can you just stay until I fall asleep?"

"Of course." He stretched out on the mat.

"You're the best," I said and snuggled up to his side.

I don't remember when Jaran left my tent because he'd

waited until I was asleep. But the howl of the werehounds in the distance woke me. Or maybe it was because I was worried about Bastien. He'd been so quiet, and it wasn't like him to leave me behind.

Wrapping my blanket around me, I wiggled my feet into my boots, then eased out of the tent. It was still dark outside, but the moon, hanging low in the sky, provided enough light for me to see where I was going. It was a familiar moon, which made me wonder if the human and Mystik worlds shared the same one. Two werehounds were lying on the ground in front of the opening. At hearing me, their heads popped up.

"Good puppies," I whispered and then shook my head. "What am I saying? You understand me. I didn't mean to call you that. I know you're human…sometimes. I'm just going over there." I pointed to the tent across from mine.

I crept to Bastien's tent and slowly pushed open the flap and slipped inside. "Bastien, can I come in?"

"Is that you, Gia?" He sounded groggy.

"Yes."

He adjusted on the mat and created a ball of light on his palm. His dark hair was tousled and a little smooshed on the right side.

Lifting the blanket, he said, "Get in."

I tugged off my boots, tossed them aside, and crawled in beside him. He was bare-chested, and I caught a glimpse of his glorious torso—tanned skin, smooth and taut over rippling muscles. "Where's your shirt?"

"I never wear one in bed," he said and pulled the cover down over me. "You can't sleep?"

"No. You left so quickly and didn't even walk me to my tent." *Stop it. You sound insecure.* "I just wanted to make sure you were okay," I added, countering the other statement.

"I needed to get out of there before I ended up being the jealous boyfriend." His breath against my neck sent shivers across my skin. The ball of light left his hand and floated above us.

"How did you do that?"

"It's magic." There was a light chuckle to his answer.

Oh gosh. Of course, it's magic.

I rolled over to face him. "You were jealous?"

His left eyebrow rose. "You're enjoying my misery, aren't you?"

"Yep," I said, nodding.

He quirked a smile, and his blue eyes sparkled under the light. "I believe my ego needs a kiss."

"And exactly where is your *ego*?"

"Right here." He pointed to his lips.

I leaned over and gave them a quick kiss. "Better?"

The corners of his lips turned down in a deliciously exaggerated frown. "That's like licking a strawberry and not being able to take a bite. Definitely not satisfying at all."

I pressed my lips together, trying not to smile. "You're *definitely* demanding."

"Only when it comes to you. *To us.*" He pulled me to him, arms tight around my waist. "Now, I might be wrong, but I believe this is a proper way to heal an ego."

His lips pressed against mine, soft and tender with a hint of mint on them. Warm. I breathed in the smell of him: lake water, cut grass, and soap from his recent bath. His hands moved over me, up my waist and moving to my back. I slipped my arms around his shoulders and leaned into him as if I couldn't get close enough. Lightly, his tongue brushed against my lips before parting them and slipping into my mouth.

The light globe above us busted. Little lights flickered overhead before going out.

We kissed.

In the dark.

Hands and lips exploring each other.

I couldn't tell if the light moan came from me, from him,

or from both of us, but it excited me, and I just wanted to let go. Let him take me to a place where there were no nightmares. A place where we never had to leave each other. A place where only love existed.

As our kiss deepened even more than I thought it could, I wrapped a leg around his. There was a catch in his breath, and it tugged at something within me.

His moan turned to a growl as he pulled back.

"What's wrong?" I felt disappointment sink in my stomach.

He sighed, soft and deep. "I don't want to be that cliché where we make love before going on a dangerous quest in case one of us doesn't survive the battle. I want to have something to look forward to—something that carries us through whatever challenges lie ahead."

"I see." He had a point. I untangled my arms from his neck and fell onto my back. My head sank into the pillow, much like my disappointment.

He propped up on his elbow to look at me. "What are you thinking?"

What am I thinking? So many things. How scared I was about the future. How worried I was about Nick. And how frightened I was for Carrig and Sinead.

For a moment in his arms, caught up in his kisses, I'd forgotten all of that.

"Your brow is furrowing." He steepled his hand with mine.

"I'm just tired." I flipped onto my side, my back to him, and nuzzled my hands under my cheek. He scooted up behind me, draping his arm over my body.

"Sleep," he said, his mouth against the back of my head. "I'm here with you."

Moonlight seeped in through the thin membrane covering the only window in the pod-like tent. I watched the many unmoving shadows. Bastien's breath tickled my neck until I finally fell asleep.

• • •

When I awoke, Bastien was on his back, an arm resting above his head. He looked peaceful sleeping. I pressed my lips against his cheek, a soft and almost unspoken kiss. His dark eyelashes flickered slightly, but he didn't wake up.

I put on my boots, wrapped myself up in my blanket, and tiptoed outside. From the dozen or so fire pits in the camp, thin streamers of smoke rose into the early morning sky. I passed my tent and went to the second one from mine. It took several raps on the flaps of Lei's tent before she answered.

"Good morning, ducky," she said, her eyes taking in my appearance as she worked a braid into her long dark hair. "Why haven't you dressed? We need to get an early start today. Jaran and I will be off after breakfast, and so should your group."

I inspected my blanket-covered body. "I probably need another bath."

"Hmm…you could use the showers. They're heavenly." Lei held the flap open and nodded for me to enter. "What's bothering you that you came in your night clothes?"

"I need help with something." I ducked inside.

She puckered her lips, her head bobbing slightly as she listened to me explain the issues of my newly obtained globes. Her fingers kept weaving her hair into the braid, seemingly without thought.

"What do you think?" I finished. "Can you give me some pointers on how to control them?"

She clucked her tongue and grabbed a hair tie off the wooden table by the bed. After securing the braid, she dropped onto the large pillows in the corner of her tent. "Have you forgotten our globe training with Sinead? It's just as you learned with the pink one. You have to feel it in your core. Go deep inside yourself to pull it out."

I sat down beside her. "I know how to do that, and I've been pulling the globes out of me, but I have no control over which one makes an appearance."

"Oh," she said. "It's like you're a beginner. We have the first years ignite their battle globes by using a charm until they learn how to make them appear at will. It's much like creating a light one."

"The light one has a charm," I said under my breath.

The light one has a charm! Why hadn't I thought of that? I'd also had to speak a charm to create my truth globe before Lorelle, an evil faery, hit me with an ancient spell that destroyed it.

"Do you know any battle globe charms?"

"Yes, it's a formula. It's one of the first things they teach us at the academy." She stood. "Get dressed. We'll have breakfast and then try it out."

"First, I must go to the curers and give them Nana's recipe and my blood before anyone else dies from the disease." My foot was tangled in the blanket, and I stumbled a little trying to get up.

Lei chuckled. "Try not to hurt yourself on the way to your tent."

"Funny. I'll see you in about an hour." I faked a scowl, hiked up the blanket, and shuffled outside.

It was great to have the old Lei back. But I wondered how she was holding up. Undoing the charm that masked her emotions must've forced her to face the pain of losing Kale. I wasn't sure how to ask her about it, and it might make her relive his loss.

After breakfast, Lei took me to a clearing down a hill at the far side of the camp. My arm was sore, the many needle marks angry red against my skin. The curer had a hard time finding a good vein to draw my blood. It was just a matter of time, and the cure would be distributed to the sick in the village. If saving lives was treason in the eyes of the council, I didn't care what the cost, I'd do it again and again and again.

"All right, then," Lei said, turning to face me. "What was the charm you used to create the truth globe?"

"Mostrami la verità," I said in Italian.

"Show me the truth," she repeated in translation. "Interesting. It's nothing like the formula we learned. I wonder if that's because it isn't really a battle globe."

"Uncle Philip told me it wasn't a typical kind. My pink one was more for battles. Since I threw it at the trap door into the Somnium, it's turned into glass."

"That's strange," she said. "How does it work?"

My thoughts went to Veronique and how I'd used my globe on her. "It shatters against things or people, cutting them."

She tapped a finger against her chin. "Oh, that is very strange."

"Where should we start?"

"I suppose we can try the formula," she said. "The first part is *accendere il* and then you'd just tag on the type of globe you want to call. For instance, mine is lightning, so I'd add *fulmine.* Make sense?"

"Yeah, I guess so."

Most likely deciding I needed a visual, she held up her open hand and said, *"Accendere il fulmine."* A bright yellow globe swirled on her palm, bolts of lightning shooting over its surface. Her fingers closed, popping it, tiny sparks zapping the air before fading out. "Now, you give it a go."

Of course, nothing ever came easy for me. It took several hours before I had ignited the fire one by speaking the charm, *accendere il fuoco*, followed by the ice globe using *accendere il ghiaccio.*

I held my palm up and summoned the final globe, *"Accendere la stun."* A purple sphere sprouted from within my palm.

Lei, her arms crossed and her braid draped over her

shoulder, nodded her approval.

With each one I created, images of their owners' deaths haunted my mind. Even though none of them would've cared if they had killed me first, I still felt sadness at their loss. The idea that many more could die in whatever battles were ahead of us scared me. There was no avoiding it.

That's what happens during war. And we were at war.

I created the fire globe again and stared at it. "Veronique wasn't a Sentinel."

"You said." Her cold gaze at the mention of Veronique's name could freeze a continent. "I can't believe she fooled us. Being Conemar's daughter explains her evil heart."

The flames swirling in a ball on my palm hypnotized me, my eyes stinging with tears. "I can't get the image of her landing on that sword out of my head. Of it ripping through her chest."

Lei pulled me into a tight hug, and I encircled her in my arms. "As days go by, the memory will fade."

"I hope so."

"Though I wanted to be the one to end her life," Lei said, "to see her eyes glaze over in death, I feel much relief knowing she's gone. It hurts missing Kale. There are times when I hold my breath in hope that I'll never take another one. But I am weak. And I want to live on. To do something good in his name. He believed in you, ducky. His faith never wavered, and he would have gone to the end with you. So I will do it. For me. For him. But mostly for you."

"I don't want anyone else to die for me," I whispered against her shoulder.

"It is an honor to die for a cause," she said, releasing me. "It's getting late. I should take you to see Carrig before Jaran and I have to leave." She locked eyes with me, most likely to emphasize what she was going to say next. "I won't fail you in Asile. We'll get Royston and the others out."

With that, she trudged up the hill to the camp.

Each step up after her was difficult. My feet felt as heavy as my heart. I hated the thought of separating from Jaran and Lei, but Bastien and I had our own mission. After I'd shown him the leather canister I found in St. Patrick's Cathedral, we devised a plan. We had to retrieve blood from the closest living heirs of the original high wizards. With Royston, we had Asile's, but I wasn't sure we'd get the other six.

When we reached the curer's building, the door was propped open, and I went inside. The Red had Carrig moved from the camp to the curers so he'd be more comfortable. It smelled of lemons and fresh cut flowers inside. The walls were a bright yellow, and a large vase with purple asters sat in the middle of a warped wooden table. I stopped in the doorframe of Carrig's room. An older woman with a crooked back rocked in a chair beside him. It seemed like most of the curers I'd met resembled her—old and hunched.

"How is he doing today?" I asked, not sure if I should enter.

She stood and offered me her seat. "Come in, dear. He could use a friendly voice. He's been restless since last evening."

My heart hurt at hearing he hadn't been comfortable. I sat down, and she closed the door behind her. His hand felt cold as I took it in mine.

"I'm not sure what to say. Please wake up. You can't leave me." I choked on the emotions clogging my throat. "We just found each other. And Deidre needs you. Sinead will die if you do. You need to fight." I leaned over, resting my forehead against his hand. "We're running out of time. I have to go, but Demos will be here to protect you."

I leaned closer to his ear. "When I was a little girl, Mom would tell me a story about a girl knight and her love. Her description of him fits you perfectly. I think she missed you until the day she died. She'd said my father had green eyes just like mine. I've held the thought of you in my heart all these years. I love you. Please—" I swallowed hard. *"Please* fight for me. For Sinead and Deidre."

His eyes twitched a little when I kissed his hand and placed it gently on the bed beside him. I held my breath, hoping he'd open his eyes. But after a few minutes passed, it was painfully clear that he wouldn't.

CHAPTER FOURTEEN

My shoulders felt heavy as I trudged back to the camp. Someone was singing a song I didn't know. It was a male voice, and I decided to investigate.

The voice led me to the base of the cliff that ran south of the camp. Embedded into the marbled side were shower stalls with thick wooden doors. Bastien scrubbed his head, lather running down his arms and the little bit of chest I could see. He belted out another chorus of the song.

When he'd finished his front, he turned to rinse his back and spotted me.

I clapped my hands enthusiastically. "Bravo!"

A smile tilted his lips as he stepped out of the water spraying from holes in the marble. Steam rose around him like a halo. "If I knew I'd have an audience, I would have worn something other than my birthday suit." He grabbed a towel hanging over the door.

"I didn't know you could sing like that," I said, watching the muscles of his shoulders and biceps flex as he dried his hair with the towel. He pulled on a thick robe, pushed the door open, and headed over to me.

"You were gone when I woke up," he said, tossing the towel over his shoulder.

"Lei was training me with the globes." I met his steps. "And I stopped by to check on Carrig."

"How is he doing?"

"The same," I said.

He stared down at me, and I brushed a strand of wet hair from his face. As I lowered my hand, he caught it and pressed his lips against my palm. "I could get used to you being around often."

"Yeah, it's sort of nice." *Sort of? Really, Gia? Way to encourage things.*

A laugh escaped him. "Only sort of? I believe you're downplaying it." He pulled me to him and leaned over to give me a kiss.

A siren blared from the village, and we instantly pulled apart.

"What's that?" I asked.

"I'm not certain," he said and took off for the camp, clutching my hand and taking me along with him. "Get in your gear. I'll meet you at the path leading to the village."

"Okay," I said, panting. He let go when we reached the tents, and I sprinted to mine. I rushed around, putting the leather breastplate from the gear Lei had given me over my white linen tunic and strapping the sword and scabbard to my waist. There was a holster holding a dagger, and I snatched it up and belted it around my thigh.

Before leaving, I tucked the leather canister with the two vials and Gian's instructions into my boot, since there were no pockets in the clothes I wore. With brisk steps, I weaved through the tents and up the hill.

Lei, Jaran, and Demos met me as I approached the pathway.

"Where's Bastien?" Demos asked.

"Right here," Bastien said, hiking up to us.

We followed him through the narrow footpaths snaking

around huts and stucco buildings of various sizes. Through a break in a flowered hedge, I spotted a small Talpar woman. A litter of seven toddler pups ran around her legs. The mole-like feelers surrounding her nose moved frantically, like fingers grasping the air. Her eyes followed us as we passed, a frightened look on her face.

The Red towered over a group of his men. Beside him, I recognized Edgar. He had been a spy for the council. The last time I saw him, he'd become Uncle Philip's personal bodyguard. His blond, stringy hair was gone, and he now sported a buzz cut that made his hair look darker. The usual look of doom sat on his face. He was thinner but still ripped. Though he was probably around twenty, his face looked aged and rugged with the many cuts and bruises marring his skin.

"The council has blocked the entry into Barmhilde," Edgar was saying as we joined them. "They aren't too happy with you, Red. It isn't wise stealing Asile's imports from the human world."

The Red growled. "They left us with no other options. We must feed our own."

"Their restrictions will only get worse." Edgar's eyes went to me. "Gia, it's good to see you alive and well. But you should know there is a price on your head. You aren't safe in the covens or havens. Why are you here? The human world is your best bet at hiding."

"She's under my protection," The Red said, not giving me a chance to answer. "If anyone from Barmhilde tries to harm her or take her from here, I will have your head." His eyes went around the group.

"A plant I have here in the village alerted me of Gia's arrival in Barmhilde." Edgar surveyed the crowd. "There could be other spies here, and you wouldn't know them."

My eyes followed where his were going. "Shouldn't we speak somewhere more private?"

"I'm with Gia," Bastien said. "We must take this someplace else."

The Red nodded his agreement before speaking to the crowd. "It will get tougher the closer we come to war with the havens. We have plenty of supplies, thanks to Bastien Renard. We should be fine for several months, though we are on high alert. You all know what that means—prepare for an attack. Should you hear another alarm, get your children and your weak to the underground shelters."

"I will place a ward over the entry," Bastien said. "It should hold or at least delay an attack."

"I'd appreciate it." The Red lowered his voice, his eyes going to Bastien. "Come to the community fire pit in the camp after you place the ward. Gia and the Sentinels from Asile, follow me. Edgar, you may join us."

We trailed The Red to a fire pit surrounded by large boulders. "Sit," he said.

"Why aren't you with Philip?" I asked Edgar, who sat on a rock beside me.

He scratched his scalp. "Have you not watched the Mystik box?"

I crossed my arms in front of my chest. "I don't know what that is."

"It's like your human telly." Lei adjusted her seat on the slanted boulder. "Except ours is holographic."

Demos plopped down next to Jaran. "I actually prefer the human one."

Bastien arrived and took the unoccupied boulder next to me. He rested his hand on my knee, and I leaned against him. This small talk was grinding on my nerves.

"Okay, so what about the Mystik box?" I asked.

Edgar dropped his hand from his head. "Philip has been arrested and is being held in the gallows under the Vatican. It's been all over the news."

"What?" It was as if a wave knocked me over and an undertow pulled me into deep water. I couldn't breathe. "Why would they arrest a high wizard?"

"That's unheard of," Bastien added.

Edgar's face held no expression. He was good at concealing his emotions, which he probably learned during spy training or something. "He's been accused of assisting you and hiding you out in Ireland. They scryered him. Everything that was once hidden in his mind has been exposed."

"The attack on our hideout was the council's doing?" Anger burned over Lei's words, and flames sparked in her eyes.

"I'm afraid so," Edgar answered.

Demos shot to his feet. "They betrayed us."

Jaran popped up and wrapped an arm around Demos. "Calm down. We have to think this through."

"Why would they do such a thing?" The Red asked.

Edgar lowered his head. "With Philip out of the way, there is only one high wizard with a pure heart. He has been sickened by the Mystik disease, and his wife, Akua, oversees the Veilig haven in his stead."

Oh my God. Of course. It was right there the whole time.

"That's why they wanted to deliver the cure to the havens themselves," I said. "They didn't want the Fey handling it so that they could make sure Veilig's high wizard would die from the disease. That way the council could put someone else in his place. Did they replace Uncle Philip?"

"Yes, they have," Edgar said. "And the wizard believes in shutting off the covens from the havens, just as the rest do. The council has placed tighter restrictions on entering the havens."

I turned to The Red. "I need some of the cure. Bastien and I have to go to all the havens to get what I need to destroy the Tetrad. We'll start with Veilig and deliver the cure to them."

"We can't go to Asile now," Lei said.

I squeezed her hand. "You can. Arik is there. They don't know you were here with me. You just have to come up with an elaborate story about being kidnapped and escaping or something. Tell them you were on your way back to Asile. That you had a lapse in judgment—"

"She's right," Edgar interrupted. "Arik got off with just an infraction. He said that his judgment had been clouded. Lei and Jaran just have to say that Carrig persuaded them to go with him. And naturally, you followed your leaders."

"That should work," I said.

His judgment was clouded? Arik probably meant by me, but I never wanted any of this. Besides, it was his idea to go into hiding. I pushed down my anger. Staying calm and focused was important for getting through whatever was coming at us.

"Have you forgotten?" The corners of Jaran's lips lowered, worry reflecting in his eyes. "The door to Barmhilde is blocked. We're trapped here."

Crap. That's right. "Is there another way out?" I asked.

"There is," The Red said. "But unfortunately, it leads to the same library that the Asile guards are in."

A thought came to me. Kale had told me once that wherever a Talpar lived, they dug escape tunnels. It was their instinct to do it.

I looked to The Red. "I saw a woman Talpar in the village. Where there are Talpars, there are escape tunnels."

"This isn't my village," he said. "We are guests, and I wasn't aware of a Talpar living in Barmhilde. We shall pay a visit to this woman. The rest of you pack what you need. You'll leave straightaway."

. . .

Bastien and I went with The Red to the Talpars' home. The woman eased the door open and peered through the crack. "What is it? I have pups to feed."

The Red towered over her. "We need to use your secret tunnel."

Examining The Red through thick glasses, she snapped, "Go away. I have no knowledge of this tunnel you speak of."

"I know where it is, Mummy," said a little boy pup attached to her leg. "We use it to visit Memaw."

She shooed the pup away. "You know I'm not allowed to tell of its whereabouts."

The Red growled before saying, "The survival of all Mystiks depends on it. Which means your life and those of your pups."

She picked up the pup who'd found his way back to her leg, her eyes going from The Red to me, then to Bastien. "Oh my," she said and clapped her flat, paddle-like hands. "You're him. Son of Renard."

"I am," Bastien said.

"Because of you, we eat." She put the pup down. "I will do what I can to help you. Come inside. My husband has maps. Possibly one of them can aid you."

The three of us barely fit inside her small home; the ceiling was so low, The Red had to hunch over. In the middle of the stack of maps, we found one of the tunnel system. All the entrances were marked with a red cross and the tunnels labeled with the name of the connecting library.

The Red rolled up the map. "This will do. Let's return to camp, eat something, then you can be on your way."

After a quick meal of meat, potatoes, and bread, we followed the map to the entry into the Talpar tunnels. I slung over my shoulder the strap to a tiny leather pouch one of the curers gave me. It held a few prepared cures along with the recipe to make more. The curers had made batches of the liquid and administered it to the inhabitants of Barmhilde. All around the village, the sick were getting better.

The map brought us to a large boulder just outside the village. It took Bastien, Demos, and Jaran together to roll the massive rock over. Underneath it was a dark hole crudely dug into the ground.

I hugged Demos. "Stay safe. And thanks for Carrig. I mean, for staying here with him."

"You worry about yourself," he said, a little misty-eyed. "We'll be fine here."

The Red clapped Demos's back. "I'll keep him out of trouble."

By the look on his face, I could tell Demos was holding his tongue about what The Red had said. Demos may be overly cocky, but he would never be careless. I smiled at him. "We'll see you in a few days."

"Until then." Demos backed up, sliding a disdainful look at The Red.

One by one, we lowered ourselves into the tunnel—Edgar, Bastien, Lei, Jaran, and me. The walls were packed tight, and roots ran in and out of the cracks. Edgar studied the map while I held a light globe up behind him.

He nodded to one of the four entries into the crevice we were in. "This way."

We had to duck-walk through the tunnels until we came to places where we could straighten. My thighs and back ached.

We came to a connecting tunnel, and Edgar stopped. "All right. This is the one. Lei and Jaran, just follow this tunnel to the end. It won't be fancy like the haven tunnels. You most likely will have to move something manually. Like the boulder in Barmhilde, or possibly a bookcase."

Bastien and I flattened against the wall for Lei and Jaran to pass. Jaran turned to me. "Don't do anything careless," he said. "I rather like you, most days."

I smirked. "Yeah, I kind of like you, too."

The pain of watching them disappear into the tunnel was almost too hard to bear. I hoped Arik wouldn't suspect them. That the council wouldn't do something to them for hiding out with me. But I told them to say Uncle Philip had ordered them into hiding, and a Sentinel never went against orders from their high wizard. Just like Arik, they had to follow them. No questions asked. Just do what they were told.

Bastien adjusted his backpack. "Come on," he said, placing his hand on my back, his touch gentle and caring. He knew it was tough for me to part ways with Jaran and Lei—they'd become more than just friends. We'd fought battles together, counted on one another for survival.

They'd become my family.

I continued following Edgar while Bastien followed me. Though the tunnel was cool and damp, squat-walking exerted so much energy, sweat dampened my hairline and dripped down the back of my neck. It smelled like a cattle farm.

Our heavy breathing was the only noise, and my thoughts kept racing. Everyone I loved was in danger. Mistakes could cost lives.

And then it hit me.

My gasp caused Bastien to grab my hand. "What's the matter?"

"If Uncle Philip was scryered, the council might know where Pop is hiding."

"Keep moving," he said, letting go of my hand. "When we get to Veilig, I'll send the Couve Sentinels to move him."

"That won't work." My thoughts went to how Arik had refused to disobey orders. "Helping us would go against the council." The farther we went, the tunnel narrowed and the ceiling lowered, and I suddenly felt claustrophobic in the tight space.

"They are loyal to me because we share the same beliefs."

Bastien had to turn sideways to avoid rubbing his shoulders against the walls. "When Augustin replaced my father as High Wizard of Couve, it became clear the council's agenda was shifting. Augustin has always been on the side that's for separating the wizard havens from the Mystik covens. After the high wizards of the other havens died, their successors aligned themselves with Augustin."

"Except Uncle Philip," I added. "And now he's in danger. What will the council do to him?"

"They will execute him after his trial," Edgar answered my question, his words rough on my ears.

My world suddenly felt like a wet painting. All the different shades ran down the canvas, mixing together and becoming mucky. The fear of losing Uncle Philip took all the color out of me.

"When will they try him?" My voice cracked over the question, and Bastien grasped my hand.

Edgar stopped at the end of the tunnel and searched the area. "A few weeks. Possibly a month."

"Above your head." Bastien pointed to the ceiling.

"Ah, a hatch." Edgar wiped the sweat from his brow with the sleeve of his shirt. He grabbed the rusty handle, eased it open, and peered through the crack before climbing into the library.

I hefted myself up after him. Bastien came out next and closed the hatch. I straightened, taking in the beautiful sight of the library. The walls were a sunny yellow with white molding edging them. Three-story galleys, holding bookcases behind railings of intricate patterns, surrounded us. There were many tall, magnificent stained-glass windows, along with a stunning stained-glass dome over the center of the library.

I stretched my back and cracked my neck, inhaling the familiar smell of old books and imagining what the library would look like in the light of day. It would be heaven to explore the shelves and discover what titles they held.

"Where are we?" I asked.

"The public library in Port Elizabeth," Bastien said. "In South Africa."

Edgar wasted no time and quickly crossed the carpet to a bookcase. He pulled books in and out, seemingly in a pattern. The case inched open, and he stepped inside.

It immediately started closing, so Bastien and I slipped through. The tunnel to the haven was beautiful. I stood there, my mouth gaping. There were veins of gold and silver shocking the sandstone walls. I could almost see my reflection in the polished ground.

Bastien slipped his hand into mine.

"It's so beautiful," I said.

"Stop gawking. We aren't tourists," Edgar growled, stomping down the tunnel. "We haven't all the time in the world."

"Someone's grumpy," Bastien whispered to me as we plodded after him.

Nearly an hour later, we came out of a sandstone building onto a beach. The sea was so blue it sparkled like glass under the sun. The tops of buildings peeked out of the water, waves smacking their roofs. It looked like there was an underwater city just beneath the surface.

"What is that?" I raised my voice to be heard over the crashing waves.

Bastien turned his head to see where I was pointing. "It's the Aqualian city. The sea is named after them." Just as he finished, a large whale-like animal with a long, flat nose and whip-thin tail jumped the waves. A bald man with blue skin and gills instead of ears rode its back, clutching a silver chain fastened to its neck. "That's a wallow. There are many unusual, creatures in the Aqualian Sea, some dangerous. For safety, the inhabitants of Veilig only swim in the bays."

"Oi," Edgar yelled, waving his hands over his head. "This way."

Just behind him, massive cliffs soared into the sky. On the very edge of the highest one was a fairy-tale castle constructed from sandstone, complete with turrets and spires, and a village of matching buildings spread out behind it. Edgar made it to the base and headed up the stone steps leading to the top.

"We're climbing those?" I stopped and glanced around. "Isn't there an elevator or bucket with a crane?"

Bastien laughed before ascending the steps.

I breathed out a long sigh and headed after him. "But it's such a long way up."

A gust of wind hit the back of my hair, so strong it whipped my ponytail across my face. Suddenly a claw wrapped around my waist and lifted me off the steps.

Bastien caught my leg. "Gia!" There was desperation in his voice.

My body jerked up, and his grip tore away. The huge bird that had snatched me flapped its golden wings, carrying me higher into the sky.

I grasped the claw and screamed.

CHAPTER FIFTEEN

The side of the cliff sped past as the bird as large as a glider soared up, holding me in its claw. It hovered over the flat surface at the top of the cliff. Somewhere a high-pitched whistle sounded; the bird chittered and lowered me to ground, my feet barely touching when it let go of me. I stumbled forward and landed on my hands and knees.

I bent over, trying to catch my breath. My leather breastplate tightened with every heavy rise of my chest. It was like time halted and the world moved slowly around me until Bastien and Edgar made it up and rushed to me.

Bastien dropped down, panting. "Are you hurt?"

I held up my hand to signal that I wasn't able to respond.

"Are you all right?" Bastien rested his hand on my back.

"I'm good." I pushed myself up and tottered on unstable legs.

Edgar dunked his head in a modest three-tier fountain, then rubbed the water across his buzz-cut hair. I hobbled over, plunged a cupped hand into the water, and splashed my face, welcoming the coolness.

Bastien dumped two hands full over his head. "Ah, that feels splendid."

"My apologies if Kiti scared you." A woman's soft voice came from behind us.

I whirled and came face-to-face with Akua, the High Wizard of Veilig's wife. We had met briefly in Asile when the Wizard Council interrogated Bastien and me about Conemar's disappearance.

"Kiti?" I looked up to the sky.

"She meant no harm," Akua said. "All she wanted was to give you a ride up."

Her kind brown eyes went from me to Bastien. She was beautiful in a cream linen sheath, her black hair tied in intricate braids that wrapped around her head. A thin crystal whistle hung from her neck by a silver chain.

"Bastien, I'm delighted to see you." She smiled, her lips turning up slightly at the corners and pressing a dimple into her left cheek. "And Gianna. You take a risk coming here. There is a price on your head. We must get you out of sight immediately."

Edgar shuffled over. "We shouldn't stay long. If we were found, there would be tough consequences for your haven."

Akua inspected him. "And who are you?"

"Philip's guard," he said. "He had me escape Asile before he was arrested."

The kindness on her face before had turned into a scowl. "Why have you come to my haven? We have enough troubles to add more to our situation. My husband is on his deathbed. The council is pushing my people to remove Enitan as high wizard and appoint a new one. Half my Sentinels and guards have fallen ill with the disease. We haven't the strength to aid you."

"But I can help you," I said and removed the pouch from around me. "I brought the cure. My nana is a Pure Witch. She gave me the recipe. Your curers can make enough to help your people."

"How do I know it will work?" The look on her face said

that she hoped it would. "It could be poison."

Bastien took a few steps forward, his stare on her. "Because it was tested."

"The council sent word that there wasn't a cure."

"They lied," I said.

"Do you mean Conemar or the council?" she asked.

"I believe the two may very well be in agreement with each other," Bastien said.

Akua uncrossed her arms. "That is my belief, as well. You have an ally in Veilig. Follow me."

She brought us inside the castle. The rooms were decorated with silver and gold accents, cream-colored furniture, flowy, pale drapes, and colorful walls. She ushered us into one of the rooms facing the sea. Statues rested in every corner of the room. A huge fireplace made out of shells and pearls dominated one of the walls. Across from it was a wide bed that could fit six people in it. Tucked under the covers slept a large man with gray streaking his black hair, and skin the color of ash. He twitched and groaned.

It was like watching a gazelle cross the room as Akua went to the man. She leaned over and kissed his cheek. "My poor lion. He used to be fierce, but gentle. His people love him. He treated them with such kindness. It breaks my heart to see him like this." And she kissed him again. "Enitan, my love, you will be well soon."

Edgar fell back into a chair by the hearth, finally showing signs of being tired.

I removed a syringe and a small bottle of the cure from the pouch and joined Akua and Enitan. After assembling the shot like Nana had shown me, I inserted the needle into Enitan's arm and administered the pink-tinged liquid. Enitan closed his eyes, and I joined Bastien on a small settee across from Edgar.

Akua pulled on a golden rope near the door, and several minutes later, a man with a stern glare, dressed in colorful clothes, entered the room.

She handed him the pouch. "Take this to the curers. It holds what they need to stop the disease."

"They'll need my blood, too," I said.

Her gaze shifted to me. "You should eat. Gain strength before giving your life's essence away."

"You don't have to go to any trouble," I said. "It only takes a few drops of blood for a hundred cures."

Edgar gave me the stink eye and rubbed his stomach.

"I am starving, though," I added.

"Very well." She nodded to the man, and he promptly left the room.

Akua pulled the drapes across the room, shutting Enitan off from us. She had fish, fruit, cheeses, and breads delivered, and we ate around the small table in front of the hearth. I gobbled down everything but the fish. Not that I had anything against fish, but I preferred them in a tank rather than on my plate.

"Why is there a party going on in my room?" Enitan's voice came from the other side of the drapes.

The man dressed in colorful clothes dragged the drapes to the other side of the room.

Enitan struggled to get up.

Akua's face lit up. "Enitan!" She rushed over and helped him sit up against the pillows. "You look better," she said, relief sounding in her voice.

He struggled to raise his arm, resting his open palm on her cheek. "My love, I'm so sorry I worried you."

It was as if my spirit elevated to the ceiling at watching Akua and Enitan. Just a little of my blood had saved him.

"Don't exert yourself," Akua urged.

"I feel well." He absentmindedly rubbed his arm where he'd received the shot. "Food smells good. I'm famished."

"I'll get you a plate." Akua crossed the room to the table and piled bread and cheeses on a small plate. There was a hop to her steps as she returned to him and sat on the bed. Lovingly, she fed him small bite after small bite.

I wiped my mouth with one of the cloth napkins on the table and went over to them. "I'm sorry to interrupt, but there is something I need."

Enitan stopped chewing. "What is it?"

"I must have a drop," I said with a shrug, "maybe two, of blood from the Fifth Heir's closest living descendent. It's needed to stop Conemar from controlling the Tetrad. I can't tell you any more than that. You'll have to trust me."

"And why should I put all my trust in you?" He coughed, and Akua lifted a glass of water to his lips.

Edgar shot to his feet and wiped his mouth with the back of his hand. "She's the presage. Not to mention she just brought your people the cure. You'd be dead by tomorrow without her."

Enitan pushed the glass of water away from him and looked up at Akua. "Is that true?"

"It is," she said.

He studied my face for a long while before saying, "All right. The oldest living heir of the Fifth is my great-grandfather. He's nearly five hundred years of age. Lives in the home of the prophets. Koluka will bring you there."

"Thank you," I said. "Can she...or he...take me to the curers first? They need some of my blood for the cure."

"She will bring you there first." Akua rose from the bed and tugged on the golden rope three times. Before, she had only tugged on it once to summon the man. The number of times must have been a code for calling a specific person.

Not too long after, a young girl of about thirteen came through the door. Her eyes stopped on Enitan sitting up in the bed, and her face brightened. "Papa, you are well?"

"I am."

She ran to the bed and hugged him. "We were so worried."

"I need you to take our guests to Oupa," Enitan said.

Koluka faced us. "When you are finished, I'm happy to do so."

"We're done," I said.

A small growl came from Edgar, and I turned. He bent in front of the table, shoved in several bites of fish, and then washed it down with water.

"Don't let us keep you," Bastien said to him. "It's not like we're trying to save the worlds."

"You're a regular clown, aren't you?" Edgar glared at Bastien and placed his fork on the plate.

Koluka held the door open. "I'll be back soon, Papa."

"Make sure to give them cloaks," Akua said. "Keep to the smaller paths. Their presence in Veilig must go unnoticed. There's a price on Gia's head. We don't want anyone alerting bounty hunters."

The curers were in a vast room on the lowest floor of the castle. After the curers had taken the needed amount of blood from me, Koluka gave us cloaks and took us out a side door. The cloaks were finely crafted. Mine was a dark hunter green, Bastien's black, and Edgar's brown.

The village was just as amazing as the castle. The homes were made out of the same stones that were in the tunnel. The silver and gold veins running through the sandstones glistened in the sunlight. The multicolored cobblestone pathways were arranged into beautiful designs—birds, unicorns, and sea creatures.

A man with a goat following him passed. I lowered my head so the hood of my cloak would hide my face.

"Hallo," he said.

"Good day, Rada," Koluka responded.

We followed her along the narrow, winding paths cutting through the village. Beautiful flowers of various colors crowded inside the hundreds of pots adorning the front doors of the homes. It was like walking in paradise.

Koluka stopped in front of a larger home with a wide golden gate. She tugged on a rope at the side. Many bells hanging from a cord that stretched from the gate to a tall, thin door chimed.

A short man rushed to the gate wearing a bright robe made out of fabric the colors of the sun and sky. "Koluka, you brought her. I am so delighted to meet the presage. Hurry, hurry." He waved us inside. "The windows have eyes, and the trees, ears. It isn't safe for you in Veilig, Gianna." He turned to Koluka. "You may go. Thank you for escorting our guests."

She beamed. "I was happy to do it. It's like a secret mission. So thrilling. Goodbye, Gianna, and you others." With a tight turn, she darted down the passageway.

"Good day," Bastien called.

"Thank you," I added.

Edgar entered. His muscled shoulders almost brushed against the doorframe.

I leaned close to Bastien. "Is it me, or is Edgar rude? He's always going in first."

Bastien stood aside to let me pass. "He does that because he's a guard, to make sure there are no dangers. No doubt, he had promised Philip he'd protect you."

"Oh. Guess it's just me, then." I crossed over the threshold. It was a bare place with hardly any decorations or furnishings.

Once inside, I lowered my hood and turned to face the man. "I'm here—"

The man held up his hand. "I know why you are here. For the Fifth heir. Follow me."

"Did someone call and tell you we were coming?" I asked.

"Call?" His little legs could sure move fast. I had to sprint-walk to keep up with him in the long hallway. "That is a curious word. In a way, I suppose she did call me through my dreams. Athela. She has been visiting you as well, I presume."

"Wait. She comes to you, too?" I'd felt a loss after the last dream. I was pretty sure she was gone.

"I am a prophet. Many spirits come to me. You sound sad." He opened a door at the end of the hall. "There is no need. She is still with you, even if she doesn't visit your dreams any longer."

"What did she tell you?"

"Showed me," he corrected. "What you saw, I have seen."

I wanted to know more. After all, he was a prophet. "Have you seen our future? Do we win the battle? Stop Conemar, I mean."

"What I see are possible outcomes. It depends on the choices you and those around you make whether good wins over evil or not. I will say that you must put aside your emotions at the end. Think with your head. Take a life without hesitation. For in that moment, you could lose it all."

My hands were shaking at his words, and I fisted them. Thinking where this quest led to scared me, but I couldn't stop. I had to go on for Nick and the others.

"Who goes there?" A low, guttural voice came from the corner of the room. An extremely old man with a crop of curly gray hair on his head and a beard sat in an overstuffed chair. Thin, wrinkled skin hung from his arms and face. His murky eyes shifted in our direction.

"Taavi, the girl I told you about has come."

"Good. Let's get this over with so I can return to my nap." He grabbed a knife from a plate of fruit and cheeses on the table beside him.

Is he going to cut himself? Yep. He just did.

Blood beaded from the red line on his palm where he'd dragged the knife across.

"A pushpin or needle would have worked." I removed the canister from my boot and took out the empty vial. "Can you hold this?" I handed the canister to Bastien.

I held the glass vial under Taavi's shaky hand.

It took some effort for him to keep his arm up. But even so, he squeezed his hand as tight as he could, letting his blood drop from the cut and into the vial. Rada wrapped a thin piece of cloth around Taavi's wounded hand.

Taavi lowered his arm and leaned back in his chair. "Now, go," he said. "I've not had this much excitement since the Fey Follies in nineteen twenty-two."

"Thank you," I said, pulling the hood back over my head. "What you've done here today could save billions of lives."

He clicked his tongue and hissed, "What do I care? It won't save mine." His eyes closed.

Taavi wasn't fooling anyone. I could feel he did care, or why would he so eagerly cut his hand?

Bastien passed me the canister. I slipped the vial inside and secured the cap over it before slipping it back into my boot.

Rada led us outside and took us down several long staircases and under footbridges. We didn't go unnoticed. People stared curiously at the three hooded figures following the prophet in the colorful robe.

He abruptly stopped. "Quickly, in here." He waved his arm to steer us into a covered alleyway. The round cobblestones were weathered and uneven. Arched doorways lined each side of the path with potted flowers between them.

"What is—?"

Rada's hand shot up like a crossing guard, cutting off my question. He opened a blue door and waved us in.

Edgar dashed in, Bastien and me on his heels. In a ready-to-fight stance, Edgar searched the room. There were shelves and barrels around the walls and brooms stacked in a corner. It had to be the back room of a shop of some sort.

"What happened back there?" Bastien asked.

Rada cracked open the door and peered outside. "I spotted some Sentinels in council gear."

Edgar snapped his head in Rada's direction. "Council

gear? What are they doing here?"

"The council has drafted all retired Sentinels under the age of forty back into service." Rada opened the door wider. "Stay here and I'll come back when the coast is clear."

A woman came through the door leading to the shop. She spoke excitedly in a lyrical language unfamiliar to me. Rada answered her back, and she nodded then returned to the front of the store.

"She will warn you if any of those Sentinels come." He closed the door behind him.

I bit my thumbnail as we waited for his return, my thoughts running like water in a cracked dam—rushing and not stopping. Were the men looking for us? Did someone tell them we were here? What would they do to us if we were caught? I grabbed the side of my head, hoping to silence my mind.

Bastien leaned against my side. "Are you all right?"

"Headache," is all I said.

The door opened, and I practically jumped to the ceiling, my elbow knocking against the shelf, causing the bottles to rattle.

Rada's head poked inside. "We're clear. Keep up and don't fall behind." He rushed down the alleyway, and we charged after him.

Through more alleyways we ran, then over a bridge and finally to a tunnel hidden behind some bushes and cut into the side of the cliffs.

"The tunnel here is more rustic than the one you arrived in, but it's safer." Rada moved a fake bush from the entrance.

"A Talpar tunnel," I said.

"It is." He leaned the bush against a boulder.

"We appreciate your assistance," Edgar said before disappearing through the carved-out entry.

"When the time comes," Rada said to me, "Veilig will stand with you. On your quest for the other heirs' blood, be careful.

Santara is in upheaval, Mantello cannot be trusted, nor can Esteril. Tearmann is our ally. With Philip removed, I'm not sure who you can trust in Asile. But I have written a name for each haven." He handed me a rolled piece of parchment. "Seek them out, and they will aid you. Go as thieves in the night and keep hidden."

"Thank you." I stuffed it into my boot with the canister.

"What have you heard from Couve?" Bastien asked.

Rada's eyes held empathy. "Augustin has appointed Odil as his commander. The French Sentinels took your mother to the Shelter, and she is safe. Your people suffer laws and restrictions Gareth never imposed on them."

Gareth. He was Bastien's father and the High Wizard of Couve before he was murdered when Conemar's little army attacked the haven. Odil had fallen in love with Veronique and had joined Conemar's cause because of her. Hearing about his mother and people suffering had to be difficult for Bastien.

But in spite of his pain, Bastien smiled. "I am grateful to you. Please extend our gratitude to Enitan and Akua. It is my hope that the troubles in the Mystik world won't lead to war."

"It is my hope, as well." Rada bowed and watched us enter the tunnel.

With the mud packed walls surrounding me, it felt like being in a grave. Not that I knew what being in one felt like, but I assumed this would be it, except tighter. Hours passed, and it felt as though we'd never arrive at the end.

The closer we got to Mantello, the louder the city just above our heads sounded. Exposed pipes on the ceiling of the tunnel shook and rattled.

A screeching groan traveled through the tunnel, followed by a loud crack. The walls shook, chunks of dirt sliding down the sides. A gush sounded behind us, and I turned. A strong current of water rushed in, knocking us off our feet.

CHAPTER SIXTEEN

Tumbling in the rushing water, mud caking my face and stinging my eyes, I tried to grab on to one of the roots sticking out of the wall, but came up short. I reached out again and caught one, my grasp slipping. My knee slammed against the ground and pain shot up my thigh. Another root brushed against my other hand, and I grabbed it, my body banging into the wall.

Bastien snatched one beside me. "Use the roots to scale the wall," he yelled over the rushing water. "It isn't far to the other tunnel."

The knot from the rope securing the cloak around my neck dug into my throat. I grabbed root after root, my boots sliding down the wall as I tried to get a foothold. Edgar made it to the other tunnel. We were moving upward so the water sped down the passage going the other way.

When I reached him, Edgar grabbed my arm and tugged me to safety and then turned back to help Bastien. Drenched, muddy, and cold, I leaned against the wall and gulped in the dank air.

Bastien bent over and grabbed his side. "That was

unfortunate. Are you hurt?"

"If I get swept away by one more flood"—I took a breath—"I'm giving up."

"A water main must have broken," Edgar said, wiping the mud from his face. "Let's find an exit before something else happens."

After recovering from the wet and wild ride, we followed the Talpar tunnel to a nearby exit. We climbed up a poorly constructed ladder and through a manhole into the city. Water and mud dripped from my hair and clothes, and I loosened the cloak's tie around my neck. Edgar shut the manhole cover. The tiles on it were arranged in a beautiful mosaic design.

We were in an alley. The back doors on either side of the road were different sizes and colors. I'd been to Mantello before with Bastien and Nick. We'd come for a trial and spent an evening at the festival there.

Edgar had many allies in the haven. He actually had them all over the Mystik world.

"This way." Edgar traipsed down the uneven cobblestones. By the slump of his shoulders and the shuffle of his feet, he was tired. We were all exhausted, actually, and I wondered if we could keep going, but then he added, "There's an inn down the way. We can get cleaned up, have a meal, and get a good night's sleep."

Bastien draped his arm around my shoulder. "What's on your mind? The night we spent here, I'm assuming."

I decided to play coy. "No. Just how muddy you are. You look like a sewer rat. And you're not always on my mind, you know." My lip twitched.

"Ah, your little quirk gives you away, *mon amour.*"

"Aren't you two adorable." Edgar's whisper held disdain. "Maybe you can save your lovey-dovey crap until we are safely out of sight and you're a bit cleaner."

Bastien removed his arm and walked silently beside me.

We took turns sneaking glances at each other. He'd smile, and I'd smile back. Yeah, he knew I was thinking about the night we spent in Mantello. And I was happy that he knew, because that meant he was reliving it, too.

Lights flickered behind curtained windows. Our boots clacked across the cobblestones, echoing off the tall slanted buildings. The alley was dark, except when we passed under the bloom of a streetlamp here and there.

We came to the end of the rows of homes. Edgar eased out into the adjoining road and glanced left, then right, before waving us over. He rushed across the cobbles to a dilapidated building just down the way. The name of the place flashed over the top of the building. Nightfall Inn. A sign in the door said only Mystiks were welcomed there.

Edgar opened the door and rushed us inside. To the right was an old-looking tavern filled with various creatures from the Mystik covens. On the other side, there was a reception counter with a wiry boy wearing thick glasses behind it.

"We only have one room available this evening," the boy said, not bothering to look up from the book he was reading.

"One will do," Edgar said, which made me shoot a startled look at him.

The boy thought it was odd, too, because he looked up from the page he was on and puckered his lips. "You're filthy. We don't let your kind stay here."

"What?" I snapped. "Our kind? That's pretty rude."

Bastien stepped in front of me. "We're tired from our travels. We obviously had an accident and need to wash."

"Did you happen to see the sign outside?" the boy asked. "Only Mystiks at this inn."

Edgar approached the counter and dropped a wet coin purse on it. "We will pay you well. And I know the owner. You might mention Edgar needs a place to stay tonight."

The boy harrumphed and walked to the door behind him.

He had a tail, and I hadn't noticed it before, but he also had a very hairy neck. He opened the door, peeked inside, and whispered something to whoever was in there.

"Edgar!" a deep voice called from behind the door. When the owner of the voice barged out to the reception counter, I was surprised to see that the voice belonged to a frail looking woman who resembled a bald cat with tiny pointy ears on the sides of her head. She was beautiful, and her big green eyes dominated her face.

Edgar stood straighter. "Calina, it's nice to see you're still running this inn."

Were they an item? The way she was looking at him suggested they had been.

"Of course we can accommodate you," she said.

"Splendid," Edgar answered.

She pulled a key off the wall and headed up a staircase. "It's a shame there's only one room. I'm not at all surprised you all are so muddy, being with Edgar. He's always in some sort of trouble—that he is."

I'm not at all surprised, either. No telling what horrible situations he'd gotten himself in before, as a spy for the Wizard Council.

Edgar nodded for us to follow. "One will do. We'll only be here this night."

"Aww, now, that makes me sad." She glanced over her shoulder at him. "No time for love, I suppose." She clomped across a landing, unlocked a door, and pushed it open.

"It's tempting," Edgar said, amusement in his voice. "But I barely recovered the last time."

What? He actually had a lighter side to his personality. I'd only seen his serious side.

I stepped inside with Bastien. Edgar glanced down both sides of the hallway, then joined us. Before he closed the door, he said, "Our presence here must stay a secret."

"I am aware," she said in a hushed voice. "Our rebels are ready to assist whenever you need us. And don't worry about the boy. He only cares about girls and the fact that his hair is coming in fast…all over his body. Werehound puberty is difficult. It won't be long before he looks as wild as his father." She laughed. "Love is a dangerous thing. It never occurs to you how your pups will turn out when choosing a mate. I fear the boy will turn into a full-blown werehound."

I tried to stifle a laugh.

"It's okay, dear," she said. "You may laugh. It's funny. But you two," she said, looking from me to Bastien. "You'll make lovely pups together."

I felt my cheeks burn and lowered my head.

She laughed this time. "Well, I'll leave you to it. I'll bring some food up in a bit."

"Thank you." Edgar shut the door.

The room had one small bed, a dresser, and tiny table with two chairs by the window. There was plenty of floor space covered with a carpet that must've seen a lot of traffic.

Bastien wrapped his arms around me and pressed a quick kiss on my temple. "We'll make beautiful pups, you and I." He winked and let me go. "But for now, this pup needs a bath. I smell like a sewer." On the way to the tiny bathroom, he removed his shirt. How could flexing back muscles be so sexy?

"You okay?" Edgar asked, eyeing me.

"Um, yeah." I'd forgotten there was someone else in the room with us. Avoiding Edgar's stare, I took off my cloak and dropped it, before sitting on the floorboards. I removed the canister and rolled parchment from my boot before taking them both off.

Edgar opened the door. "I'll see if I can get us some clean clothes. You need anything else?"

"I don't think so. Thank you."

He shut the door.

The parchment was wet, and I gingerly unrolled it. The ink was smudged, but I could still make out the names Rada had written on it. The name listed for the first heir in Mantello was Mardiana Acardi. He wrote notes beside the names about where to find them. Mardiana spent every morning on a bench across from the bookstore in the village. I'd sat on that same bench the time I came to Mantello with Bastien and Nick.

Nick had squished grapes with the local girls during the festival. He was drunk on wine by the end of the evening. I smiled at the memory and wiped away the tears that normally followed after I'd thought of him.

The steam from the shower seeped under the bathroom door. Bastien was singing again. This time it was a Beatles' song. "She loves you, yeah, yeah, yeah …"

I chuckled and removed my socks. My feet were aching and cold. My body protested as I laid back on the floor. The water turned off, and Bastien was still humming. I imagined he was drying off.

A few moments later, the bathroom door flew open, and I sat up. Bastien strolled out, a towel wrapped around his waist.

"That felt great," he said, stretching his hands over his head, the towel inching down a little below his waist. His skin wasn't completely dry, his biceps and abs glistening in the light from the lamp on the table. I couldn't help but stare at his glorious torso.

"You should take one," he said, breaking the spell the ripple of his muscles had on me. "Mantello has the best showers. The water is always hot."

"Sounds great." I scrambled to my feet, darted to the bathroom, and snuck another look at Bastien in his towel as I shut the door. I leaned my back against the door, the steam engulfing me.

Okay, calm down. It's just Bastien. A. Partially. Naked. Bastien. I sighed.

By the time I'd finished with my shower, Edgar had returned. He knocked on the door, and I eased it open a crack to let him pass me the clothes he'd found.

A cloud of steam followed me out of the bathroom. The nightgown I had on looked like something a princess would wear. I'd prefer pajama bottoms and a tank top, but at least it was clean. I had the bed to myself. Bastien and Edgar were on mats on the floor.

Bastien was already asleep. I pulled back the covers and slipped into the bed. Edgar was mud-free and in a white linen shirt and loose pants. "You're clean. Where did you shower?"

"Never you mind about that." He gave me a mischievous smile and rolled onto his side, his back to me. I hadn't noticed it before—how could I with all that hair he had when I first saw him—but he was a good-looking guy. Especially when he smiled. I could see the females of any species falling for him.

I rested my head on the flat pillow and pulled the rough blanket up to my chin. The window was cracked open, the Mantello breeze pushing the sheer curtains in and out, and I stared at the ceiling.

I hated quiet moments like this. It was when all the worry would catch up to my mind. And regardless of how tired I was, I couldn't sleep.

Edgar came over to the side of the bed. "You're awake."

"Yeah, my mind is whirling." I sat up and rested on my elbows. "Edgar, what are you? Are you a Sentinel…wizard?"

"I'm a guard. Some children with wizard parents are born without magic. I happen to be one. We tend to go into services where magic isn't needed." He turned his hand and showed me a scar the shape of a cross between his thumb and index finger. "When we graduate our academy, we're branded so we can jump the gateways. My scores were higher than any guard before me, so Merl recruited me to be a spy for him." He held out a cup to me. "Drink this. It'll help you sleep."

The cup was warm when I wrapped my fingers around it. "What is it?"

"Fey Water," he whispered. I hadn't noticed his eyes were such a dark green before. There was pain in them, as though they'd seen horrible things.

I took a sip from the cup, and it was as if a fire went down my throat and blazed through my body to my stomach. I coughed. "That's not water."

"Well, of course not." He returned to his mat. "It's Fey Water. There's magic in it. Pretty potent stuff."

The walls were breathing in and out, and I felt dizzy. I fell back against the pillows.

"Just lay there and don't move. You will sleep soon."

I couldn't move if I wanted. My eyes closed, even though I tried to keep them open.

Several or tons of hours later, I couldn't tell, I woke up to someone shaking my shoulder. Beautiful birdsong came through the open window, and the scent of something delicious just recently cooked wafted in the air. I stretched my arms above my head and opened my eyes.

Edgar stared down at me. "You shouldn't speak in your sleep."

Startled, I sat up and glanced around. "Wh-what did I say? Where's Bastien?"

He scowled at me. "Which question would you like me to answer first?"

I shrugged. "Bastien?"

"He went to buy a *Mystik Observer*. It's an underground newspaper. You can get arrested for just having it in your possession." He went over to the table and picked up a slice of bacon. "Calina made breakfast. You should eat. When Bastien returns, we'll be on our way."

"Wait. Why would he do that? It's risky."

"Bastien can take care of himself."

My feet were tangled in the sheets, which meant I'd had another restless night, but I couldn't remember a thing. "You didn't answer my other question."

"Let's just say"—he smiled around a piece of bacon—"if Bastien ever doubted your feelings for him, he no longer does."

What the hell did I say?

He threw his head back and laughed.

Bastien opened the door carrying a newspaper and mug with steaming liquid inside. "You're awake," he said, stating the obvious.

"Um, yeah, I was just going to get dressed." I grabbed my clothes from the chair. Calina must have had them cleaned and folded for me.

"Here." Bastien handed the mug to Edgar. "Calina said it's a fireball coffee."

The mention of the drink reminded me of Arik. He loved the stuff. Said the coffee was made with chocolate and hot spices. A Djallican girl behind the coffee bar in the Asile castle's game room had offered him one. We were on our way to the exit that led to some ancient ruins—an outdoor theatre where the Mystik Games were once held—to train with my battle globe. It had rained on us that day, and I'd fallen for Arik.

Back then, staring at Arik in the rain, I would've never believed I'd be where I was now. Life changed so quickly. Sometimes what might look right just wasn't. And we weren't. But that didn't change the fact that I cared about Arik. I missed his friendship. Missed my battle partner.

And then, there was Bastien, with his eyes on me as if he could read my mind. He lifted a smile, and it reminded me that I'd apparently done a sportscaster thing while I was sleeping and given him and Edgar a play-by-play of my feelings for him.

"Is something the matter?" Bastien asked.

My eyes widened, as I realized I had been standing there

staring when I should be getting dressed. "No. Just enjoying the view." I glanced at the window and the sheers were closed. My cheeks burned.

Oh gosh.

"It's even better when the curtains are open." Bastien winked and slid the sheers to one side. "Get dressed. Wear your hair down. The images of you flashing across the various screens around the Mystik world have it up. And you may wish to hurry, or your breakfast will be cold. We should be on our way soon."

After shutting the bathroom door, I leaned against it, trying to remember what I'd dreamt about last night. I did witness Bastien in all his bare-chested-towel-only glory. There was no telling what played out in my dreams, or what I mumbled while getting some serious REMs. All courtesy of Fey Water.

When I'd dressed and returned to the room, Bastien and Edgar were in deep conversation, their empty plates between them. Their tall frames didn't fit at the tiny table, and they had pushed it over to the bed. Edgar was on the mattress, Bastien on one of the chairs, and the other one sat empty for me. The *Mystik Observer* lay open in the middle of the table. My stomach rumbled, so I took the empty seat and picked up a piece of toast.

"So, what are we talking about?" I took a bite.

Bastien pointed out the top article in the newspaper. "We can't use the tunnels any longer. Haven guards discovered an entry and are searching them for you."

"Then what are we going to do?"

Edgar lifted his mug. "We're splitting up."

I dropped the remainder of my toast onto my plate. "No, we're not. That's a bad idea."

Bastien placed his hand on my knee. "We must use the gateway. It's faster. No one knows that Edgar is with us. He'll go to Esteril and gather the heir's blood there. I've contacted the French Sentinels to meet me in the Senate Library. They'll be on their way back from delivering your father to the Shelter. I trust them to get me into Couve safely, where I'll gather our heir's donation."

"And me?" I didn't like this idea. And I didn't like that it made sense for them to go without me.

"You'll stay here and find Mantello's heir." Bastien squeezed my knee as if it would ease my worry.

"Here." Edgar dropped some gold coins in my hand. "In case you need money."

"I don't know how to use them," I said. "How much to pay for stuff."

"Just give them a gold coin," Edgar said. "Don't use the silvers. Always use the gold. It's a lot, and they'll have to give you change."

Another headline caught my eye, and I turned the paper to read it. council sentinels kill three in library. The deceased had been traveling illegally through the gateway books. A fight broke out between the Sentinels and a group of protestors from the Santara haven. It went on to say that more guards were stationed throughout the libraries. The guards were given orders to stop all illegal jumps, by any means, even death.

"How can the Couve Sentinels jump with Pop?" I worried my lip, almost breaking the skin. "It's too dangerous."

Bastien glanced over the article I'd been reading. "They do a library hop with your father between two Sentinels. The Monitors will sense human, but the Sentinel presence will register higher. It should confuse the Monitors."

"Should." I grimaced. "That's not at all comforting."

"My Sentinels are some of the best," he said. "They will give their lives to protect your father."

The council's Sentinels killing people at will in the libraries caused a lead ball to drop in my stomach. I fingered the gold coins in my hand. The thought of separating from Bastien and

Edgar scared me, but it made sense. We'd get what we needed from the heirs quicker. Suddenly, I wasn't hungry anymore.

After I put on my breastplate and my cloak, Bastien took my hands in his. "Avoid crowds. Stay away from the main roads. You know where you're going?"

"Yes. Three blocks up. Four right."

He released my hands and lifted the hood of my cloak over my head. "If something happens to me, get back to Barmhilde and stay with The Red. He'll protect you."

I touched his cheek and fought back my emotions, not wanting to upset him. "You're the one traveling through the gateways. You be careful. I don't know what I'd do if—"

His lips on mine stopped me. He kissed me deeply, as if it would be the last chance we'd ever have. I wrapped my arms around his neck, wanting desperately to keep him there with me. Tears slipped from my eyes.

Cupping my face in his hands, he wiped them away with his thumbs and said, "I'll be back before morning. Nothing will stop me from getting back to you. Have you forgotten? I'm a wizard. Best in my class. Let them try stopping me." He flashed me that arrogant smile of his that stilled my heart.

I smiled. "I feel sorry for them."

He smirked. "Besides, we'll have to fulfill your fantasies one day."

The blood rushed to my cheeks again. "Exactly what did I say? And it's Edgar's fault he gave me that drink. That Fey Water."

"A gentleman never divulges such things." He winked.

"All right, now," Edgar said. "I am in the room with you. Let's get this done."

I followed them out into the hall, my embarrassment trailing me. Edgar stopped at what looked like a broom closet and opened the door. "Gia, you go through this back way. It leads down to the alley. Keep your head covered and your face down. Calina will be here should you need her."

"Okay," I said, nodding. "Good luck."

Before I went inside, Bastien caught my hand and kissed my temple. "Stay strong, Gianna." It was the first time I saw fear in his striking blue eyes. We'd been through scarier things than this, and he had never flinched. An uneasy feeling settled in my stomach.

"We've got this," I said, holding his stare.

Bastien bounded down the stairs after Edgar. As I watched him disappear around the corner, my mind screaming that I shouldn't let him go, I realized he was going without knowing my feelings.

I called out for him, but there was no sound of boots returning up the stairs.

He was gone.

CHAPTER SEVENTEEN

The alley outside the inn was narrow. The cobblestones were cracked and broken. A white cat nosing in a tipped-over trashcan hissed at me as I passed on my way to the road. A noise sounded behind me, and I glanced back. The cat was following me.

"Go home," I told it and continued on my way.

Mantello was alive with people rushing across the streets. Carts pushed by men and women or pulled by horses and goats bumped over the uneven stones in the road. It was like walking back in time.

There were no vehicles in the Mystik world. The Wizard Council had voted to ban them. They didn't want their air polluted by them like in the human world. But the villages were small and walking made more sense anyway.

The small Tuscany-like village was beautiful with all its different-colored stucco buildings, cobbled roads, and flowerpots stuffed with beautiful flowers. I kept my head down, the hood blocking my face, and went three blocks up, then four right, and stopped in front of the bookstore. The sign above the door read, *Libreria*. I'd been here before when Bastien brought Nick and me to Mantello for Toad's trial. Acting as nonchalant as I could, I sneaked a view of the bench.

A woman dressed in black with silver streaking her black hair waved.

I glanced behind me then back at her, pointing to my chest. *Me?* I mouthed.

She nodded. The woman was beautiful and resembled Sophie Loren, the actor from all those old movies Nana loved to watch.

Okay. It must be her.

"Hello," I said approaching her. "Are you Mardiana Acardi?"

"I am. Now, I'm going to point at the bakery." She did. "Go inside. Buy yourself a pastry and coffee. Then sit on the bench beside me. And act as if you aren't talking to me."

"Okay."

"And remove your hood," she said. "You look more suspicious with it on. Only wear it if it rains."

I slipped off my hood and headed for the bakery. The smells inside were delicious, and I wanted to buy everything behind the display case. I chose a frosted pastry and a buttered coffee at the suggestion of the woman serving me.

The sky darkened as I crossed the street and sat on the bench next to Mardiana.

"I suppose you were told that I come here every morning."

"Yes," I said, took a sip of the coffee, and wrinkled my nose. It wasn't bad, but I missed the sweetness of my caramel lattes.

The white cat from the alley sat in front of Mardiana. "You've done great, Angel Kitty. Come rest." She patted her lap. The cat jumped and curled up on her black skirt.

"You had her following me?" I asked.

Her warm brown eyes were fixed on the bookstore. "Naturally, she's my familiar. My spirit friends told me you were coming."

"You're a witch?" I took a bite of the pastry. The sweet goodness melted on my tongue and made up for the bland coffee.

She petted Angel Kitty, which was such a silly name to give a cat. "My granddaughter named her. It made her proud to have the honor."

"So you're intuitive?"

A thin-lipped smile wrinkled the corners of her mouth. "Actually, I am an enchantress. We have familiars just as witches do. Athela speaks to me, as well. I've known for years you'd come seeking me, even before you were born. I am Gian's cousin. The oldest living heir of the First Wizard, Galante."

Gian's cousin. Does she know he's dead?

"I do know," she said. "He gave his life for you. For what you mean to both worlds. And you wonder if he cared that you were his great-granddaughter. I can assure you he was very proud and filled with much love for you. Wizards from his generation were taught never to show their emotions. But know I tell the truth."

The look on Gian's face before Conemar had killed him played across my mind. His peaceful eyes stared at me as if to tell me he'd accepted his fate. He had made the ultimate sacrifice for me, for his belief in what I could do for both worlds. Mardiana saying he was proud of me filled me with resolve. I would make sure he hadn't died for nothing. I might not win, but it wouldn't be for giving up.

"Good girl." Her slender, wrinkled hand covered mine resting on my lap. "Now, I believe you need something of mine. Turn your hand over." I did as she asked and she dropped a small silver container on my palm. "What you need is inside."

I leaned over, pretended to fix my boot, and stuffed the container next to the leather canister.

"Don't you wonder why I sit here every day?"

"I'm guessing I should?" I straightened. "You weren't just

waiting for me all this time, right?"

"Correct. I haven't been waiting for you," she said, nudging the cat off her lap before standing.

I reached my hand down to pet the white furry creature, and she hissed at me, again. *Angel? More like Devil Kitty.*

"Mantello is the city of Gian's birth," she said. "That bookstore there holds many works by him, including one that may have great interest for you. One you should never let out of your sight."

"I won't."

Mardiana stared down at me. "Do not wait for the two young men you're traveling with to return to Mantello. You must go to Tearmann straightaway. There's a storm heading for the haven. You won't want to miss your opportunity to retrieve what you need there." She bowed her head slightly. "It's been a pleasure meeting you, cousin. May Agnes guide you in your travels."

I kept my eyes on the bookstore as Mardiana walked off, only sneaking a glance when the sound of her heels softened with distance. Angel Kitty kept close to Mardiana's heels as she clipped down the road.

Does she mean an actual storm or metaphoric one? Whichever one she meant, I decided to go with her warning. Tearmann was an ally. I'd be safe there.

After wiping the frosting from my hands and face, I threw my trash in a fancy nearby can.

A cart, pulled by a brown horse with white hoofs, bumped over the road. I waited for it to pass before crossing over to the bookstore. Everything in the haven was quaint and old-world feeling. I tugged the door open.

"*Buongiorno,*" said the same scholarly looking young man with glasses and a bright smile from the last time I was there.

"Morning," I said and leafed through a stack of magazines on a table.

"English?"

"*Sì*."

He straightened his glasses. "Please to tell me if you're in need of *assistenza*."

Déjà vu. I could've sworn we'd had the same exact exchange when I was here before.

"*Grazie*," I said.

It would be a lot easier to find Gian's books if I asked him for their location, but I didn't know if it would raise suspicion. And I didn't know who in Mantello had seen my face and knew that the Wizard Council had a warrant, or whatever they called it in the Mystik world, out for me.

My finger bounced across the spines of books as I searched the shelves for Gian's name. I finally came across them in the special studies area. There were a few I'd already read, one about Mystik creatures and another on charms and spells. I paused on one titled *My Magnificent Journeys*. I removed it from the shelf and flipped through the pages, leafing through the photographs until I came to it. A picture of three large mountains capped with snow.

I recalled Gian's message. *You shall find the entry into a mountainous, frozen land. The Four sleeps under the tallest peak…*

I ran my fingers across the photograph, and it tugged at my fingers. I'd found it. Mardiana came here every day, sat on that bench from the time the bookstore opened until it closed. She was here to watch over the book. The entry to where the Tetrad was caged was in its pages. Until today. Her job was done. It was now my turn to protect it. I grabbed another book of Gian's, not wanting the one containing the Tetrad's prison to stand out, and went to the counter.

"Just the two?" the man asked in his broken English.

I handed him a gold coin. "Yes, please."

His gaze went to the window. "Signora Acardi never leaves

the bench until the sun lowers past the buildings. Strange, no?"

It didn't seem like he was talking to me so I stayed quiet.

"*Buona giornata.*" He handed me a few silver coins in various sizes, his eyes still watching the window.

I hugged the books to my chest and rushed outside, worried that he'd look closer at me. My boots pounded against the cobblestones as I hurried down the road.

One you should never let out of your sight. Mardiana's warning went off in my head. I had to keep Gian's book with me.

Bags in the window of a store stopped me, and I went inside. With my head down, I grabbed a satchel with long straps, paid the girl operating the register, and tucked Gian's books inside.

Mardiana had told me not to wait. But it was early. Bastien and Edgar wouldn't be back until late that night or in the morning. I decided to listen to her and go to Tearmann. They were allies. There hadn't been an uprising there like in Santara. Besides, I was shielded. I could sneak in and out without being noticed.

It took me nearly an hour to find the outbuilding with the tunnel leading to the Riccaidiana Library in Florence, Italy. I'd been there before, but I was following Bastien and hadn't paid attention to where we were going. I kept running into dead ends until I noticed the stucco structure just down the hill from the haven.

The store windows with their displays and decorations were enticing. I passed a costume shop with a long blond wig sitting on a porcelain head. The door stuck a little, and I tugged it open. A round woman dressed in a black dress and wearing a red cape took a gold coin for the wig and handed me a small silver one. She let me put it on in front of the mirror.

I didn't look too bad as a blonde. It actually seemed like real hair—long with a little wave. Hopefully, no one would recognize me.

"*Bellissimo,*" the woman said.

"*Grazie,*" I said and exited the shop. The hill was steep, and my steps were fast on the way to the outbuilding.

I thumped down the stairs to the tunnel. It was narrow, just like most of them were, with a series of stone steps going up and down and twisting left to right. The light from my globe bounced across the rock walls. As I neared the end, there was a line of people. I held tight to the straps of the bag holding Gian's books.

They're inspecting people. Panic fluttered in my chest, and I clenched the cloak closed to hide my Sentinel gear underneath. I turned to go back the way I'd come, but was stopped by an older couple's approach. They looked like parents who had just walked out of a Norman Rockwell painting, the man in his suit and the woman in a flowery dress. The man studied my face before I whirled back around.

"The libraries are crowded," the woman said. "It seems quite unnecessary to make everyone return to the place of their births to reregister."

With every movement of the line, my heart stopped, and I caught my breath. I should have stayed in Mantello as Bastien and Edgar told me. I was second in line, and my stomach clenched.

"Next," said a guard with a hawkish nose and barrels for arms.

The man in front of me stepped up to the guard.

"Identification," the guard said holding out his hand.

Identification? I didn't have any. The panic in my chest nosedived to my gut.

The man held up a metal card. The guard studied it and then nodded the man through.

I approached the guard, playing in my head all the scenarios on how to get out of this.

"What's in the bag?" he asked.

"Books," I said in a soft, timid tone. He motioned for me to open the bag. I did and he searched inside.

Okay. There're two guards. I'd have to use my globes.

"Identification," he said.

"Just a second." I squatted, put my bag on the floor, and pretended to search inside.

I opened my hand by my side and whispered, "*Accendere la stun.*" The power of the globe tugged at my palm. Leaping to my feet, I slammed the purple sphere against his shoulder. It spread across his body, encasing him in a purple glow.

A sharp intake of breath came from the woman behind me.

I glanced over my shoulder. "Make sure to call someone to remove the stun, or he'll run out of air and die. Okay?"

His eyes wide, the older man nodded.

I darted through the entrance, creating another stun globe and hurling it at the other guard pacing the library. It smacked him the chest, and he fell to the floor like a chopped down tree.

The Riccardiana Library's warm woodwork and gold accents flashed in my peripheral vision as I dashed for the main reading room. My boots clacking against the checkered tiles resounded against the fresco ceiling. Moonlight came in through the tall window, casting shadows over the bookcases.

I called for the gateway book and spun around listening for it. Above the fresco was a circular window, the frame resembling a lemon slice. Though it was day in the havens, it was nighttime in Florence. Tables were lined up in the center of the room, gold-painted chairs with pink cushions pushed up against them.

The book wasn't chained to anything. It floated to me and I flipped to the photograph of the Trinity College library in Dublin.

"*Aprire La Porta.*" I said the charm and jumped into the book, an alarm sounding as I disappeared into the gateway.

I searched the Long Room in the Trinity library for the

spiral staircase Jaran had said led to Tearmann haven. The arched ceiling soaring overhead made me feel small. I walked past the display of the Book of Kells, which was an illuminated manuscript of the Christian Gospels created around 800 AD. Jaran would be impressed that I remembered what he had told me.

Finally, I found the spiral staircase tucked away in a tiny alcove surrounded by bookcases and beside a bust of Shakespeare. I stepped onto the first stair and clutched the black rod iron banister swirling up to the top.

Admit the pure. That's what the charm to open the doorways into the havens meant. It was spelled to let only those without evil intentions into the haven. But I wondered if it really worked, because some of the wizards on the council weren't playing nice. Could they have altered the charm? Most likely.

I took a deep breath and said, *"Ammettere il pura."*

The rod iron shook in my grasp, the floor slid aside, and the staircase spun down. My grasp tightened. It landed with a bang, and I ended up in a rock tunnel, one that was surprisingly empty. I stepped off, and the staircase returned to the library above, the floor shutting me inside the tunnel.

"Okay, whatever happens, there better not be a flood." I removed the itchy wig and shoved it into my bag.

Water leaked from the arched ceiling and plunked into puddles forming on the uneven stone floor. The tunnel walls were covered in beautiful graffiti art of wizards, Mystik creatures, and unusual landscapes. I stopped when I spotted one of me, a sense of pride swelling inside. Someone had actually painted me. By the details, whoever it was took a lot of time doing it. I looked fierce in my Sentinel gear with my pink battle globe, the wind blowing back my ponytail.

I bent and dipped my finger in the mud where a stone in the ground was missing. With the tip of my finger, I drew a

hairline scar across my cheek. I'd earn the scar and was proud
of it because it was a badge of survival. I wiped my finger on
my pants and continued down the tunnel.

The passage dipped and rose until it came to a series of
steps carved out of the rock, twisting down and then spiraling
up. I had to duck to avoid hitting my head on the low arches,
and I almost felt dizzy with all the turns. The final stairs were
so long, I had to stop several times to catch my breath. The
steps stopped at a heavy wooden door that I had to use all my
weight to push open.

Bright light blinded me, and I squinted until my eyes got
used to it. As my focus cleared, I caught glimpses of lush green
grass with thousands of yellow cup-shaped flowers. A swarm
of colorful humming birds rushed by me. Tall trees drooped
with red and purple fruit.

"Toto, I have a feeling we're not in Kansas anymore," I
recited, and laughed. "Now all I need are ruby slippers."

"You always be talking to yourself like that?" a grumpy
sounding male voice said from somewhere nearby.

The accent and syntax reminded me of Carrig.

I whirled around. "Where are you? Better yet, who are you?"

A guy a little bit older than me, with dark red hair and
bushy brows of the same color, came out from behind a tree
carrying a basket full of the red and purple fruit. He dropped
the basket, the fruit tumbling and disappearing into the long
grass.

"Be it you?" he asked, gaping.

I raised an eyebrow. "Last I checked, it was me."

"I don't understand."

"Who do you think I am?" I asked.

"Gianna," he said with uncertainty in his voice.

Do I tell him he's right? He could turn me in.

He ran his sleeve across his forehead. "I'm not going to
harm you. If you were she, we'd protect you. The council is

up to no good."

I paused and studied him, not sure if he was trustworthy. He didn't seem dangerous, but that didn't mean anything. Lining the basket was a copy of the *Mystik Observer.*

"Why do you have an *Observer*?" I asked.

"Because it's the only true news out there nowadays. The others are filled with false stories the council wants us to believe."

I decided to take my chance. If he turned on me, I'd fry his ass.

"I am her, but you can call me Gia."

"All right, then, Gia," he said. "Never in all me days would I have thought I'd meet the presage. You be a hero in Tearmann. One of our own, you are."

I smiled, strangling the handle of my bag draped over my shoulder. "Do you think you could take me to your leader?"

Take me to your leader? Really? I sound like a cartoon alien or something.

"Most certainly," he said, oblivious to the alien-like comment. "I will take you to our queen, but first I must pick these up. Me *máthair* won't be able to make her pies for the bakery without them." He sat on his heels and started picking up the fruit and placing it in the basket.

I bent down and helped him. "Why does your haven have a queen and the others have high wizards?"

"Briony be the daughter of our fallen high wizard and a princess from the Fey nation. After his death, Tearmann voted to have her rule the haven. We have a parliament of high wizards." He piled the last purple fruit on top of the others. "They be the best of the wizards. Most pure hearted. If you be asking me, our system should be how they govern the entire Mystik world." With that, he lifted the basket.

"You're probably right," I said, following him. "A responsible government or even a democracy would be ideal."

"I don't know what you speak of, but ours would work best."

"Okay, same thing probably." I wasn't sure, but so far, Tearmann haven wasn't after my head. That had to be a good thing. "So, what's your name?"

"Buach," he said, taking a dirt path that weaved around what looked like a large Hobbit village. The houses had colorful doors and stained-glass windows, and some were even dug into the many hills.

"How do you say your name, again?" I asked.

"*Boo-ock,*" he empathized for me.

"That's a strong"—*odd*—"name."

He stopped at one of the homes with a yellow door. "Can you open it for me?"

I grabbed the big brass knob and tried to turn it, but it wouldn't move.

He snickered. "They don't have doors where you come from? You push."

"Oh." I shoved open the door and stepped aside to let him pass. "We do have doors, but our knobs actually do something."

"Too bad my ma isn't home," he said over his shoulder. "She would be beside herself for a month after meeting you."

This was all taking too long. "I really have to be going. I'm running out of time." I shrugged a shoulder. "You know, the whole *I have to save both worlds* thing."

His eyes widened. "For the love of taffy flowers. I be as dense as a wicket. We go straightaway." The basket thumped against the counter as he dropped it and rushed outside with me. "You'll cause a ruckus if anybody recognizes you."

Pretty much, I had to hide from everyone—bad and good. I drew the hood of my cloak over my head.

All the roads in that haven were twisty and turny. We'd walked nearly five miles when we approached a massive gate made of thick silver twisted to look like flowers, trees, and birds. Several guards flanked each side, and more kept watch from balconies carved into the rock above the gate.

"Lower your hood," Buach said.

I pushed it off my head and suddenly felt vulnerable.

"Who do you have here, Buach?" said one of the guards with big biceps, wearing a helmet with flaps covering his cheeks and a bar hanging down that pressed against his nose.

Buach narrowed his eyes at him. "Blimey, Galach, don't you recognize her?"

"What did I tell you?" Galach could narrow his eyes in a way more menacing manner than Buach. It made me take a step back. "Outside of home, you are to address me formally."

"Just let us through, already," Buach said. "Do you want to be known as the bumble head who didn't recognize her?"

Galach studied me harder. His eyes widened. "The presage."

"I'm here to see your queen," I said. He was just staring at me, not saying a word. "Please?"

He shook out of his stupor, motioned for the other guards to open the gates, and escorted us inside.

"Contact the queen," Galach ordered a smaller guard with red hair sticking out from his helmet. "Inform her she has a guest."

We were led to an elevator that resembled the outside gate—silver rods bent and turned to look like flowers and birds.

The elevator took a while to reach the bottom. It bounced and my breath hitched. When the door slid open, I hurried out, only to discover it was freezing. The cold settled into my bones, and I shivered. We were inside a gigantic cavern. I wrapped my cape tighter around me.

"Is this real?" I asked, trying to take in all the tiny details, like the carvings of people and faeries and landscapes on the walls.

The hum of the electric lanterns—hanging on wires strung from elaborate spears sticking out of the rock on either side of the walkway—mixed with the plopping of a thousand drips of water. Surrounded by crystal stalactites and stalagmites was a castle that had been carved into the side of the cavern.

At the end of the walkway, we crossed a drawbridge and entered the castle. If the outside was cold, the interior was warm and decorated in brown and burnt orange furnishings with sculptures of strange looking animals lining the main corridor. We ended up in a room where a wiry woman, maybe in her early twenties, with hair almost the color of paper and even paler skin, stood up from her seat at a long table. She wore a cream jumpsuit made of some sort of chiffon material, a thick leather belt cinching her tiny waist.

She glided over to us. As she neared, her amber eyes held me. With her hair pulled half up in intricate braids, her pointy ears stood out.

"Gianna, it's a pleasure to finally meet you." Her voice was as sweet as honey. "I'm Briony. Come sit down. You must be hungry. Our meal will be delivered soon."

"I am," I said.

A man in a stiff suit pulled out a chair for me. It was beside the head of the table where Briony sat.

Briony's eyes inspected Buach. "And you are?"

"He be me brother, Buach, Your Highness," Galach said. "He works in our family's bakery."

"Oh yes. Well, thank you for bringing our guest to me." She gave him a warm smile. "You may go."

Buach bowed, and before he turned to leave, he said, "When there be peace, Gia, might you come and have a slice of pie? Our bakery be the best in all the havens."

"Definitely," I said. "I look forward to it. Thank you for everything, Buach."

"I should be the one to thank you." His smile was sad, or

maybe it was pity for me, the sacrificial lamb on her way to slaughter. "All right, then. Goodbye."

It was as if he didn't want to leave me there, so I gave him a reassuring smile. "Goodbye."

After Buach and Galach exited the room, several men and women came in carrying trays. There were meats, cheeses, steamed vegetables, fruits, and baked goods. A man placed a white plate with etched flowers in front of me and served a helping from each tray onto it.

"This is a lot of food," I said. "Is anyone else joining us?"

"No, it's just us." A woman showed her a bottle of wine, Briony nodded, and the woman poured it into her glass. The liquid was bright purple like the fruit that was in Buach's basket. "When we are finished, they will sit and eat what is left over."

"Oh, I see."

"Now, leave us," Briony said in a commanding tone. The room emptied, and she adjusted in her seat to look at me. "So, what brings you to Tearmann? I assure you we are allies. This is your father's home. Carrig is one of our greatest Sentinels. Your father must be proud of you."

Tears stung my eyes at the thought of him. I wished he were in Tearmann with me. He could show me his home, the people he knew. I didn't want to think about what would happen if he never woke up.

Briony covered my hand resting on the table with hers. "What is it, dear one?"

"He's in a coma."

Her face was questioning. "A what?"

"It's like an endless sleep." I picked up the napkin on the table and dabbed the wetness from my eyes. "The thing is, his wife, Sinead, is also in a sleep. They're tied to each other or something."

"So she's Fey." She frowned, removing her hand from

mine. "The same thing happened to my mother. When the Fey marry outside of our species, their lives are forever tied to their beloved's."

I placed the napkin back down. "Did your mother die with your father?"

She took a sip of the purple drink and nodded. "It was devastating. But enough about things we can't change. You need something here in Tearmann. What is it?"

Well, she gets straight to the point.

"I need blood from the oldest living heir of the Third Wizard." I pulled out the list Rada gave me. "A Cashel Deasmhumhain?" I totally butchered that last name.

"That is all?" She tilted her head back and laughed.

"Why is that funny?"

Recovered, she picked up her glass again. "I thought you were going to ask for an army."

"Why? Would you give me an army?"

"Of course. We're on the same side." She glanced over her glass at me, took a sip, then placed it back on the table. "Here in Tearmann, we follow the rules of the Fey. We believe all living creatures should be cared for, and no one life is more important than another. When you need us, we will be there for you."

"It's how I feel, too."

"I know you do," she said. "I felt your empathy when you entered the castle. And, about the reason you are here, I am the heir. Cashel was my grandfather. He passed last autumn. I'm the only one left in the Third Wizard's family. How shall we draw my blood?"

"Just a few drops are needed. You only have to prick your finger." I bent over, retrieved the leather canister from my boot, and removed the vial containing the other heir's blood.

"I'm curious to know why you need this, but it's best you don't say. Keep your secrets close, Gianna; not everyone is trustworthy." She snatched up a knife and poked her finger with the tip. I held out the vial, and she squeezed her finger, letting a few drops fall into it.

Tell me about it. I wish I still had my truth globe.

As I turned my foot slightly, I could feel the small silver container Mardiana had given me. I took it out and added her blood to the vial.

"Who does that belong to?" she asked, her brow slightly up as she watched me.

"The Mantello heir."

"I see. My curiosity has risen again."

I ignored her. As she said, I should tell no one what I was doing. I secured the top of the vial, eased it into the canister, and returned it to the inside of my boot.

A siren went off somewhere in the castle, and Briony shot to her feet. "Oh dear. That's not good at all. We're being attacked."

I stood, not knowing what to do.

They found me.

CHAPTER EIGHTEEN

Galach and Buach rushed into the room with many guards behind them. "Your Highness, we must be leaving at once. The Asile guards be here to arrest you."

Arrest her? Not me? If they didn't know I was there, they'd find out soon. "We need to get out of here."

"What do they want with me?" Briony asked, ignoring my plea.

"It is uncertain." The expression on Galach's face held concern. "We received word that High Wizard Murtagh be arrested today during the council meeting."

Briony crossed over to him. "What reason did they give for his arrest?"

"He voted against removing all charges from Conemar's records. We haven't time. I must get you to safety."

"Um, we should go," I said. "Like, *now.*"

Galach waved the guards to the corridor and held out his hand to Briony.

She grabbed it. "Gia is coming with us. Buach, you come, as well."

Galach rushed out with Briony and Buach and I went after them.

"I just don't understand," Briony was saying when I caught up to them. "By removing his charges, Conemar can resume his position as Esteril's high wizard. Why would the council arrest Murtagh for voting against this?"

"Who's Murtagh?" I whispered to Buach.

He darted looks behind us. "He's our highest wizard. He attends council meetings in Briony's stead."

"The council stated that Tearmann sided with the Mystik League," Galach said. "That we be traitors. They believe the covens be responsible for the recent attacks on the havens."

Briony glanced over her shoulder. "Why aren't the guards coming? And what about our people? I can't leave them."

"The guards stay to slow them down while we make our escape." Galach guided her around a corner. "Asile won't harm Tearmann's people, just her leaders."

I couldn't believe what I was hearing. Conemar had to be behind all the prior high wizards' deaths. This was his plan: to take over the council.

"This is bad," I said. "They can't put him on the council."

"They must have a unanimous vote," Briony said. "That is why they want me removed, and most likely my parliament. They'll replace them and me with one high wizard sympathetic to Conemar."

We entered a corridor with large paintings of regal looking people, and many statues. In the middle of the room were two marble sarcophagi with the likeness of a man carved into one and a woman in the other.

Briony must have noticed me staring at them. "My parents. They'll remain until my death. When I'm placed here, they will be moved to a crypt outside the village."

Galach pushed something under the lip of the sarcophagus of the man. The two caskets separated, exposing stairs leading down into darkness.

I created a light globe and motioned for Galach and Briony

to go. Buach and I pounded down the steps behind them. The sarcophagi came back together, sealing us in.

"Where does this lead?" I asked, watching my steps. The ground was uneven, with sharp rises and potholes.

"To a different library," Briony said. "It's the national one in Dublin."

Buach was silent beside me, his breathing heavy.

"Are you doing okay?" I asked, clutching my bag to my side.

He rubbed the back of his neck. "Only worrying about me ma and da."

"Sorry, Buach," Galach said. "But I could not risk you being taken and questioned. As it be now, they won't know you be part of this escape. Once safe in the library, you can jump to Tearmann. Tell them you visited friends in Mantello. Give me ma and da me love."

When we reached the end, we entered the library through a moving bookcase. I checked the time on Carrig's watch. It was nearing three in the morning in Dublin.

After calling out the charm to summon the gateway book, I glanced around waiting for the book to fly over. White wood trim crisscrossed the large dome with different shadow of teal colored squares inside them. Tall arched windows wrapped around the lower part of the dome. A line of sculpted cupids, linked by garlands of fruit, encircled its base. Just below, lofty wooden bookcases surrounded the room.

I strolled down one of the many rows of desk-like tables in the middle of the room, scanning the bookcases. This book had remained strapped to the back of a bookcase and it knocked against a nearby shelf, trying to come to me. I trotted over to it, removed the binding, and carried it to the others.

Galach let go of Briony's arm. "Right then, Buach, you jump first. Don't be doing anything rash. Keep to your work and mind Ma and Da."

Buach hugged his brother. "Come back to us."

"Ah, you know I can't be promising you that." Galach clapped Buach's back. "Now on your way, you."

"See you for that pie," I said.

"That you will." He smiled and jumped into the book.

"Now, where are we going?" Briony asked.

Galach removed his helmet and dropped it onto the wooden floor with a *thump* that traveled up to the dome ceiling. "Do you know how to get to the Fey realm?"

Briony shook her head. "The last I went there, I was not even six years of age. I only remember a beautiful garden."

I glanced at the silver butterfly hinting on my wrist.

Of course. I blew on it. The tracer pulled from my skin, flapping its wings to hover in front of me.

"I need Aetnae, please," I said.

The tracer *swooshed* up above our heads, then dove into the gateway book.

Briony's amber eyes looked darker in the dim light of the library. "Whom did you send it after?"

"A book faery," I said, pulling out one of the chairs from the desk and plopping down on it.

My stomach knotted as we waited for Aetnae. The sky outside the windows was getting lighter, which meant it was getting dark in Mantello. Bastien would return to the inn soon, and I wouldn't be there. He would be angry that I'd decided to go to Tearmann by myself.

The pages in the gateway book turned and the tracer flew out of the book with Aetnae right behind it.

The butterfly came over to me and bounced in front of my face.

"It wants your wrist," Aetnae said, flying over to me. "Looks like it has claimed you as its owner."

"That's cool." I turned my wrist over so the tracer could land on it. "How about friends instead?" It seemed like the tracer brightened a little at my words before seeping into my skin.

Aetnae spotted the others. "Why did you call me? What's going on—" A surprised look crossed her face and she bowed, then straightened, all while hovering in front of us. "Your Highness. What happened?"

"The council sent guards to Tearmann to arrest me and my parliament members," she said. "I must seek asylum in *Tír na nÓg.*"

"I can't take you," Aetnae said, landing on my shoulder and holding on to a strand of my hair. "Your jump will register."

"But they will arrest her," Galach said. "There be no telling what Conemar will do to her once he's in power."

A thought came to me. "I have an idea. But Galach won't be able to jump with us. He'll have to return to Tearmann."

Galach squared his shoulders. "No. I won't leave her."

Briony placed a tender hand on Galach's cheek. "I will be fine with the Fey; they are my people. You must protect our haven. But stay safe. My heart cannot survive your loss."

He touched her hand for a brief second before taking a step back and bowing. "Your order be my wish. I will wait until after you have gone before going back to Tearmann."

Was there a love thing going on between them? It definitely looked like there was.

"I'll be right back," I said and headed for the door.

"Where are you going?" Aetnae asked.

"I need privacy," I said over my shoulder and exited.

Standing in the hallway leading to a wide staircase, I lifted my shirt and placed my right pointer and index finger on the crown. The Chiave would make the wearer invisible in the gateway.

My fingers hovered over the brand. I should keep it hidden, but I had to get Briony to safety. Her jump would register without it, and she could get caught. Uncle Philip, Akua, and Briony were the only council members not corrupted.

We needed them. The havens and covens needed them.

"*Reditum*," I spoke the charm to release the Chiave, my thoughts only on the crown. The Chiave ripped from my side, and I dropped to my knees in pain, clenching my teeth. The crown grew to its actual size and floated in front of me. I grasped it and rushed back to the others.

Briony and Galach were standing close, their voices low. His face told me he didn't like what she was saying.

Aetnae flew up to me and landed on my shoulder. "Lovers' spat," she whispered. "You thought forbidden love was bad for you and Arik—" She stopped, her eyes widening. "Sorry. But you get what I mean. It's worse for them. She's a ruler, he's a guard…never the two shall mix."

"I don't get what's the problem." I frowned at them. "So what if a ruler and a guard love each other? It's just their jobs, not who they are. Everyone should be equal."

"Tell that to a bunch of uptight wizards with their noses in the law books." Her eyes went to the crown. "What's that for?"

"It will shield her jump," I said.

She darted off my shoulder. "Well, let's get out of here before we're discovered."

I stalked after her. As we approached Briony and Galach, they backed away from each other.

I held the crown out to Briony. "We're ready to go. You'll need to wear this, but don't put it on until we're about to jump. Now, Aetnae and I are going to turn our backs while you two kiss goodbye." Briony opened her mouth to protest, and I put up my hand to stop her. "Look at him. No telling when you'll get this opportunity again."

Aetnae touched down on my shoulder, and I turned around. "Your grandmother will be happy to see you," she said, obviously making small talk.

I'd give anything in the worlds to see Nana, but I couldn't. There was too much at stake for me to stop now.

"I'm not going with you," I whispered. "Bastien is waiting

for me in Mantello. I just have to figure out how to get by the guards in the library."

"I can help you there. Jump to Mantello. The book faeries will meet you. While we cause a diversion, you can slip by the guards. Simple." She hopped a little and hit a nerve in my neck, making me flinch. "Oh sorry. Got a bit excited there. It will be so much fun."

"Yeah, fun," I droned.

It must've been a long kiss because it felt like minutes passed before Briony said, "All right, we're ready."

The gateway book had put itself away, so I had to call for it again. I flipped to a photograph of the Central Library in Edinburgh, Scotland, and glanced at Briony. "Okay. Ready?"

Her eyes went to Galach, and he gave her a reassuring nod back.

"I am," she said.

"Put on the crown."

She put it on, and I grasped her hand.

"*Aprire la porta*," I said and jumped with her into the book.

After we arrived in the Edinburgh library, Aetnae opened *The Secret Garden* pop-up book.

Briony turned to me, her eyes glistening. "One day, when there is peace, we will meet again. Stay strong, Gianna Bianchi McCabe."

"I will," I said. "And I *will* see you again."

"If you need me," Aetnae said, "you know how to find me."

"I do. Now go."

She nodded and led Briony into *The Secret Garden*.

With much pain, I used the spell to brand the crown back into my skin. Then I put on the blond wig and jumped to the Riccardiana Library.

There was a line to go through the bookcase leading to Mantello. It had to be longer than the one when I had left the haven. As I neared the front of the line, I twisted my hands in front of me.

Where is she? I bit my lip and adjusted my bag on my shoulder, my eyes darting to every corner of the reading room and scanning each bookcase.

The line moved again.

My heart sprinted in my chest. I glanced behind me. *Maybe I should go back. Would they notice if I got out of line?* The guard was too near, so I decided to stay where I was.

And the line moved once more, making me the next up.

I swallowed hard.

Something tickled my ear and I swatted at it.

"Whoa there," Aetnae hiss-whispered. "Have you not learned that you shouldn't swipe at what you believe are bugs? You're going to bend a wing or something."

I tried not to move my lips when answering her. "Where have you been? I'm almost up."

"You need to get out of line," she said. "We'll make a diversion and you jump through the gateway to the El Escorial library in Spain."

"To Santara? Why?"

The man and woman in front of me were in an intense argument with the guards.

"I must go to Mantello first," I said. "Bastien is waiting for me."

She heaved a sigh. "No. He was there, but you weren't, so he went looking for you in Santara. Guess he picked the wrong haven. Your distraction is happening now; you best go."

The man in front of me slammed his bag down and yelled something in a language I didn't know, his arms flailing around him. Books dropped from a nearby shelf.

A woman screeched, spinning around, looking for something in the air. "What is it? A moth?"

People and creatures in line scattered. The guards' heads snapped in the direction of the commotion.

I backed up and quickly walked to the other room. I called for the gateway book and waited. There were so many travelers coming through that it took several minutes before it came to me. I searched for the page with El Escorial on it.

"Hey, you!" a deep voice called to me.

I glanced up. One of the guards, a little smaller than the others with thinning hair and bushy sideburns, headed in my direction, his boots pounding against the tiles.

Crap. Focus, Gia.

I found the page with the El Escorial Monastery Library in Spain near the back of the book.

"I'm talking to you, mademoiselle—" His words and footfalls stopped, so I gave him another look. "It is you. Gianna Bianchi." He picked up his pace.

Aetnae darted around the guard's face, and he swung his hands around his head. I created an ice globe and pelted the floor with it, right in front of the guard's feet. He slipped and landed hard on his back.

"*Aprire la porta*," I blurted and jumped into the book, turning the page before I was fully through. I didn't need a bunch of guards knowing where I went.

The darkness of the gateway surrounded me, and I breathed in the cool air.

"That was close," Aetnae hollered over the wailing wind. Her voice was so faint, I wouldn't have heard her if she wasn't as close as she was to my ear. She held tight to my hair.

I landed out of the book and onto a black and white marble floor. The welcoming smell of old books and old-world air filled my nose. Aetnae let go of my hair and floated beside me, her iridescent wings barely visible while flapping to keep her up. My eyes went to the arched ceiling with gold trim. I'd studied this library in art class once. Afton had forced me to take it with her. It was a boring hour filled with the history of murals, frescos, and something else I couldn't even remember. Out of all the different places, the libraries interested me the most. And here I was standing in one.

The panels of the ceiling were filled with beautiful frescos depicting the seven liberal arts—arithmetic, geometry, music, grammar, astronomy, rhetoric, and dialectic. Why I remembered this stuff was beyond me.

"You just going to stare at the ceiling?" Aetnae asked from where she stood on one of the display cases in the middle of the room.

I pulled my eyes away from a woman in one of the frescos—or it could have been a man, it was hard to tell in paintings sometimes. The woman had a crown floating above her head and religious men with beards and bishop-like hats surrounded her. Afton had chosen to paint it once for the class. Hers was almost identical; mine put stick figure art to shame.

I missed Afton. I missed Nick. I missed that long-lost time where the biggest fear we had was receiving our grades.

"Where is the entry into the haven?" I asked, pushing back the homesickness hardening in my chest.

Aetnae took off from the display case and hovered in front of a portrait of a royal-looking man. "This is it."

I went over and faced it. *"Ammettere il pura,"* I said.

Nothing happened.

"Ammettere il pura."

Still nothing.

"Are you sure this is it?"

"Yes," Aetnae said. "It looks as if someone has changed the entry charm."

"Do you know if there is a Talpar tunnel around here?"

Aetnae landed on my shoulder, her breathing heavy. "Why do you assume I'd know where their tunnels were located?"

"Because book faeries know everything in the libraries." I craned my neck to see her. "Isn't that what you told me?"

She lifted her face and frowned at me. "Well, you better

not tell anyone I did. And you're not going to like this. We need to go down to the basement."

"Why am I not going to like it?"

"You'll see. That way." She pointed.

I hurried down the long stairs, clutching my bag to my chest, Aetnae bouncing in the air ahead of me. She brought me to a room with black marble, red jasper, and gilt decorations, with twenty-six marble caskets stacked four high on the shelves surrounding the room. An alter with a cross above it was on one wall.

"What is this place?"

"The royal crypt. Kings and queens are buried here."

"I don't like this," I said.

"Told you."

She flew over to one of the golden cupids attached to the wall holding a candlestick over his head. "Pull him forward."

I placed my hand on his head and tugged on it. A panel in the wall slid aside. I stepped inside the roughly dug tunnel and turned to face Aetnae. She waited outside. "You're not coming?"

"No. I'm not allowed to leave the libraries. I can only enter the Fey realm." Her smile was as small as the tip of a fingernail. "Just go until you can't go any farther, and it'll lead you to Santara."

"Okay. Thanks." I wasn't too happy about being in a scary tunnel by myself. The panel slid back into place, and the darkness wrapped around me like thick velvet, a sense of doom hanging in the damp, moldy air.

CHAPTER NINETEEN

The light from my globe reached out into the tunnel until I made it to the end. All that was there was a rustic brick wall with black smudges all over it. I searched for a lever or something to open the entrance. A large pile of used candles lay on the ground to the right.

I shone the light globe over the bricks. Not one was out of place.

"How do you get in?" I asked, as if the wall would answer me. Then I spotted it. Something was written above the door. It wasn't in a language I understood, but one word stood out. *Fuego.* Fire.

My eyes went to the candles then to the soot on the wall. *Fire triggers the door.*

I closed my fingers on my light globe and held up my open hand.

"*Accendere il fuoco,*" I said and a fireball formed on my palm. I touched the bricks with it, and the wall separated at the seams and opened.

The countryside was green, with many trees. I tugged my hood over my head and followed the road carved into the grass. It led me to a village with white stucco buildings and red tiled roofs. A few of them were crumbling or had burned in a fire. People stepped out of their homes as I walked along the road. In the distance, a beautiful castle was built into the side of a tall mountain.

My eyes took in the destruction around me.

It looked like there had been a battle there. Tears stung my eyes, thinking about how the men, women, and children now lining the road must have suffered. They watched me—not with hatred. Not loathing. But what looked to be hope in their eyes. An older man, dirt on the knees of his pants, skin weathered, and his white hair like cotton in the wind, approached me and handed me a cup.

I studied the water inside before drinking it down and handing him back the cup. "What happened here?"

"Our rebels were defeated," he said. "Are you she? Gianna?"

I nodded, tears falling from my eyelashes and tumbling down my cheeks.

He bowed and hobbled along the middle of the road. "Gianna Bianchi," he yelled. "Gianna Bianchi! *Nuestra salvación!*"

More heads bowed as I passed.

That last word sounded like *salvation*. I was just a girl. How could I be that for them? This was too big for me. I wiped my eyes with the flap of the cloak and swallowed hard, gathering the courage to continue.

As I neared the end of the street, Bastien stepped out from one of the houses. He shielded his eyes from the sun with his hand. From the condition of his clothes, he looked like he'd just climbed out of a dirt pit.

He was gorgeous in all his filthy glory, and it was like my entire body lifted, as if I could take flight and soar through the sky. And I couldn't stay still. Couldn't hold back. I ran for him, and he caught me in his arms.

"You're here," I mumbled against his shoulder, my breath heavy, my arms shaky. One of his hands cradled the back of my head while the other squeezed me to him.

"Gianna, you scared me," he whispered. "Why weren't you in Mantello?"

"I went to Tearmann to get the heir's blood." I inhaled the scent that was only him. No one ever smelled as good as he did, even covered in dirt. "I thought I would be back before—"

He released me, his brows pushed together as he studied my face. "You were careless. Why did you go off on your own? You could have been caught."

The anger on his face made me back away from him. "I had to go."

"Why? You could have waited for us."

"Because Mardiana told me to go." Now the anger in my voice matched his. "She said there was a storm coming, and we'd lose our chance to get what we needed in Tearmann."

He ran his hand over his head, dust wafting from his hair. "And you went knowing there'd be a *storm*?"

"Oh, stop it, you two," Edgar said, passing us. With my eyes stuck on Bastien, I hadn't seen him approach. "Kiss and make up. We need to get out of here."

I ignored Edgar's comment. There was no way I was going to kiss and make up, not with Bastien looking at me with venom.

"I can handle myself."

The bite in my voice startled Bastien. He pulled at his neck and lowered his head. "You frightened me. I thought—"

"You thought what?" I cut him off. "That I was a helpless girl?"

His head shot up, his focus on me. "No. I don't think that. I was worried you'd be harmed."

"Well, I'm fine. And why didn't you wait for me in Mantello?"

"I knew you'd go on your own. You're not very patient. It

was either Santara or Tearmann."

"So you chose the one that had a recent uprising?"

"Well," he said, his voice softening. "I thought it best to try the most dangerous one first. In case you had chosen it." He held up a small bottle with what looked to be blood inside. "I did get this from the woman inside."

Edgar came back, eating a big chunk of bread. "We also have Esteril and Couve's donations."

I smiled, a half one, not fully felt. "Good. Then, Royston's the seventh. We have everything we need."

Bastien shielded his eyes again and inspected the road. "There is still the matter of finding the Tetrad."

"I found it," I said, my eyes going to where he was looking. "What is it?"

"We need to take these people with us." He spun around to look at the castle. "How did you get here? Asile guards have blocked the entrance into Santara, and I placed a charm on it to block them."

"Through a Talpar tunnel."

"There is no way to take an entire village with us," Edgar said. "They won't harm the villagers. A king needs subjects to rule."

Edgar was right. The council wouldn't harm people who could work and make them rich. There was a cart on the side of the road. I climbed up on it.

Bastien reached out a hand to me. "What are you doing? Get down."

I ignored him and yelled, "Hello, everyone." Those who weren't watching us already turned their heads. "Um...I am Gianna Bianchi McCabe. Great-granddaughter of Gian Bianchi, and the presage from Agnost's prophesy." The people gathered closer to the cart. "I know this is a scary time."

The old man who had given me water translated what I was saying to the crowd.

"What I have to do is risky. If I fail, the storm will come."
I waited for the man to translate. Concern crossed their faces,
and they whispered among themselves. I swallowed a deep
breath to calm my nerves, to push down my fear.

Okay, get out of your own head, Gia. You can do this.

"But I won't give up," I continued. "I will fight to the end.
You must go about your routines as usual and not provoke
the authorities. Keep your families safe." I paused again for
the man as he repeated my words in Spanish. "There will be
a time to rise, but now is not it. We will send word when you
are needed. I guess that's all."

The concern on their faces changed to hope as the man
finished translating what I'd said. I hopped off the cart.

Bastien's eyes met mine. There was so much love in them
that it caused me to pause. He placed an open palm on my
cheek, and I leaned into it even though I was still mad at him
and he hadn't apologized. "I wish we could run away from all
this madness. Spend time alone, and truly enjoy each other
without mayhem and ruin clouding over us."

"Me, too."

"And I do think you're strong. I apologize if my concern
made you feel differently. I was just scared for your safety."

Though his anger earlier still stung, his words were a start
at tamping down mine. "I worry about you, too."

Edgar put a hand on Bastien's back. "We must get out of
here before your charm is broken."

I glanced at the faces around me. Old and young, men,
women, and children, all helpless to what could come if the
Tetrad ended up in the wrong hands. Really, were there any
right hands? I didn't think so. Power changed people.

That's why Athela wants me to destroy it.

It made me wonder why she chose me. Because she had
used her magic to set all this in motion after her father created
the monster. It should have happened way before this time, but

the Wizard Council threw an ax at her plans, first by killing her, and then by keeping Sentinels from marrying other Sentinels.

I led Bastien and Edgar through the Talpar tunnel and into the library. We jumped through the gateway book and returned to Barmhilde. It was the raining cycle in the coven. Lightning shot across the sky like a synchronized dance against the clouds. Rain smacked the hood covering my head and clapped the ground around me. Mud sucked at my boots with each step.

The Red met us when we entered his camp. "Ah, it's good to see you made it back. There have been some unsettling things happening in the havens. Tearmann was invaded."

"Gia filled us in about Tearmann." Bastien pushed his wet hair from his face. "What else has happened?"

"Let's get you somewhere dry," The Red said, motioning us to follow him.

Demos peeked out of his tent as we passed. "I wondered what all the commotion was about."

Shyna looked over his shoulder. "Hello, Gia."

I gave them a puzzled look. "What are you two doing? And why is she here?"

Demos turned and said something to Shyna. She nodded, and he darted after us.

The Red held the flap to his tent open for us to enter. I removed my cloak and dropped it by the entry. Bastien dropped a flaming ball onto the logs stacked in the fire pit.

I stood over the fire and held my hands above it. My fingers thawed, and a final shiver shook my body. Bastien came up behind me and rubbed my arms.

"Better?" he asked.

"Yes," I said, nodding. "I could sleep forever."

"Please don't. I'd be lonely if you did."

I flashed a smile over my shoulder at him. *That was sweet.*

Bastien took a seat on one of the pillows.

Edgar warmed his hands beside me, glancing from me to

Bastien. "You know, when all this is over, if our side wins, there will no longer be a Wizard Council," he said under his breath, for only me to hear. "The talk is that there will be one ruler over a united council with both Mystik and wizard representatives. And that ruler would be Bastien. He's sacrificed and given much to take care of both the covens and havens. He hasn't hesitated in denouncing the council."

Edgar walked off, not expecting a response from me. It hadn't surprised me. I'd heard it mentioned when I first arrived in the Mystik world that his people loved him and that they wanted him to be high wizard of their haven one day. But what would it do to our relationship? I was too young for all this. Too young to fight beasts. Too young to have everything counting on me. Too young to wonder what the future held for Bastien and me. I just wanted to survive and go to college next year.

All the dreams I had for myself before I was sucked into the Mystik world were like the smoke rising from the fire—a hazy, thin line dissipating into the air.

The Red cleared his throat while rubbing the wetness from the stubble on his scalp. "So Tearmann's queen is in exile, and her parliament has been removed from power, replaced by Comyn MacColgan. Horrible man and wizard, that one. Once bit a man's nose off just for looking at him wrongly."

"What's happening to the guards and their families?" I asked, my thoughts going to Buach and Galach.

"We sent word for them to show no resistance," The Red said. "A few ignored us. Some are dead. Others are in the gallows under the Vatican."

"I see." I lowered my head, hoping neither Buach nor Galach was one of the dead.

"Once the new high wizard is in place," Bastien said, "they plan on expunging Conemar's criminal record and allowing him to resume his role as Esteril's high wizard."

Demos slammed his fist against a pillow. "This is felonious.

They can't reverse a court's finding."

Bastien nodded, staring at his folded hands in front of him. "If they're in control, they can do whatever pleases them."

The Red picked up a bottle with dark red liquid inside and poured himself a glass. He downed it in one gulp. "There's more. The High Wizard of Veilig and his family escaped before the guards sent by the council to arrest them arrived in their haven. We received word from Greyhill that the family is hiding within their coven." A quick look passed between The Red and Demos.

Shyna must have brought the message.

"You have some time to rest," The Red said. "Make sure to use it wisely. We must plan for our library invasion. So get some grub and some sleep, and we'll meet again in the morning."

The smell of breakfast wafted on the cool morning air. Rain plunking against the hard shell of my pod-like tent had kept me up all night. I yawned and picked at the eggs on my plate with the bent tines of a fork. The uneven surfaces of the log tables caused the dishes to tilt, and the chairs, made of stumps, rocked if not positioned just right on the lumpy grass.

Bastien placed a plate of food down and sat beside me, his stump rocking. He scooted it around until it was steady. "You dressed for a battle?"

My fingers went to my scabbard on the table. "Lei ordered us to be ready at all times. Just in case."

One of his eyebrows shot up. "Ordered you?"

"Since—" I stopped before mentioning Arik. It hurt to think of him against us. "Anyway, she was next in line to lead our Sentinel group."

He picked up his cup. "I see."

"Where's Demos and Edgar?" I asked, changing the subject. "I haven't seen them around this morning. And both of them usually wake early."

He took a sip from his cup and put it down. "They're going over the distraction plan for the libraries with The Red's forces."

I rubbed my eyes.

"Didn't sleep well, huh?"

"No." I yawned again. The air between us was as thick as the porridge in the bowl beside my plate. Though he'd apologized for getting angry with me, I still felt the sting of it. I didn't like him scolding me as if I were a child. I'd faced many dangers before. Even if I was scared, I was a Sentinel born with the natural ability to fight, armed with more than one battle globe.

He gave me his signature cocky smile. The one a little higher on one side of his mouth than the other. "You could've slept in my room."

"Yeah, thank you, but no." I shoved a fork full of egg in my mouth.

"What? Are my arms not warm enough for you?"

"Oh, they're warm, all right," I said, going back to poking at my eggs. "I'm just not sure I could *handle* myself."

"I detect sarcasm in your tone," he said and took a bite of his potatoes.

I picked up a slice of toast, tore off a piece, and dipped it in the egg yolk. "Sorry. I just need some time alone. I'm worried about everyone. It feels like I'm juggling a bunch of globes and any moment they're all going to fall around me." I swung my leg over the stump and faced him. "It's everyone. Pop, Nana, Nick, Afton, Carrig, Sinead, Royston…Uncle Philip. I see them all ready to drop. And which ones do I catch? I can't grab them all at the same time." I'd omitted Arik's name, but I was concerned for him, and for Emily.

Bastien wrapped his arms around me, and I rested my head

on his shoulder. "I'll help you catch them. So will Demos. Lei and Jaran will be there, as well. You're not alone, Gianna."

I tilted my head to look at him. He gently kissed my lips, and my heart finally forgave him.

"I'm most terrified of losing you," I said.

He flashed a crooked smile. "Never going to happen."

"Are you always so sure of everything?"

"Not everything," he said. "I doubted you would ever come to your senses and realize I was the better man for you."

"You never doubted that."

"All right." He laughed. "I knew you'd come around. Besides, who could resist me?"

I laughed that time. "You're so full of yourself sometimes."

"I was raised to never lie, weren't you?"

"Yes, of course."

"Then tell me a truth about yourself." Amusement sparkled in his eyes and flipped my stomach.

This game made me uneasy. "I have a mean uppercut and knee strike."

He frowned. "How about something about you, not something you can do."

"I have thick hair."

He stifled a laugh. "This makes you uncomfortable, doesn't it?"

"*So* uncomfortable."

"How about I start?"

"Okay."

"I once caught the pantry on fire," he said. "Odil and I were nine and eight, respectively. He warned me not to play with matches. My brother was my best friend growing up. I looked up to him. Then he changed, became more self-centered. I miss the Odil from our youth. It crushes my heart to see how he's turned out."

"That has to be hard," I said.

"Now you."

"I wish my mother was still alive. She's a shadow in my mind. I'm not sure which memories are my own and which are ones I've made up from the photographs and videos I've seen of her." I glanced away, hiding the sadness noticeable in my eyes.

"That must be difficult." He lifted my chin and kissed me again, his lips soft and tender. "All right, then, I'll stop torturing you."

Screams broke out somewhere in the distance, and I pulled away from him. "That can't be good."

Bastien scrambled off the stump at the same time as I grabbed my scabbard and jumped to my feet. We dashed out of the dining tent. Shouts and screams came from the village. We ran toward the sound.

I struggled to strap my scabbard to my waist as we sprinted up the hill. It slipped a couple of times before I got the buckle fastened. The closer we got to the area, the more my heart sank. It was coming from the curer's building.

Oh no. Carrig.

The Red stopped me before I could charge inside.

"Let me through." I pushed against him. "Carrig!"

"What is happening in there?" Bastien asked.

"A mad woman is inside," The Red said. "The coven's guards are handling it."

"That won't do. They haven't any magic." Bastien brushed by him and produced an electric charge in his upturned hand.

I hurried behind him. A Laniar with dark hair falling to his shoulders blocked the entry into the room. Beside him was a Djallican girl, not much older than me, with small horns sticking out of her wide forehead, long earlobes, and short spikey hair the color of cinnamon. The two guards pointed their swords at a woman whose face I couldn't see with the uniformed bodies blocking my view.

"Let us through," Bastien commanded.

The guards glanced behind them and, spotting the electricity in Bastien's hand, stepped aside.

"*Accendere il ghiaccio.*" I ignited an ice globe and weaved around the guards, almost tripping when I saw the woman. Fear grabbed my breath, and I gasped.

Lorelle. She stood over Carrig, a large dagger to his throat. I hadn't seen her since she hit me with an ancient spell that stole my truth globe from me. She had murdered my aunt Eileen and posed as her to spy on Nana and to find me.

"Step away from him, Lorelle," I warned, holding my globe up higher for her to see.

Her screeching laugh scratched across my scalp and rattled down my bones. "I'm not Lorelle. Her brain was a blank canvas after the scryers had their way with her. Easy for me to move in. Usually, I can only claim the mind of a magical child, but here I am in the shell of a Fey. Drop your magic, or I'll cut him."

I stumbled back, fear choking my throat. *Not Lorelle?*

Bastien lowered his hands, the electric spark between them snuffing out, but I refused to bust my globe. I processed the information she'd given us.

The scryers had used their magic to gain information on Conemar after Lorelle's arrest for trying to destroy me. If she wasn't Lorelle, then who was she? And it hit me.

No. It can't be. But the clues in her statement gave me all I needed to know who she was.

"What do you want with Carrig, Ruth Ann?"

"Conemar was right," she said. "You are a smart little girl, aren't you?"

Ruth Ann was a Bane Witch from Branford, Connecticut, who had been sentenced to death during the witch trials in the sixteen hundreds.

"You didn't answer me. Why Carrig? He isn't a threat to anyone in his state."

"He may wake up. He is the leader of the Sentinels and is

too powerful and persuasive to let live. Too much of a risk for Conemar." Her grin looked sinister, and her eyes held evil, her hand lifting a little and the blade leaving Carrig's neck.

She noticed her hand had moved, and she returned the blade to Carrig's skin.

The ice globe on my palm bit at my skin. I could stop her. Throw my globe when she was distracted again. So I waited, not feeling scared, not panicking, just watching her and waiting for my moment to strike.

"I will trade his life for Katy Kearns," she said.

"We cannot make that trade," a voice came from a hologram image on the counter opposite Carrig's bed. It was Queen Titania, and beside her was Nana. In the background, Sinead slept in her hospital bed. My heart crushed in my chest.

"Hell, no, they can't," I affirmed. "What do you need her for—?" I stopped, knowing exactly what Ruth Ann was after. "You want to possess her body because she's skilled in the magic of Incantora."

Bastien slid a confused look at me. I couldn't explain it to him, so I shook my head.

Nana had never used the Incantora, saying with that power came responsibility. She had been a young girl when it was discovered that she had the power. Her mother had forced Nana to make a witch's pledge to only use it when preventing a major disaster that could cost many lives, not just one or a few. Since there was magic behind her promise, she'd face grave consequences if she ever broke it.

"This is not a deal we are willing to make," Queen Titania said.

Nana turned her head toward me. "I'm sorry, Gia."

"Not your fault." I focused back on Lorelle before my eyes could fill with tears.

Ruth Ann glared at the hologram. "I'll give you one minute. That is all. Make the deal, or I will kill him." She held the long dagger above Carrig's chest and watched the antique clock on the table beside the bed.

And that was her mistake.

One minute. So much could change in just a moment. I could lose a father I'd only recently discovered. The Mystik world could lose one of the greatest Sentinels in their history. Deidre could lose the only father she'd ever known. And her mother, since Sinead would die with him. Such a small amount of time to lose so much.

One minute.

CHAPTER TWENTY

Ruth Ann's decision to move Lorelle's hand away from Carrig's neck to above his chest gave me a better opportunity to hit her.

I eased my hand back, the glittery white globe spinning on my palm.

"No, you'll hit Carrig," Bastien hissed, grabbing my arm and causing my globe to slip from my hand.

It busted against the floor, and ice shot across the wooden planks.

Anger twisted Ruth Ann's face. A guttural growl escaped her lips and she slammed the dagger into Carrig's chest.

NO!

Electricity ignited between Bastien's hands, and he released the charge. The powerful stream hit Lorelle's body, and it crumpled to the ground. Ruth Ann's dark, smoky spirit shot out of Lorelle and frantically flew around the room, hitting things off the table and slamming into the two guards. She knocked Bastien to the floor.

My eyes followed her spirit, waiting for the perfect time when she crossed in front of me, then I shot my ice globe at her. The hazy form froze in the air and dropped, shattering against the ground in thousands of little pieces.

I darted to Carrig's side. His blood seeped into the sheet covering him. "No, no, *no*. Carrig! Someone help him." My pleading screams were almost incoherent.

Two curers, an older woman and a young man, came to his side.

"Get her back," the man said, pushing me aside and starting to work on Carrig.

Bastien wrapped his arms around me, and I yanked away from him.

The image of the curers working on Carrig was blurry with the tears pouring from my eyes. "Please. You have to save him. Please. *Please*."

The woman's eyes went to the hologram. "He's too weak. His wife's connection is draining his strength. They both will die."

"*No*," came out of me as a painful wail. Bastien reached for me again, and I shrugged him off.

"We must remove the bond," the man said, "or we'll lose them both. If we break it, he'll have a chance to survive."

I hung my head. The nightmare wouldn't end. I would lose him. Lose Sinead. The pain was too great.

"Gia, you're his daughter." Queen Titania's voice was staticky over the hologram. "We must save one of them. Do you agree? It's your choice."

I knew what my answer would mean. That in choosing one, I would lose the other. But I couldn't let them both die. One life. But what would that life be without the other?

You'd lose both. Reason broke through my irrational thoughts. *You can save one.*

"Remove the bond," I said firmly and assuredly.

Queen Titania nodded to a faery woman in a white jacket with a severe stare. The woman injected Sinead with a long syringe that had a silver liquid inside. I watched as the fluid emptied into Sinead's arm. I wanted to hold her. To tell her I loved her, and that I was sorry this had happened.

"She's gone," the woman said and walked out of view.

I slumped, wailing. Bastien captured me in his arms before I hit the floor. With each sob, pain ripped through my chest.

Deidre. Oh, Deidre. This would be a blow to her. Sinead was her mother. They loved each other deeply. I never had a mother relationship, and I'd been envious watching theirs.

I wiped my eyes with my sleeve. The tears kept coming, and the pain I felt in my chest sharpened.

The Djallican girl bowed her head slightly on her way to the exit. "I am truly sorry for your loss. I wish—" She cleared her throat. "I wish we could've stopped her." I knew her. She had been behind the counter in Asile's basement common room when Arik and I had gone to practice my globe.

Since I was just staring at her and couldn't speak with the emotions gutting my stomach, Bastien answered for me. "Thank you. No one is to blame here. We all tried our best."

No one is to blame? It was as if a black fog hung over me. The voices around me were muffled, and the bodies were distorted by the pooling tears blurring my vision.

She nodded and followed the other guard outside.

"He's improving," the older woman said, checking Carrig's vitals with some sort of clear tablet. "The dagger missed his heart. I believe he'll pull through."

The man beside her turned to us. "We must operate. I'll send for you once we've finished. Please leave us."

We turned to go, and the room felt like it was spinning. Bastien held me, helping me out the door.

No one is to blame? The words stung. But there was someone to blame. I shoved Bastien away from me.

"It's *your* fault!" The words came out guttural, scraping my throat. "*You stopped me.* I could have hit her with my globe and you stopped me."

Bastien looked like my words had slapped him. "I'm sorry. I thought—"

"You didn't think! You don't trust my abilities. Because of you, Sinead is dead." I ran from him.

"Gia! Wait!"

I ignored his call, sprinting down the hill. My foot hit a rock, and I crashed to the ground.

"Gia!"

My boot slipped as I scrambled up to my feet. I tore into my tent and paced, my breaths loud and painful, coming quick and hard. Too quick. Panic rose in my chest like bile bubbling up and burning my throat.

"Gia, may I enter?" Bastien's voice came from the other side of the tent's flap.

"Go away."

There was silence and then a deep sigh. "All right. I'll be back to check on you."

I didn't answer him.

The sound of him plodding off caused another sob to rip from my lips. I removed my boots, lowered myself onto the mat, and pulled the covers over me.

I cried until I couldn't cry any more.

Demos pushed open the flap and charged into the tent. "What happened? There are rumors that someone tried to kill Carrig."

I just stared at him.

Bastien barged in after him. "What are you doing in here?" he asked and pulled Demos to the side.

"I heard about Carrig," Demos said.

Bastien whispered a play-by-play of what had happened at the curer's building. Demos's face changed from concern to anger. Tears filled his eyes. When Bastien mentioned that Sinead had died, Demos fisted his eyes and dropped into a squat.

"No," Demos cried. "I'll kill that woman."

"She's gone," Bastien said. "Gia destroyed her with her globe."

Demos looked at me. "I'm so sorry, Gia. What can I do for you?"

"Can you ask Edgar for some Fey Water?" I asked. "I just want to sleep."

"No," Bastien said, stopping Demos before he left. "It's too risky. She's already had a taste of it and could get addicted. Just get ready for tomorrow. We're still going as planned."

Too tired and distraught to comment on what Bastien had said, I tugged the covers up to my chin and turned onto my side.

The flap rustled as Bastien and Demos left the tent.

I cried for a long while before falling asleep. Dreams rushed in and out of the darkness behind my eyes. Faces of my family, friends, and the Sentinels. The first day I met Sinead was so vivid it felt real. I was walking through a corridor in the Asile castle after being drugged. She'd caught me before I fell to the hard floor. She was beautiful with her perfectly angled face, choppy red hair, and pointy ears, her movements graceful.

Would she be mad that I chose to save Carrig? *Never*, I could almost hear her say.

Wake up, Gia. You are the Assassin of Truths. Show them what they do not see. Show them all.

"Sinead?" I opened my eyes. Bastien held a *Mystik Observer* in one hand and a cup of something steaming in his other.

"How long have I've been sleeping?"

He folded the paper. "For a long while. It's morning. How are you feeling?"

"I'm okay. Just extremely sad."

"I can imagine." He placed the illegal newspaper on his lap and studied my face. "Can I get you something?"

"No—" My eyes went to the newspaper, and I sat up. "The *Mystik Observer*."

"Yes." He raised an eyebrow at me. "You want to read it?"

I shook my head, picking it up. "Where do they print this? Do you know?"

The look on his face said he was trying to figure out why I'd asked. "I don't, but possibly The Red does. Do you care to explain what's turning inside that pretty head of yours?"

I glared at him. "Don't call my head pretty."

"You're still angry with me."

It was a statement, so I didn't feel like answering it. "We can use the paper to expose the council's lies and tell the people what they're planning to do."

A smile slowly pulled on his lips as he studied the paper. "That's a brilliant plan."

Someone knocked on the side of the tent.

"Come in," I called.

Demos ducked his head in. "Your nana and Afton just arrived in Barmhilde."

"No. They can't be here. They're supposed to stay in the Fey realm where they'll be safe." I grabbed my boots and shoved my feet into them. "Where are they?"

"With Carrig. He's awake," he said, holding the flap open for me as I charged out. He and Bastien sprint-walked trying to keep up with me.

When I entered Carrig's room, he was propped up against the pillows. Tall glass cylinders glowed red and hummed in the corners of the room. By how hot it was inside, they had to be heat lamps. Afton fed Carrig a spoonful of broth from a ceramic bowl with a chipped lip. Nana sat on a chair beside Afton, saying something to him that I couldn't catch.

Carrig's red-rimmed eyes landed on me. Afton and Nana turned to see what he was looking at.

"Oh Gia," Afton said and placed the bowl on the table beside the bed. Three brisk steps and she had me in her arms. "I'm so sorry. What you went through—had to do—it was awful."

I hugged her back, inhaling the rose scent in her hair. "I'm okay. But why are you here? It's not safe. You should have stayed in the Fey realm." I gazed over her shoulder at Nana. "You both should have."

Nana pushed herself up from the chair. "I'm perfectly capable of taking care of Afton and myself." She hobbled a little as she came over to me. "Now give me a hug."

After releasing Afton, I stepped into Nana's embrace and she whispered against my ear, "You are never to feel guilty about the decision you made. We would have lost them both. The bond Sinead accepted to marry Carrig would never let her live without him."

"Come here." Carrig's voice was hoarse and weak.

I shuffled over to him. He motioned for me to get closer, and I bent over him. It took a lot of effort for him to give me a simple kiss on my cheek, but it meant so much to me. Tears dropped from my eyes and blotted his sheet.

Nana handed me a handkerchief.

"Thank you." I took it and wiped my eyes.

"You aren't to be worrying about me," he said.

With the redness in his eyes and the moisture on his eyelashes, it was obvious he'd been crying. I couldn't imagine what losing Sinead felt like to him. It was a blow to my heart, and it had to be a hundred times worse for him.

When I hadn't spoken, he continued. "You did the right thing. I have you and Deidre. I'll be fine. My love is waiting for me, and we'll be together again one day. Now then, get prepared for what you must do today. Sinead would want us to keep fighting. My apologies for not being able to take up arms with you today."

I dabbed at my eyes again. "You don't have to apologize. I have plenty of fighters going with me."

It took him some effort to smile. His eyes drooped, and he forced them open.

"We should go and let Carrig sleep," Nana said.

Afton turned to Carrig. "Do you want some more soup? I can stay and—" She stopped, realizing he had already fallen asleep. "I guess I'll come back later and try to feed him again."

The cool air outside felt good after being in the hot room. I noticed the Mystik newspaper still clutched in Bastien's hand. He must've carried it with him without thinking when he'd chased me up to the curers.

Nana dabbed at her forehead with her floral scarf. "I'm getting tired. Is there a hotel someplace in the village?"

"Not sure. We haven't seen any." I turned to Demos. "Could you show Nana to my tent?"

"I'd be delighted," he said and held his elbow out to her. "Shall we?"

Nana grasped his arm. "I bet you're a real charmer with the ladies."

He led her down the hill. "It's been mentioned a time or two."

My cold eyes met Bastien's worried ones. Guessing I was still angry with him, he excused himself and plodded after Nana and Demos.

I faced Afton. "You were on the news staff at school. Do you think you could help write something for me?"

Her eyes studied me. "I'm not sure I like the expression on your face. Every time you look at me that way, you want to do something that could get us in trouble."

"Okay, so it could be a little illegal," I said. "And if we're caught, it may be punishable by death here in the Mystik world."

"Well," Afton said, "it'd better be worth it, then."

"It is. We're going to assassinate the council's truths."

Her eyebrows crinkled together. "Assassinate their truths? What does that even mean?"

"Expose their lies."

Afton crossed her arms. "I'm in. What do you need me to do?"

"Write an article. I'll tell you what to say, and you make it sound legit."

"It's fabricated?" She gave me that look that said she drew a line at false news.

"No, I just need you to make it sound eloquent."

"Oh," she said. "Well, I can do that."

"Splendid. Then we should find The Red and see what he knows about the *Observer*." I glanced back, not wanting to leave Carrig but knowing I had to. There was much to do, and we still needed to get Royston away from Asile.

The rain streamed down the window of the small village library. It had television and, apparently, spotty wifi and the oldest computer I'd ever seen. I sat on a short file cabinet and tapped my boot against the leg of the desk, watching Afton's fingers fly over the keyboard.

"How do you have human world technology here?" I asked, hoping to make the time pass faster.

The Red leaned against a wall, inspecting the sharpness of his long, claw-like nails. I imagined he'd use them as a weapon while fighting. "The capability is there, but the Wizard Council forbids it. They argue that we should cherish a simpler life and that technology has ruined the human world. You can't miss something you've never had. So the people of the Mystik world are in the dark as far as human technology is concerned."

"I see." I glanced over Afton's shoulder.

"You know that makes me nervous," she snapped. "Stop watching me type."

I returned to my seat on the file cabinet and continued

tapping my boot.

Demos had joined us after leaving Nana in my tent. He stood guard at the window to make sure no one interrupted us.

Afton glared at my foot. "Do you mind? You're shaking the desk, and I can't concentrate with that noise."

I shrugged a shoulder at Demos and mouthed, *Whoops*.

He quirked a smile. "She's just anxious. We all are."

"Well, good thing I'm done, then." She reclined against the back of the chair. "Now what?"

"Do they have an email address where we can send it?" I asked The Red.

"They do have an illegal computer like this one here," he said. "But it isn't a good idea to send an email. There's no telling who can intercept it. We can print it out, and I'll have it delivered it to the *Mystik Observer* in Greyhill."

"Shyna could take it," Demos said. "Since she's a Greyhillian, she wouldn't raise suspicion."

"That's a great idea." I hopped down from the cabinet. "Let's go ask her."

The Red pushed himself off the wall. "If we send her, we put her in jeopardy. No telling what they would do to her if she's caught with that article."

"I will deliver it," a Talpar woman said from behind the other desk. I'd forgotten she was there. She was the librarian, and she was the woman who'd given us the map to the Talpar tunnels.

I shook my head. "No. You can't. What about your pups?"

"My mother will take care of them," she said, her small, mousy voice shaking a little at the beginning of each word. "I want to be part of the Resistance. Because of the council, my husband died of that disease. There was a cure, and they refused to distribute it to us."

"But the council's guards discovered an entry into your tunnels," I said. "They've been searching them for me. You could run into one of their groups."

The feelers on the side of her nose wiggled. "I can sense movement in the tunnels for miles. Besides, since we knew our tunnels were discovered, we've dug new ones and filled the old with water. A few guards were lost in the flood."

And Bastien, Edgar, and I were almost lost, too.

"I will send two of my men with her," The Red said. "It's best we prepare for the library distraction. Jaran and Lei depend on us. If they're caught trying to get Royston out of Asile, they'll welcome death to avoid what the scryers will do to them."

The wind outside kissed my tent and flapped the doors. Nana reclined against the large pillows on the mat covering the ground. A note had arrived from the underground for me from Buach. Briony, a few faeries, and Couve guards had sneaked into Tearmann and rescued Galach and his guards from their captors.

Bastien. He knew how worried I was for Galach and the others, and I was pretty certain this rescue was his doing.

"You look as if you belong in Sherwood Forest in that get-up," Nana said.

I glanced down at the leather breastplate, tunic, and army green pants before giving her a questioning look. "I guess so. All I need now is a bow and arrow, and I'd be Robin Hood." The leather strap creaked as I tightened the belt of the holster around my thigh.

Nana rolled over to her hands and knees and pushed herself up into a standing position. "Getting old is such an annoyance," she said, her breaths heavy.

I slid the dagger into the sheath. "I never think of you as old."

"Thank you, dear," she said with a smile. "Never stop lying to me."

Afton came in the tent carrying straps of leather. "This is all I could find to tie your hair up. Maybe I can braid it?"

"I was thinking a high, tight bun. Nothing loose where my hair can get pulled." The first time I met The Red, he'd yanked me up by my ponytail, and it was painful.

Afton dug her fingers into my hair and started weaving it. "Okay. Something warrior chic. Got it."

"Gia, are you ready?" Bastien called from outside the tent.

"Just about," I called.

"What's wrong with you two?" Afton asked, tugging my hair as she worked to braid it.

"Nothing."

Everything. I wanted to say. When he prevented me from using my globe, it had caused us to lose Sinead. But I couldn't tell them that. I cared about Bastien, and I didn't want them having negative opinions about him.

Nana's soft green eyes glistened. "Your pop would be terrified if he knew what you were about to do."

It was her way of letting me know she was terrified for me, too.

"Don't worry. I'll be fine. I just don't like leaving you guys here alone." I glanced from Nana to Afton. "Maybe we can get you to the Shelter with Pop?"

"I'd rather go to the Shelter than stay here." Afton tied the ends of the leather straps securing my hair.

Nana studied Afton's work. "Looks good. Almost romantic."

Afton frowned at the top of my head. "Is it tight enough?"

I shook my head hard and nothing moved. "It's perfect."

Bastien's head poked into the tent. "What's taking you so long?"

"I'm ready," I said, picking up my bag with Gian's book inside. "Can we get Nana and Afton to the Shelter beforehand?"

"If we leave now," he said.

Nana exited the tent first, and before Afton went through, she gave me a hug. "You got this. You've met every challenge head on. Don't hesitate, ever. Remember what your coach said once."

"The toughest opponent is the one in your head."

Her lips hinted at a smile. "That's it. Love you, G. Stay strong."

"I love you, too."

We scrambled out of the tent together. The setting sun blinded me as I trotted down the hill with Afton. I could barely make out Nana and Bastien's silhouettes against the brightness. Just past the hill, a group gathered in a circle. When we neared them, Demos broke away from The Red and his gang of misfits and met us.

"Are you all ready?" I asked, approaching.

Demos gave me an incredulous look. "We've been waiting on you."

I flashed a wide grin. "Oh, then I guess we're ready."

Bastien stood beside me, looking everywhere but at me.

"I know what you did," I said.

He gave me a questioning look. "What have I done now?"

"Galach's rescue. Thank you for helping Briony."

"It's the least I could do," he said. "And we'll need as many guards as we can find for whatever is ahead. They should be at the Shelter by now."

Of course he'd downplay it. Whenever he'd done good deeds for others, he was humble.

"Everyone has their assignments," The Red hollered. "We're off. Remember, you start jumping at two in the morning London time."

The group broke up and headed in different directions.

"Red," I said, approaching him.

He rotated to face me. "You need something, Gianna?"

I reached behind my neck, unfastened Faith's pendant,

and handed it out to him. "I wanted you to have this. It was Faith's, and it should belong to you. Maybe it'll bring you luck."

He inspected the pendant that was connected to the dainty chain dangling from his large hand. "Thank you. It's as beautiful as she was." He sniffed and strained his face, trying not to cry, but he couldn't hide the emotion in his voice. "I miss her every day."

I glanced off, not wanting to catch the emotions choking him up. "I do, too."

The Red squared his shoulders. "Enough sap. It's time we be warriors. Stop Conemar and his followers. That's what Faith would want us to do." He secured the necklace around his neck, tucked it into his shirt, and stomped off.

Enoon, the tough man with boar features and tusks who we ran into at Barmhilde, was first. "It is our custom to show respect to our greatest warrior by a slap on the back. Not many receive such an honor. Don't worry, the others won't hurt you." He clapped my back. "Death be a stranger."

Another Mystik with ashen skin and twig-like hair came up and repeated Enoon's words and actions. The line continued with men and women from the many different Mystik covens— Laniars with their sharp canines and greyhound shaped bodies, horned men and women, a few older Sentinels, and many others. Their various colored and shaped eyes held hope and so much warmth for me.

A Writhe, one not turned into an evil, ominous creature by Conemar, stopped in front of me. He moved his bald head from side to side, studying me. Raised veins just under his pale skin branched out like roots of a tree.

The Writhes were the first coven to fall to Conemar. He'd used the ones who hadn't escaped or he hadn't killed as experiments for an ancient potion he'd found in Esteril. It turned them into evil creatures driven by the thirst to kill, but controlled by their master. The first high wizard of that haven and Athela's father, Mykyl, had come up with the recipe to create the Tetrad—four warriors made into terrifying creatures joined by one soul with the power of all the elements.

"I do this for the loss of my people." He lightly tapped my shoulder as if afraid to hurt me, which completely surprised me. All this time I had been afraid of every Writhe because of my encounter with the ones Conemar had changed into feral beasts. But I was wrong. The Writhe standing in front of me was proof that not all of them were bad. "Death be a stranger," he said and walked off with his head high and determination in his gait. He joined a group of Writhes up the hill. There were about a dozen of them joining the fight with us.

Two hounds paced around the Writhes. They looked like nightmares on four legs, resembling demon-possessed rhinos with a large tusk curving up from their snouts. Nick, Afton, and I had encountered one that first night I accidentally jumped with them to a Paris library. Most of them had died during Conemar's attack on the Writhe's coven.

After each Mystik performed the ritual on me, they headed for the village. A rush of pride caused me to stand straighter. Their respect and the hope they placed in me sent fire through my veins. We had to stop the council's plan. We couldn't fail. Too many lives depended on it.

Taking up the end of the line, Bastien smiled as he approached me. "I thought it would never end."

"Me, either." I glanced over my shoulder at the Writhes. "I'm surprised they came."

He looked to where my eyes were set. "They have had it harder than most. Those men and women are the last of their warriors. It was hard for them to leave their hideout. They know the remaining survivors are vulnerable without them."

"There are more of them? Survivors?"

"Yes. Their hope is to one day return to their coven and rebuild. That is their motivation for joining us." Bastien slid a glance at me. "You all right?"

"Yeah. Just a little overwhelmed by that ceremony."

"It's a great honor," he said.

An uncomfortable silence settled around us. Ever since Sinead's death, things were off with us. Everything felt numb—my body, my mind, my soul. Nana said I was just grieving, and that with time, I'd feel better. I sure hoped so, because the funk I was in made me feel like there was a black hole eating up my insides.

When it was obvious I wasn't going to respond to his last statement, he said, "I forgot to tell The Red something. Excuse me."

My eyes followed Bastien as he jogged over to The Red, who was in a deep conversation with Edgar.

Demos came up to my side. "Hey, it's going to be tough tonight. I just wanted to say—"

"Wait." I stopped him. "You're not going to say you love me, are you?"

His eyebrows pushed together. "Have you lost your senses? Why would I say that?"

Because Nana and Afton had? I shrugged a shoulder. "Um, I don't know."

Okay…awkward.

"I was going to tell you to stay alert," he said. "And that I like you most days, so try to make it back alive, all right?"

"You watch yourself, too. You're kind of nice to have around…*most days.*"

He smirked and took long strides up the hill, following The Red's gang.

There was no certainty our plan would work, but watching the determination in the creatures storming up the hill, I felt ready to face it.

CHAPTER TWENTY-ONE

The neoclassical manor of the Shelter seemed quiet compared to the last time I'd been there. The makeshift camp that housed many Mystiks, wizards, and guards during the uprising was gone. To the south of the manor, the lake was a dark gray, with clouds covering the moon.

With labored breaths, struggling with her tote bag, Nana tried to keep up with us.

"Here. Let me carry it for a while," Afton said, adjusting the pack on her back before taking Nana's bag from her.

Nana smiled and patted Afton's arm. "Thank you, dear."

We crossed a bridge arching over the river and walked on a cobbled pathway that cut through the tiny rows of cottages. Not a single villager was out as they were the first time I had walked the roads. Only a few of the windows had flickering lights behind their thick glass windows. No voices greeted us when we came into the foyer of the Shelter.

"Something isn't right." I held on tighter to my bag with Gian's book inside as I quietly walked into the den. The furniture resembled hunched ghosts covered with sheets. "No one is here."

Panic fluttered in my chest. *Where are they? Pop?*

Bastien crossed the room to the large brick hearth that dominated one of the walls. He grabbed a metal rod leaning in a stand beside it and poked at the charcoaled logs.

"It's wet," he said. "Someone put it out with water. They were here not too long ago."

"This is bad, isn't it?" Afton twisted the handles of Nana's tote bag.

Nana clicked her tongue. "Now, now, dear, we always stay positive in moments like this. We wouldn't want to invite bad karma, now, would we?"

My chest tightened as all the horrible things that could have happened raced through my mind.

Pop was supposed to be there with Afton's parents. Bastien's mother and her guards had been hiding at the Shelter for months. Briony and Galach should have already arrived there, too. But they hadn't. They were gone—or worse, taken.

"Where are they?" I asked, frustration in my voice.

"By the looks of things, they were covering up their presence here." Bastien stood and wiped the wet cinders from his fingers onto his pant leg. "Perhaps they went to the basement. There's a hideout there."

I followed him down the basement steps. Nana and Afton waited at the top of the stairs for us. As I landed on the bottom floor, my hands shook. Bastien went to the farthest wall to a heavy mahogany wardrobe.

At first, I thought he would open the doors and we would travel through the wardrobe to another magical realm just like in one of my favorite books, but instead he searched the side of it. His arm jerked and a *click* sounded.

"Stand back," he warned me before calling, "Hello! Is there anyone inside? I am Bastien Renard of Couve."

"Bastien?" a woman's voice came from the other side of the wall.

The wardrobe swung out. A guard with huge muscles and a receding hairline, his sword extended in front of him, eased through the opening. "*C'est lui*," the guard said. "Bastien."

Sabine, wearing a tunic with pants and boots, squeezed by the guard. "*Mon cher fils*," she said, throwing her arms around Bastien. They had the same dark hair, except gray streaked hers.

He hugged her back. "*Mère.*"

Another guard, taller, with fewer muscles and more hair, came out.

The moment a tuft of red hair peeked out from behind the door, I knew who it was. "Pop," I cried and ran into his arms before he had a chance to enter the basement. "I was so worried."

"Welcome to my world," he muttered against my head. "I've been out of my mind worrying about you."

I pulled back to get a better look at him. There were more wrinkles pressing into his forehead and around his eyes, and the bags under them had deepened.

"I can take care of myself."

His thumb gently traced the scar across my cheek and there was a sadness in his eyes. "Doesn't stop my fear of losing you."

"Where are my parents?" Afton bit her bottom lip. I hadn't even heard her come downstairs.

Pop glanced over at her. "They weren't home when the guards came for me. They're in New Mexico. Your grandmother had a fall."

Concern struck her face. "*Abuelita*? What happened to her?"

"She broke her wrist," Pop said. "But is doing much better. Thankfully, it wasn't a hip."

She stopped worrying her lip. "So they're all safe?"

"They are," he said.

To our side, Briony, Galach, and a few guards shuffled out

from behind the wardrobe. Kayla Bagley, wearing a guard's uniform, her apricot hair pulled tightly back, was right behind them.

I pushed away from Pop, pulling the dagger out of the holster around my thigh. "What is she doing here?"

Kayla was the guard sent to Branford to watch over the gateway book in the library there. She was supposed to help us with our search for the Chiavi. Instead, she was a spy for Conemar, and she'd turned on us. Not to mention she had been dating Pop and broke his heart into pieces.

Pop grasped my hand, the one strangling the dagger, and lowered my arm. "We are safe because of her."

"Nick is gone because of her," I snapped.

"No," Kayla said. "You don't understand. I was a double agent for Merl. Conemar thought I had turned to his side. If I hadn't helped him escape that day on your front lawn, more of you would have died. It was either Nick or all of you. And I knew Conemar would never kill his son."

"How do we know you're not lying?" I asked.

She removed a cell phone from her pants pocket and searched for something on the screen, then handed it to me. "I have proof. It's a video from Merl in case I was ever caught."

Hearing Merl's name twisted my heart. He had been Asile's high wizard before he was murdered and Uncle Philip took his place.

I inspected the cell phone. It was the exact match to the one Ricardo, a Laniar who'd died helping me, had once. It also had a message from Merl to me. I pressed play.

Merl's weary face popped on the screen. "Whoever receives this video, know that Kayla Bagley is a guard for Asile. I enlisted her to spy on Conemar. To become a turncoat, so to speak. She is to receive complete immunity from any crime committed while in my service. May Agnes guide you... in your duties and in removing this threat on ours and the human world." A loud *boom* went off somewhere off screen.

He glanced behind him. "We're under attack. Kayla, you must go. Use the secret passage." The video was still playing as he handed her the phone.

"Your Highness, come with me," she pleaded. The images of his office were jumpy as she moved.

"No," he said. "They know I'm in here, and will assume I had a secret escape. I can't risk them finding you. You must get back to Branford. Besides, I won't leave my people." I could barely see what he was doing with the screen jerking all over the place. He tugged on the side of a portrait of Taurin, the Seventh Wizard, and it opened like a door. The video stopped and Kayla's legs froze on the screen.

The words clogging my throat wouldn't come out. I gave her back the phone and turned away from everyone. Facing the brick wall, I tried to gather my emotions. Merl. It was right before he died. He could have saved himself. Instead, he felt saving Kayla was more important than his own life.

I turned back around and found Kayla's gaze. "Why were you hiding down here?"

"I overheard Conemar order Odil to take some of Couve's guards and search the Shelter for Sabine," Kayla said.

"How come they didn't find you in the hiding place?" I asked.

"Because my husband had it built," Sabine said. "He only told me and his most trusted son, Bastien, about its existence. Never had he put such faith in Odil." There was regret in her eyes at the mention of her older son's name.

I found Bastien's gaze. "I need to get to the library. My first duty is to Royston. But you have to get everyone here to a safe place."

"I won't let you go by yourself," he said.

"They need someone more powerful than guards to protect them, Bastien," I said. "They need a wizard. You couldn't go all the way with me, anyway, just to the first library. We don't have time to argue. I need to go *now*."

"All right," he said. Though his head was nodding his agreement, his eyes were protesting. "Where should I take them?"

"To the New York Public Library," I said. "Jump with them at the same time the Mystiks make the library hop diversion. Go to the lowest level and then to the north wall. At the bottom is a tiny starburst. Push on it and a door will open. Follow the tunnel. It will lead you to Saint Patrick's Cathedral. Your entry will alert Father Peter, and he will meet you."

"Right. Father Peter. Got it."

"Okay, we have to hurry. I'll go with you to the library, make sure you get through before I leave."

Their concerned faces touched my heart. Though I was afraid to go alone, I knew it was the only way to ensure that Pop and the others were safe. Guards were great fighters, but they would be no match for a wizard.

I stormed up the stairs, the clomping of boots shaking the steps behind me as the others followed. They couldn't see the fear in my eyes or the tears gathering in them. I had to be strong.

Bastien needed to go with them. It was the only way. I wanted to tell him every secret in my heart. Tell him how I felt the spark between us the first time we met. Tell him I forgave him and that I was scared to lose him.

But there wasn't time.

We never had enough time.

I'd chosen the George Peabody Library in Baltimore because it was large enough to hide Gian's book containing the entry into the uninhabited coven where the Tetrad's prison was

located. And I didn't want anyone discovering it while we
were gone.

The stark room contained five stories of galleries behind
ornamental cast-iron banisters. Walls rose dramatically up
to a skylight of several glass panels with metal crisscrossing
inside, framed with white painted wood. The huge open room
was like an atrium for books.

There was a small movement in the shadows on the floor.
I whirled on my heel, searching the library, but there was
nothing there.

"Stop freaking yourself out," I said. "It was just a trick of
the light."

Placing my bag down, I stood on the black-and-white tiled
floor and watched the gateway book, listening to the sound of
silence. The cool air swirling inside the library brushed the
back of my neck and kissed my cheeks. I turned my wrist over
and checked the time on Carrig's watch.

It was just turning two in London.

Anytime now.

The pages of the gateway book flipped, and I backed up.

"*Accendere il fuoco*," I said, creating a fire globe on my
palm.

Royston flew out of the gateway book, that cocky grin on
his face. His light brown hair had been cut, and soft waves
brushed his jawline; he'd also shaven. He towered over me
with his wide shoulders and long, muscular torso.

It took me by surprise when he snatched me up in a hug.
"Milady is well?"

I wiggled out of his arms. "I'm good."

He intently watched me before nodding, his eyes on my
cheek. "You were hurt."

"It's nothing. I'm much better now." I picked up my bag with
Gian's *My Magnificent Journeys* inside. The gateway book lifted
and flew off to wherever it belonged. "We need to get going."

"Aren't we meeting the others?" he asked, following me across the tiled floor.

I turned to face him. "I didn't want anyone else to know. They have no idea what I have planned for us. We need to end things. It's getting bad."

"What about the mission?"

"It's finished," I said. "You're out of Asile. So are the others. Now we have another one to complete."

He lowered his head, nodding. "I will do whatever you wish."

"We're going to destroy the Tetrad on our own."

He lifted his hazel eyes to mine, his stare boring into me. "Then that is what we will do. I only wished to make my farewells. Can you deliver them for me?"

"Yes, of course." I swallowed. The resolve on his face, the knowing that he only had a little time left to live, threatened to break me. "I'm so sorry."

"You did nothing but be my friend."

There was something noble about Royston. He would give his life to save two worlds full of strangers, not even people from his own time. What did he owe us? Nothing. Atheia had made him our sacrificial lamb, and we didn't deserve his offering.

"I am your friend, Royston," I said. "I won't leave your side. You won't be alone."

"Thank you, Gianna." Grabbing the back of my neck, his massive biceps flexing, he pulled me closer and kissed the top of my head. "I have complete faith in you."

He released me, and I took a few steps back from him. "What do you want me to say to the others?"

"Thank Cadby for his service. Tell him he was cherished as a father. Deidre, I cared deeply for her and wished we could have had more time together. The others, thank them for making me feel as if I belonged to a family for the first time in a long while. I shall miss our times in the hideout."

"I will," came out so quiet, I wasn't sure he'd heard me.

"I am ready," he said. "My father is waiting for me."

We needed to find a more private place where the book would be safe until our return. I led Royston up the stairs to the fifth level and between two lines of bookcases. Below us, boots hitting the marble floor resounded through the library. I dropped to my knees and pulled Royston down beside me.

"Someone's here," I said, barely audible.

Shit. What do I do? Think of a plan.

"You are in the light." Royston dragged me back like a rag doll. "What shall we do?"

I have to get him out of here.

I removed Gian's book from the bag and retrieved the leather canister from inside my boot, then shoved them both behind the books on the shelf beside us.

"I'm going to distract them," I whispered. "You jump through the gateway book to Chetham's library in Manchester, England. Wait there. A book faery will show you to the Barmhilde coven. Tell The Red who you are. He'll protect you. Okay? Did you get that?"

He nodded. "Chetham. Wait for a faery. Go to Barmhilde. Seek The Red."

"Good," I said.

Lifting my wrist, I blew on the silver butterfly embedded in my skin, gave her instructions, and she flitted off. I untied my breastplate and lifted my shirt under Royston's questioning look. My fingers shook as I placed them on the crown and whispered the charm. I bit the back of my hand as the Chiave ripped from my skin.

"Take it," I said, grunting through the fading pain. "Wear it while jumping. It will shield you. Don't lose it. Keep it safe until I make it back to you. We need it to release the Tetrad."

He grasped it. "I will do as you say."

The boots below us were shuffling around fast as they searched the library. How did they know to follow Royston's jump? The guard's mark that enabled him to jump was old. Maybe the Monitors could tell it was ancient.

I stood and motioned for Royston to go the other way. With quick, quiet steps, I found the stairs and went down to the lower level. When I came into the main room, my breath punched out of me.

Arik turned at the sound of my boots against the marble floor.

CHAPTER TWENTY-TWO

Arik's cold, dark eyes fell on me. He had several guards and two Sentinels I didn't know with him. "Gia, where is he?"

I shrugged a shoulder, turning my right palm up. "I have no clue who you mean. *Accendere la stun.*" A purple globe formed in my hand.

His eyes widened. "How did you do that?"

"It belongs to one of those Sentinels who died when Veronique attacked me in the New York Public Library. I guess I absorb Sentinels' globes after I kill them, even if it's an accident."

He stared at me, most likely trying to process what I'd said.

"Arik, just let me go. I don't want to fight you."

"Drop it," he said, creating his fire globe. "Have we come to a place where we are enemies?"

"I don't know." I glared at him. "You tell me."

A book falling to the floor above us sent a *smack* sound through the library.

"Up there. Go!" Arik ordered his guards and Sentinels. He manipulated his fireball into a whip.

The guards charged to the upper levels using different

stairs. I popped the stun globe, purple flickers of light dying on the air.

Arik lowered his hand, his fire globe snuffing out. "You did that to distract us."

"I was taught by the best."

"Flattery won't help you out of your predicament." Even as he was being cruel, his accent made it sound so proper.

"He's gone," one of the Sentinels shouted from the fifth level. "Jumped through the gateway book. It closed, so we can't determine where he went."

"Bring the book and get down here," Arik said.

His dark eyes narrowed on me, and those beautiful lips that I'd kissed so many times pressed together in disappointment, shattering my soul. He closed the distance between us.

Tears formed in my eyes as I looked up at him. "How did we get here, Arik?"

"Don't speak. Because if you do, I won't have the strength to follow my orders." He lowered his lips to my ears. "Gia, everything comes back to you. I loved you. My heart is ruined. You've broken me."

"I'm sorry." The hurt in his eyes made something inside me implode. "It wasn't my fault. I wish…" What did I wish? That Emily never came between us? That Arik and I never broke up? That Bastien and I never fell through that trap? I didn't wish any of those things. My wish would be for Arik and me to find a common ground. To be friends.

"Why can't you follow orders?" His voice was softer then.

"Because it's wrong. Can't you see that?" I stepped back from him. "I thought I knew you. That you knew right from wrong. I put my faith in you. And *I* broke *you*?" The laugh that burst from my lips was weak and shaky. "You tore me to pieces."

Footsteps pounded across the tiles, and Arik took a step back from me before the guards and Sentinels joined us.

"The shackles," Arik said, his jaw tensed.

My face heated with the anger burning inside me like a furnace.

One of the guards pulled out a long chain with two metal plates at the end.

Avoiding eye contact with me, Arik said, "Hold out your hands."

I lifted my arms. "Don't do this. We don't have much time."

Another guard helped put the metal plates against my palms and fastened the chains around them.

Arik couldn't look me in the eyes. "Gianna Bianchi McCabe, you are under arrest for treason and will be allowed a trial. Take her to the gallows."

"Arik, please. You're wrong. The new council is with Conemar—"

"You'll be safer in the gallows than running loose in the covens."

The two guards dragged me over to the gateway book and jumped with me to the Vatican Library. I struggled in their grasp, trying to break free. We came out of the book and crashed against the floor, one of the guards landing on top of me.

"You had to struggle," the guard grunted as she rolled off.

The second guard pulled me to my feet. Arik and the other guards and Sentinels came through one by one.

Arik stayed in the back as the rest rushed me through the tunnel and down to the gallows. The faeries attending there were ancient-looking and tall. I glanced around for Odran, the only one I knew. He was the faery who let Nick, Deidre, and I visit Toad when we'd come to get a Chiave from him. But the faery wasn't there.

"You can remove the bindings," Arik said. "Her magic won't work down here."

A woman guard undid the metal plates from my hands.

Two faeries, a tall, lanky woman and a stout man, shuffled me along the long narrow corridor. There were prison cells on both sides. I glanced over my shoulder, my tear-filled eyes finding Arik. I stared him down until he turned and exited the gallows.

He left me here.

I wanted to scream out, but I couldn't. It was like a concrete slab fell on top of me, crushing me to the ground, knocking the air out of me.

When I'd first entered the Mystik world, I had thought Arik would always protect me. I once trusted him with my life. He taught me how to survive in this new world. How could he care so little for me? After everything we've been through...

He had said I'd broken him. But I wasn't about to let him break me. I didn't know how, but I was getting out of there. And if it came to blows between Arik and me, I'd go down fighting.

As we passed a cell on my right, I recognized the man staring through the barred window of the door.

"Uncle Philip!" I struggled against the hands gripping my arms.

He grasped the bars. "Gia, what are you doing here?"

"For treason," I said. "Arik arrested me."

The faeries stopped and unlocked one of the cells.

"I'm so sorry. I never wanted this for you." He had a beard, and his usually perfectly cut hair was shaggy. There were bruises on his face and bags under his eyes. "Stay strong."

The faeries shoved me into the cell and locked it.

"Well, well, you never know who will join you in the gallows."

I spun around.

Pia lay on one of the cots. "Hey, roomie."

The last time we saw each other, she and her twin sister had buried arrows into guards and some of the high wizards attending Toad's trial in Mantello. And they'd killed him. Her sister ended up dying that day, too.

"What are you in for?" Pia sat up and swung her legs over the side.

I sat down on the cot opposite hers. "You know, trying to save the worlds."

"You were always so ambitious. And such a softy."

"Unlike your evil heart." I lay back on the cot. There was no way we could share a cell without me killing her. Toad had been innocent. He didn't deserve to die. Actually, the wizards she'd killed were *all* good. The council was now corrupted because of their deaths.

She leaned back against her pillow. "Word trickles down here, believe it or not. And the rumor is we're on the same side now."

I shot off the cot and grabbed the collar of her shirt. "Because of you, Conemar will take over the Wizard Council. Because of you, bad leaders are in control of the council. Because of you, Mystiks died of a disease when said bad council refused to give them the cure they knew would save them. Because of you—"

The tears rushing down her cheeks stopped me, and I released her.

"You're not worth it." I kicked the air and fell back on the cot.

"I'm sorry, Gia." She sniffed and swiped at her eyes. "I believed it was the right thing to do. When Santara was attacked, her distress call went unanswered. We thought the council ignored it. About Toad, we believed he murdered Gian, the father of the resistance. Philip told me everything. We were fools. Anger made us act on the lies fed to us. And I lost my sister because of it."

I turned my head and was about to answer her, but three guards came to the cell door. "That's her," the woman said, her blond hair cut short and her eyes the brightest blue. "Gianna

Bianchi, come with us."

Pia stood. "Where are you taking her?"

"Sit," the short, stocky guy hissed between the bars in the window.

The fear on her face as she sat back down shook me. What had they done to her? More importantly, why did they want me?

The other guy, with arms bigger than my thighs, charged in and pulled me up by my arm.

"Okay," I said. "You don't have to be so rough. I'm coming."

They brought me to what looked to be an interrogating room and forced me down on the only chair in the place. The stocky man chained my arms to the chair.

"This can be easy or it can be hard," the woman said. "It's your choice. Now, where are the Chiavi?"

"I guess it's going to be hard," I said, acting all brave while being completely terrified.

The woman's fist slammed into my cheek. An explosion of pain rattled my jaw, and I screamed as tears stung my eyes. "The Chiavi," she growled.

Another fist to the cheek.

And another shock of pain.

Flashes of light sparked my vision. I took deep breaths. *How can I stay strong? I can't do this.*

I wanted to give in. Tell them where the Chiavi were. Anything to stop her from hitting me again.

I'm too weak.

Gia, you can do it. Leave your body. Come to me.

"Nick?"

The woman glanced behind her. "Who do you see? A ghost?"

I closed my eyes, waiting for the next blow. The grass under my feet felt real, my face warmed by the sun. I opened my eyes and sat up. I was in a beautiful meadow. But I wasn't alone. Nick, with that silly smile on his face, the one where he'd just played a big prank on me and I'd fallen for it for the thousandth time.

But this wasn't a prank. It was real life, and he wasn't there. He was somewhere living a nightmare, same as I was living one.

"Of course you'd have to put a damper on a beautiful dream," he said, smirking.

"I wish you were real." I started picking wildflowers, because that's what you do in a dream.

"What are you going to do with those?" Nick asked. "Make a crown?"

I turned my back to him. "Maybe. What's it to you?"

When I looked back, he was gone.

I stood and dropped the flowers. "Nick? Come back. Don't leave me."

Dark clouds rolled overhead, and I fell to the grass. I shivered.

"Gia?"

A girl's voice?

Something scratchy dragged over my shoulder. It smelled like dust and a bit moldy. A wet cloth wiped my cheek. I opened my eyes, except the left one wouldn't fully open.

"Those animals," Pia said. "They really hurt you."

"Did I tell them anything?" My voice sounded strained and scratchy.

The sounds of boots traveled down the corridor and got louder the closer they came to our cell.

"Gianna," a guy's voice I'd heard before called from the window.

"What do you want?" Pia asked.

"Unlock the door," the voice commanded someone.

Antonio? The Vatican's Sentinel had to be there to get me out. If I weren't in so much pain, my spirits would be lifted.

The door opened and he came in. "Get on your cot," he ordered Pia. He bent down beside me and brushed the hair out of my face. "What have they've done to you? This is your fault," he said to someone behind him.

He ran his fingers through his dark, curly hair. His large nose was now crooked. I wondered if he'd broken it when he fell out of the gateway book after being attacked. It was when Nick and I were looking for the Chiave.

"Get out of my way," Arik said.

Antonio straightened and moved to the side.

Arik crouched down. The only eye I could open met his stare. Tears formed in his eyes. "I'm so sorry, Gia." He shook his head, trying to gather his emotions, and he glared at Antonio. "Your guards did this. If anyone touches her again, I will kill them."

"They aren't my guards," Antonio said. "They're the Wizard Council's. We have to get her out of here."

"Time's up," the guard snarled.

Arik brushed my hair back and leaned close to my ear. "They won't hurt you again. I'll get you out of here."

The guard rattled his keys. "I said time's up."

Arik stood and walked out of the cell. "Send a curer to her straightaway."

Antonio rushed after him. "Arik, they'll hurt her again. We must get her out."

The guard slammed the door and locked it.

"What have you done to her?" Uncle Philip shouted from his cell.

"Shut your mouth, you," the guard said.

"Arik, come back," Uncle Philip pleaded. "Listen to me. They'll scryer her. You can't leave her in here."

"They won't harm her." Arik's voice sounded farther away.

There was a bang as if Uncle Philip had kicked his door. "Gia, are you all right?"

Pia went to the door. "She's been beaten badly, but she's talking."

"Thank you," he said, sounding defeated.

She came back to me and continued washing my face with what little water she had. "I can't believe Arik would let them do this."

My mouth was dry. "Water?"

She put down the cloth, picked up a metal cup, and put it to my mouth. I flinched when it touched my cracked lip. "Too bad I can't create my water globe. This stuff isn't the best, but it's wet."

I drank it and choked a little. "That is horrible."

The curer, a young woman with curly red hair, arrived and slathered gunk all over me. Before leaving, she placed a tattooed hand on my head. "Don't give up. Keep fighting. And don't be scared if the power goes out tonight. It'll be extremely dark down here, but it's only a few moments." She slanted closer to me and whispered, "Even the wards and charms will be down."

After the curer was gone, Pia came and sat at the edge of my bed. "I've been here for months and the power has never gone out. Why do you think she told you that?"

"Whoever she's with is giving us a window to escape," I said. "But what can we do with a few minutes? I doubt our battle globes could do anything to that thick steel door."

"Then why did she even tell you that?"

"I don't know." I rolled over and faced the wall. "Let me think."

She adjusted on her squeaky bed.

The pain made me restless. I stared at the dimmer lights just above our door, thinking about my globes. Glass would just shatter. Fire wouldn't do anything. The ice and stun globes would be useless. Pia's water globe would probably only drown us.

A dimmer next to the door glinted against one of the hinges. I needed a tool or something to undo them. There wasn't anything in the room that could break them.

Hinges.

I sat up at the memory of when I'd used the Chiave to get Carrig out of a cell. The Chiave could cut metal. I just had to wait for the power outage to get the sword off my skin.

A yawn stretched my mouth. "No. You can't sleep now," I scolded myself.

"What?" Pia groaned and pulled the pillow over her head.

Worried I'd fall asleep and miss the power outage, I stood and paced the cell, keeping my eye on the dimmers above the door. Hours passed, and I paced.

Memories played through my mind.

And I paced.

Sweet memories of the past when Faith, Kale, and Sinead were alive. When my birth father, Carrig, had first found me outside the Boston Athenæum. When Arik wasn't such an ass.

And I paced.

When it was just Nick and me, before Afton. And then when Afton had joined us. And when Pop and I were alone after my mom had died. Sunday dinners and Saturday picnics on the Boston Common with Pop.

And I stopped.

The light flickered. I pulled up my shirt, found the raised sword in my skin, and pressed my fingers to it.

The lights flickered again.

A loud *pop* sounded somewhere in the gallows.

And dark.

"*Reditum.*" I grimaced as the sword ripped from my body. It grew and floated in front of me, and I grasped it.

"Get up, Pia."

I waited until the light came back on and hit the sword against the top hinge. Metal sang against metal.

"What's happening?" Pia stumbled out of bed.

"We're getting out of here." I hit the next one, then the bottom.

With all the strength I could gather, I threw my body against the door and crashed with it into the hall. Pia helped mc to my feet. Footsteps and voices came from farther down the corridor. I limped to Uncle Philip's door and broke each hinge with the sword.

"Back up," he warned before pushing the door out. It hit the floor like thunder. When he was out, I hugged him tight.

"Come on," Pia said. "Where are we going?"

"This way." I bolted up the corridor in the direction Odran had taken Nick, Deidre, Toad, and me when we'd come to get a Chiave from Toad. At the end, I found the narrow door Odran had brought us to and tugged it open. With every step up the tight, winding stairwell, my head felt as if it would fall off.

Suddenly the door below us flew open.

CHAPTER TWENTY-THREE

U ncle Philip struggled up the spiraling steps behind me. I hadn't realized he was hurt, and when I stretched my hand back to him, he grasped it.

"We're almost there," I said. "Keep going."

We reached the top and another lean door, and pushed it open. On the other side, Arik stood with his fire globe balancing on his hand. I stumbled, practically falling back on Uncle Philip.

Emily darted around Arik and caught my wrist. "Hurry up. Get inside." She dragged me up the final steps into the Vatican Library. The familiar scent of dusty books and pine cleaner filled my nose.

Uncle Philip, then Pia, darted inside. Arik tossed his globe and slammed the door.

A deep yelp and then a series of thumps, like someone falling down the stairs, came from behind the door.

I threw up my hand, created a white globe, and slammed it against the panels. Ice shot across the door and onto the wall, sealing the opening. After creating another one, I turned to Arik.

It was ironic to see him framed by the murals of saints and

bible scenes painted on the walls, pillars, and arches, since I was pretty sure he was the devil incarnate.

"Gia, put it down," he said, his hands up in surrender.

Emily leaped between Arik and me. "Stop. Because of him you're out."

I glared over her shoulder at him. "Because of him, I was in there in the first place. Move out of the way." The wound in my lip split as I spoke, blood seeping onto my tongue.

Uncle Philip hobbled over, still breathing heavily, and placed a shaky hand on my forearm. "Drop it. This can wait. We must get out of here."

With anger firing through my veins, I spat, "I hate you," at Arik and dropped the globe. It hit the floor, ice spreading across the tiles.

Arik pulled his eyes from me, opened the gateway book to a page, and placed it on the floor. "You jump first," he said to me.

"No. Uncle Philip and Pia will go, then me."

I didn't trust Arik enough to leave them behind with him. And he knew that's how I felt, because it showed on his face like the bruises on mine.

The guards were banging on the door, trying to get it open.

After Uncle Philip and Pia made it through the book, Arik jumped into the page, and I flew after him, landing with a *thud* on the floorboards. Every beaten part of my body screamed in pain. Going from the bright gold of the Vatican Library to the high bookcases and dark wood in the Chetham's Library in Manchester was like going from day to night.

I was surrounded by familiar faces—Lei, Jaran, Demos, and a few guards with Tearmann uniforms. I stumbled on my feet and cried out with the memory of every blow to my face and rib cage catching up to me.

Pia supported Uncle Philip. He looked about as bad as I felt.

A feral growl came from Lei, and she turned an angry stare on Arik. "See what all your loyalty has gotten us."

Jaran caught me as I swayed on my feet. "Easy there. I've got you." His eyes took in my condition. Anger flashed on his face, and he glared at Arik. "You let them do this to her?"

"I never thought they'd—"

"What did you think?" Jaran cut him off. "That they'd nicely interrogate her?"

Arik's stare was on me. "I only wanted to protect her. She was being reckless, and I thought she'd be safe in the gallows. She hasn't had a trial. They aren't allowed to do anything but—"

"Torture her," Pia interjected.

"*Interrogate* her until she's been sentenced," Arik finished, ignoring her comment.

"You were with us in Asile," Jaran continued to press him. "You saw all the messed-up stuff going on. Have you not witnessed the corruption of the Wizard Council? It was evident to Lei and me the moment we arrived there."

"Did you not know it when I was arrested?" Uncle Philip added.

Arik lowered his head. "They gave good reason for your detainment. And when Veronique attacked Gia in New York, and you were the only one who knew she'd be there, I thought you were behind it." He lifted his eyes to Uncle Philip. "I believed you were with Conemar."

He turned to Jaran. "As far as the corruption and unethical incidents going on in Asile, I'd just returned to the haven from the Fey realm after being detained in Greyhill, then I was immediately sent on a mission. There wasn't time to notice any corruption."

"I've known you since you were a boy," Uncle Philip said, disappointment or sadness in his eyes. "How could you ever assume I would have turned against Gia?"

"I am sorry," Arik said, looking at him.

"I can see you're absolutely gutted," Demos said. "Why did you stop Gia from delivering the cure? She saved so many with it."

Arik lowered his head again. "There were reports broadcasted in the havens showing the drug to be dangerous to those who took it. Images of children suffering after having the cure. I was fooled by the propaganda, but I see now they were lies. That the council only wanted to let the disease to run its course through the covens. My eyes are open now, and I'm truly ashamed of my actions."

Someone came through the book, and we all turned at once to see who it was.

"Bastien." My voice sounded rough and dry.

He hurried to me and grasped my arms. "I was so worried."

"I see what clouded your judgment," Uncle Philip said, his gaze going from Arik to Bastien and me. "It's because you lost her."

Bastien glanced down at me, and his face twisted with concern. "Who did this to you?"

"I'm fine," I said, but my gaze instinctually went to Arik.

Bastien noticed—his eyes narrow and sharp as they followed mine. He let me go and charged at Arik, tackling him to the ground, fist after fist pummeling into his side and face. "How does it feel? What were you thinking arresting her? You're as evil as the council...as Conemar."

"Leave him alone," Emily shouted. "You're hurting him!" She caught one of Bastien's arms, and he yanked it away from her. "Someone stop him."

Arik didn't fight back. He just lay there, letting Bastien's anger punish him. The expression on his face said it all—he was ashamed.

I stumbled away from Jaran, grabbed Bastien's arm before it fell on Arik's face again. "Please stop. He's not fighting you back."

Fist readied to strike, Bastien paused, his eyes going to mine.

"He's had enough," I said softly.

Bastien dropped his hand, stood, and brushed his palms across his pant legs.

His anger scared me. It was a brutal attack. I'd never seen Bastien lose control like that.

"How are you here?" Jaran asked.

"Arik sent a message through the Couve guards loyal to me," Bastien said.

Emily dropped down beside Arik, her hands going to his face, but he grasped them, stopping her. A cry escaped her lips.

"I'm all right," Arik mumbled, blood trickling from his right nostril. "I've been worse."

She guided him to his feet. "I was in Asile," she said. "The people there have been brainwashed by what's being fed to them. I almost started to believe their lies. Lei and Jaran, you've seen it, too. You just weren't there long enough to feel the pull of it."

"We're finished here," Lei said in a commanding voice. "Arik and I will discuss his role in our group once we're back in Barmhilde."

Lei's new role as our leader fit her. She was firm, but there was empathy toward Arik written all over her face.

I kept my head down, my feelings and thoughts all over the place. Everything was processing slowly. My injuries were sharp, and it was hard to concentrate. I just wanted to lie down, and I couldn't wait to get back to camp.

The lake water felt cool on my feet as I walked in the shallows watching the Mystik children from Barmhilde dart in and out of the water. Their mothers gathered stringy plant life that resembled seaweed from under the water and around the rocks. One of the children called it bimcord and said they used it for ropes because it was nearly indestructible.

The sun heated my skin, and I raised my face toward the sky to take in the warmth. Strangely shaped birds with long wings and thick bodies flew in synchronized patterns in the purplish-blue sky.

Royston came down the hill, heading in my direction, looking like a god with his powerful muscles. He had a bad habit—or good depending on how you saw it—of going without his shirt on warm days. The sun lit up the golden highlights in his light brown hair.

I hadn't seen much of Deidre since Jaran and Lei brought her back from Asile. She spent most of her time with Carrig, helping him recover. She'd taken Sinead's death hard, wouldn't eat anything for days. Royston pulled her through it, forcing her to finish the plates of food he'd brought her.

Overhead, Cadby darted between the flocks of birds, guarding Royston. He resembled a yellow, human bat soaring back and forth in the sky.

Royston's feet splashed into the shallows as he came up to my side. "You look well."

I kicked up some water. "I feel better."

"Did you get the crown from Cadby?"

He knew I had, because Cadby always followed his orders.

I patted my side. "It's safely tucked away."

"I am ready." He knotted his hands behind his back.

"Ready?"

He faced me. "You've gone soft. Afraid."

"I have not." I totally had. Images of me chained to a chair without any control of what those guards did to me haunted my sleep. But there was no way I could keep ignoring what I had to do, even if it terrified me.

His eyes followed a little boy with four arms carrying a pail full of water. "The longer we wait, the more people suffer and the better prepared our foes become. I suggest we leave tonight. Just you and me. No need to put anyone else in danger."

I glanced up at him, the sun haloing around his head. He was right—the longer I waited the more everyone suffered.

"For so many years I have lived in a wasteland alone," he continued, eyes still on the children playing. "I shall never know a child's voice calling me father. The memory of my own has faded. When I close my eyes at night, I no longer can recall the image of him."

It was so unfair that he was given such a long life with no one to live for. He deserved a happily ever after, but he'd never get one. Maybe he would welcome death. Was that why he was ready now?

As if knowing my question, he said, "When I struggled in the Somnium, I prayed for death, but when faced with the opportunity, I fought for life. My feelings for Deidre are growing each day, and so we must do this now, or I might not have the strength to leave her."

I wish you didn't have to do it." I wrapped my arms around myself, digging my toes into the wet sand.

He grasped my shoulders and turned me to face him. "You are not to feel sorry for me. Live and love. Enjoy the world for the gifts it presents. Don't dwell on her evils. The good outweighs the bad, or there wouldn't be a fight for it."

Emily coming down the hill caused him to release my shoulders.

"Tonight, then?"

"Tonight," I said.

He smiled with a nod and headed for the path. His long strides had him passing Emily before she reached the bottom of the hill.

"Hey," she said, worry on her face.

I crinkled my brows at her. "What is it?"

Her frown deepened. "I'm concerned about Philip. Today, he couldn't remember how to use a fork."

"Has this been happening often?"

"Yes," she said. "He asked me not to tell you. Deidre noticed and sent me here right away. I thought he was just recovering, but it's not getting better. You know, Pia said he was scryered. Do you think...?" She couldn't finish what we both feared.

Fighting a scryer could ruin your brain, and I had no doubt Uncle Philip had resisted it during his interrogations in the gallows.

"I'll check on him," I said, rinsing the mud off my feet and slipping on the sandals I'd bought in the village.

Emily kept in step with me. "Can I ask you something?"

"Sure."

"It's about Arik."

I glanced sideways at her. "What about him?"

She hesitated before spilling it. "I'm in love with him. Is that wrong? I know it was because of me that you two broke up."

"We both know there were other forces at play there." I stopped to look pointedly at her. "All we have in this world that is worth anything is love. I don't know why you feel the need to tell me, other than you're worried I still have feelings for him and that you'll get in the way of us getting back together."

She bit her bottom lip. Her dark hair had grown past her shoulders. Her widow's peak lowered with the frown lines in her forehead. Her once pale skin was now tanned from the sun.

"That's it exactly," she said.

I continued up the hill with her by my side. "You don't need to worry about me. Arik and I are damaged beyond repair."

Emily struggled to get a good footing until finally catching up with me. "I just want you to know I'm really sorry for what happened."

"I see you are." I smiled at her, hoping to ease her concern. "You know what they say—actions speak louder than words, and you've more than made up for it. Saved my ass a few times. I think that gets you a Get out of Jail Free card."

"Thank you," she said, keeping pace with me. "Oh, I almost forgot. Pia was searching for you earlier. She's returned from Santara. Said the Talpar tunnel will work. Her rebels are ready when needed."

"Thanks." I had mixed feelings about Pia. I liked her during our time hiding in Branford together. But she had killed Toad and some high wizards. Her and her sister's actions had caused the council to fall under the control of high wizards greedy for power and loyal to Conemar. But I'd been to Santara, seen the destruction and suffering. How could I blame her?

When we walked into Uncle Philip's tent, he was staring at the framed mirror propped up against a washbasin on a dresser in the corner.

"How are you doing?" I asked, going over to him.

He looked at me through the mirror. "Someone replaced my face."

My heart thudded to my feet. "Why do you say that?"

"I can't remember this one. It's older." He turned his head from side to side. "Do you have any more of that candy?"

I gave Emily a questioning look.

"I can get you some more," she said.

"That would be quite agreeable." His eyes returned to the mirror. "Now rather than later if at all possible."

With a heavy heart, I slowly backed away, trying desperately not to cry. "I'll be back soon, Uncle Philip."

He rubbed his chin, ignoring my statement.

I pushed the flap aside and exited the tent, panic rising in my chest and causing me to gulp for air. I covered my face with my hands. Tears slipped from my eyes and ran between my fingers. Emily hugged me.

"It just keeps getting worse." I sniffed. "Will they take everyone away from me?"

She rubbed circles on my back. "No. He's still here, just different. We'll work with him. You'll see. We can help him remember."

It was sweet how she comforted me, but she hadn't read all the stories I had. Resisting a scryer damaged the brain. But she was also right. With therapy, we could get as much back as we could. There were curers skilled in that type of recovery. He'd never be the same, but he was alive. And I was determined to make the life he had left full of love and happiness. He deserved that.

"What's going on here?" Arik asked, approaching.

Emily released me. "Nothing. Just having one of those days."

"I see," he said. "Gia, can I have a word with you?"

Disappointment crossed Emily's face.

"Sure," I said.

Emily forced a smile. "I'll catch you later."

As she walked off, Arik called out to her, "Dinner later?"

At my angle, I could see her face brighten. "Sounds good," she said and turned the corner of the tent.

"What did you want?" I asked.

He came closer to me. "Rumor has it that Conemar is now seated on the council as representative for Esteril. The council is gathering all the havens' armies for an attack. No one knows what the council is planning, but my bet is an attack on Barmhilde. There was talk in Asile. They fear The Red."

Arik had been working really hard to regain everyone's trust. He didn't have to with me, because I knew him. I'd known he'd side with the council. And I'd known he'd come around once he saw what they were up to. Plus, I could tell by how ashamed he was when he let Bastien beat him up.

"I'm going with Royston tonight."

"I think you must," he said. "I have all the faith in the world in you, Gia. Don't worry about things here. The others and I will handle it. We'll take care of Carrig, Uncle Philip, Deidre, and...Emily."

Why had he paused at Emily's name?

"Thanks," I said and started walking away, but his next question stopped me.

"Will you tell Bastien?"

I was avoiding Bastien. We hadn't really talked much since returning three days ago. It hurt to think about how Sinead would still be alive if he hadn't stopped me from using my globe to stop Ruth Ann from stabbing Carrig. And I couldn't get him beating up Arik out of my mind.

"I'm not sure," I said and rounded the corner of the tent.

Bastien was kicked back against a large pole that held a lantern. "What aren't you sure about telling Bastien?"

"Are you spying on me?"

"No." He unhitched himself from the pole. "Should I be?"

"Then what are you doing?" I suddenly felt guilty for no apparent reason. So what if I was keeping something from him?

He walked in that confident swagger over to me and his hands landed on my shoulders. "When will you forgive me?"

"Why did you stop me? Sinead..."

"I misjudged the situation." His beautiful blue eyes were haunting and sad. "Your globe wouldn't have stopped her. She would have stabbed Carrig before it hit her. I thought by preventing you from throwing it, we would've had more time to find a way to disable her. She'd allowed us a minute to give her what she wanted. I thought she'd wait. Bargain."

I took in a deep breath, digesting his comments. I'd played that moment in the curer's room several times in my dreams. There was a second. A second where my globe could've hit Ruth Ann right before she stabbed Carrig. And a second where the dagger could've stabbed him right before the globe hit its mark.

Then there was the thought that if I hadn't tried to throw my globe, Ruth Ann wouldn't have panicked and stabbed Carrig.

The only one to blame for Sinead's death was Ruth Ann.

"I'm sorry, Bastien," I said. My voice didn't sound like my own. It was tired, drained of energy. "It wasn't your fault. I haven't been fair to you."

"We both made mistakes. And you were grieving."

"I was," I said.

"You're leaving tonight to find the Tetrad, aren't you?"

"So you *were* spying on me."

He quirked a smile, taking a few steps until there was almost no space between us. "Is it spying if the person was in the right place at the right time?"

"I suppose not," I said with a small smile.

"My guards will stand watch in the library when you leave," he said. "Make sure you can return safely."

"Yeah, okay. I'd feel better knowing they're there." I grasped his hand and he towed me to him.

His hand slid behind my neck, and as he lowered his lips to mine, I tangled my fingers in his hair. A surge of heat rushed through my body, my heart pumping like a runner on the last lap of a five-mile run. I wanted to get lost in him. Forget the storm building around us. Forget the pain of injuries and loss. Forget my fear that we'd never have a normal life together.

Rain dropped on us and clapped against the taut skin of the tents. It plastered our hair to our faces and our clothes to our skin, but it didn't pull us apart. We kissed as if we'd never kiss again, and I hungrily devoured his lips, wanting more from him. Wanting all of him.

I pushed my body harder against his, causing him to lose his footing, and we tumbled to the muddy ground. He rolled onto his back to keep me from ending up in the mud. And his consideration made me want him more.

"If you keep that up, you'll both drown, duckies," Lei hollered over the rain drumming around us.

Jaran laughed. "Good one."

Bastien let me go, and we held each other's arms as we struggled to stand, our feet slipping in the mud until we gained our footing.

"That's determination," Demos said. "There's dozens of tents around them, and they chose a mud pit to do that in."

"You're just jealous you didn't think of it," I said and walked off to a chorus of their laughs behind me.

After washing up the best I could in a basin full of water, I met the others in the dining tent. Carrig sat at one of the tables with Deidre fussing over him—placing his napkin on his lap, then picking up his fork and knife to cut his food.

When I reached them, I bent and kissed Carrig's cheek. "You look well."

"I be feeling good, if not a bit pampered," he said. Deidre tried to feed him a fork full of potatoes, but he took the utensil from her. "I'm quite capable of feeding me self. Me arms aren't broken."

Emily brought Uncle Philip over. "They're serving meat and potatoes. It's your favorite. Sit and I'll get you a plate."

Uncle Philip took a seat across from Carrig. "I'm not the only one being treated as a baby, I see."

Carrig stabbed a piece of meat. "They think we be fragile."

Uncle Philip folded his hands on the table. "I would have to admit that I'm in and out of stability." He winked at me, and I knew stable Uncle Philip was the one who had come to dinner.

I took a seat next to him and rested my head on his shoulder. "I love you both. You know that?"

Uncle Philip's lips pushed into a smile. "That's good to know."

Freshly showered, and with a mischievous grin plastered on his face, Bastien sat beside me, placing a plate in front of me and one for himself on the table. He leaned over. "You need to eat. Keep up your strength."

The rest of the Sentinels joined us. Arik took a seat beside Emily. As we shared jokes and stories of our short past together, it felt good to laugh. To have what could be our final meal together.

My eyes went to Emily and Arik. She fed him something from her plate that he hadn't gotten for himself. There was this easiness to them, as if they were comfortable with each other. The smile on Emily's face warmed me inside, and I couldn't help the smile pulling on my lips. She had come through for me time and again, and she was growing on me.

Taking a slow drink from my cup, my eyes scanned the smiling faces around me. I wanted to stay in this moment forever. Remember every detail so I could recall it in later years when I would miss them.

We spent hours there, telling stories and reliving memories. When those we'd lost would come up, we'd go silent until someone would bring up another story. And then the laughs and smiles would continue. And it was over too soon. One by one, they left for their tents, turning in for the night.

When they awoke in the morning, the world would either be changed or destroyed.

CHAPTER TWENTY-FOUR

Royston and I would have to jump alone to the George Peabody Library in Baltimore, Maryland, where I had left Gian's book and the leather canister. I was uneasy about it, but Bastien and his guards would be sensed in the gateway, and our whereabouts would be discovered. Bastien would wait for us by the gateway book in the Chetham's Library with two of the guards from Couve who had joined us in Barmhilde.

The Red and his army had forced the council's forces out of the library, which allowed Bastien to put a spell on the page into Chetham to lock them out.

Bastien gave me one of the guard's window rods to contact him should we run into trouble.

Trouble? The end of our quest would bring us smack in the middle of it. To the Tetrad.

I hugged the fur jacket The Red had given me. All the talk about releasing the Tetrad and no one ever mentioned what would happen when the beast was released. Supposedly, whoever opened its prison could control it. But how were they so certain it would work? A prophecy? I had my doubts.

Royston put the strap holding a canteen over his shoulder

and then the crown I had removed from my body onto his head. He nodded at me then jumped into the book.

Bastien cradled my head in his hands and pressed a long kiss on my lips. "Take your time. Don't make rash decisions." His hands fell away, the warmth of them leaving my skin.

"I will. And Bastien, I, well, I—" I considered telling him how I felt about him, but the words wouldn't roll off my tongue. Maybe it was better to leave it unsaid. I worried he would think me saying it was only fueled by our situation and not my real feelings.

"What is it?" He watched me curiously.

"I'll see you soon," I said and kissed him one last time before leaping into the open page.

After I landed, Royston and I didn't speak. He handed me the crown, and I returned it to my body. We climbed to the fifth level of the cathedral-like room and went straight to the bookcase where I'd hidden Gian's book and leather canister. Thankfully, they were still where I had shoved them behind the books.

Royston paused in the middle of putting on his fur coat. "Did you see that?"

I buried the canister into my boot and darted glances around us. "What was it?"

"Might have been a bug."

A shiver tickled up my spine, and I scratched my neck. "I hope not."

I had thought we could only jump into libraries, but Emily had found a charm in the ancient spell book that could create a gateway to anywhere. Gian must've used it for his book. I slipped on my coat and opened the book to the page with the three-peaked mountain range on it.

"Let's go."

We grasped each other's hands and jumped into the photograph.

Like a million needles, the icy wind stabbed at my exposed skin. I pulled the fur hood over my head. We were at the foot of the tallest peak of the mountains. In front of us, a trail spiraled up to the mouth of a large cave.

With shaky fingers, I opened the leather canister and carefully removed the parchment with Gian's instructions. "We have to look for etchings. There are clues for getting past traps."

We followed the trail to a wall made out of some sort of metal. It had to be over twenty feet tall, stretching from one side of the mountain to the other.

"Possibly we need a Chiave for this?" His breath froze in front of his face.

"I think you're right." I touched the slick wall and instantly wished I hadn't. The frozen metal bit my fingertips. "Crap. That was real smart."

"You should never touch metal that is frozen," Royston warned, a little too late.

As I rolled my eyes at him, I spotted an etching in the wall. There was a shape of a cross cut into the metal. The spirit of the Chiave had told me the wearer or owner would see things that had come before them. I couldn't see over the wall, so I guessed using the cross would show me something. Like the other side maybe.

The wind picked up as I opened my jacket, pulled aside my leather breastplate, and lifted up my shirt. I placed my cold fingers on the cross branded into my skin and shivered.

"*Reditum*," I said. The cross tugged from my skin, and I fell to one knee from the pain.

Royston caught the cross and slipped it into the etching on the wall. It fit as perfectly as a puzzle piece. The ground shook as the wall separated in the middle, leaving just enough space for one person to pass through it at a time.

I removed the cross from the wall. Holding it on my palm,

I chanted the charm to return it to its original form.

"*Modificare.*"

The cross flattened and twisted into a long metal rod with a blue tint to it. I stuffed it into the deep pocket of my fur coat and shimmied through the opening in the wall.

We traveled up to a fork in the pathway. At a loss for which way to go, I searched for one of the etchings. After several minutes searching, I sat on a large rock and pulled the fur jacket tight around me.

"There's nothing," I said.

Royston sat down beside me. Something on a nearby tree distracted him, and he pointed at it. "Is that an eye?"

I popped up. "It is. We must have to use the telescope here."

After removing the telescope from my side, I peered through the lens at the forked path. One of the paths was blurry while the other was clear. I worried that it was just me and maybe I'd squinted wrong, so I had Royston look.

He lowered the telescope. "The left path is clear."

"It was for me, too," I said. "So we go that way."

I changed the telescope into a rod and continued up the pathway behind Royston.

The trail spiraling upward was difficult to travel with the ice slicking the rocks. I fell twice, landing on my knees. Eventually, we came to a flat part of the path. A large boulder secured with a metal net blocked our way.

A sweep of the area gave us no clues. I stared at the boulder, shivering against the cold. The sun came out from behind a cloud and glistened against the metal surrounding the boulder.

"Search the net," I said, combing every bit of it until my eyes came to a tiny sword cut into the metal. "Here it is," I said, opening my jacket to retrieve the sword.

The pain wasn't as bad this time when the sword tore from me, either because I'd gotten used to it, or because I was a walking Popsicle and couldn't feel anything. I had to focus to keep my frozen fingers wrapped around the hilt of the sword.

The etching on the net didn't match the size of the sword as the cross had in the wall. My gaze ran across the circumference of the boulder. There had to be some mark or even a hole the Chiave fit in…

Nothing.

There was nothing.

The clouds drifted overhead, the sun warming the back of my neck, its light glinting against the netting.

Of course.

The Chiave could cut metal.

I swung the sword at the lock securing the netting around the boulder. The hilt shook violently in my hands when it made contact.

"Gia! The boulder will crush you," Royston yelled from an alcove in the side of the mountain.

The net fell away and the boulder rocked back and forth.

I sprinted for Royston. My foot caught on a raised rock, and I fell to my hands and knees, the sword knocked out of my hand. Royston caught my arm and dragged me out of the way. He held me against him in the alcove as the boulder flew past.

"Thank you," I said.

He didn't move.

"Are you okay?" I asked when he hadn't let me go.

"You scared the life out of me." He released my arm. "Please be more careful."

It was sweet that Royston worried about me. "I will."

I picked up the sword and changed it to its original rod form.

"Come on," I said. "Let's keep going."

The trail grew steeper the farther up we went. I could barely climb with the freezing wind whipping around my body. My fingers froze against rocks as I grasped them to pull myself up. I glanced behind us and instantly wished I hadn't—it was a long way down. One slip of the foot and I'd roll all the way to the bottom.

We finally reached a landing. Royston climbed up first and reached a hand out to me, and when I caught it, he pulled me up the rest of the way. In front of us was a gorge and no bridge to cross it.

"Now what?" My arms were weak and my legs wobbly. We had come all so far and there wasn't a bridge. There wasn't a way across the gorge. It was like my soul imploded within my body at my disappointment.

Royston pointed his finger at something across the gorge from us. "See there. It's a drawbridge."

In a rock by the edge of the gorge was a handprint. There wasn't a Chiave shaped like a hand. I ran the list of the Chiavi still left through my mind—*crown, badge, hourglass, and scroll.*

None of them matched the imprint in the rock.

What is it? I bit at my lip. There was a tiny lump from where the cut was still healing. My mouth was dry. Every single muscle in my body ached from climbing.

"Can I have the canteen?" I asked, reaching a hand out to Royston. He removed the strap from his shoulder and passed it to me, and I unscrewed the top. Royston kicked rocks around as he hunted for clues.

My eyes ran over the drawbridge as I took a big swig of the cold, sweet water. I gave the canteen back to Royston, and our hands touched. *His hand.*

I looked back at the handprint on the boulder.

Of course. The scroll.

It had Royston's name on it. I opened my jacket again and placed my fingers to the scroll. The Chiave easily pulled from my skin.

"It's you," I said. "Your hand goes in the print."

He surveyed the gorge. "How do we get over there?"

"There must be one on this side."

We checked the boulders on either side of us and found it.

I handed him the scroll. "I guess you just place your hand in the print."

Royston bent and pressed his palm into the etching. The drawbridge lowered, banging hard against the edge. He handed me the scroll and, before leaving, I changed it into a rod.

The bridge shook and swayed as we crossed it to the other side. There was less of a slope on this part of the pathway, and it felt good to walk on flat ground. I could totally sleep on one of the large boulders, and I wouldn't even care if I froze. But I had to push on.

After nearly twenty minutes of hiking, Royston asked, "Why do you suppose there were two handprints?"

Why were there two? A thought came to me. *Shit.* "Maybe to raise the drawbridge again." Dread settled in my stomach. I glanced behind me. It would slow us down if we went back and would cost us forty minutes. Twenty to get there, twenty to return where we were now. But only Bastien and his guards knew we'd jumped into this book. It would be okay to leave the bridge down. I returned my focus to the path in front of me. We ended up at a steaming waterfall. It was so hot I could feel the heat as we approached it.

We searched for another etching for nearly ten minutes. Finally, I paused and stretched my back. "Where could it be?"

"This is maddening," he said. "Why not just put it where we can find it easily?"

I shielded my eyes from the sun with my hand, searching the sides of the mountain. My gaze traveled over the top of the waterfall, and then down. On the other side of the dropping stream, against the rock wall, was an outline of a crown.

"Found it. You wear the crown and pass through the waterfall," I said.

"How can you be certain?"

"I'm getting the hang of this, I guess."

He gave me a doubtful look.

"The crown. When I got it, the spirit told me *the wearer* would be invisible. I thought it was just in the gateways, but it's for this."

Royston shot me an uncertain look. "I refuse. The water will burn my skin."

"I don't think it will."

He shook his head at me.

"Come on," I said with a sigh. "We're almost there. It looks like there's a cave on the other side of that waterfall."

He studied the steaming water clapping down on the rocks. "Very well. Hand over the crown."

I removed it from my side and gave it to him.

"How will you pass?" he asked, placing the crown on his head.

"I don't know." That was a good question. "The keeper of the Chiave said it wouldn't shield the wearer for that long. So I'm assuming, if I follow you, I could get caught in the water."

Royston scratched his hair under the crown. "Hop on my back."

"What if it just keeps the water from burning you and not me because I'm not wearing it?"

"I suppose it is the chance we must take," he said, removing his coat. "Put this on top of yours and cover your head."

"Great." I took the coat from him and put it on.

He laughed at the sight of me, then turned and bent over for me to hop on his back. "You are a bear."

"I'm glad you're amused." I jumped on and he grabbed my thighs, hiking me up higher.

He placed the crown on his head.

As he neared the pool surrounding the waterfall, the water level lowered, exposing a raised beam. Royston adjusted his balance and stepped on it. As we neared the waterfall, the water stopped falling. He wobbled a little, and I gripped his shoulders tighter.

"Be careful."

"I am," he grunted.

Foot after foot landed on the narrow beam. It rocked under Royston's weight, and I held my breath. Something snapped, and the beam started to drop. Royston darted for the other side, and I clung to his neck.

"You're choking me," he grunted.

I loosened my hold, bouncing on his back until we reached the other side. "We made it!" My heart pounded fast and furious. I took several breaths, trying to calm down.

He lowered me to the ground, took off the crown, and handed it to me.

We glanced back at the waterfall at the same time.

"We broke it," he said. "It has stopped falling."

"I guess so. The beam must be connected to the waterfall." I stared at the crown in my hand before saying the charm to change it into its original form. "*Modificare*," I said.

The crown shrunk and thinned until it became a metal rod. I turned it in my hand, the blue tint to the metal reflecting in the rays of the sun. I followed Royston around a corner in the cave to a sealed entry.

Beside the rock barrier was an imprint the shape of the Chiave badge. I removed it from my skin and put it into the wall. The rocks tumbled inward and rolled left, down an inclining trough big enough to fit a person. It reminded me of how marbles rushed down the ball shooter lane in a pinball machine.

I converted the badge into its rod form and tucked it into my pocket with the others. There was one Chiave left. We followed the tunnel to a large cavern at the end.

There were torches on the wall, so I created a fire globe and lit them. The minerals in the rocks glittered under the light.

Turning on my heel, I inspected every wall. "It's a dead end."

"Impossible. It must be hidden." Royston ran his hands across the smooth surface. "What is the last Chiave?"

"An hourglass," I said, joining him in the search.

We'd combed every bit of the cave and came up with nothing. I rested my back against the wall and slid down to sit on the ground. Tired and cold, I just wanted to go home.

Home.

It was a foreign word to me now. Could I ever go back to Boston? To our cute apartment in the North End? I seriously doubted I'd ever see that place again. Basically, I was homeless. And then I remembered what Nana Kearns always said. The place didn't make a home. People you loved did.

Royston sat beside me, crossing his legs. "What shall we do? Sit on our backsides and wait until it magically appears?"

I opened my coat, lifted my shirt, and placed my pointer and index finger on the final Chiave. *"Reditum,"* I said, releasing the hourglass from my skin. It grew and floated in front of my face, the sand in it glittering in the light coming from the torches.

The sand. It's the same as the minerals in the wall.

There had to be a reason they matched. I snatched the hourglass from the air and turned it around, inspecting every inch. There was nothing on it. I tugged on both bases and the arms. They didn't budge. When I pushed on the glass, it moved slightly.

"There's something here," I said, gently pushing the hourglass until it popped out of the stand. Engraved on the inside of one of the wooden bases were instructions.

Royston glanced over my shoulder as I read: "Sprinkle the sand into the crevice aligning the wall without torches, and light it. Then shall past meet present, stopping time and revealing the Tetrad's prison. Make haste for once the granules burn out, the spell will be broken."

Pushing myself up the wall, I stood and crossed the cave to

the other side. A thin line had been dug into the ground, and it ran the length of the wall. Gingerly, I sprinkled the sand in the crevice and down the line.

Royston grabbed one of the torches and touched it to the sand. Like a fuse, the fire rushed across the crevice. The wall of the cave lowered into the floor, exposing a metal door with seven holes forming a circle in the middle.

"We found it!" Excitement flushed my cheeks, and I hugged Royston tight.

When he didn't respond, I let him go. He wasn't as excited as I was. His stare on the door said it all. This was the end of the line for him. The end of his life.

"What is next?" he asked, his eyes still stuck on the door.

"The rods go in those holes. Then the door will unlock and the Tetrad will be freed. You drink the potion, and you will be able to destroy it. I'm not sure how. I have no idea what will happen."

"Then we shall see. I am ready."

I put the glass back in its wooden case. "*Modificare*," I said, and the hourglass changed its form to match the others. One by one, I removed the rods from my pocket and placed them on the ground. Next, I tugged the leather canister from my boot, uncapped it, and removed Gian's notes.

"Let's see what's next." I unfolded the parchment and read Gian's notes. "You have to light each Chiave, by saying *accendere* and then insert it into one of the locks—the holes."

Royston picked up the first one and said, "*Accendere*."

The rod didn't light.

"I haven't magic. You must do it."

I took the rod from him and said the charm. It glowed blue, and I inserted the key into the door. I picked up another one and repeated the process for each Chiave until I had one left to insert.

An electric charge hit the ground by my foot, and I dropped

the rod and parchment. I spun around.

"Bravo, Gianna." Conemar's voice came from the entrance to the cave. He was in Sentinel gear, shorter than the Sentinels flanking him, yet more menacing with his fierce glare on me. "You led us here, and you even left the traps open for us. Such a considerate girl, you are."

On Conemar's right stood Nick, an electric ball zapping between his hands. His eyes were almost gray. It wasn't Nick. Some other wizard was compelling him.

"*Accendere la stun*," I said, creating a purple globe and pitching it at Nick.

He released his power and it exploded my globe, snuffing it out before it could hit him. I quickly formed a fire globe.

"Grab the Chiave," I ordered Royston, nodding to the final one on the ground.

As he reached for it, Nick shot an electric charge that barely missed Royston and hit the rod, sending it flying across the cave.

Royston stepped back.

"Nick. Stop. It's me, Gia," I pleaded with him.

He ignored me and formed a fireball between his hands this time. Two Sentinels came to Nick's side wielding their battle globes, one green and one yellow—wind and lightning. Conemar created an electric charge on his palm.

"They outnumber us!" Royston stated the obvious.

One of the Sentinels shot her green globe. I threw an ice one at the blast of wind with so much force that frozen shards flew back, hitting the Sentinel and knocking her to the ground. The other Sentinel released his lightning, and I stunned it with mine.

My eyes went to the canister on the ground by my boot, then to the rod against the wall a few feet away. "They'll control the Tetrad," I said.

"Before we could release the creature," Royston said.

"They'd have us. If we do not run, you will not have me," he whispered. "They will kill me. Then no one will be able to destroy the monster."

They had us trapped. I glanced around trying to find an escape. The trough where the rocks went down was our best bet, but I had to drive back Conemar, Nick, and the two Sentinels so we could have a chance to make it.

"Get ready to run to the trough where the rocks went down."

He nodded his understanding.

Dashing for the rod, I created fire globe after fire globe and hurled them at Conemar and the others. Nick dodged the exploding flames and charged after me. He collided into me, and we crashed into the metal wall.

I pushed him off me and threw a knee strike to his stomach. He stumbled back, and I snatched up the rod. A wind globe hit me, and I landed hard on the ground, the rod jarred from my hand and pain exploding across my back.

My head throbbed, and fear shook my body.

Get up. Don't stop. I rolled onto my knees and grasped for the rod. Nick's boot came down on my hand, and I shrieked. He picked up the rod.

"No, Nick," I pleaded. "Don't give it to him."

Nick tossed the rod to Conemar.

"No!" It was as if the ceiling of the cave crashed on top of me and all hope punched out of my soul.

Conemar caught the rod, a sinister grin twisting his lips.

Royston tackled Nick and slammed a fist against his jaw, and then another. Nick lay motionless on the ground.

Nick. I couldn't think about him right then. I had to get Royston out of there.

I repeatedly launched fire globes at Conemar and his Sentinels. The balls bursting into flames created a wall between them and us.

Conemar and his Sentinels backed out of the cave.

"Run!" I yelled.

I grabbed the canister and note and shoved them inside my boot. Royston took off for the trough, and I sprinted after him. I ignited another fireball and threw it at the entrance before jumping into the trough behind Royston. We rode it down like a slide, pebbles flying up, pelting my face. It went a long distance before I shot out of it and landed on top of Royston at the bottom.

Crawling over the rocks, Royston and I went out of an opening in the cave. The light blinded me for a few seconds before my eyes adjusted. We'd ended up at the base of the mountain. We needed Bastien's and his guards' help. I fumbled to get the window rod out of my pocket. It was broken in half. I tossed it to the ground.

"We have a head start," I said. "They're going take time releasing the Tetrad." Saying that caused my stomach to drop. I'd failed. Because of me, both worlds were in danger. No telling what Conemar would do with his new weapon.

"How do we get out of this place?" he asked.

I hadn't thought about that. "Let's just go to where we entered. There has to be a way out."

Screeches sounded above us. A half dozen Writhes, changed into menacing creatures by Conemar, slithered down the mountain heading in our direction. Their deformed bodies, contorting over boulders and through cracks, moved inhumanly fast.

"Go, go, go," I yelled, and took off down the trail.

I sprinted behind Royston. My lungs burned with the cold air rushing fast and heavy into them. The place we had entered came into view—a floating image of the library. Royston slowed down, seemingly not knowing what to do.

"Keep going," I shouted, passing him and jumping into the image. I dropped into the library and landed on my hands and knees.

Royston flew out and crashed into the bookcase to my right. A Writhe's claw reached out of the book, but I kicked it shut and sat on it. The book bucked with so much force, I could hardly keep it closed. The Writhe's wailing stung my ears.

"*Sei zero sette periodo zero due DOR*," I spurted out the numbered charm to call the gateway book.

The Writhe kept knocking the book. It was like riding a bronco across the floor. The gateway book flew over and Royston caught it.

"Find the entry into Chetham's Library," I said, grasping the side of the book underneath me.

Royston flipped the page to the photograph. "Give me your hand," he shouted over the siren-like screech coming from the Writhes.

I reached my hand out to him and he grasped it.

"*Aprire la porta,*" he spoke the charm and jumped into the page, pulling me in with him. I stretched to turn the page but Royston's larger body yanked me too fast into the gateway and I missed it, my fingers brushing over the edges.

We flew out of the book, and my side smacked against the floorboards. Royston landed hard on his feet and stumbled forward.

"Gia!" Bastien ran over and helped me to my feet. "What happened?"

Arik, our Sentinels, and the Couve guards stood ready for a fight.

Two Writhes came sailing out of the book. One charged after Demos, and the other knocked me to the floor on my back. Royston backhanded the creature, and it flew off me. Another one jumped out. Bastien shot an electric charge at it, and it thudded to the floor, shaking and wailing on its back.

Demos and Jaran sliced one of the creatures down with their swords.

"How are they transporting through the book?" I shouted

to whoever would listen.

Lei blasted a lightning bolt into a Writhe climbing a bookcase, missing by an inch. Books flew off the shelf, and burned paper floated down. "See that silver mark on the back of their hands? It's a charm. Only the council knows how to create one of those." She sent another strike at the beast and hit it this time. It fell back and thumped against the floorboards.

Several more Writhes shot out of the pages. I created an ice globe and threw it at one, freezing the beast. I landed a front kick to its body and it shattered, the pieces thumping to the floor. My stomach roiled at the bloodied flesh and rotting smell.

Arik had one of the Writhes caught in his fiery whip.

Bastien, with an electric charge dancing between his hands, faced off with another one. The gateway book shook on the floor behind him.

"Bastien, the book!" He didn't hear me, so I barreled for it, landing my butt on the cover.

The book bucked. And bucked. On the third one, I flew off, hitting the floor hard on my side. A Writhe shot out and grabbed Bastien's legs, pulling him into the book.

I scrambled for them and caught Bastien's hands before he was pulled fully inside. "Don't let go," I said, tightening my grip. He was half out and half in the gateway.

Bastien cried out.

"Oh my God, what?" Panic fluttered in my stomach.

"Its claws are digging into my legs." He clenched his jaw and groaned.

"Kick it," I said, then yelled over my shoulder. "Help! Someone help me!" I slid forward as the beast tugged Bastien harder into the book.

"Let me go," Bastien pleaded, pain twisting his face. "It'll take you, as well."

"I won't," I said, tears pouring from my eyes. "You didn't let go for me. I won't, either. You go, I go. We'll fight them together."

Bastien smiled before wincing in pain again.

His hand slipped a little inside my right one.

As he was yanked back again, I was yanked forward.

"That won't do this time. The worlds need you." He pulled one of his hands from my grip and formed a charge on his fingertips.

"What are you doing? Stop!" My voice cracked with the panic releasing from my chest.

He touched my hand with the charge, causing me to let go of his other hand.

The Writhe pulled him into the gateway, and just as I started to jump in after him, the pages caught on fire. Strong arms wrapped around me and dragged me back from the flaming book.

CHAPTER TWENTY-FIVE

I struggled in Arik's arms, pushing my back hard against his chest, trying to break free of his embrace. "Let me go. I have to go. They'll kill him."

"The gateway is lost," Arik said against the back of my head.

"No, no, no, no." I gulped in several breaths. "Please, *let me go*. He—he can't be gone."

Arik's arms tightened, and I pushed against them harder.

He held me for a long while as I cried, painful sobs shaking my body. His warm breaths puffed against my hair and the back of my ear.

Oh Bastien.

I prayed for him to be all right. I asked every saint I'd learned about in Sunday school to watch out for him. I begged God to trade me for him. To bring him back. And I doubted any of them would listen. I wasn't even sure I had faith anymore. So why would they care that my heart had been ripped from me? That Bastien was gone?

Jaran sat on his heels in front of me and wiped my eyes with some tissues he must have found in the library. "Come on. We need to go."

I took a deep breath and shook my head hard. "No. I can't leave him."

"He's gone," Jaran said. "We can't help him here. Not if we are caught. Can you stand?"

I nodded.

Arik released me, and I stood on shaky legs. Jaran wrapped an arm behind my back and guided me to the entrance into Barmhilde. My knees buckled as another sob tore from my throat.

Jaran lifted me into his arms, and I wrapped mine around his neck. "I'm here," he said. "You're not alone."

Jaran's eyes followed my pacing. The tent felt hot and suffocating. "Why are they making us wait? We have to go after Bastien." I fisted my hands to stop them from shaking. The fear of what Bastien could be going through clenched my stomach and twisted it tight.

Please, let him be okay.

A light tapping came from the outside of my tent. Jaran pushed the flap aside.

Arik ran his hand through his hair, shifting his weight.

Emily smiled, a tray of food in her hands. "I brought you something to eat. You need to get your strength up." She pushed past me.

"We must talk about what happened," Arik said. "I hope you're up for it. I believe it will help Bastien if…"

We all knew what Arik couldn't finish.

If he is alive.

"I wasn't sure what you liked, so I brought a little of everything," Emily said and placed the tray of food beside the pillows on the floor.

I crossed the carpet to the corner of the room and sat on a pillow. Arik dropped down on one opposite me. "Tell me about the events leading up to the Writhes' attack in the library," he said.

Jaran adjusted on a pillow beside me. "She might need more time to recover."

"We haven't the luxury of time," Arik said.

"It's okay. I'm fine." A sense of doom weighed on me when I thought about what had happened in the cave only hours ago. "Conemar ambushed us."

Demos came in balancing a metal box in his arms. "It's all over the Mystik news." He set the box down and pushed some buttons on it. A hologram image snapped on above the box. Screaming came from the speakers. Between the hurricane and cracking earth, the Tetrad moved like a glacier, destroying everything in its path.

Four beasts, each threatening and scary.

The despair on the people's faces matched what was in my heart.

"What coven is that?" I asked.

"Nymhold," Jaran said, ignoring the platter of food beside him.

I covered my face with my hands. "It's my fault. I failed."

"You're alive," Arik said, going into his leader mode. "That's all that matters. We'll have to figure out a way to stop the beast." He must've remembered he was no longer our leader and added, "We must ask Lei what she wants to do."

"We have a way," I said. "Royston."

Arik's eyes were stuck on the hologram. "Then we'll make a plan. This time you'll include us. We would've been better prepared for what happened in the library if we knew what you were doing. Someone needs to get Lei."

The flap opened and Lei came in. "I'm here. Everyone in the camp has a Mystik box on." She slanted a look at me.

"How could you have been so careless?"

"I didn't think…" I said. "I don't know how they knew where to find us. Royston and I were both shielded."

Royston came into my tent, his arm raised. Deidre was right behind him, a frown on her face. The silver tracer Aetnae had given me shook on Royston's wrist like it was stuck on a flytrap. "What is this thing doing? It won't leave me alone and has been annoying me for hours."

"It wants free," I said. "Blow on it."

He did as I said, and the tracer lifted off his skin. It swirled in the air around us before hovering in front of me. "Gia," a ghostly voice came from it. "Go to the library."

"It's Aetnae," I said, watching the tracer escape through the opening of the tent.

We passed questioning looks. "I guess we should go," I said.

"Get your gear on," Arik said, standing. "We'll meet at the entrance into the library."

The others followed him out, except Deidre—she turned to me as I straightened. "I'm going. You're not leaving me behind, again. I've been trained to fight like a guard."

No," I said. "You're not going with us. You don't have magic."

And I can't lose anyone else.

"You can't protect everyone, Gia," she said, crossing her arms. "And you can't prevent me from fighting for a cause and avenging my mother's death."

My fear finally dropped to my feet, and she must've seen it on my face.

"I know." She grasped my arm and looked tenderly into my eyes. "I love you, too. And I'm afraid of losing you, but I'd never stop you. It would be selfish of me. So let's kick some bad guys' asses and win the day, okay?"

I chuckled. "I think Pop should limit your Netflix binging. You're sounding more like an American teen every day. Sinead would be mad if—" I stopped myself. "I'm sorry."

A sadness settled in her eyes. "Don't worry about mentioning her. We can talk about my mother. Laugh and cry while remembering her time with us. But let's not omit her from our lives, okay?" A smile turned the corners of her mouth. "Besides, she'd be angry if we forgot her."

"I don't think I've ever seen her angry."

"That's because she missed your puberty years." She went to the exit. "Trust me. She got frustrated with me often. Get dressed. See you in a few." She disappeared around the flap.

B eing back in the Chetham's library caused all my fears and sadness over Bastien to rush back to me. There was no telling what Conemar and his creatures were doing to him. I pushed that thought to the back of my mind. Crumbling wouldn't get him back if he was alive. I had to press on and stop Conemar.

Dressed in proper Sentinel gear—metal breastplates, helmets, swords, and shields—which the Couve guards had brought for us, we eased down the row of bookcases in teams, back to back, covering one another.

Arik glanced over his shoulder at me. "Keep an eye on the top of the bookcases."

"Okay," I said. I felt uneasy partnering with him again. Though we made a great team, I wasn't sure I could trust him anymore. The cut healing on my lip reminded me he was the one who put me in the gallows. But I decided to go with it. *Keep your enemies closer.*

Jaran and Demos, back to back, were a few steps down from us. Lei had teamed up with one of the French Sentinels, Abre, an athletic girl with short brown hair and bee-stung lips.

I wondered how Lei felt having a different partner. Before Kale had died, she'd been with him since the first year at the Asile Academy.

The silver tracer came out from behind a bookcase and darted in the air around us. We followed it to a room with a round table and more than a dozen red leather chairs surrounding it. We stepped inside.

Across the room, the tracer flew into the stone hearth, which, with the chairs and cabinet in front of it, looked to be out of use. The fireplace moved forward, pushing the furniture with it. We backed up as the table approached us. It stopped, and footsteps sounded from inside the opening.

A Talpar poked his head out from around the side of the hearth, the feelers on his nose sensing the air. He moved all the way out, carrying a gateway book. His large feet shuffled across the wooden floor, his eyes shifting from face to face.

The silver tracer rushed to me. I held up my wrist, and it landed, its butterfly body sinking into my skin.

Arik went to the Talpar and accepted the book he offered.

"When we had our own coven, just outside of Esteril," the Talpar said, his nose twitching, "this was ours. But Conemar has destroyed our home, forcing us to move into the tunnels. By the kindness of strangers, we made new homes within their covens. We gladly relinquish this gateway book to stop the same fate falling upon other Mystik races."

The Talpar returned to the hearth and disappeared around it. The fireplace moved back into place, the furniture staying where it had been pushed.

The book in Arik's hand shook. He placed it on the floor. The pages flipped, stopped, and Aetnae darted out.

"Oh my, oh my," she said, zipping around excitedly.

"Aetnae, slow down," I said.

She landed on my shoulder, but she could barely stay still. "The worlds are ending. Have you seen the *Mystik Observer*?

The live news?"

"Yes," Arik said. "We are aware of what's going on."

"Did you know there was an article about what the council was up to? They arrested a group of Greyhillians who ran the underground press, and then...and then the Tetrad attacked the coven. A massive earthquake." She took a deep breath.

"Slow down," I said, "you're going to fall off."

Demos stepped closer to us. "Have you heard anything of a bird girl named Shyna there?"

"No," she said. "I'm sorry. But I could have the curers ask about her when they go to aid the injured."

"I'd appreciate it," Demos said, his head lowering.

"There's more," she continued. "The Tetrad caused a tsunami in Veilig. The Aqualian undersea village was destroyed and many died."

"Oh no," I said, looking at Arik. "We have to stop it."

Aetnae tugged at my hair. "I followed that boy you said liked me. The one with cropped brown hair and large wings. It was innocent, really. It's not as if I was being nosy. A girl just needs to know what a boy is like before—"

"Do you mean Sen?" I had to stop her. She was making my head hurt.

"Yep." She stomped her foot against my shoulder. "He's a spy. That bug. I'm going to smoosh him flat if ever I see him again. He told Conemar what you were up to."

"So that's how Conemar found us," I said.

Then I had an idea. "Aetnae, do you think you can follow him again? Bastien"—I swallowed, his name touching my lips tearing at my heart—"was taken by Conemar's Writhes."

"I don't have to follow him," she said. "Conemar is bringing his army and the Tetrad to Barmhilde. Sen told him where you are hiding."

My heart felt like it had collapsed. The Tetrad was coming. There were so many families in the coven. And because of me, they were in danger.

"All right," Lei said, walking around, giving each of us a stern look. "We know what's coming. We must get with The Red and Edgar and prepare the coven for an attack. We're on the defense, so we must gear our plan toward holding our ground and preventing loss of life."

"There isn't a gateway book registered to this library," Jaran said. "That should slow them down."

"It should," Arik agreed. "So we'll use the time to our advantage."

"Let him come," Lei said with a fierce glare in her eyes. "Because of him, Kale is dead. I want a piece of him."

Because of him, Bastien is missing. I hoped she'd save a piece for me.

We returned to the coven and prepared for the attack we knew would come soon.

I sat on a bench near the fire pit in the middle of the camp and ran the blade of my sword across a sharpening stone. Arik dropped his canteen on the ground and took a seat beside me, picked up a stone, and started sharpening his own weapon.

Emily approached carrying a basket of sandwiches wrapped in wax paper. "Are you hungry?"

"Famished," Arik said.

She extended the basket to him, and he took one.

"Take two." She smiled. "You have to keep up your strength."

He grabbed another one and put both on the rock beside him.

She moved the basket in front of me. "How about you?"

"Thanks." I took two and put one down beside me.

She headed over to Jaran and Lei, practicing their sword skills. I placed my sword on the ground.

"How are you holding up?" Arik ran his blade across the stone with a *shiiiiing.*

I focused on unwrapping the sandwich in my hand, letting my hair fall against my cheek so he wouldn't see the tears. "What happened keeps popping into my head. It's like a horror film on replay. I lose my grip on Bastien, and those creatures pull him into the gateway."

Arik dragged his sword across the stone again. "It was the same with me when my parent faery was taken by that hound. It will get better."

"It will never get better," I said. Or maybe getting better meant not having a heart at all. Never wanting to love another person again.

"I understand," he said. "You care for him. Loss is painful. I'm just starting to feel again." He glanced at Emily.

My eyes went from Emily to him. They were falling for each other. I took a bite of the sandwich. It was chicken salad, but I couldn't taste it. There was no enjoyment in food or much of anything else for me since Bastien was taken. I forced myself to eat to keep up my strength like Emily had suggested.

He lifted a smile. "Good to see you have your appetite back."

"Yeah." I brushed away a strand of hair stuck to my eyelash. "About the plan. I don't think we should have the weaker adults and children leave by way of the Talpar tunnels. It's not safe. If the Tetrad creates earthquakes, the tunnels could collapse. I think we hide them in the woods behind the cliffs."

"That is a better plan," he said. "What other thoughts do you have?"

I smiled at his reassurance. "The women gather something called bimcord. They use it to make indestructible rope. Maybe we get the locals to make a net or something out of it. We can use it to snare the Tetrad. If anything, it might slow the creature down."

"Another great idea." He put his sword and stone down and picked up one of his sandwiches.

"Those are just things I would do if we're staying here."

"You believe we should go after the Tetrad," he said.

"Stop the creature, and we'd have a better chance against Conemar." I unwrapped my other sandwich. "Once we get rid of Conemar and the Tetrad, we have to take down the council."

"I can present this plan to Lei."

"Good."

After Royston destroyed the Tetrad, I would search for Bastien. I had to find him, bring him home for his mother and for his people. But mostly, for me. I couldn't live with the knowledge that he was out there somewhere—dead or alive.

Arik reached over and removed another strand of hair that had stuck to my eyelashes. "One day, we'll feel less awkward around each other."

"One day, you'll tell Emily you have feelings for her."

He stared down at his sandwich. "One day," he repeated.

Faran and I jogged along a trail that circled the lake. It felt good to stretch my muscles. I was growing stronger. Two days had gone by since losing Bastien—the same number of days we'd been on alert for an attack from Conemar and the Tetrad.

The last televised news report was yesterday. The Tetrad had caused several "natural" disasters in the human world. It was part of Conemar's plan to make the human world weak so he could take over. He'd already brought many of the covens to their knees—both Greyhill and Darkton had surrendered.

The article Afton and I wrote for the *Mystik Observer* exposing the council's corruption had circulated wildly. I just hoped when war came, the covens and our allies in the havens would join the fight with us.

High wizards loyal to Conemar now ruled the havens.

Taxes and tariffs had increased by nearly 30 percent. The Mystiks and the people in the havens were growing poorer every day. Curfews and travel restrictions had been put into place.

I welcomed Conemar's arrival to Barmhilde. The sooner he got here, the sooner we could be done with this.

Jaran rounded the corner and noticed it first. Barmhilde's green and red flag with a large sunburst in the middle was at half-mast. We picked up our speed and ran to the other side of the lake and past the outdoor showers. When we'd made it to the fire pit in the middle of the camp, The Red, Edgar, and Arik were speaking to the crowd gathering around them.

"I've just come back from Esteril," Edgar was saying. "Conemar's forces and the Tetrad are there. Your plan to burrow in and wait for him to come to you is careless. To win this fight, we must go on the offensive. Keep them away from here. Away from your loved ones."

I pushed my way to the front. "There isn't a way to get an army through the libraries without the Monitors sensing it."

"We don't need an army," Edgar said. "We have you and Royston. We just need to get you to the Tetrad."

"That's suicide," Lei said. "We must draw the Tetrad into the open. Distract it so Gia and Royston can have a chance of destroying it."

Edgar walked along the group. He had dark circles under his eyes as if he hadn't slept for days.

"Do you not see?" he asked. "If you bring the beast here, it will cause destruction and death you could never imagine. Not only was I in Esteril. I was there when the creature attacked Darkton." He lowered his head and scratched the blond stubble on his scalp. "It was horrible."

The Red patted Edgar's back. "That's enough. You need to rest, my friend. Your concerns are noted. Our leaders will meet and discuss what you have told us."

Edgar raised his eyes to him. "You're pacifying me. You believe your way is the only way. Do as you wish. Kill your people." He walked off, following the row between the tents.

I charged after him with Jaran on my heels. "Edgar, hold up."

He turned and waited for me to reach him.

"I think you're right about going to Esteril."

"You do, huh?" He rubbed his chin. "Lei will go along with whatever The Red decides, which means her Sentinels will have to follow suit."

Jaran darted a quick look over his shoulder before saying, "She's coming."

"We need to meet," Lei said, approaching our group.

"There isn't time for it," I said. "We should go to Esteril and stop the Tetrad before it gets here."

Lei nodded as she processed what I'd said.

"What's going on?" Arik asked, coming around the corner of a tent with Demos.

"We're going on the attack tonight," Lei said. "Get your gear ready."

Arik turned to Edgar. "Are you with us?"

"The moment you said 'going on the attack,' I was with you." Edgar headed down the row between the tents. "Meet me in the library at two."

In the morning? Why did every nefarious thing have to happen so early, when a person should be sleeping and not dancing with death.

CHAPTER TWENTY-SIX

N ot wanting to alert The Red's men or the villagers of our departure, we took different routes through Barmhilde. Royston and I kept to the shadows as we moved swiftly across the uneven road to the library.

"Cadby was not pleased that I made him stay behind," Royston said. "The old bird won't know what to do without me."

"Why did you make him stay?"

Royston watched his feet. "He would die trying to protect me from the beast. Might even get in the way. Seems like a waste. Will you care for him once I'm gone? He is an excellent guard."

"Of course I will."

I looked like a Ninja Turtle with my shield strapped to my back. The sheath holding my borrowed sword bounced against my side. The French Sentinels had given us a mismatch of Sentinel gear. The helmet was too big, so I left it on the mat in my tent.

Arik and Emily were already at the entrance when we arrived.

The others soon joined us, and Arik spoke the charm to open the entrance. The dark wood-paneled wall shimmied to the side, and we crept inside the library. Emily kept close to

Arik. She had a horribly knitted scarf wrapped around her neck and a size too small jacket on.

"What is she doing here?" I asked. "She isn't coming with us. It's too dangerous."

"Oh please. I am, too," she snapped. "I'm a witch. I can help."

I gave Arik a scolding glare, and he shrugged. "She followed me. And she's stubborn, like someone else I know."

I knew he was talking about me, but I ignored it. Having her along with us made my anxiety rise another notch.

"Don't worry," Deidre said. "I'll stick with her."

Emily smiled at her. "Yeah, see? With her fighting skills and my magic abilities, we'll be like one Sentinel."

"Great." I forced a smile to match hers.

"I know that's not your real smile, Gia," Emily said, a frown replacing hers.

With the two Sentinels and four guards from Couve, there were fifteen of us in the library. Since Edgar knew Esteril the best, he jumped first. We did a library hop, all picking different places to go before ending up at the Saint Petersburg library. By the time the Monitors followed our paths and sent an alarm, we'd be in Esteril.

Once all of us were in the library, Edgar led us around the many display cases crowded by elaborate, cherry wood bookcases. We went by arched beams and more bookcases, passing the one that I knew would take us to Esteril.

"Isn't that bookcase the entry?" I asked, keeping up with him.

He rounded a corner. "We can't very well go through the front door."

Made sense.

He stopped at another bookcase and pushed in one of the wooden carvings of a rose. The bookcase rattled across the floor, exposing an opening in the floorboards. "We'll take the Talpar tunnel. I'm not sure what state it's in, so watch your step." His boot clunked down the rough slope.

I went next, with the others going after me. Jaran and Lei ignited their light globes. The tunnel wall had rocks and roots sticking out of it. I scratched at my hair, feeling a little twitchy at seeing the bugs scurry and slither into the cracks as we passed.

The tunnel inclined, and we went up. It grew steep, and my boots slid over the loose gravel. There was a thick rope with knots for handgrips off to the side, and I grasped it. Hand over hand, I went up after Edgar.

He pushed open the hatch at the top and hoisted himself out. Turning around, he grasped my hand and helped me up. I adjusted my breastplate and sheath, pushing on the hilt to make sure my sword was secured inside.

The flat land with sparse trees was familiar to me. I had come here with Ricardo, a Laniar, who sacrificed his life to save Carrig. Edgar had been there. Sinead, as well. It seemed like ages ago, not almost a year. Thinking of the loss Ricardo and Sinead choked me up, and I cleared my throat.

When the others were up, Edgar kept us to the shadows under the skeletal trees. Our boots crunched through the snow, and I worried about the footprints we were leaving behind. A strong wind swept across the field, sending waves of snow over us, and rattling my teeth and bones. I glanced back to find our prints had been covered.

Demos smiled, lowering his hand, green flashes of light snapping at his palm. He'd used his wind globe to cover our prints.

Esteril's dark gray castle on top of a rocky hill looked like something out of a horror movie. From a pole on the tallest tower, the black flag with a red flame in the middle waved violently in the wind.

Edgar squatted behind a gardener's building, and we dropped down around him. "See over there." He pointed in the distance. "Conemar must have the Tetrad in the basement or the barn."

"What are those?" I asked, pointing at the horizon across the field.

Edgar looked to where I indicated. "Animals. Conemar most likely had them removed from the barn to keep the Tetrad there."

Arik scooted up to Edgar's side. "So what's the plan? We go to the barn and Royston destroys the Tetrad?"

"You have it wrong," Uncle Philip's voice came from behind us, and I almost fell over.

I shot up, rushed over, and pulled him down to the ground. "What are you doing here?" I whispered.

"My mind is good today," he whispered back. "I still have my magic, and it's a high wizard's power. You'll need it going up against Conemar."

"What if—?" I couldn't say it, but he could.

"I lose my mind?" He touched my cheek. "It's a risk I'm willing to take."

"I'm not," I said.

"It isn't your choice." Uncle Philip smiled. "You have been the best surprise of my life. Let me do this for you. If I die, so be it. Soon, my quality of life will diminish."

I stared at him for a long moment. It was wrong of me to stop him from fighting for a cause he believed in. Or even fighting an unfathomable beast that could kill us all. History had shown that sometimes it took great sacrifices to ensure that good prevailed over evil. The memory of Bastien zapping my hand so that the Writhe didn't take me along with him punched my heart with a life-threatening blow. It was Uncle Philip's choice to make, not mine. I had to let go.

Tears stung the back of my eyes, and I nodded silently to Uncle Philip.

He gave me a knowing nod back, then crouch-walked over to Edgar and Arik. "He'd never leave the Tetrad in such an unsecured place. It would be in the basement. There's an old torture chamber just off the corridor to the prison cells. It's large enough to hold the beast."

Though we left at two in the morning from Barmhilde, the sun would be rising in Esteril soon.

I moved closer to Edgar. "We can't bring all these people in there. It'll be a parade. I have to go on my own with Royston. I've been to the basement before; I know my way. You have to get the others to a shelter or something. They'll freeze out here."

"She's right," Arik said and turned to me. "But I'm going with you."

Edgar surveyed the others. "All right. We go to the barn. Lei?"

"Sounds good to me," she said.

"A covered passageway leads from the barn to the castle." Edgar inclined his head in that direction. "You can access the castle from there. We won't be too far away if needed."

"Okay, let's move," I said.

The wind blew blankets of snow that threatened to bury us. Each step was a struggle, and my exposed skin burned as the frozen air smacked me. Finally, we reached the barn and relief from the torturous storm. There was a large hole there where some of the animals must have escaped. Uncle Philip had made the right call. Conemar would never keep the Tetrad in such an unsecured place.

Our group found warm corners and settled in for the wait. One of the Couve guards, a young guy with big ears, gave Arik a window rod to contact Edgar if we needed help.

Emily removed her scarf and wrapped it around Arik's neck.

"I shan't be outside," he said.

"It's for luck."

He glanced down at it and gave her a dimpled smile. "Thanks."

Royston took Deidre's hand in his. "You are like the sun in this dark world. Thank you for allowing me a small bit of life."

"I wish we had more time," she said softly. "There's so

much I could show you."

"See it all for me." He released her hand.

Demos gave me a tight hug. "I thought you should have some sort of emotional parting like the others."

I laughed and pulled away from him. "I'll carry your hug with me."

"You do that." He winked.

Jaran came in for a hug and Lei joined him. "Keep your head on the goal," she said at the same time he whispered, "I love you like a sister."

When we parted, Uncle Philip kissed my cheek. "Don't worry about us out here. You keep your mind on what you have to do. Think of nothing else."

"I will."

I created a light globe and led Arik and Royston into the passageway. The wind whistled through the cracks and shook the walls violently. Arik ignited his fire globe and moved beside me with Royston following.

We came to a large fissure in the wall. Snow rushed through it and covered the stone floor of the passageway. A chittering sound came from the rafters above, and I glanced up, A bat or a miniature dragon was perched on one of the wooden beams, staring down at us.

I raised my globe to see it better and it took off squawking. It circled around and dove for us, and I ducked. It hit Royston square on the chest, knocking him to the ground. He was back on his feet fast.

"She's protecting her nest," Arik said, climbing over the crumbled rocks in front of the opening. "Keep moving, and she'll leave you alone. And, hopefully, her attack hasn't announced our arrival here."

Keeping my head down, I continued after Arik.

"Evil bird," Royston snapped under his breath.

The passageway ended at a metal double door with a large

sliding latch secured by a thick lock. Arik inspected it. "This may be complicated. It's tungsten. Hard to break."

"The lock is ancient," Royston said. "When I was a boy, I would unlock the one securing the pantry by using a sharp object. It requires a few tools."

I gave him an incredulous look. "Let me just grab my toolbox for you."

Royston raised an eyebrow at me. "Are you being sarcastic again?"

A noise came from the other side of the door, and Arik waved us back. We shuffled fast the way we'd come, trying to prevent our boots from making too much noise, and we were around the corner and out of sight just as the doors opened and slammed against the walls.

Arik squeezed through the broken opening in the wall with me, then Royston behind him. Flattened against the outside wall, the blizzard-like snow smacked my face. The mumbling of voices grew nearer. The dragon-esque bird squawked.

"Damn thing," a man grumbled. "Why won't Conemar let us kill that nuisance?"

"He said it's the only one left of its kind," a woman answered.

"Let's just feed the animals quickly," another man added. "This weather is going to freeze my man parts off. Tonella will have hot stew for us when we return."

When they had passed and were a ways down from us, Arik pulled out the window rod and called one of the Couve's guards. "You have company coming," he said and closed the rods. "Let's move."

After single-filing back into the passageway, we sprinted to the entrance, my shield bouncing on my back. Thankfully, the door had been left open. Arik and Royston kept close behind me as I moved us swiftly through the bare, cold corridors, ducking into corners or other rooms whenever I heard someone approaching.

We came to a wide staircase with a corridor on each side of it. The one on the right led to the kitchen, and the left one to a stairway to the dungeon.

I went left with Arik and Royston on my heels.

The stairs were slick, and I took them carefully down to a narrow hall. The small sconces on the walls of the corridor didn't provide much light. We passed several iron doors with small barred windows lining the walls. The door I'd cut the hinges off with the Chiave sword when I rescued Carrig from his cell was still missing.

If I weren't rushing so fast, I would've realized making it this far into the castle had been too easy. Maybe Arik would have noticed, too. I crossed the guards' room to the door leading to what I believed to be the torture chamber.

Arik and I created fire globes and he slowly opened the door. Except for the shackles hanging from the ceiling and a number of bloody torturing tools, the room was empty. The Tetrad wasn't there.

"I'm thinking Edgar's source lied," I said, backing up. I didn't want to be in a room where people had most likely lost their lives.

"What's that noise?" Royston asked, weaving through the torture racks, surgical-like tables with bindings, and baskets of tools.

I followed close behind him. "This is so creepy."

The closer we got to where the sound originated, I realized it was a tiny voice. I peeked around Royston's arm. Sen hung from manacles fastened around his wrists and nailed to the wall. A book faery sat in a birdcage on a table nearby. She was much younger than Sen. Her hair was brown like his, but her wings were almost transparent.

"Help her," he said weakly.

"How did you end up here?" I searched a nearby table for keys.

Royston joined the search.

"Conemar took my sister," he said. "If I refused to spy for him, he threatened to kill her. He wanted to know the goings-on in the libraries. Specifically, your whereabouts."

Arik inspected the birdcage.

I opened a drawer and found two tiny keys threaded together with a thin wire. "Found something." I handed them to Arik.

He unlocked the birdcage, reached in, and picked up the girl. "You're safe now. We'll take care of you."

"My brother?"

"Him, too," he said, passing the keys to Royston. "Can you do the honors?"

Royston took them. I cupped my hands underneath Sen as Royston removed the manacles, and the faery dropped into them.

"I'm truly sorry," he said, sitting down on my palms. "I had no choice."

My gaze went to his sister in Arik's hands. "Of course you didn't."

"This will do." Arik set the girl faery into a box and handed it to me. "They'll have to ride in it. It's all I could find."

"It'll work," I said, placing Sen inside next to his sister. The girl hugged him and he wrapped his arms around her. "Royston, can you carry this?"

He snatched the box from me, the faeries bracing themselves from the force. "I have been demoted to a faery nursemaid," he snapped.

"I should contact the others." Arik pulled out the window rod and called the guard in the barn again. "What happened with your guests?"

"We have them tied to the poles," the guard said.

"I must speak to Edgar."

Edgar cleared his throat before answering. "What is the problem?"

"The Tetrad isn't here."

"The castle grounds are a bit too quiet, as well," Edgar said.

"Can you get any information from your captives? Use force if need be. We'll be back shortly."

As we passed through the corridors to the passageway back to the barn, I noticed just how quiet it was. Two women carrying linens came around the corner and, spotting us, quickly turned back the way they had come, yelling something in a language I couldn't understand.

Next, we heard boots clapping against the tiles, coming from where the women had gone.

"Get ready," Arik said.

I created a stun globe, thinking that whoever was about to fight us was probably forced by Conemar. They could have families, and I was tired of death.

Four Esteril guards, all men of various sizes, came around the corner. I threw my stun globe at one, and he dropped to the floor. Arik wrapped his fire whip around another guard's wrist and the man dropped his drawn sword. Before I could ignite another battle globe, the tallest guard swung his sword, hitting my breastplate, which stopped the blade. I spun away from him and pulled my sword out of its sheath.

Royston made to go after the guard, and I yelled, "Stay back! You can't die. Remember? And be careful with that box."

He pushed out a heavy sigh. "I was a great warrior in my time."

"Good to know," I said, keeping my eyes on the guard. "Now sit back and relax. Watch the show or something." So I wasn't as good as Demos with the quips.

Arik's sword connected with the other guard's, and the man stumbled back.

The guard in front of me hesitated, studying my face. "Gianna Bianchi," he said like a statement with a thick accent.

"Yes?" I wasn't sure where this was going.

He dropped his sword and yelled something to the other guard, who stepped back from Arik and lowered his weapon.

"We are with you," the man said in choppy English. "We do not want Conemar as a leader. End him. End the Tetrad. Go in peace."

The men walked off down the corridor.

"Well, that was unexpected." I returned my sword to its sheath. And then, a thought hit me. I ran after the men. "Hey, wait."

The guard who could speak English turned. "Yes. What is it?"

"A wizard," I said, hope sounding behind my words. "He would have been a prisoner. Bastien Renard."

"He was here."

My spirits lifted. *He was here. Alive.*

"Where is he now?"

The man studied my face again. "Conemar. He took him. Earlier, with the Tetrad and his army."

"Where were they going?" Arik asked.

"That is all I know," the man said.

I wanted to cry; whether with relief or with fear, I didn't know. He was alive but still with Conemar. He could be hurt. The thought of what Conemar was doing to him, and the image of the torture chamber with all the bloodstains, made my stomach lurch and my hands shake.

Though blood was already on my hands, I never wanted to kill anyone. Life was too precious to take. But if I had the opportunity, I wouldn't hesitate cutting Conemar down. It scared me that I wanted to watch the life leave his body. For all the Mystiks and humans he had harmed or murdered, I would witness that for their revenge.

Arik put a hand on my back. "We must keep moving. It's the only way to save him and our worlds."

He was right. I couldn't give up. Giving up was losing.

Not bothering to be quiet, we darted through the passageway, our boots thudding against the floor. The strange bird squawked at us as we passed it. Royston leaned over the box, most likely worried the bird would snatch Sen and his sister up for food. For not wanting to be a nursemaid, he sure was gentle with the box.

We were met with grave faces as we entered the barn.

"What's the matter?" I searched their eyes.

Edgar rubbed the back of his neck. "We missed Conemar by an hour. He was on his way to Barmhilde with his army and the Tetrad. We sent a message through the window rod to warn The Red. Rebels from Tearmann, Veilig, and Santara are rushing to Barmhilde's aid."

The sound of his voice was grave and dark, like the wasteland surrounding us. We couldn't catch a break.

"Wait," I said. "How are they getting there? They think there isn't a gateway book in Chetham's Library. It burned up after they took Bastien."

In what had to be Russian, Edgar asked the three Esterilians tied to the poles barely holding up the barn. The woman answered him.

"She says they took the Talpar tunnels."

Demos hopped off a gate he was sitting on. "That could take hours to move that many through the tunnels. And the Tetrad might be too big for them."

Edgar asked the woman another question, and she wrung her hands while answering. "The Tetrad can use their powers to widen them as they go."

"Then we run," Arik said. "We can get there faster through the gateway."

The Red was right—we should have burrowed in and waited for the attack. This mission was a complete waste of time. How many would die because of our mistake?

CHAPTER TWENTY-SEVEN

When we reached Chetham's Library, I sent the tracer for Aetnae. Our band of rebels followed Edgar to the coven while Arik and Royston waited for Aetnae with me.

Royston sat the box on a display case.

It didn't take Aetnae long to show up. "What is going on here?" she asked.

"Come see," I said, showing her the box. "I'll let Sen explain things to you. Can you get them safely to the Fey realm? And stay there. Conemar is coming with the Tetrad to attack Barmhilde."

"I will." Her voice sounded solemn.

My boots felt heavy as I headed down the aisle after Arik and Royston.

"And Gia?" Aetnae stopped me.

I turned. "Yes?"

"Be careful."

"You, too."

Arik straddled the entry into the haven, waiting for me. I stepped through the open panel and joined Royston.

The Barmhilde village looked like a ghost town. Doors

closed and windows shuttered, not a single living person or creature crowded the usually busy streets. Coming to a rescue in the Mystik world would prove difficult. Having so many jump through the gateway books would take forever.

We met Edgar and the others on the outskirts of the camp.

Cadby circled the sky before landing. He took up his guard at Royston's side. "The Red and his army are at the entrance to the Talpar tunnel," he said, a little out of breath.

Lei stood on a rock to look at everyone. "All right. Our objective is to protect Gia and Royston so they can destroy the Tetrad. They are center. Demos, Edgar, and Arik will take forward. Jaran and I will each take a side. Divvy up Couve's Sentinels and guards to aid you. Deidre, Emily, and Philip, you're in the rear. Get ready for battle. Arik is lead."

Arik's eyes snapped in her direction and a grin pushed dimples into his cheek. Lei was a great leader. She knew Arik had more training than she had. Leading came naturally to him.

She hopped off the rock, waved her hand over her head for us to get information, and charged in the direction of the battle. We reached the top of the hill that looked down on the field. To the left, cliffs dropped to the lake below. The Red's army surrounded the boulder covering the Talpar tunnel. Arik stopped our group.

I held my side and panted, welcoming the rest.

"What is The Red thinking?" Edgar shouted to Arik. "If the Tetrad is blowing through the tunnels, it'll hit those men closest to the entry. We must get them back to a safer distance."

Lei studied the field. "All right. Go put them in a better formation."

"Gladly," Edgar said and jogged down the hill.

Jaran came to my side. "How are you holding up?"

"Terrified and ready at the same time," I said. "The waiting is killing me."

Edgar reached The Red. His arms flailed around him as he spoke.

The sound of boots on the packed dirt, marching up the hill caused Jaran and me to turn. I recognized the people right off. The men and women were from Tearmann. A few looked to be my age. I spotted Buach and made a beeline for him.

"What are you doing here?" I asked.

Buach, his back straight and chest out, side-glanced me. "I be here to fight. What else would I be doing?"

"No, you're not." I pulled him away from the others. "You're too young. Galach wouldn't like this at all."

"He isn't me father." He inspected my gear. "You're my age, and you're in the fight."

"That's different."

"How so?"

"Okay, if you're going to be in the battle, then you're going to be with me." I grabbed his arm and stormed off.

Buach kept up with me. "What are you up to? Don't be embarrassing me."

I ignored him and stopped in front of a man who looked in charge of the rebels. His hair was longish with gray streaking it. I released Buach's arm.

"Sir," I said. "Can I have a word?"

The man held his nose up in the air and rested his hand on his not so flat belly. "You may."

"I need this…um, what are you called? A soldier?"

"That would work," the man said.

"Well, I need him to aid my group."

"And you are?" He looked down at me.

"Gianna Bianchi."

He lifted his helmet. "That you be. You be much younger than your likeness painted in our tunnel. A little scrawny to

be the Assassin of Truths as mentioned in your article in the
Mystik Observer."

Scrawny? How rude.

I didn't know what to say to that, but I guessed a response
wasn't needed. The man's hand dropped from his belly. "It is
an honor to meet you. We are here to aid you." His eyes went
to Buach. "Do as she wishes."

Buach gave the man a slight nod.

I headed back to Arik and the others, with Buach not so
anxious to follow me. The field looked like a living thing, with
the Mystiks all shifting their positions. Birds took off from
the cliffs and flew over the lake. The purplish-blue sky was
clear of clouds.

Buach stomped up to my side. "What will you have me do?"

I stopped in front of Deidre, Emily, and Uncle Philip.
"You stick with them. Our gang is bringing down the Tetrad."

Leaving him there, I returned to my spot beside Royston.

Cadby's wings twitched. He looked ready to take off. "This
wait is agonizing."

"Tell me about it," I murmured.

The Couve's Sentinels and guards were evenly spaced
around our formation.

Edgar was still working on getting The Red's army to move
back. The Tearmann rebels continued down the hill to join
Barmhilde. Dust rose, kicked up by the many feet pounding
against the ground.

At first, I thought Tearmann's army had shaken the ground,
but it was an explosion at the entrance to the tunnel. Clumps
of earth and dirt sprayed into the air. The boulder covering the
tunnel shot out and dropped onto two Mystiks by the opening,
crushing them underneath it. The Red's army scrambled back.

The Red and Edgar shouted orders, trying to get the
people back into formation. They'd just about gotten everyone
under control when the Tetrad came out of the hole. Screams

and shouts rushed up the hill.

I glanced back. Buach was viewing the field with a gadget that looked like old-fashioned binoculars.

"Can I see those?" I asked.

He nodded, shuffled over, and handed them to me. I peered through the lens at the field.

The creature of my dreams was alive. It stomped toward the army. The lead beast had a lion-like face. A dirty-yellow mane framed his scarred face, his nose was flat, and he had a cleft upper lip. Claw-like nails twitched at his sides as his fierce eyes glared at the Mystiks readying to fire a cannon.

Three other beasts followed him. One had two large ram horns coming out of his forehead. He was human, except for his forearms and legs, which were more beast-like. Another one had a boar's head with sharp tusks and bristly black hair covering most of his body. The final beast had scales coating his arms and legs, which bent like a lizard's limbs. His forked tongue tasted the air; drool dripped from his rows of razor-sharp teeth. The only human parts to him were his muscled chest, neck, and abdomen. All four looked as if someone had cut them up and haphazardly sewed them back together.

The beasts moved together on the field. It was as if something invisible tethered them together in a diamond formation as they descended on the army. The Lion Man led them like a puppet master pulling invisible strings. Whatever move he made, the others made with him.

Conemar came out of the tunnel with Nick by his side. His army then poured out onto the field. He climbed onto the boulder and yelled a command to the Tetrad, and it stopped. His army lined up behind the creature.

He motioned to someone in the tunnel, and several Esteril guards brought up eight people with sacks covering their heads and hands tied behind their backs. A dozen or so Writhes flowed out of the cavity in the ground. And I almost crumpled to the ground when a guard pulled Bastien onto the field.

Arik glanced back at me. "Stay strong, Gia."

I took a deep breath. If I panicked, I'd fail Bastien. I'd fail them all.

Conemar raised his hand, and a blue light shaped like a cone formed. He put his lips to one end of it and spoke. "Surrender or lose your lives." The cone was a speaker, making his voice boom over the valley. "We are embarking on a new era. One where wizards rule both the human and Mystik realms. You will be treated well. Your families fed. Everyone will be equal. If one has a slice of bread, all have a slice of bread. I am not the enemy."

Murmurs rose from the Mystik army.

"Don't listen to him," The Red shouted. "You will all be slaves to him and his council. Ready your weapons."

"Fools!" Conemar's voice rang over the field. "He will lead you to your deaths."

Arik gave me another look. "Are you ready? We have to move. Stop him before he turns the Mystiks against us."

"I'm ready."

"Lei?" Arik sought her approval

"All right," Lei commanded. "Tighten our formation. Keep close to Gia and Royston."

Five werehounds surrounded us. One pushed her head against my leg. It was her way of telling me they were with us.

Arik motioned for us to follow him.

"Should I drink the potion?" Royston asked.

My gaze went to the Tetrad. "No. It might not last long. We have to get closer."

"My creature can kill you in one quick, swift blow," Conemar continued.

Nick looked like a zombie as he stood just to the right of his father.

In front of us, Arik's and Demos's paces picked up. They

led us behind the bushes on the hill.

"Stay low," Arik said.

I crouched. "We must find a way to stall him."

"I'll distract him." Buach broke formation and headed down the hill.

"No, Buach," I hissed. "Buach. Come back here."

My eyes followed him down the hill. *What's he up to?*

I found Bastien on the field. His eyes closed and palms turned up, he looked like he was mumbling something. The people with their heads covered seemed familiar to me, but I couldn't figure out why.

Buach ran along the outside of the Mystik rebels, then he slowed down when he reached the end. He approached Conemar, and I couldn't hear what Buach was saying. Conemar nodded as he listened, then put his lips to the magical bullhorn.

"This lad has an excellent question."

"Move," Arik said, taking advantage of Buach's distraction. We shuffled after him.

Conemar continued. "He wants to know if being part of this uprising would hurt his chances of being a guard for the council. If you put down your arms and walk away, your actions here will be forgiven."

The hill steepened, and we slid down it on our butts. The werehounds trotted beside us. At the bottom, I pushed myself up. Arik shot to his feet. Royston grasped Deidre's arm and helped her up. Cadby's wings stretched out before flattening on his back.

Lei came close to my side. "We need a fight to break out. Not this question and answer stuff. We can get lost better in a fight."

"I agree," Jaran said.

Buach said something that made Conemar throw his head back and laugh. "The boy wonders if he'd get paid. Certainly, you will receive a hundred crown coins a week."

We made it to the field and mixed in with the Mystiks. I could hear what was being said better from where we stood.

Murmurs broke out among the Mystiks again.

"Lies!" Edgar shouted. "He lies to you. I have spies close to the council. They will only give you enough so that you don't starve. They want to enslave you. They will make you equal, all right. He says if one gets bread, all get bread. Well, you'll be lucky to get that. His promises are lies."

Conemar's face twisted in anger. "Will you believe a turncoat over a high wizard? I did not come to fight you. I am here for one reason."

Buach's stare went up to the hill. Conemar glanced to where Buach was looking.

"Get back with the others," Conemar ordered, watching Buach suspiciously.

Get out of there, Buach.

It was as if Buach heard me. He crossed over to the Mystiks and found a spot in the line.

Conemar brought the magical bullhorn back to his mouth. "People of Barmhilde, there is a fugitive in your midst. Turn over Gianna Bianchi. Those harboring her will receive a death sentence. Whoever brings her to me now will receive a thousand crowns."

I had no idea what a thousand of those golden coins with a crown on them meant in dollars, but the gasps coming from The Red's army made me think it was a lot.

Conemar scanned the crowd. "No takers? Reveal our guests," he said to the guards standing behind the prisoners.

The guards removed the sacks from their heads. I gasped, my eyes going from face to face—Sabine, Pop, Nana, Afton, Kayla, Briony, Galach, and Father Peter.

Buach made a run for his brother.

With a flick of his wrist, Conemar created an electric ball and threw it at Buach. It hit the boy in the chest, and he flew back, landing hard on the ground.

"No!" I shouted at the same time Galach had.

Galach broke from the others, but he only got a few steps before one of the guards grabbed his arms and pulled him back.

Conemar watched Galach curiously. "Was he a loved one of yours?" He nodded to the guard behind Briony. The guard put a knife to her throat. "Move again and my guard will kill your queen," he said.

With the bodies in front of me shifting, I couldn't get a good view of Buach. Was he breathing? Still alive? I didn't know. *Please be okay,* I prayed.

"Gianna, only you can save them," Conemar continued. "Come to me now."

I tried to move past Lei, but she stopped me. "No. He'll kill you."

"He has my family...Afton. He'll kill them all." I retrieved the canister from my boot and placed it in her hands. "I got Royston here. I gathered the blood for the potion. I've done my part. Because of my mistakes, we're here. I should have been more careful. I left a drawbridge down—"

"What are you saying?" Her eyes danced over my face.

"I am what the presage saw. The Doomsday Child." I glanced back at the field. "I can change it. I must go."

Jaran huddled with us. "What are you doing?"

"You guys need to get Royston close enough to the Tetrad," I said. "Have him drink this, and he knows what to do. I will be the distraction you need. Please trust me on this."

Lei's eyebrows pushed together as she watched me, my words processing in her mind. "I trust you."

"I do, as well," Jaran said.

"Arik and Demos may try to stop me," I said. "Don't let them."

The werehounds followed me.

I eased into an opening in between a Laniar and a man

resembling a bull, and disappeared into the crowd. It was as if the sea parted when Mystiks realized it was Gianna Bianchi pushing to get by them.

"Gia!" Arik's voice came from where I'd just left.

Gasps and murmurs moved like waves over the Mystiks when I stepped from the crowd into the front.

"Stay here," I told the werehounds. They whimpered but obeyed me.

Conemar was about half a football field away from me. I squared my shoulders and crossed halfway to him.

His eyes landed on me. "Good girl. I knew you would do the sensible thing. And I'm certain your loved ones appreciate your sacrifice."

"No, Gia, get back," Pop pleaded.

"What do you want me to do?" I slid a glance to Nick. His eyes were almost marble-like.

The Tetrad stood slack, heads down, like puppets waiting for their master to bring them to life.

Conemar turned his head from side to side while he studied me. "Don't you wonder why I have your Bastien?"

Bastien's tortured eyes lifted and found mine.

I didn't answer Conemar. My heart was slowly tearing from my chest.

A sinister smile tightened his lips. He hopped off the boulder and paced in front of Nick. "Too afraid to know, huh? I needed wizards to compel my son. Children these days don't obey their parents as they did in my day. I've been running through wizards like cheap batteries, their lives snuffed out too fast."

I didn't speak, just stood there, listening and searching for weaknesses in his plan.

"Compelling runs out a wizard's life. We live almost three hundred years. But I had to be careful not to let any of them die while compelling my son. I'm not that evil. I don't want a vegetable for an heir. You'd be surprised what someone will sacrifice for loved ones. They'd let me run out their lives to save them."

I had no options. He could kill any one of his hostages. He could kill Bastien.

"Bastien is controlling my son as we speak," Conemar was saying. "While you're standing there watching him, your beloved Bastien's life is slowly diminishing."

Whatever was left of my heart exploded, the pain so great I could barely stay upright.

Conemar scanned the Mystik army. "While I have a captive audience, and because I've dreamt of this revenge ever since you sent me into the Somnium, let's play a game. Shall we?"

Sure, Conemar. I'll play your game. Because while he was being a typical evil dumbass seeking revenge, Lei and Jaran were getting Royston to the Tetrad.

He stopped pacing and turned his menacing glare on me. "Bastien will do what I want because eight innocent victims, one his own mother, will die if he doesn't do as I command. What will you do for the lives of those you love, Gianna?"

My gaze found Pop. Worry weighed on his face. Tears streamed from Afton's eyes. Nana was gagged, probably so she couldn't use her spells. Sabine stood regal, as if she was ready to die if need be. Briony looked the same way. It must be something they learned when becoming rulers or something. Galach's head hung, blood dripping from his mouth. With worry on her face, Kayla kept glancing at Pop. Father Peter's gaze met mine. He had no fear in his eyes or on his face. His lips moved as if he were saying a silent prayer.

I returned my focus to Conemar. "What do you want from me?"

He went over and placed his hand on Nick's back. "A fight to the death."

My stomach lurched.

"All you have to do is kill Nick," he continued. "That is, before Bastien's life runs out. If Bastien goes easy on you, I'll kill one of the prisoners. If he doesn't compel Nick, I'll kill them all. Bastien is young. His life span is long. But the sooner you kill Nick, the better for Bastien."

There was no way I could kill Nick.

I could just kill myself. End his game. But did I have the courage to do it? I wondered what was happening behind me. Were Lei and Jaran moving with Royston? Was Arik trying to reach me or come up with a plan to save us? I had to put my faith in them. That they were doing what they could to stop this madness. And I did have faith. I trusted my life to my brother and sister Sentinels. We were born to fight as a team. To have each other's back. They would die for me, as I would for them. And there was comfort in that thought.

"If you kill yourself," Conemar said, as if he'd read my mind, "they all will die. Are we clear on the rules of the game?"

Tears blurred my vision as I stared into Bastien's eyes. "Go at me hard," I told him. "Don't stop. You can't. Promise me you will choose them over me."

"Gia, I＿"

"No!" I stopped him before he could finish. "You have to promise me. I can take care of myself. Trust me."

He nodded, tears pooling in eyes. "I promise."

"I couldn't have written a better script," Conemar said, amusement in his voice. "Bastien, take control of Nick and kill her."

I just have to make it look good before I give in. I removed the shield from my back.

Bastien's head lowered, and Nick charged for me.

CHAPTER TWENTY-EIGHT

Nick stopped halfway between Conemar and me. He formed a fireball in his hand and threw it at me.

I shot an ice one at it. The flames froze and dropped to the ground, shattering into a hundred pieces.

He sent an electric bolt at me that I stopped with a stun globe.

The rage in his eyes stunned me to my spot. He threw a series of electric charges, and I blocked them with my shield.

The crowd behind me shifted and called out my name. A horn sounded somewhere to my right. I didn't dare look, but the cheers coming from the Mystiks and the look on Conemar's face told me it had to be something in our favor.

Nick took several heavy steps forward. His jaw tensed. He closed his eyes tight and dropped his head.

I held my fighting stance, readying for his next move.

His head flew up before he sprinted the rest of the way to me, pushing his body against mine. "Gia." He struggled to say my name, his voice deep and shaky. "I can't fight it. Kill me."

"No." I shook my head hard. "I can't. Fight, Nick, or they'll all die. Afton will die."

The muscles in his face tensed. "I love you, Gia. You're my family." He flinched and groaned. "Whatever happens, know that."

"I feel the same way," I said. "I love you. My death won't be your fault. It's on Conemar."

A cracking sound came from his body as Bastien regained control of him. I took the opportunity to quickly back away from Nick.

Conemar's stare on the hill caused me to take a quick look. The rebels from Veilig had arrived for the fight. Above their heads, flocks of Greyhillians circled the sky. The shock on Conemar's face turned to anger. To their right, I could make out Pia with the Santara rebels. Doylis and others like him pounded down the hill.

"Tetrad, earthquake!" Conemar pointed at the hill.

The Tetrad straightened, and the Boar Man roared and shot his hand in the direction of the hill, and it split in half. Many Veiligicans and Santarans tumbled into the fissure. Greyhillians dove and rescued several of them. It didn't stop Doylis and his team. They continued.

Conemar's army passed Nick and me, charging at the Mystiks behind me.

The noises of a battle exploded on the field.

"Hurricane," Conemar commanded the Tetrad again.

An electric charge hit my shoulder, and I flew back to the ground. I quickly rolled over and jumped to my feet just as another hit the ground to my right. The distraction cost me. I ignited a fire globe and threw it at Nick, hitting his leg.

The rain and wind rushed across the field in a violent fury, punching Mystiks and Conemar's fighters to the ground. It knocked me flat and pushed me across the mud. I'd lost my shield, and I could barely lift my head to view the destruction. Greyhillians dropped from the sky. Bastien was on his back. Pop and the others huddled together, hopeless with their hands bound.

I spotted Arik and Demos pushing through the rain and wind, trying to get to me.

It was over in minutes, but the damage was immense. Mystiks, wizards, and guards had been beaten down and struggled to their feet, while those not hurt aided the fallen.

Conemar pulled Bastien to his feet and turned him to view his mother. A guard held her, his dagger at her side. "Continue or she dies."

I met Bastien's gaze and nodded. "Do it."

Those tortured eyes of his, once bright blue, were almost a stormy gray. He closed them and Nick stood.

I thought of my stun globe, and without my saying the charm, it sprouted on my palm, and I lobbed it. The purple sphere soared through the air and smacked into Nick. He dropped to the ground, unmoving and gasping for air.

It was over. Nick was down. Unless I removed the stun, he would run out of air and die. The thought soured my stomach, and I stumbled forward, my knees slamming against the ground.

In my peripheral vision, I spotted Lei and Jaran flanking Royston.

They made it. I have to keep up the distraction. I staggered to my feet and tossed another stun globe on Nick, countering the one before.

He gasped for air.

"You are weak because you love, Gianna." Conemar turned to Nick. "Finish her."

Nick rolled to his hands and knees and pushed himself up from the muddy ground.

Conemar's downfall was his desire for revenge. He hated anyone getting the better of him, and I had beaten him in battles twice. He wasn't about to let me best him in a third. And I would use that weakness against him.

My foot slid across some pebbles and I glanced back. I hadn't realized we were so close to the cliffs. I was trapped between Nick and a deadly fall.

A wide smile spread across Conemar's lips "You have nowhere to go, Gianna."

From where I stood, I could see the field better.

Arik and Demos were almost to Pop and the others. Lei and Jaran with Royston and Cadby were almost in range of the Tetrad. Lei shot her lightning spheres and blasted several of Conemar's guards blocking their way. Jaran tossed a water globe at another guard, a wave pushing the man across the muddy field.

The Red ran back and forth in front of the Mystiks yelling for them to attack Conemar's guards.

Near Pop and the others, Edgar lay facedown in a puddle, his blood mixing with the mud. He must've been cut down before he could reach them. My glare turned to Conemar.

"I will kill you," I cried out, created an ice globe, and hurled it at him.

Conemar shot a charge at the frozen sphere and it exploded, ice raining down and plunking into the puddles.

Distracted, I didn't see Nick coming until he tackled me. I slammed my fist into his side, but it didn't stop him. He rolled me over and sat on my chest. My head sank into the mud. Nick could never beat me in wrestling.

He swung his right fist at my face, and I blocked it with my arm. I hugged his neck and pulled him down against me, wrapping my right leg around his left. Bridging up with my left foot, I thrusted my hips forward and rotated him over onto his back.

"I'm sorry," I said before slamming my fist into his face and scrambling off him.

He was to his feet in a flash. Another fireball formed between his hands.

I backed up, watching his shoulders. His muscles in his neck tightened, and I readied for his throw. The flaming sphere rushed for me, and I dodged it. My foot slipped on the edge of the cliff—I hadn't realized we'd gotten that close to the fringe. Before Nick could reach me, I moved away from the drop off.

Needing a break, I slammed another stun globe against Nick, and he plummeted to the ground.

Fatigue was getting to me. I surveyed the situation on the field. Arik and Demos were back to back fighting Conemar's guards. The Red was on all fours. He sprang for a guard, his sharp canines puncturing the man's neck. Odil fought alongside Conemar's men; I hadn't noticed he was there. He shot fire at The Red, just missing his head. The Red swiped a sharp claw at Odil, cutting open his throat. Odil grabbed his neck and folded to the ground.

Sabine cried out before bowing her head and sobbing. My heart split in two watching her. She loved her son, even though he'd turned bad. I pulled my gaze away, not able to watch her pain.

Jaran held the vial with the black liquid as Lei poured the heirs' blood into it. She shook it before handing it to Royston.

Bastien's face was drawn, his shoulders stooped. He was burning his life span, and I wasn't sure how much time he had left. Uncle Philip approached Conemar. He was yelling and flinging his arms. Conemar watched him intently.

No, no, no. What is he doing?

Before Nick was completely out of air, I dropped a stun globe on him and took off for Uncle Philip. My chest burned as I pushed myself to move faster. Conemar played with an electric charge, bouncing it between his hands.

"Stop!"

Conemar glanced at me.

It was déjà vu. The memory of Conemar hitting Gian with a charge and killing him smacked my heart. My foot slipped in the mud, and I fell to my knees. A guard behind Uncle Philip thrust his sword into Uncle Philip's back and he collapsed.

"*No!*" ripped from my throat. I couldn't move. Couldn't breathe.

"Gia!" Pop shouted. "He's coming for you."

Pop's desperate cry caused me to look up, but I couldn't move. I was frozen with grief or fear or both.

Deidre, her sword drawn, reached Pop and the others. A guard cut her off, swinging his weapon at her. She parried it and buried her sword in his gut. Emily headed toward them, moving her hands as she mumbled charms to control the earth. She manipulated rocks, hitting the guards hard with them.

Arik slid behind me with his shield and blocked Nick's electric charge from hitting me. "Get up," he snapped. "You quit, we lose."

I stood, cold and covered in mud.

Another charge dinged against his shield. He flew backward, smacking against the hard clay.

Emily darted in front of Arik and stretched her hands out. With her fingers spread wide, she mumbled a charm and a wall of mud shot up and flew at Nick, knocking him over.

"Get up. *Get up*," she said to Arik. "Don't just lie there."

"Hey, stop worrying." He pushed to his feet. "I just needed a breather."

She hit his shoulder. "Well, do that later. You scared me."

Arik quirked a smile at her. "I like you, too. So will you get to a safer spot, please?"

"Since you put it like that, I will." She rushed off, heading for the outer side of the battle.

He gave me a once-over. "You hurt?"

"No. I'm good."

"I have your back," he said, just before an electric charge hit his leg. He yelped and toppled a little before straightening. "That smarts."

Anger replaced my fear, and I held up both hands, two fire globes springing to life on my palms.

"Impressive." Arik winked.

"Thanks."

"You may have to kill Nick. Stay strong."

Nick matched my fire globes with a large storm of lightning bolts between his hands.

"How about you take Nick and don't kill him," I said. "The only way to end this is for me to take down Conemar."

I hit Nick with my globes, and he screamed in pain, dropping the charge in his hands. His knees crashed to the ground.

"Are you certain?" Arik glanced back.

I followed his gaze. Conemar had lost track of Nick and me. He was yelling at his guards, who were losing to the Mystiks.

"Yeah," I said. "Try not to kill Nick."

I took off for Conemar, dodging guards on my way. Before I reached him, he had turned, spotting Royston drinking down the potion.

"Tetrad, attack!"

The four beasts looked at once to where Conemar was pointing, and like a thundering stampede, they ran for Royston. Lei rapid-fired her lightning globes at the Tetrad. One hit the Boar Man on the shoulder, and he threw his head back and screeched. The Lion Man roared when one grazed his neck.

Royston screamed as his body contorted and grew. The sound of popping bones and growing flesh curdled my stomach.

Everyone in the battle froze. Conemar stood with his mouth wide. I couldn't move, either. But the Tetrad kept going.

Jaran threw a water globe and knocked the Tetrad to the ground. They slipped in the mud trying to get back to their feet.

When Royston had fully changed, he was as tall and wide as the Tetrad. A monster like the Writhes, his skin became thick and leathery, his teeth sharp, his hands clawed.

The Tetrad finally made it to their feet and collided with Royston. The Lion Man swiped his nails at Royston, and he wailed. It was as if the world's biggest siren went off.

The pain hit my ears, and I covered them.

Somewhere on the battlefield, the werehounds howled.

I pulled my attention from the battle of the beasts. Conemar was distracted—this was my chance. I sprinted for him. Coming at him from behind, I thrust my sword into his back, just as his guard had done to Uncle Philip. I yanked it out, and he turned to face me with a surprised expression. An electric sphere balanced on his hand.

"Gianna, I'm impressed." Blood spread across his white shirt. He whirled around and fired the electric charge in his hands with so much force a bolt flew high and far. My eyes followed it.

Arik had Nick backed against the edge of the cliff, and it was heading for them.

"Arik! Behind you," I yelled.

He spun around, spotted it, and dived to the ground. The charge hit Nick in the arm and knocked him off the edge.

I was numb. Nick was gone, and I couldn't feel. I wanted to cry. Scream. But nothing came. Staring at the spot he went over, I expected him to jump up and say he was only joking around. He was okay.

But he wasn't. He was gone.

My numbness was replaced by a boiling anger, and I faced Conemar. He was struggling to stay standing.

The werehounds attacked the guards surrounding Pop and the others, their teeth sinking into legs and arms. Heavy paws hit the earth as the largest of the pack chased the guard who cut down Uncle Philip.

Another charge left Conemar's hands and hit me in the shoulder. I landed hard on my back. My flesh felt on fire, and I rolled to my side, screaming. A fire globe whizzed by and hit Conemar.

He howled and stumbled back.

I shot a glance over my shoulder. Arik had another fire globe dancing on his palm.

Rada's prophecy repeated in my head. *What I see is possible outcomes. It depends on the choices you make, and those of the ones around you, whether good wins over evil or not. I will say that you must put aside your emotions at the end. Think with your head. Take a life without hesitation. For in that moment, you could lose it all.*

I had been distracted when Nick went over the edge, and Conemar bested me.

Rage overtook me, and I struggled to my feet. Conemar rocked on his feet, and I charged him, burying my sword into his belly, delivering him the final blow. He staggered back, and I watched him. Watched as he collapsed to the ground and the life left his body. I watched him die for all those he took from me. For those he took from others.

I watched him take his last breath.

CHAPTER TWENTY-NINE

B lood blossomed from Conemar's body and mixed in the muddy water rushing down the cracks in the ground. All noises were muffled. Dazed, I felt like an outsider to the battle still going on around me.

Across the field, Royston fought the Tetrad, his claws swiping across the Lion Man's face, blackish-red blood spilling down the lion's cheek.

Arik grabbed my shoulders. "Gia, are you hurt?"

I shook my head. He pulled me into a hug. But I didn't hug him back. My arms were like dead weights at my side.

"Bastien needs you," he said against my ear.

And that snapped me out of my stupor. I pulled away from Arik and dashed to Bastien. His eyes still closed, he chanted under his breath.

I grasped both sides of his head. "Bastien, stop. Nick's gone. Conemar is dead. You have to stop."

He kept chanting.

"Bastien, stop!" I slapped his face hard.

The chanting stopped, and his eyes flew open. "Gia."

I wrapped my arms around his neck, and we dropped to

our knees. "Oh Bastien. You're okay. I love you. I love you so much. I was so scared. You're okay."

His arms went around me and he pulled me closer. "I love you, *mon amour.*"

Deidre and Emily untied Pop, Nana, Afton, and the others. Pop rushed to us. "Let me check him out."

I released Bastien and stood. "We're not done here. I have to help Royston."

Deidre held Afton, who sobbed on her shoulder. I forgot she had seen Nick go over the cliff. I couldn't go to her. We could comfort each other when all this was done.

The Red's men, along with the Writhes that hadn't been changed by Conemar, rounded up the possessed Writhes with bimcord ropes. They didn't kill them. I knew what The Red was doing. He wanted to find a way to return them to their original states.

I sprinted across the field toward Royston and the Tetrad.

The Lion Man fell forward, and Royston grabbed his throat in his claws. His father's corpse had been used to make the Lion Man. It was son against father.

The Tetrad spun, and Royston lost his hold on the Lion Man. The Horned Man came around and rammed his horns into Royston's side. Royston's heavy feet thundered as he stumbled back. This time the Lizard Man whipped him with his tail. Royston smacked against the ground.

The Boar Man stomped his hoofs against Royston's beast-like chest. Cadby flew above the beast and swooped down, his boot connecting to the Boar Man's face. The impact barely made him sway on his feet. I threw an ice globe at the creature, freezing his leg to stop it from pounding Royston again. But the freeze didn't last long, and the Boar Man continued hitting Royston's chest.

When the Boar Man stopped pounding Royston, the Tetrad turned and charged at us.

I sprinted in the opposite direction with the others on either side of me. The Mystiks and Conemar's guards on the field scattered.

Royston scrambled to his feet, throwing his head back and roaring. It was an earsplitting roar that stopped the Tetrad. Joined together, the Tetrad marched around until it faced Royston, the Lion Man in the lead, and it stormed toward Royston.

I remembered something I had learned while visiting Athela's past. The Tetrad was four beings with one soul. The lion was the heart. Remove him and the others would die.

I took off after the Tetrad—I had to get closer. My feet pounded against the mud. When I was close enough for him to hear me, I yelled, "Royston! Take down the lion and the others will fall!"

A beautiful beast with a fierce stare, Royston braced himself. The Tetrad neared. Royston's clawed hands rose at his sides. The Lion Man reached him first.

Royston's right claw cut across the Lion Man's chest. He swung his left and his nails cut the lion's throat. The lion dropped to the ground, disconnecting from the other three. The Boar Man and Horned Man collapsed beside him. The Lizard Man spun, his tail whipping around, knocking down those in his path. Heading for me.

I darted out of his way.

Nana took measured steps forward, her hands at her sides and her eyes red and focused on the lizard.

"Move back," I yelled at her. "Nana, stop."

Nana kept going, ignoring my pleas. When I got closer to her, I could hear her mumbling some sort of charm. She was in a trance.

The sound of the lizard's thundering steps stopped. An earsplitting wail came from behind me.

I whirled on my heel. The Lizard Man clawed at his skin,

his painful cries rising in intensity. Fire shot out of his eyes, mouth, and nose. Flames crackled over his skin, consuming him until he collapsed—a burning pile of flesh.

Royston buckled to his knees and fell to his side.

I ran over and bent down beside him. His body contorted and snapped until it returned to its normal state.

Cadby knelt at his head, his wings flapping nervously on his back.

"Royston?"

He opened his eyes. "Gia. Did we win the battle?"

"We did."

"I am thirsty," he said.

I glanced up at Arik. "Water. Get him some water, please."

Deidre dropped down on the other side of Royston. "You're alive," she said, tears slipping from her eyes.

"Not for long, my beautiful Deidre." He turned his head and watched my eyes. "You did well, Gianna."

"I don't understand," she said. "You won. You've made it."

Royston turned his head back, his breaths growing shallow. "I have always known this would be my end. The potion is poisonous."

Deidre leaned over and hugged him. "No, please stay with me."

"I have heard of a place where loved ones meet again after death." He coughed, his voice strained. "If it truly exists, I will meet you there."

His eyes closed, and Deidre laid her head on his chest and cried.

He's gone. Tears puddled my eyes, and a sadness bubbled up in my chest. It wasn't fair. He was still young and never really got to live, except for the five months he spent with us. I hated Athela, then. Hated her for sacrificing Royston.

Cadby lowered his head. I couldn't see his face, but his wings shuddering on his back was a sign he was crying.

I stood, swiping my tears away with muddy hands. Emily brought me a long strip of cloth, and I wiped my face with it.

Nana came over, grasped my chin, and kissed my cheek. "You're safe. I was so frightened for you."

I wrapped my arms around her and cried against her shoulder.

A sharp pain stabbed my chest. We had to recover Nick's body. But I would wait. Because if I waited, I could pretend he was alive for a little longer.

I released Nana and searched the field for Bastien. Sabine and Bastien covered Odil's body. Nearby them, Father Peter prayed over Uncle Philip. Every bit of me wanted to go over there, but I'd have to wait until Father Peter finished. Saying goodbye to Uncle Philip would tear me apart, and I wasn't sure I was ready to do it. I wiped the tears from my eyes.

In the middle of the field, Galach's arm was around Briony as she wiped the mud from Buach's peaceful face. The Red carried Edgar's lifeless body to a place under a large shade tree where others were taking their dead. A man lay Pia's body beside the other Santaran fallen.

Doylis nodded at me before following his men back up the hill. Shyna stood at the top of the hill searching the field below. Her eyes found Demos, and she smiled, then turned to join her people gathering their dead.

I pulled my eyes from them and combed the field. Pop held a sobbing Afton, while Kayla rubbed her back.

Nana hobbled across the field in their direction.

Jaran wrapped an arm around my shoulder. "Are you hurt anywhere?"

"I don't think so. You?"

"Surprisingly not."

Demos sat in the mud beside us. "I'm knackered. I have never seen so much blood in my life."

Lei came to my other side and slipped her arm around my

waist. "You did good, ducky."

"Help!" A faint cry came from the cliffs. "Can someone give me hand? Or a rope would be good."

Nick?

Another faint cry: "*Help.*"

"Nick!" The sound of his voice replaced the darkness shadowing my heart with the light of hope. He was alive. Alive!

I ran so hard to the cliff my thighs burned. After dropping to my stomach, I scooted out to the edge and peered over. Thick bramble covered the entire side of the mountain. Lying on his back, Nick balanced on the prickly branches.

Arik skidded to a stop and glanced over. "I'll find a rope." He hurried off.

"What are you doing?" I said, which was probably the most ridiculous question to ask in this situation.

"Oh, just hanging around." Nick gave me that annoyed look that used to drive me crazy but totally lifted my heart right then.

He was alive.

Afton dropped down beside me. "Nick, you're alive! I'm going to give you the biggest kiss when you get up here."

"Deal." He looked down, shaking the bramble, and he grabbed the branches. A frightened look crossed his face.

"Don't move," Afton said.

"Good idea," he said.

The shadow of a large bird passed over us. Cadby sailed through the air and dove, scooping Nick into his arms.

"Oh my God," Afton squealed. "I love that bird guy."

Cadby lowered Nick to the ground, and I pushed past Afton, not caring that she wanted to kiss him or whatever. Not caring about anything but Nick. I almost tackled him in a hug and cried.

"Oh Nick. You were dead." I took a breath. "I thought you were dead."

"Gia," he whispered. "I'm here. We're okay. But can we make a deal, though?"

I pulled back and nodded. "What is it?"

"Let's stay in our own world for a while, okay?"

I laughed. I laughed *hard*. Nick was alive. *We* were alive.

"Um, do you think...?" Afton bit her lip. "I mean, can I get a hug, at least?"

Nick snaked an arm around Afton's waist and tugged her to us. We held each other so tightly I could hardly breathe. Over Nick's shoulder, I spotted Bastien heading our way. I kissed Nick's cheek, and then Afton's, before untangling myself from their arms.

Shortening the distance between us, I met Bastien almost in the middle. He cupped my face in his strong hands and kissed my lips. He kissed them as if he'd never kissed them before, urgent and frightened. My hands, dirty from battle, gently touched his cheeks.

"Bastien," I whispered around his kisses. "I love you."

"You could never love me as much as I do you." His warm breath tickled my lips.

I smiled against his mouth. "Says you."

Uncle Philip.

"There's something I need to do," I said.

He followed me as I made my way to Uncle Philip. Father Peter was making the sign of the cross over Uncle Philip's lifeless body as I approached. He stood and nodded at me.

I dropped to my knees beside my uncle. "We did it," I said, lowering my head and resting my forehead against his chest. "I'm going to miss you bad. You've been the best uncle a girl could ask for. Say hello to my mom for me when you get to wherever you're going. She'd be proud of you for taking such good care of me. I couldn't have survived this without you." I lifted my head and kissed his cold cheek, tears dropping from my eyes and falling on his skin. "I love you and will carry you with me for the rest of my life."

My legs shook as I stood. Two men waited with a makeshift stretcher to take Uncle Philip's body. A cry tore from my mouth, and I covered my face with my hands. Bastien's arms went around me, and I bawled against his chest. I couldn't hold myself up anymore, so he held me instead.

"I'm here," he said.

We had lost so much, but gained even more. There had been so much pain, so much suffering, but the sun was coming up, and a new Mystik world was dawning.

CHAPTER THIRTY

Normal life. I wasn't sure I knew what that was anymore. The mirror was not my friend. It distorted my reflection, making me look a little askew. I frowned and straightened my black cocktail dress.

The pendant with Pip's feather inside hung from the corner of the frame. I touched it, thinking about Uncle Philip. It had been a month since his funeral in Aoile. Thousands of Mystiks had been in attendance.

There were so many funerals we attended in the week following the battle. Buach's in Tearmann. Edgar's in Asile. And Pia's in Santara. I wondered if the hole in my chest from all our losses would ever heal.

But none of the funerals compared to Sinead's ceremony in the Fey nation. Sinead was draped in a shimmery white dress and glitter dusted her skin. It was private and in the most beautiful garden. Carrig was proud that day. Having known her love would carry him to the end of his days.

He and Deidre had moved into a house down the street from us in Branford. Carrig was now the guardian of Peyton, Dag, and Knox. He'd train and raise them in the human world.

No one knew there were three from the eight-year-old Sentinels who had survived the disease, and Carrig was determined to keep it that way.

In the last few weeks, Deidre and I spent many hours together playing basketball at the park or watching comedies late at night. I'd abandoned my love for horror movies. I'd seen enough of them in my nightmares lately.

Lei, Arik, and Demos had returned to Asile to help get things in order.

And Jaran? Well, he moved in with Pop, Nana, and me. Pop and Carrig had finally finished renovating that extra bedroom in our Victorian home, which sat at the end of a quiet road with a crooked street sign.

When Pop had asked where we wanted to move, we all voted for Branford, Connecticut. It surprised me, too. I never believed I wouldn't return to Boston. But I was ready for a quieter life with less traffic until I went to college, which could be a year from now, since I'd missed sending in my applications. And Jaran was ready to get to know a certain student body president better.

"Are you going to stare at yourself all night?" Deidre sighed from her old bed.

Emily shifted on my bed to give her a stern look. "We're not rushing her tonight. Take your time, Gia."

Deidre groaned. "By all means. Take forever."

Nana's familiar, Baron, and my cat, Cleo, lay at Deidre's feet bathing each other with their tongues. Momo climbed up on the bed and sniffed them. Carrig had brought Momo back from Asile for me. Momo was living the good life since leaving the Somnium. It was the least I could do for the ferret for alerting me when danger was around while in the Somnium. Pop spoiled her with sips of the last bit of his creamy coffee in the morning and dry cereal when I wasn't looking.

Momo burrowed under Deidre's leg. "Hey, girl." She picked Momo up and ran a finger over her fur.

"I don't get why we have to do something so fancy," I said. "Can't we order pizza delivery instead? It's just a girls' night. We could rent movies."

"We have to go out," Emily said and crossed the area carpet to me. "Remember your therapist said getting out was a good thing. And it's November first."

My therapist was an eccentric woman from Asile—because there was no way I could see a human one, not with my stories. She'd jump to the Branford library for our sessions, since I needed time away from the Mystik world.

I picked up my root beer flavored Lip Smacker and slathered my lips with it. Yes, I had reverted back to balm over lipstick.

"What's so special about November first?" I asked.

Emily gave me a shocked expression. "It's All Saint's Day."

I pushed a loose strand of hair behind my ear. "Then shouldn't we go to church instead of dinner?"

"Your neck looks so long with your hair pulled up," Emily said, glancing over my shoulder and smiling through the mirror at me. "You're beautiful."

My cheeks warmed, and I lowered my eyes. "Thanks. You look amazing, too. I love that dress on you."

She ran her hands down her blue dress, which matched her eyes perfectly. "Now I'm blushing."

"You guys going to kiss now or what?" Deidre stood. "We have reservations. How about we not be late for them."

"Reservations? You guys really went all out for tonight."

"Yeah, we thought it would be nice." Emily grabbed her jacket from the bedpost. "Let's go."

Emily drove five miles per hour under the speed limit for me. She parked in front of the D'Marco's restaurant, and I raised an eyebrow at her.

"We never have to make reservations here," I said, getting out of the car and following them to the host stand.

Deidre walked by it and headed for the banquet room.

I caught Emily's arm. "What's going on?"

She grasped my hand and pulled me along with her. "Stop being so suspicious and just go with it," she said.

We walked into the banquet room.

"Surprise!" everyone yelled.

I stumbled back, my heart leaping into my throat. "Oh my gosh. What's going on?"

"It's a party for you," Emily said.

The room was decorated with purple and green balloons floating on strings tied to the back of chairs, and matching flower arrangements added color to the white tablecloths.

Nick strolled over with a smile plastered on his face. "Surprise," he droned. "They shouted at me when I walked in, too."

"What's this for?"

"Happy birthday," he said, waving understated jazz hands. "Yay."

"My birthday was a few months ago," I said.

"Yeah, I heard something about you being in hiding. Me being tortured. Us not getting to celebrate them. Blah. Blah. Blah."

I chuckled. "Your mom?"

"No. Afton."

"Afton's here?"

"You called?" She slipped her arm through his and rested her head on his shoulder.

"You're here," I said and gave her tight hug, my smile as bright as hers. "This is great. Really. Thank you for putting this together."

"You're welcome," she said. "Mrs. D'Marco helped me. I arrived from Boston last night, and it took all my willpower not to go over and see you."

"It's a great surprise," I said.

Afton glanced up at Nick. "Your mom wants to take a

family pic." She smiled at me and said, "Come over when you're done being a wallflower."

Nick took her hand, and Afton adjusted his collar. It was great to see them finally together.

My eyes toured the room. Nana, Pop, and Kayla stood by one of the long tables arguing over seating arrangements. Mrs. D'Marco poured water into empty glasses at the place settings. Mr. D'Marco set baskets of bread between the flower arrangements.

Kayla laughed at something Pop had said. He was giving her another chance, and I was happy for him. It was time he had someone special in his life.

"There you are." Deidre rushed over and planted a kiss on my cheek. "Do you love it?"

"I do." I wrapped my arm around hers. "I can't believe you hid this from me."

"It was hard. Believe me. You're so nosy." Her eyes narrowed on Peyton, Dag, and Knox standing by the cake table. Dag glanced around before stabbing his finger into the frosting of the cake.

I laughed.

"That little brat," she hissed. But it wasn't an angry kind of hiss; it held amusement. "Excuse me." She marched over to them.

Lei rushed in, her arm wrapped around a very attractive guy, just a little taller than her, with black hair. "Happy birthday, ducky. You look beautiful. You need lipstick, though."

"Thanks. I think." I nodded at the guy and mouthed, *Who's this?*

"Oh, sorry. This is Gamon. He doesn't talk much."

"Nice to meet you, Gamon. I'm Gia."

He bowed his head slightly. "The pleasure is mine."

"We'll talk later," Lei said. "I want to make sure Nana doesn't sit us by Demos. I can do without him teasing me or interrogating Gamon." She dragged him away.

I snickered. My family and friends were the best, if not a little on the unusual side.

Jaran came in holding Cole's hand. "Happy birthday, Gia," Cole said. "Hey, there are appetizers. You want a plate?"

"Sure," Jaran said. "Whatever you're having is fine."

"Be right back." Cole made a beeline for the hors d'oeuvres table.

Jaran handed me a small box wrapped with pink paper. "Here. It's from Aetnae."

"It's not my birthday," I said, inspecting the box. "My birthday was months ago. It's actually Nick's this Wednesday, though."

He bumped my shoulder with his. "I was told we were celebrating it anyway. Aetnae said to tell you not to stay away for too long."

Stay away too long? I couldn't imagine ever going back. There were too many painful memories and too many people who wouldn't be there.

"Want a drink?" Jaran asked.

"No, thank you."

He smiled. "I'll get you one anyway. I'll be back in a few."

Emily stood close to Arik listening to Carrig tell them one of his many stories. Arik's arm rested on Emily's back. When Carrig said something that made Arik laugh, Emily would smile up at him. She adored Arik, and I think her charms were winning him over more and more every day.

Arik's and my eyes met. He gave me a bright smile, and I returned a brighter one. After fighting alongside each other in the epic battle against Conemar and his followers, we'd become partners again. Though we were on hiatus from training for a while, we still sparred together to keep in shape. Most importantly, we had become close friends.

He returned his attention to whatever Carrig was saying, and I studied my hands.

Demos entered the room wearing jeans and a nice black

shirt. "Hullo, Gia. Happy birthday."

"It's—" I gave up. "Thank you."

"I guess I got the dress code wrong."

"You look great," I said. "How's Shyna?"

"Seeing someone else." He winked. "It was a fly-by-night kind of relationship. Pun intended."

"I see."

"Oh, there's food," he said. "Excuse me. I'll be back."

I smirked. *Guys and food.*

Watching everyone together touched my heart. I wanted to keep them there forever in that room. Safe from the outside world. From the Mystik world. Even though the havens and covens were coming together to form one nation where all the Mystiks were equal, the government was being restructured, and The Red, Sabine, Briony, and Bastien had important roles to play in its formation. Briony was training Bastien to one day take over her role as head of the new parliamentary system. Though he was busy, he made a point to meet me often at one of the most beautiful libraries in the world.

Strong arms wrapped around me from behind. "Why is the birthday girl alone at her party?" Bastien whispered, his breath brushing against my neck. He kissed my collarbone. "You are simply beautiful in this dress."

I spun in his arms to face him. He looked amazing in his dark blue suit, pressed white shirt, and matching tie. His sleeves stretched across his biceps as he held me.

"I didn't think you would make it," I said, staring up into blue eyes that matched his suit. Eyes so dazzling that they caused my breath to hold in my lungs and warmth to rush to my cheeks. I exhaled.

He kissed me. Mint hinted on his lips, as if he'd just brushed his teeth. "I will always make time for you," he said.

"How come you always say the most perfect things?"

A smile twisted on his lips. "Because I am perfect."

"And arrogant," I added.

"You love that most about me."

"You're wrong. I love your kisses most."

He kissed me again. "There will be more of those later."

His smile was infectious, and I pressed my lips together trying to stifle my own.

"Come with me," he said, grasping my hand and leading me out of the room.

"Where are we going?" I asked as he weaved around tables.

We passed the host stand. "You'll see."

When we walked outside, he removed his jacket and placed it over my shoulders.

"No," I protested. "You'll freeze out here without a jacket."

He grabbed the lapels and pulled the jacket tighter around me. "Then I'll hurry. Now, you have a habit of interrupting me—"

"I do not."

His eyebrow lifted, and he placed a finger on my lips. "I love you, Gianna. You've been moody lately, wondering where you fit in both worlds. Pop said you missed applying for university." He reached inside the jacket, removed an envelope from the inside pocket, and handed it to me. "We have many connections in the human world. It just so happens there is a wizard who works in admissions, and I called in a favor."

Boston University was in the upper left-hand corner, and my name was in the middle.

"What is it?" I asked, shivering against the cold.

"Your acceptance for next fall," he said. "You'll be rooming with Afton."

"Really?" I hugged him tight and shrieked. The jacket slipped from my shoulders, and he caught it. "I can't believe it."

"There's more." He returned the coat to my shoulders.

"More?"

He removed a small square box from the inside pocket of his jacket, his hand brushing my waist caused a shiver to tickle up my spine.

My eyes widened.

"Before you panic, it's not what you think."

"Okay," I said.

He opened the black box. A sapphire ring sat on a tiny red pillow.

"That *is* a ring."

"It's a promise," he said. "You can wear it on your right hand. I read up on rings in your world. In ours, we don't give them for engagements. They're simply tokens of affection."

"What are we promising, Bastien?"

"I'm promising to wait for you until you are ready to join me in the Mystik world. I promise to be there whenever you need me. I promise to watch those horrible black and white movies with you and Nana. I promise no one will ever love you or cherish you as much as I do. I promise to love you until my last breath."

Tears gathered in my eyes. "And I promise to not annoy you."

"I don't think you should make promises you can't keep."

He gathered me into his arms, and I lifted my face to meet his kiss. A warmth rushed over me, and I no longer felt cold. I would make a million promises for Bastien. And it didn't matter what world we ended up living in. Because I knew when things got bad, Bastien would jump into a trap with me, and I'd do the same for him.

"This is just the beginning," he said, his lips hovering over mine.

It was the beginning, all right: the beginning of my new life in the human world and the beginning of a beautiful relationship that never would have happened if I hadn't been sucked into that damn book. I pulled back to look into his beautiful blue eyes—and I wouldn't have it any other way.

ACKNOWLEDGMENTS

Finishing a series is such an amazing feeling. I am both thrilled to have finished and sad to be leaving the Library Jumpers world and the characters I love so dearly. This journey through the most beautiful libraries in the world and through the magical Mystik world wouldn't have happened without the help of many special people along the way.

I want to thank my agent, Peter Knapp, for guiding me through this daunting process. Your kindness and care is always appreciated.

Thank you to my publisher and editor, Liz Pelletier, for giving this series a chance and for helping to make it so much better than how it started. A special thank you to Stacy Abrams for all the rounds of edits on this book. It was a great experience working with you and having you push me to delve deeper into the characters.

And many thanks to the entire Entangled Publishing team that worked on this book from editing to cover design to marketing and everything in between. Thank you for making my books pretty and getting them into readers' hands.

A gigantic thank you to Pintip Dunn for being so hard on me with the critique of this book. I'm in awe of your talent. Our daily phone calls are the brightest moments of my day. To Heather Cashman for helping get the first draft in shape and for working with me on Pitch Wars so that I could get this book done. You are simply the best!

To my writer friends here in Albuquerque who meet for coffee whenever we can, to the wonderful Pitch Wars community, and my online friends—thank you for keeping me company on this journey.

Thank you to my family and friends for all your support and for understanding when I have to pass on things because I have a deadline or some other pressing matter.

And to my husband and desk mate, Richard Drake, for all your support so I can chase after my dreams. I'd jump through any gateway book with you no matter how dark and scary it is.

I dedicated this novel to my beautiful son, Jacob Maez. He was my inspiration for Nick. When Jacob was five, he conquered cancer and during the final edits of this book, he's now fighting liver disease. He has always been a warrior and keeps his humor through some of the toughest battles of his life. I am truly blessed to be his mother.

And finally, to you, dear reader, thank you for going along with me on Gia's journey. I hope you enjoy the series as much as I enjoyed writing it.

INTERVIEW WITH THE AUTHOR

Pintip Dunn: Hi Brenda! Thanks so much for agreeing to let me torture…ehr, interview you! I've been dying to get the answers to some of these questions.

Brenda Drake: This is sort of scaring me. Ha! But really, thank you for doing this!

PD: Don't be scared. Much. *rubs hands together* Okay, let's start with a question that all writers get. And I know I'm a writer myself, but I have to ask it anyway—

BD: No, Pintip, this book is *not* based on you.

PD: *pouts* Really? But I kinda thought Gia was inspired by me! You know, kick-ass girl, super-cool magical powers, has two hot guys fighting over her…

BD: Actually, Gia was based on a combination of my nieces. I was hanging out with them a lot at the time. One is an athlete and the other is a bookworm.

PD: Now the *real* question I wanted to ask you—the one all writers get—is about your amazing imagination. I'm always so impressed with all your creative details. How do you come up with your ideas?

BD: Thank you! This has to be the hardest question for a writer to answer. The ideas just pop into my head. But seriously, I think our surroundings and experiences influences our imagination. For me, it can be an object or some other visual that spurs an idea. A coffee table book on the most beautiful libraries in the world was the inspiration behind the Library Jumpers series.

PD: Do you have a favorite library? Did you spend a lot of time in libraries as you were growing up?

BD: My favorite library has to be the Boston Athenæum. The first time I had visited, I was about ten. It was spacious and awe-inspiring with its beautiful artwork and balcony bookcases.

PD: Let's talk about cute boys instead. I have to ask: Are you Team Bastien or Team Arik? Did you know Gia's perfect match all along, or did you change your mind during the writing of this series?

BD: Ha! This is tricky. I'm Team Nick all the way! But seriously, I can't choose between Bastien and Arik. I love them both for different reasons. Bastien for his empathy and his flirty arrogance and Arik for his loyalty and protectiveness. My feelings about whom Gia should end up with vacillated between the two so many times. In the end, I believe she makes the right choice.

PD: You don't hesitate to put your characters into difficult situations. In fact, you kill quite a few characters in this book. Why did you feel like they had to die?

BD: In a world where there is magic, swords, and epic battles, someone has to die. I tend to choose characters who sacrifice themselves out of love. I never set out to kill my characters. It just feels right for the story when it happens. If it doesn't, I spare them. There are a few characters I wish I could bring back to life. I miss them.

PD: I miss them, too! But so long as you leave my favorites alone, I'll give you a pass. Did you hide any secrets in your books? Meaning, are there any details with special significance that only you and a few close friends understand?

BD: There are many secrets in all three books. Things I've pulled from my life that my family and friends will recognize. It could be a conversation or an item. Gia's cat, Cleo, and a ferret named Momo in Book 2 represent my real pets.

PD: I want to meet Momo! Was it harder to write the second book in a series? What's the difference between writing a Book 1 and a Book 2 (or a Book 3, for that matter)?

BD: The hard part about writing Book 2 was doing it on a deadline. When I wrote Book 1, I didn't have that pressure. But with Book 2, I already had the world established and could delve deeper into the characters. Book 3 was difficult to write. Ending a series is tough. You have to make sure you tie everything up in a neat bow. I cried several times while writing it.

PD: And I cried several times while reading it!

BD: I'm still crying...

PD: Aw, we have to end this interview on a happy note! What was your favorite scene in this book and why?

BD: Fight scenes are my favorite ones to write. But I will surprise you and say it's a scene where one of the characters makes a huge sacrifice for Gia.

PD: Ooh, I love that scene! I bet that scene is probably all of your readers' favorite, too. Well, I am looking forward to reading many more heart-melting scenes from you. Thanks so much for answering my questions, Brenda! As always, it was a blast to hang out with you!

BD: It's always a wonderful time talking with you, Pintip! Thank you for going on this journey with me. It wouldn't be as fun without you!

Pintip Dunn is the *New York Times* bestselling and RITA ® award-winning author of the Forget Tomorrow series as well as the upcoming *Star-Crossed* and *Malice*. Visit her online at www.pintipdunn.com.

entangled teen

an imprint of Entangled Publishing LLC